THE
POSTMAN
POET

THE
POSTMAN
POET

Liz Shakespeare

LETTERBOX BOOKS

First published 2017
by
Letterbox Books
Littleham
Bideford
Devon
EX39 5HW

www.lizshakespeare.co.uk

ISBN 978-0-9516879-4-9

Printed and bound by SRP Ltd, Exeter

ACKNOWLEDGEMENTS

I am very grateful to Edward Capern's great-great-granddaughter, Lady Ilfra Goldberg, for sharing documents and her family history with me, and for her support and encouragement. Her biography, *Edward Capern: The Postman-Poet*, has been a useful resource. Alison Harding has given me invaluable advice and reassurance throughout the three years I have been working on this project. Many thanks to Kate Cryan for her careful reading; and to my son Ben, as ever, for designing the cover.

I would also like to thank Peter Christie, Janet Few and the Buckland Brewer History Group, the North Devon Record Office and Local Studies Library, and the Royal Mail Museum in London for their help with research.
I am grateful to the Gilcrease Museum for permission to use the image on the cover.

All poems quoted are by Edward Capern unless stated otherwise.

Prologue

Braunton, Devon, 1884

The secluded country station is tranquil in the late afternoon sunshine. The only sounds are the chirping of sparrows in the eaves and the murmur of voices from the group of gentlemen gathered on the platform, staring expectantly along the railway tracks that run across low-lying meadows.

After a few minutes a cloud of steam can be seen in the distance and as the engine comes into view a low roar is heard, drowning out all other sounds as the train approaches. When it hisses slowly to a standstill, just one carriage door opens and a stout man with a long white beard steps eagerly down on to the platform, followed by an elderly woman with two small children.

A gentleman steps forward. 'Edward, hello! How wonderful to see you back in Devon!'

The new arrival smiles broadly at the welcoming party. 'Thank you, thank you all! So many friends to greet us! This is a great day for me and a long-awaited one!'

He shakes hands warmly with each of them and then with the stationmaster hovering nearby, who looks rather taken aback at the unaccustomed familiarity.

'Welcome, Mr Capern. Can us take your bags for you, Sir?'

The lady holds on to the children's hands to restrain their excitement as the guard blows his whistle and the train wheezes and chuggs away from the platform. The four make their way out to the waiting cart for the last stage of their long journey, but the boy with the barrow who has been staring open-mouthed at the important passenger can contain his news no longer.

'Us used to learn your poems in school, Mr Capern, Sir.'

As the station cart creaked and swayed along the narrow lane, Edward contemplated the landscape he loved, and listened with pleasure to the children's chatter. He named the small village of Wrafton for them and pointed out the Manor Farm with its old cob linhays, then a brook that ran sparkling under the road bridge; he reassured his wife that in only a few more minutes they would arrive at their new home.

As soon as the cart came to a halt and the horse stood patiently with downcast head, he rose and negotiated the steps without waiting for a hand from the driver. He landed heavily on his feet and gazed spellbound at his surroundings. The sun was low, shining on to the cottage windows and some little trees and fields, and now that the clopping of hooves had ceased, all was silent but for the rich, celebratory warbling of a thrush.

When he saw his favourite flowers growing in the hedge, Edward almost ran to them, cupped his hand around them and inhaled deeply.

'Janie! Primroses!'

His wife was standing in the cart waiting for the driver to help her down so he hurried over to his two grandchildren who had already clambered out.

'Look, Ilfra, Archie, primroses waiting for our arrival! Can you smell them?' He held out a flower to each obedient child. 'And there are bluebells and buttercups –'

How good it was to be back in Devon! He flung out his arms excitedly while the horse jerked its head up in surprise.

'There's balm in the air, love, and bloom on the trees,
    And warbling of woodlands, and humming of bees.'

'Never mind the poetry, Edward. Is this our new home?'

Jane was standing in the lane, staring up at the cottages. In the centre of the terrace stood a well-proportioned house, its porticoed entrance and sash windows looking down on the humble doorways and casements of the smaller dwellings. Edward hoped it would please her.

'It's not quite as grand as your drawing showed,' she said, 'but 'tis all the better for that. Look, children, here's the house Grandpa told us about, so no need to ask any more if we're nearly there.'

Ilfra went to lean against her grandmother's comforting side. 'And we're to live here with you and Grandpa forever?'

Jane met Edward's concerned glance before taking Ilfra's hand. 'Yes, chiel, you're to live here with us. See, Grandpa has the key so hold it between the two of you so's we can unlock our new door. There, you can go right on in, it's our home now, nobody else's.'

The children rushed in but Edward paused on the doorstep. A rambling rose clambered up the porch to provide a canopy at the entrance; across the lane he could see the vegetable plot, a little neglected but of sufficient size to feed him and Jane and their two charges. The village would give them sanctuary, just as the lush hedgebank provided a haven for countless plants, birds and other creatures. In recent years such scenes had often featured in his dreams, as he imagined he strode again through narrow byways, greeting the flowers that had inspired his thoughts and the birds and brooks that lent him their melodies. The Devon lanes had been his greatest muse. Perhaps they would again prove generous. He shielded his eyes from the lowering sun. Away to the west a luminescence, suggestive of a large body of water invisible from where he stood, was drawn up into the sky. Devon!

He was home again, at last.

Later that evening, with the children finally settled in their makeshift beds and Jane resting in her chair, Edward stood at the window of the upstairs room that would become his library. The light was almost gone but as his gaze travelled over the panorama before him, he could still make out the silvery line of the river Taw below a sheltering shoulder of hills, Chanter's Folly towering above Appledore and the estuary of his beloved Torridge; then, between the rolling dunes of Braunton Burrows and the distant finger of Hartland Point, a narrow gleam which he knew to be the great ocean, where in daylight he would see stately ships gliding into the estuary to unload their cargoes on the quays at Fremington and Bideford.

Slowly, he turned his back to the window. The bookshelves he had described to the village carpenter had been fitted to two walls and seemed to be well-executed; they would do nicely. The trunks of books lay haphazardly where they had been placed with groans of relief by the removers. He had fretted about the trunks. If the weather was very wet they *must* be covered with oilcloth and he feared they would not be; the consequences of a drenching were too awful to consider. He got down painfully on to his knees, undid the clasp of the first trunk and lifted the lid. The books were a little shaken but appeared dry. He ran his hand over their covers; books bound in blue, brown and dark green cloth, books bound in leather with gold tooling and marbled edges, books with cracked spines and titles too faded to read; more than two thousand of them. Edward knew them all and loved them all; they were his companions, his inspiration.

He took one up and caressed it; this was the first of several given to him by his dear friend Elihu Burritt, and this, the first volume of poems by John Gregory with whom he had been friends since his early days in Bideford. These four lying side by side were all inscribed to him by their authors; and this one, this was his most treasured possession – *Antony and Octavius* by the great man Walter Savage Landor. He opened it reverently as he had hundreds of times to see the dedication, printed so every purchaser of the book could read it: '*These scenes are dedicated to Edward Capern, poet and day-labourer at Bideford, Devon.*' He sighed and replaced the book carefully in the trunk. Here was another – should this not have pride of place on his new shelves? It was a cheap edition of Bunyan's *Pilgrim's Progress*, its faded cover frayed at the edges, the spine broken and the pages loose, yet it was this very book that had opened his eyes to the world around him and set him on the path of poetry and learning, this book that had made him the man he was.

1819 – 1846

Early Life

O give me back the dreams of youth,
Those visions bright and glowing,
When all was innocence and truth,
And joy a cup o'erflowing.

Chapter One

There was only one book in his childhood home. The Bible was kept on a high shelf in the kitchen above the pots and pans and Edward was the only one allowed to look at it, because he was the eldest. Perhaps it was not often that his mother lifted it down for him; but in his memory he would have been racing through Barnstaple's narrow streets with a gang of other boys, the October evening drawing in and smoke hanging above the terraced houses, until their mothers' voices called them in one by one. His mother would look up from her sewing as he came to sit at the candlelit table, and he would feel the warmth of her glance.

Perhaps it was because of his fidgeting that she would put down her sewing and place a clean cloth on the table, reach up to the shelf and place the Bible in front of him as carefully as if it were a delicate piece of china. The cover was heavy and creaked slightly as he opened it, releasing a sweet, earthy aroma. The writing on the first page was his mother's. When he looked at it in later years he saw, with a rush of sympathy that brought tears to his eyes, that the letters were laboriously and badly formed. Her name and his father's were at the top; they both began with E, Elizabeth and Edward. His own name was underneath along with the date of his birth, Thomas was next and then his two little brothers who had the word 'died' next to their names, then came his two sisters. He knew, although he had not been told, that there would soon be another name to add to the list.

The pages were as delicate and rustling as autumn leaves. Sometimes he turned several at once, indiscriminately, to prove to himself that every single page contained as many words as the one before. He could read a lot of the words and sometimes a whole sentence but it was difficult to make a story unless his mother showed him where to start, so he would turn back to the first page and read again the story he knew. *In the beginning God created the heaven and the earth.* The words made him feel dizzy; he read them again and again until his mother leaned over and found a passage for him, prompting him when he reached a difficult word, until he could match the words to her voice.

He could read quite well because he had been to school, last year, for four months. One of his mother's relatives, who came from a branch of the family she admired, paid the pennies each week for him to learn his catechism and trace letters in a tray of sand. At the end of his second week Miss Thomas brought him up to stand at the front of the class, and he saw the other children staring blankly at him with open mouths as she told them that Edward knew all his letters and they should all work as hard as he. Before he returned to his place she whispered, *'You show great promise, Edward. You can be a great man if you try.'* His mother told him the same, not always with words but with looks and hugs.

'Your cousin, Sir Matthew Wood, he had a poor start too, but he became Lord Mayor of London and a Member of Parliament,' she would say. 'Of course, my side of the family, the Woods, are known throughout the land. Your cousin Sir Matthew Wood will help you make your way in the world.'

She would write to him, she said, and ask him to find a position for Edward when he was a little older. It was a member of this family who paid for him to go to school, but when the money stopped coming after only four months he had to leave. Most days he wandered through the streets to the school and sat on the steps outside to hear the lesson, until he grew tired of trying to make sense of the muffled words and ran off to play.

Edward understood that they must be poor because they did not have fine clothes and a table heaped with food like Sir Matthew Wood; but everyone who lived in Vicarage Street and the Derby area of Barnstaple was the same. Many were worse off than his family because when the lace factory was on short time they could not always afford to buy the bread that his father baked. At the end of each day when his father came through from the bakery, his mother would turn away to the fireplace and the children fall silent until they knew his mood; sometimes he brought bread home because it had not sold and then he was angry and shouted that it was the fault of the government who had fixed the price of corn, and if he did not sell the bread, he could not afford to buy more flour. The children had to avoid their father's eyes and eat the bread in silence, as if they did not like it. Edward knew that his parents had moved from Tiverton when he was only three, because his father thought there would be more people in Barnstaple needing to buy bread when the lace factory opened.

The day came when Edward was given baked potatoes wrapped in a cloth for lunch and told to take all the children out of the house while Mrs Harvey came to sit with his mother. As he closed the door, he heard his mother groan upstairs and understood that before long another name would be written in the Bible.

He told Thomas that they must carry the little ones to save their bare feet being hurt by the rough surface of the road; Elizabeth struggled to get down so to distract her he sang her the rhymes, some plaintive and some jolly, that had become part of him through hearing his mother sing them. He and Thomas walked until they left the grey, narrow streets behind and came to a flower-studded meadow that sloped down to the River Yeo. It was somewhere their mother liked to take them when she could spare an hour or two, because here the river ran clean and bright, quite unlike the offensive brown sludge it became as it passed through the town.

They took turns minding the babies. While Thomas climbed the trees that overhung the river and dangled by his hands to swing his feet through the deepest water, Edward sat with Thomazine in his lap and Elizabeth by his side on the grassy bank, picking flowers for their hair to keep them amused. The sunlight glinted through the branches, silvering the river as it burbled over the stony riverbed and lighting on a kingfisher that appeared, suddenly, on the opposite bank, making him gasp before it flew upstream in flash of azure. When Thomas returned, Edward leapt up and ran as fast as he could through the long grass alongside the river, jumping over thistles and frightening the sheep in his excitement at discovering the glorious beauty that was in the world.

They returned home when the shadows were lengthening. The house was silent; his father sat in the corner of the dark kitchen with a bundle in his arms.

'Here, Edward. I'm glad you'm home.' His new little sister was passed to him. 'Your ma's bad.'

His mother was still upstairs a week later. Her face was grey and drawn as he crept into the small room, his nose wrinkling at the stale air, but she turned her head and there was love in her eyes for him.

'I shall write to your cousin, Sir Matthew Wood,' she whispered. 'He will help us. What your father wants – that wouldn't be the right start in life for you.' She looked down at baby Caroline tucked in the crook of her arm and smiled up at him. 'She has the same look about her as you did at this age.'

The letter was sent despite his father's protestations that, if a reply came, they would not be able to afford the shilling it would cost to receive it. His fears were unfounded because no letter arrived, and the following week the doctor had to visit on two more occasions which meant more expense. Edward heard his parents' voices after he went to bed, his mother pleading and his father persuasive.

The next morning his father called him into the kitchen and sat him down. 'You'm a man now, and you can earn a wage like a man to help your mother and your sisters. I'm not about to start beggin' for parish relief.'

Edward was to start as a threading boy at the lace factory the following Monday. He was nine years old.

His mother was up to see him off before 5 a.m., the first time she had been out of bed since the birth. She leaned on the furniture as she moved slowly around the kitchen, packing up some bread and a bottle of cold tea for his breakfast. When the knock on the door came, she hugged him tightly and he felt proud to be such a comfort to her.

Although it was still dark, the streets were thronged with silent people walking with bowed heads towards the factory bell that sounded in the distance. Edward walked with Mr Glover, on whose machine he was to work. It seemed a great adventure and he asked lots of questions as he skipped along, unconcerned that Mr Glover's replies were indistinct mutters. The factory was as long as a whole street of houses and so high he had to crane his neck to see up to the fourth storey; he stopped to stare, having never taken much notice of it before, and had to run after his master before he lost him in the crowd.

The machinery was starting up as they entered the factory, a tremendous rattling, clattering and banging that increased in intensity until it was louder than any noise he had heard before. He covered his ears and was ready to run if the revolving wheels and cranking levers of the huge animal-like machines started moving towards him, but Mr Glover grabbed his arm and pulled him to one side.

They stood next to a massive iron frame containing an immense complexity of inert parts, seemingly asleep despite the din from its neighbours. From a box containing numerous identical items, Mr Glover picked up a small brass wheel wound with cotton thread. He tried to show Edward how to take the end of the thread and pass it through a hole in a small steel carriage, but his fingers were too big and after a few fumbled attempts he called to a boy working by the next machine. Edward knew him as Jed; he was an older boy who lived in the next street. Jed demonstrated the required action but with such speed that it was impossible to follow. After glancing nervously over to his own machine, he repeated the action again: pass the thread through the eye, hold back the spring, drop the bobbin into its carriage and release the spring. Edward tried and, after a failed first attempt, met with success. He stood back, looking up at Mr Glover for the expected praise.

'Don't stop now, boy, there's 'undreds more, thousands, and they have to be done fast so's I can set 'em in place.'

Jed demonstrated the required speed and completed a dozen or more in seconds, before returning to his own work. After a couple of failed attempts, Edward set to again and gradually built up speed until he felt that his fingers were flying along, yet Mr Glover seemed always to be waiting for the next bobbin and sometimes wandered off a short distance. Edward was taking advantage of his absence to rest for a moment, stretch his overworked fingers and gaze at the active machines when he felt a sudden blow to the side of his head which almost threw him off balance. For a second he couldn't think what had hit him, until Mr Glover roared in his ear.

'Don't stop, numbskull! I'm waiting for 'ee and losing money as it is!'

His face burning with shame, Edward set to again and forced his fumbling fingers to move even faster; his chest felt tight and he struggled to breathe but he knew he must not cry. It was impossible to look up while performing the task because he had to focus closely in order to pass the fine thread through the tiny eye, and sometimes the end of the thread was slightly frayed making the job much harder; hours passed before he dared to glance in Mr Glover's direction again. He saw that his master was working in a leisurely but steady manner and was no longer having to stand and wait for bobbins. Edward had worked his way through four boxes and was starting on the fifth. Mr Glover, speaking for the first time since his outburst, told him that each box contained five hundred bobbins. When the final box was finished it would be time to start the machine.

'We're well behind time, but you'm learning fast.' This time he felt he might cry from pride and his fingers seemed to fly still faster despite his aching legs and smarting eyes. He longed to see the machine in action and know that his work had made it possible.

Finally, the last bobbin was in place. Mr Glover adjusted some small parts, pulled some levers and the machine started to move, building up speed and finding a steady rhythm. Edward stared in astonishment. The monster which had stood idle was now engaged in an almost maddening variety of movements, the bobbins he had threaded swinging from side to side in a pendulum-like motion while travelling the length of the machine, other components moving steadily back and forth, up and down, so that all were dancing around each other in perfect harmony and producing their own rhythmic clanks and jangles which combined to create a deafening clatter. An immense roller above it all steadily turned to draw up a sheet of lace netting the length of the entire machine, lace that he had helped to make. He stood captivated by the spectacle until he suddenly broke away and ran to the back of the machine. There was no one there!

'Who's making it all work?'

Mr Glover stood in front, watching the movement intently and making occasional adjustments, but *he* wasn't making it all move. Could someone be underneath? He went to dive below the workings until Mr Glover grabbed him and dragged him up.

''Tis steam, boy. I'll show 'ee the engine room later.'

A man brought several wooden boxes of bobbins, piled them on the floor and removed those that Edward had emptied. Mr Glover gestured at the stack of boxes, slightly higher than the one just completed. 'On with the next, boy.'

Edward stared in disbelief. 'But I have to watch the machine!'

'Not your job, boy. Get moving. Get a head start.'

He could scarcely believe his ears. 'What? I got to do more?'

'What d'you expect! Get going!' Then in a milder tone, ''Twill be dinner time dreckly.'

Edward started on the first box, his eyes pricking with tears and his head bowed. He could not believe that his work consisted only of this one endless task.

After dinner they set to again. He knew he was getting faster and was even able to glance up occasionally at the frenetic activity of the nearest machine, but the task did not engage his mind. He longed to explore the factory and speak to the other boys. As more hours passed his legs began to ache horribly from standing still for so long and his fingertips tingled painfully; several times he felt himself swaying with exhaustion. After what seemed an interminable length of time, the bell finally rang. It was seven o'clock; he had worked for fourteen hours with two short breaks.

He walked home in a daze, barely aware of the group of boys who invited him to join them in kicking an old knuckle bone from one to another along the street. His mother was waiting anxiously for him at the door; she enveloped him in her arms and he let her lead him into the kitchen, hardly able to walk another step unaided. He fell asleep while eating his broth and woke to find her feeding him with a spoon like a baby, then his father carried him up to bed and he was asleep again before reaching the curtained alcove he shared with Thomas.

He never became inured to the tedium of the task and he longed for each day to be the last. He was never woken by the knocker-up who went from house to house at 4.30, and had to be roused by his father who started work in the bakery even earlier, but Edward rarely fell asleep at his work as some boys did. As he worked through the long afternoon and evening, he would hear from time to time a shout above the din of the machinery and would look up to see one of the boys on the floor, having fallen over through exhaustion. The lace twister would usually yell at his assistant and haul him to his feet, but Edward twice saw boys being beaten for their crime. As he became more adept, he found that there was a second or two while reaching for the next bobbin when he could glance at the boy at the next machine, or the one across the way. If they could make their glances coincide, one or both could pull a face or make a gesture which was sufficiently amusing to break the monotony of the task. Sometimes it was possible to build up a rhythm of working that enabled their eyes to meet after every bobbin, but this generally led to a build-up of hilarity and resulted in one or both of them receiving a blow from their masters. On occasion one of the boys would acquire a scrap of wood or a stone which could be kicked surreptitiously from one to another, sometimes passing it right around the factory before it was discovered and confiscated.

Some of the boys were allowed to help set up and attend the machines. Mr Glover did not permit such a pleasurable activity but Edward stopped regretting this when, one day, a boy got his arm caught in a machine and was almost dragged in. His arm was badly broken in two places and he did not return to work again.

The high point of his week was coming home on a Saturday night to see his mother waiting, as always, on the doorstep for him, and handing her his 3s 6d weekly wage. The hours of work were increased or reduced according to the lace orders received. When he was put on short time, it was a huge relief to be sent home early while there was still time to rush around the streets in a frenzy of excitement with other children; however, his wages were reduced along with his hours and his father's income fell because the lace workers were short of money for buying bread. His mother made sure that he did not go to bed hungry, but he knew there was not enough food for everyone in the family. When there was an increase in orders for the factory, his hours became almost insupportable and there were several occasions when he worked twenty hours out of twenty-four; the rest of the family then flourished because the whole Derby area could afford to eat well.

Sunday was now a bright light towards which he struggled all week. To wake feeling refreshed and to eat breakfast with the rest of the family, to play with his three little sisters; then, dressed in clean clothes and with his hair oiled, to go to the Wesleyan Sunday School with Thomas – it was a day of undiluted pleasure. For many children, Sunday School seemed to be almost as much of a trial as going to work, but he loved the hushed atmosphere of the chapel schoolroom and the lilting rhythm of the teacher's voice when she read to the class.

Recognising that Edward had ability, she allowed him to read her Bible while the other children were being taught their letters. He read some passages again and again in his head, thrilled by the sound of the words even when he didn't understand their meaning. *Chronicles* was his favourite, especially David's adventures. He tried to imagine a thousand chariots and seven thousand horsemen crowding the streets of Barnstaple in place of the few tired horses pulling farm carts. Unlike the Bible at home, some of the pages carried illustrations showing bare-chested men with wings, plump babies peeping from clouds, and long-haired men draped in cloth dramatically brandishing swords or holding flaming torches aloft before a fantastical backdrop of wooded mountain crags. It was after studying some of these pictures that he was asked to read a passage to the class while the teacher prepared the next lesson.

So fired up was he by the images that he started off loudly and dramatically, 'Yea!' The class sat up, shocked. 'Though I walk through the valley of the shadow of death, I will fear *no* evil.' He was exhilarated; no one laughed, they were as caught up in it as he was himself and the room was strangely silent when he eventually sat down, shaky with excitement.

In the afternoon he and Thomas were free to do as they wished. They roamed the streets and surrounding countryside with a gang of other boys, running races and playing leapfrog, climbing trees, fighting and sometimes stealing. Apples from the orchards at Pitt were a favourite and some of the boys stole potatoes and cabbages from gardens but Edward would never have been able to take anything home without his mother asking searching questions. He avoided the worst crimes by wandering from the outskirts of the town into deep lanes where the only sounds were the songs of birds. Sometimes he climbed a gate into a field and lay on his back in the long grass, listening to the rustling of leaves and letting his eyes follow the shifting patterns made by clouds. After these occasions he would give his mother a bunch of wild flowers instead of stolen vegetables and would tell her about the wonderful things he had seen, knowing that she never tired of listening to his stories.

Once, when he was part of the group, they targeted Vicarage Lawn, a large house set in its own grounds which was run as a boys' boarding school. They sauntered past the gates while concocting a plan to scale the garden wall at the back in search of an open window. Edward stopped at the gates and watched the boys in the garden. Dressed in clothes that made even his Sunday best look poor, pairs of boys deep in conversation wandered along the flower-lined paths, some played with bats and a ball, others lay reading on the grass. One boy was engrossed in a book and had a pile of three or four more next to him. Edward longed to call out to him and ask him what he was reading, but knew that he would only receive a scornful glance. The gate was locked and he could not pass through, but he stood for a long time, watching.

Chapter Two

Edward sat in a corner of the dark, wood-panelled workshop studying the book he had found on a shelf. He should have been working, so while he read he remained alert for Mr East's return. The book was an encyclopaedia. It had taken him a while to understand the title and to realise that all the entries in the book began with F, G or H.

Edward ran his finger under the words again. 'GARTER, ORDER OF THE, one of the most ancient and illustrious of the military orders of knighthood in Europe, was founded by Edward III.' He didn't know when Edward III had been king, and he couldn't find out because he didn't have the volume that contained the letter E. He couldn't look up Europe either. Was England in Europe? There was so much he didn't know.

Mr East was good at answering his questions but became impatient after a while: 'I'm not your schoolmaster, you'm here to learn shoemaking, boy!'

He had been with Mr East for several years. After four years at the lace factory, it was decided he should move on because the constant close work in poor light had damaged his eyesight, and his fingers were becoming too large for the fine threading. His mother was keen for him to learn a trade so it was arranged that he would be apprenticed to Samuel East, a shoemaker in Barnstaple High Street; the premium was paid from a sum she had managed to put aside for the purpose. He had felt humbled that she should manage to do so whilst in continuing poor health since the death of the most recent baby, Susannah.

He heard the outer door open so he quickly put the book down and bent low over the leather he was supposed to be shaping, as if concentrating intently; but the shuffling footsteps and pungent smell of unwashed clothes told him that it was only old Mr Tucker.

'Need a stitch again, do they, Mr Tucker?'

'Ah, they do, boy.' The old man eased his boot off, revealing a very dirty and gnarled foot. The leather was deeply corrugated and cracked and carried an odour which caused Edward to hold it at arm's length. The welt and edges of the upper were torn in many places but he managed to stitch the sole to an intact area.

'Won't last much longer, Mr Tucker.'

'Ah, 'twill see me out.'

He hobbled away and Edward looked longingly at the book but he was already behind with the tasks awaiting him on the bench, so reluctantly he set to work.

When Mr East returned, Edward ate his dinner quickly and asked for permission to go out for ten minutes. The breezy March day revitalised him as he strode along the busy High Street; looking up beyond the roofs and clusters of chimneys, he saw gleaming white seagulls floating gracefully against an azure sky and regretted the seven hours still to be endured in the close, cluttered atmosphere of the workshop.

Reaching Mr Brightwell's bookshop, he hesitated for a moment then boldly opened the door. Mr Brightwell was serving a gentleman so did not greet him with the usual 'What! You again!' Edward was able to sidle straight over to the box on the shop floor. He was not allowed to touch the new books on the shelves but this box contained second-hand books, and amongst the religious tracts and old prayer books was one that had caught his interest; he had returned three times to look at it.

The cheap cloth cover was scuffed but the lettering was easily read: *Pilgrim's Progress by John Bunyan*. The first page of the book was already deeply scored in his memory, he did not fully understand the meaning but there was music in the rhythm of the lines. He read the words again, and again they carried him high above the rooftops, dizzying him with their ambition; he heard again their whispered promise that here, amongst words and their tantalising meanings, lay the key to his future.

The shop bell rang and he saw that he was alone with Mr Brightwell.

'I got my threepence, Sir. My mother give it me.'

And then he was walking down the street with *Pilgrim's Progress* in his pocket, the very first book that he ever owned.

Mr East was poring over the newspaper and Edward leaned in, trying to see. Mr East ran his finger down the closely-spaced columns and jabbed at a paragraph.

'Here it is! "The woman who died..." Yes! of starvation it is said and the Poor Law Officials are blamed for their heartlessness. Just as I heard. Didn't I say this would happen? What do they care as long as they've one less mouth to feed?'

'Shall us write the letter then, like us planned? To the Mayor?' It made his legs feel weak to think of it – a letter in the paper with his name and others underneath.

He was the youngest of a dozen men who squeezed into the workshop each week to discuss whatever seemed of greatest importance; but the topic was very often the Poor Law Amendment Act and the terrible effects of it throughout the town. They discussed the fate of William Laskey who had lived in the old Workhouse for years, but had been moved to the new building and told he must work, and then was thrown out when he was unable to do so. He had wandered the town, a wretched figure in rags with badly ulcerated legs. Edward saw him one day while walking to work and, shocked at his appearance, gave him his lunch packet. The old man clutched on to his arm. 'Thank 'ee, my boy, thank 'ee.' Edward thought he would never let go.

William was eventually taken into the workhouse infirmary where he died soon after. Others were forced to walk from villages up to eighteen miles away to apply for relief and, if admitted to the Workhouse, were too far away for relatives to visit. The Act did not work well for North Devon's remote community. It had been suggested that the Mayor should petition Parliament against certain provisions of the Act, but when Mr East approached him, he was brushed away as one would a bothersome fly. So the group now planned to put their names to a letter, demanding a public meeting.

'Won't it get us in trouble, doing that?'

'Don't 'ee worry about it boy, us must stand up for them as can't stand up for theirselves.'

Edward knew Mr East had lost one or two customers through his outspoken views, and he admired his employer for being so firm in his beliefs.

Edward paid a penny a week along with three other men for the weekly copy of the *North Devon Journal*, which was then shared between them. Each was able to take it home for a night and when it was Edward's turn, he stayed up until he had read every word, then often had difficulty sleeping as his mind raced over all the information he had taken in. All the men read the newspaper and he tried to guess what they would say about the articles; he was used to believing everything he read, but Mr East distrusted anyone who supported the New Poor Law or the introduction of the police force, or who spoke out against Chartists.

It was the column headed 'Literary Gleanings' that secretly interested Edward most. Sometimes there was an amusing story or a weighty opinion, but best of all was when a poem was included and he could marvel at the power of words to simultaneously arouse his emotions and stimulate his thoughts. Apart from those in the group, he did not have any friends who could read. The men had created a small lending library between them by sharing any books they owned. He had his copy of *Pilgrim's Progress* and others possessed *Robinson Crusoe*, *Sartor Resartus* and Shakespeare's *Sonnets*; while Mr East now owned eleven volumes of the *Penny Cyclopaedia of the Society for the Diffusion of Useful Knowledge*. Edward once brought in a religious tract which he had been sold for a penny on the street, but Mr East said it was written only to persuade poor people to be satisfied with their situation in life.

Sometimes when he became engrossed in a book, he stayed at home on a Sunday to read instead of going to chapel, but the Minister noticed his absence and came to visit him, warning that he would be forever lost unless he renounced all books except those that the Minister approved.

'Consider the condition of your soul if you died while reading an irreligious book!'

After the warning, Edward made sure he went to chapel at least once on a Sunday but he did not give up his reading.

Mr East's grunt of displeasure as he read the newspaper brought Edward back to the current situation. He peered over his employer's shoulder to read the article about the inquest. It made him shiver; he and his family had known hunger but had always assumed that aid would be available if they were forced to seek it. Mr East stood up.

'Us needs to meet tonight and write this letter. I'll go and see Mr Edwards and he can spread the word. While I'm gone there's them two repairs to do and the new leather to skive.'

Edward's heart sank. 'Tonight? Can't it be another day?'

Mr East stood in the doorway removing his apron. 'Why wait? Us wants to get the letter in next week's paper. I know Mr Avery will print it for us because he's unhappy with this new law, along with us. Get that leather done now, I'll be ten minutes.'

Edward held the leather taut on the workbench, picked up a blade and pushed it carefully along the edge in long, slow strokes to create a quarter-inch skive. He had had other plans for tonight; there was someone he hoped to see and he had thought of little else all day. Her name was Jane Trick.

Jane had recently moved into Barnstaple with her grandmother. This time, she met the upheaval in her life with eagerness as well as apprehension.

Her childhood had been disrupted when she was still very young. She did not remember much about that time, but she did recall being carried in her father's arms as he walked. She knew now that he must have walked for many hours. Gradually it became light and she was able to see the empty lanes through which they passed, and hear the first birds as they started to sing. She was tired of being jolted around and wanted to get down, but his silence made her afraid. When it came on to rain he pulled the blanket up over her head and walked on. She never saw her father again after that long walk.

Her next memory was of sitting on the floor in her grandmother's house in Ashford playing with a box of buttons, and realising that one of them matched the buttons on her mother's dress. She stroked it and held it close to her face, remembering how she had repeatedly run her finger over the smooth surface when cradled on her mother's lap. It was only later that she came to realise that her mother was dead.

Her grandmother was a warm, comforting presence. As Jane got older, they worked side by side from first light, cleaning, cooking, tending the hens and the vegetable garden, gathering firewood and then sewing, always sewing. Sometimes they sewed together by candlelight well into the night, until her back was aching and her fingertips were stinging. The only time she spoke to other children was at Sunday School or when she went with her grandmother to take healing herbs to the sick; she would glance up at the window to watch them playing outside, but it never occurred to her to want to leave her sewing and join in.

Her grandmother was a talented dressmaker and milliner and she taught Jane carefully and systematically, starting with the plain sewing then moving on to copying designs and cutting out. She taught her how to examine dresses – through surreptitious glances if they were being worn by their owners – to gauge the length and position of seams, the number of gathers on the shoulder and the width of the skirt at the hem, until she could copy any dress she saw. When her grandmother's hands started to be affected by rheumatism, Jane was able to take on all the work. One day a week she went to Strand House to do the family's mending, and eventually she was trusted to make Mrs Langdon's dresses. She and her grandmother only went hungry when orders stopped due to a bad harvest.

Jane was nineteen when they were told their cottage in Ashford was needed for a farm-worker. She walked to Barnstaple to look for a new home, hoping there would be regular work in the town. Following her grandmother's directions, she visited a cousin on Well Street to ask if he knew of any cottages to rent. She was told of two; the first cost more than they could afford but the second was cheaper, and she asked to see it.

The afternoon light was beginning to fade and she was anxious to return home before dark. Her guide took her through a narrow street where lace workers lived to reach the cottage in the Derby area of Barnstaple. The houses were crowded so close that the darkness seemed further advanced than elsewhere; there was scarcely room to pass between them, and further rows lay behind.

'Bain't there no gardens?' she asked.

'No, just small backlets. But some keep a pig there.'

She was familiar with the smell of pigs but the stench here was worse and seemed to rise from the open drain in the middle of the street where children, dirtier and poorer even than those in the village, played amongst the filth. A crowd of boys on the corner eyed her and called out things that made her scarlet with embarrassment.

They came to a wider street where the houses were larger, making her feel more hopeful; but she was taken to a tiny cottage which had just two rooms plus a small scullery and an even smaller yard. She hesitated. It wasn't anything like she or her grandmother had imagined.

'How much is the rent?'

'Sixpence a week.'

It was a little less than they had been paying. She wished she could talk to her grandmother but there wasn't time because they had to leave the Ashford house the following week. She went to the front door and looked down the street.

It was more respectable than the narrow ways that ran off it. Her cousin seemed to read her thoughts.

'You can walk that way to the High Street, don't have to go through they places.'

She told him she would take the cottage. As she walked the three miles back to Ashford with the sun descending beyond the sweeping view over the estuary, her mind raced with anxiety and excitement.

The cottage to which Jane and her grandmother moved was in Vicarage Street, a broad street of large terraced houses and smaller cottages. Once they were settled in, Jane ventured out to find work. She still had her day at Strand House and two customers in Barnstaple who were related to people in Ashford, but it wasn't enough. Carrying a dress and a bonnet she had recently made, she began to knock on doors in Vicarage Street. She was not used to approaching strangers and each time she heard footsteps she had to prevent herself from hurrying back to her home. Most people made it clear that they had no money for such things, but Jane tried to answer politely even when met with rudeness.

'If you do ever need anything, or hear tell of someone wanting a dressmaker, I live just over in that house there.'

One woman seemed impressed with the standard of work and was interested when Jane explained how she could remake an old dress in a new style; another was very taken with the bonnet. Her confidence began to grow a little.

A young man of about her own age opened the next door.

'Hello!' He leaned against the doorframe, smiling at her. He had a broad, expressive face, sandy hair and a small reddish beard.

'Oh! Is your mother at home?'

'Her's in bed, not very well. My name's Edward Capern. Can I help?'

He had a very direct gaze. She felt rather flustered.

'I'm a dressmaker, I live a few doors down– '

'I know. I saw you moving in. Got anything to suit me, then?' He held out his arms with a flourish. He was quite sturdy and the thought of him in a dress made her giggle, but she put her hand over her mouth and tried to be serious.

'Could I call in to see her when she's better? Show her these things? I can make anything– dresses, coats, plain hats or fancy hats…'

His smile and the way he kept looking at her were confusing her; she was more used to the boys in the village who stared at their boots and mumbled.

'Or I can remake dresses. Will 'ee tell her?'

'Shall I compare thee to a summer's day?'

'What?' She didn't know what he was talking about and he would keep looking at her! She could feel the giggles coming on again. 'I'd better go…'

'No, wait!' He put his hand gently on her arm. She could feel it long after she got home. 'Come back when my sisters are in. Ma doesn't get out much but they'll be interested. Come when I'm at home too!' She was backing away in embarrassment but he didn't let go of her arm. 'Promise!'

She promised.

Edward had never walked out with a girl. He sometimes talked with Mary Coates who lived around the corner in Lower Maudlin Street and had thought of asking her to walk with him. She wore her bodice very tight but she shrieked with laughter at things which were not very amusing.

Jane had dark eyes that drew his to them and her lips were full of life as if she was trying not to laugh. He had noticed her before she knocked at his door, and the next evening she came to his house to show his sisters some clothes. He stood nonchalantly in the corner of the kitchen while she talked to Elizabeth and Thomazine, who were visibly enchanted by her.

'That's a fine hat', he said, although he knew nothing of hats, ''tis as pretty as a meadow full of flowers!' She looked at him from under her dark lashes and laughed, and he liked the sound so much he tried to think of ways to make her laugh again. That was three days ago.

The knife cut deep into the leather. He was not concentrating hard enough. He shaved off a little each side of the cut then smoothed it with his thumb, hoping that Mr East would not notice.

His memories of the evening were with him all the time and mingled in his imagination with what was surely to come, one day. When he closed his eyes he saw her, heard her breathing and the rustle of her dress, and when he was out on the street he searched for her face. She had a small, neat figure and her movements were quick and light. It occurred to him for the first time how heavy Mary Coates was on her feet.

When Jane took off her bonnet to show the girls how it was made, he saw how her very dark hair curled on her cheek.

'Where did 'ee get those dark good looks then?'

She looked up at him, trying again not to smile. 'My mother used to say we have Spanish blood, perhaps from a sailor who settled here.' She turned back to Elizabeth. 'See, if you've no ribbon, you can use a long strip of cotton, perhaps from a dress you've shortened, hem it like this and tie it round the bonnet.'

He could tell that she knew his sisters had no money to pay a dressmaker, but she was happy to make friends with them and share some of her knowledge. He liked her for that. She offered to come back one day and help Elizabeth make a bonnet. When she left, he went to the door with her.

'I know it's just you and your grandmother over there– if you ever need anything done…'

'Thank you, but I know how to do most things.' She looked straight at him this time and he had a feeling she was better at practical tasks than he was.

'But, as we'm neighbours, we'm bound to meet.' She smiled and he couldn't even think of a reply.

Later, as he helped his mother downstairs, he told her about their new neighbour.

'You'm sweet on her already,' she said, but then had to stop for her cough. It sometimes seemed as if her cough was the only strong thing left in her.

He had intended to stand out in the road this evening, to talk to whoever was around and perhaps wander up and down a little, hoping Jane would see him and come out on an errand. But now there was this meeting with Mr East. In his irritation, he cut into the leather again.

Three months later, after a day's work in Ashford, Jane was walking quickly down the narrow country lane that led towards Barnstaple. It was a fine August evening and it would be several hours before dusk fell; the glaring heat of the middle of the day had dissipated into a soft, warm breeze which played on her cheek and bare forearms. Her breath came fast and her boots tap-tapped on the stony path in a rhythm that was even faster than the beating of her heart. She was late and would have liked to run.

The sound of low voices and a rhythmic swish, swish, reached her from the far side of the high hedgerow; as she passed a gateway, she saw half a dozen men turning hay. They seemed part of a graceful dance as one by one they bent over the soft heaps with their pitchforks, lifted a huge swathe of hay and tossed it high so it turned and fell back to the ground with a sigh, wafting its sweet, earthy scent in her direction. She recognised two or three of the men but just lifted her hand to them and hurried on. The hedgebanks, bright with meadowsweet and red campion, obscured her view until she reached a stile and could look down on the River Taw gleaming like a silver ribbon as it snaked through the green and tawny landscape to the broad estuary. Running alongside the river was the long straight road where she was to meet Edward.

Until now their meetings had been in the company of his sisters. She had been helping Thomazine to decorate a bonnet and when that was done she had suggested that they should make one together from start to finish. Edward usually managed to be at home, asking questions as he watched them work, talking about things that were going on in the town or pretending to read a book. She knew he was pretending because he never turned the pages and was often looking at her instead. They had developed a game; she would try to avoid his eyes when she knew he was looking at her, but she could only manage it for a little while.

'What be you two laughing at?' Thomazine would ask suspiciously, and Edward gave a clever reply. Jane loved to hear his voice; it was rich and musical. Sometimes as she and Thomazine worked, he read to them from a book.

Jane had visited her cousin in Well Street and asked him to teach her to read. She was afraid Edward would no longer like her if he discovered that she could not. She now knew her letters and her cousin had lent her a chapbook which she propped open on the table while she was sewing or put on a shelf in front of her on washday with the pages fastened back with a clothes-peg, so she could try to make out some of the words while she was working. Much of it bored her. She hoped one day to be able to read the sort of books that Edward enjoyed, because he had so many strange and interesting things to say which he must have learned from books. She had never met anyone like him.

Last Sunday she, Thomazine and Edward had gone to Pitt Farm to buy some straw for making bonnets. As they walked, Edward picked delicate blue flowers and wove their stems together to fasten in his sister's hair.

'Would 'ee like some too?' She knew by the way he looked at her that he wanted very much to put flowers in her hair. She felt too confused to reply but she nodded, then he stood so close to her she could smell his sun-warmed skin, and the hairs on his arm brushed against her cheek. He moved away slowly and they both walked in silence for a while.

Later he started to sing and soon Thomazine joined in. When they had finished, he turned to Jane,

'Don't 'ee want to sing along with us then?'

She was embarrassed. 'I would, but I don't know the words.' He leaned closer to her.

'What songs do you know then? You sing, and us'll join in.'

Reluctantly she told him she knew no songs.

'Didn't your mother sing to 'ee when you were small?' He put his arm around her shoulder as if to console her and she leant in for a moment, but the desire to be held and comforted was so strong that she had to move away again.

'Us'll teach you the words then, won't us, Thomazine?

"Now's the time for mirth and play,

Saturday's a holyday

Praise to heaven's unceasing yield

I've found a lark's nest in a field."'

He had a deep, mellow voice. He sang the first two lines again and made her join in. Singing together felt strangely intimate, as if they walked hand-in-hand.

As they approached Pitt Farm they heard a prolonged and repeated call echoing from across the hedge: 'Caow! Caow! Caow!'

The human call was accompanied by the barking of a dog and from a gateway ahead on their right the leader of a herd of dark red cows swayed into the lane which was muddied by their twice-daily passage. They walked slowly behind the jostling cows and when Edward moved closer to Jane to accommodate the farmer, his arm brushed repeatedly against hers. She was careful not to glance up at him, but looked straight ahead at the shuffling, swaying cows, their great bags of milk swinging and dripping under them, and she inhaled their powerful milky aroma. When the farmer stepped ahead to chivvy a cow, Edward did not move away from her.

And now she was to meet him on her own. All day she had both longed for and feared the moment. As she sat sewing in the window seat at Ashford Parsonage, she had pictured his broad, kind face and tried to imagine what he might say. She was afraid he might be annoyed that she was late; he might have grown tired of waiting for her and walked back to Barnstaple. She could not walk any faster without breaking into a run. As she approached the stile where the path met the road, she saw him just as he turned to look up the hill towards her, and they walked towards each other as if drawn by magnets. Jane saw that he was smiling, and when they met at the stile he took both her hands in his. For once, he did not seem to know what to say, so she had to break the silence.

'I'm sorry I'm late, there was so much work to do and I've walked so fast down the hill – ' She was a little out of breath.

'Ssshh, it don't matter.' He pulled her towards him and they stood for a moment with the wooden bars of the stile between them.

'Here, climb over to me.'

He held her hand to help her on to the stile, then lifted her down with his hands around her waist and drew her to him. She felt herself enveloped in warmth; her heart was beating hard against the pressure of his chest and his thighs were warm against hers. His hands slowly stroked her back. He moved away a little and she knew he was looking at her, but she could not at first meet his eyes.

'Janie!'

She lifted her head and her gaze was drawn in by his warm brown eyes; she could not look away as he drew her closer again, and their lips met. He kissed her gently two, three times, and she felt herself relaxing into his embrace.

'Janie! I've wanted so much to hold you like this.' When he spoke, his breath tickled her ear. They looked at each other again, and she felt her smile coming from somewhere deep inside.

They stayed beside the stile for a long time. Then, gradually starting to talk and to laugh, they linked arms and barely noticed the dust clouds thrown up by farmers' carts or the curious stares of passers-by as they walked slowly back to Barnstaple, while the sun sank behind them towards the estuary.

Chapter Three

Edward woke at dawn and turned to lie on his back, his hands behind his head. The space where he lay was separated from his parents' room by a curtain and had no window, so it was not the light from the rising sun that had woken him; it was dreams of Jane. Every morning his first thought was of her waking just a few yards away in the bed she shared with her grandmother, a distance that might as well have been miles for all the walls that separated them.

It was three years since she had agreed to marry him but they were still unable to make the dream a reality. He could not imagine leaving his mother while she was so unwell, and Jane's grandmother was crippled with rheumatism and could not live alone. Even if they had been free to marry, he had not yet achieved the steady income that would allow them to do so. His regular work with Mr East had ceased due to lack of orders; many people in Barnstaple did not have enough money for food, and the ache of an empty belly was more demanding than the discomfort of a boot sole that flapped at every step.

For the poor, each year had been harder than the one before. First there was a drought that caused crops to wither in the parched ground and the following year the weather was cold, resulting in poor harvests and higher food prices; now there was talk of potato crops being hit by a plague. The lace industry was in a depression. Edward worked for his father occasionally but the bakery made very little profit and could not sustain two men; yet some people imagined that bakers were becoming rich while the poor starved, so they made their discontent known through daily complaints. Once Edward came down in the morning to find the bakery window broken and a half-brick on the floor inside; another time a badly written note was pushed under the door threatening to set fire to the building. It was unfair, but he grew tired of hearing his father railing at his treatment.

'I ask 7½ pence for a 4lb loaf – in London it is 10 pence yet *I* am accused of charging too much! If I lower the price any further I'll be giving it away.'

Edward watched as his friends aimlessly wandered the streets, their faces growing hard and bleak as they saw the prospect of a decent life vanishing before them. It distressed him to see his neighbour's children dressed in rags, sitting listlessly on their doorstep and lacking the energy even to play. He knew they slept on the bare floor of the room inside, the furniture having been sold to pay the rent. How would he feel if he and Jane had married, and these were his children? He crouched down to talk to them but his father reacted angrily when he asked for a loaf to give them.

'What! Would you feed your neighbours and see your mother starve? The children'd not be so hungry if their father didn't spend money on ale!'

His own family were not as badly off as some. They were sometimes hungry, but they did not starve. Edward found work where he could and collected wood for fuel; to save on candles he read by the light of fireflies caught in a glass jar. Caroline and Thomazine were in work and Elizabeth, being the eldest daughter, looked after the house and nursed her mother. Thomas had married and made the treacherous journey over the sea to America in hope of a better life, but neither Edward nor Jane wanted to leave Devon when they married, despite the unrest in the area.

As the burden on the poor became more intolerable, the mood amongst them turned increasingly to anger. He heard about a riot in Appledore when it was discovered that potato vendors were buying for 7 pence a peck and selling at 13 pence. A mob of women from West Appledore took over, seizing the potatoes and paying only what they felt they were worth.

His own anger at the suffering of his friends and neighbours burst forth at the meetings held in Mr East's workshop. Together the men wrote impassioned letters to deliver to the Mayor and the newspaper, asking for less stringent application of the Poor Law, for support of teetotalism and for Parliament to be petitioned for the repeal of the Corn Laws which only benefitted landowners. They knew things were unlikely to change until every man had the vote. Edward studied the newspaper carefully and learned how to employ words in a persuasive and authoritative way, using phrases like 'it is well known that', and 'it is only to be regretted,' and to ask a string of questions followed by the answers. Before long the group came to depend on him to find the best words and he found himself sitting at the centre with the pen in his hand.

But his success with writing did not extend to his attempts to find employment. He repaired shoes for friends and neighbours but it was not often that Mr East had work for more than one man. In desperation Edward obtained a week's work in the tanner's yard, humping the reeking skins on his back from the carts to the tanning vats like a beast of burden. The skin of the men working in the pits was stained brown and their eyes regarded him blankly as if they had long ago ceased to feel pain or joy; they seemed barely human and his greatest fear was of becoming like them. It was a relief when he was told that there was no more work. He worked occasionally for a house carpenter and had recently helped to lay joists and rafters for the new wing of a large house near Tawstock. For the first time he could observe the workings of a wealthy household. He saw whole cheeses and huge joints of beef being brought into the house, and cakes and pies fresh from the oven when he went to the kitchen for a cup of tea. One day he saw buckets of waste being carried down to the farm for the pigs. He called across to his employer.

'Look at that! There's enough to feed a family in each of they buckets! I think those who have plenty should be duty-bound to help the hungry, or else they should be made to feel what it's like to have an empty belly – that's what I think!'

'Think? What right have *you* to think? Let's 'ave less thinking and more working – can't you see I need a hand here?'

He had to bite his tongue because if he had said what he felt, he would have been laid off immediately. His anger burned inside him all afternoon.

One evening he was reading at home when he heard shouting and the scurrying of feet and went to the door to see what was going on.

'Come on then, boy! Us is going to stop them buggers starvin' us anymore!'

'Why? What's happening?'

'Potatoes – a girt load of 'em! They'm going to be shipped out of the town if us don't stop those buggers! Us needs cheaper food and us is going to get it!'

The people of Barnstaple were hungry, yet the merchants were only interested in maximising their profits! His passion rose and he joined the throng hurrying through the narrow streets to reach the Quay. A ship was moored ready for the loading of the potatoes but the way was blocked by a large crowd of women, their gaunt, determined faces lit by the light of a full moon as they jostled at the river's edge, shouting abuse at any man considered to be the perpetrator of the crime. Edward fought his way to the front, then a shout went up as the crowd surged towards the merchant's house and he was carried along by the pressure of the bodies behind him until he was looking up at the three-storey dwelling. His anger grew at the thought of the comfort and plenty within and he found himself shouting in unison with the women around him;

'Starve us, would you! Give us food for our children!'

Then a chant formed and grew in strength, 'Give us food! Give us food!'

A figure was seen to appear at an upstairs window and quickly withdraw as a roar went up from the crowd and the chanting grew in strength. He saw that a dozen or so men had started to congregate on the edge of the crowd; recognising

Mr East, William Ching and John Dart in the near darkness, he pushed his way through to join them. William grasped Edward's arm.

'Come on! Us'll tell him us'll burn the house down if the potatoes leave the town! He'll have to take more notice of us than the women!'

Edward would gladly have done it but Mr East broke in.

'No! We want no arrests here tonight! Here comes Mr Avery. Wait, and listen.'

The magistrate, Mr Avery, crossed the road with two other men to stand on the steps of a house and look out over the crowd. The women, sensing that here was someone in authority, turned to face him and their chanting grew in strength.

'Give us food! Give us food!'

Edward felt almost frightened by the desperate and determined faces; he was thankful that Jane was not amongst them.

Mr Avery raised his hands.

'Quiet, please! Quiet!' The chanting died down a little.

'Let me talk to the person concerned. I shall see what I can do. Now, please, go home to your beds.'

Edward joined in the roar of indignation and, after a clamour of shouted refusals and insults, they all started to chant again.

Mr East spoke in Edward's ear. 'He'll have to do more than that. They won't be easily appeased.'

For several minutes Mr Avery consulted with the other men, then he climbed the steps again.

'Listen. Listen! I will buy the potatoes myself.' The shouting abated. 'I will buy the potatoes myself and tomorrow I will sell them in the market at a reduced price. Sevenpence a peck, a price you can all afford. That is my promise to you!'

Edward heard women nearest to him saying, 'You can't say fairer than that.' 'Should us believe him?' 'He's a man of his word, I've heard.'

'Now please, go home to your beds. The potatoes will be in the market tomorrow morning.'

Edward watched as the women gradually drifted away. A few remained, insisting they would stay all night to ensure that the potatoes were not loaded on to the ship under cover of darkness, and William Ching and John Dart offered to stay with them.

Edward walked slowly back to the High Street with Mr East, feeling stunned by what he had seen. Mr East was hopeful that the authorities would now take more notice of the grievances of the poor.

'They have to realise that folks can't take much more. There'll be more trouble if something isn't done. Other towns make a better job of things.'

Edward was despondent. There was so much he wanted to do! He wanted to help create a fairer society where everyone had enough to eat and the chance of an education; he wanted to read books and become a wise and cultured man; he wanted to marry Jane. But he could not even find regular employment.

Slowly he got out of bed, still thinking of Jane. When a solution to their problems could be found, a new and splendid life would begin. How long would they have to wait? Would they be old before they could be together? He went downstairs and ate several slices of bread while standing at the kitchen window looking out at the grey September day. Elizabeth had already lit the fire and was upstairs making her mother comfortable for the day, but the room was cold and he saw that there was no more wood to burn, so when he had finished eating he went into the yard and chopped what little was left. It was his habit to collect fallen branches in the woods around Barnstaple so that they did not need to buy as much coal. He was glad that there would be something to do today even if it did not put money in his pocket.

He heard the rhythmic gushing of pump water from beyond the high walls that divided the back yards, and a sweet low voice.

'Janie?' She was singing one of the songs he had taught her.

'Hello! What be 'ee doing?'

He leaned against the wall in order to feel a little closer to her. He knew she would have helped her grandmother dress, lit the fire, cleaned the house and prepared food for the day before she settled down to sew. They rarely saw each other before evening, then only briefly. Every week they looked forward to Sunday because after chapel they could have some time alone together.

'I be going for some wood. Any errands for me?'

'You could take some sheets for me, far side of Pilton.'Twas only hemming but better than nought.'

He teased her and whispered some endearments so he could hear her laugh. When she went back indoors he stood and stared at the bleak little yard, which seemed even more desolate now that her voice no longer floated over the wall. How many more years before they could be together?

He did not find any wood. There were only a few places where it was permissible to search and other desperate people must have been there before him. He called at a few houses to ask whether any of the servants needed shoes repairing. He had been lucky at two houses but had only earned sixpence all day. Twenty-six years old and he was only earning sixpence! How could he marry on sixpence a day?

He took a longer route home, passing through Tutshill Woods. The trees had turned but there was no sun to pick out the colours and they failed to improve his mood.

That evening, he sat with his mother for an hour as was customary. He thought of amusing stories to keep up her spirits and to distract himself from the trial he had to face that evening, but his mother would not let him forget.

'Go on now; put your Sunday clothes on. You mustn't be late.' Although she whispered, the effort set off her cough again.

'I'm wasting my time.' he said, 'They won't want the likes of me in that place.'

'They'll soon see that you'm cleverer than any of them. They'll be honoured to have 'ee. Now go.' She tried to push him away but she had as much strength as a kitten. 'Show me when you'm dressed.'

He was to have an interview at the Literary and Scientific Institution that had opened earlier in the year. There was an opportunity for free second-class membership for poor people considered to be suitable candidates. Edward could not believe someone like himself would be allowed in; but he had been encouraged to apply and was told he would be subject to a personal interview with the founder and benefactor, Mr Rock. If accepted, he would be allowed to use the Library.

The Institution was housed in an imposing building half-way along the High Street. Edward hesitated at the door, feeling conspicuous and uncomfortable in his best clothes. Should he just walk in? He grasped the brass knocker, remembering childhood games of knock and run, and winced at the loud retort. He was taken to an office on the ground floor where a gentleman stood up and shook hands in a most friendly manner, while introducing himself as Mr Rock. His long face and high forehead surrounded by rather wild hair and beard gave him the look of a man of high intellect, but the effect was softened by the warmth of his gaze. He explained the purpose of the Institution and told Edward that there was indeed an opportunity for the poorer classes to be involved.

'It is true,' he said, 'that there are those who think it dangerous to instruct their fellow men and even believe that the lowly are incapable of appreciating the advantages of literature. They forget that Shakespeare and Milton were themselves of lowly birth. I do not forget such a thing, as I too spring from the working class.'

He had the manners of a gentleman; it was hard to believe that he had such beginnings. Edward knew that, although born in Barnstaple, he was now a successful businessman in London, a stationer whose company produced steel-engraved views of places of interest. Mr Rock did not have a family and chose to spend his money supporting his home town.

'There will be great benefit in bringing the classes together,' he went on. 'The poorer classes will see that the rich are not so inattentive to their wants as they are often represented to be, and the rich will find that we of the working classes are not the vulgar and offensive creatures that they imagined. Now, tell me, where do your interests lie? Have you had the opportunity to read books other than the Bible?'

Edward stammered a little as he started to name the books he had read but Mr Rock responded with enthusiasm. Bunyan was one of his great favourites too, he said, and he had even been inspired to write a little himself.

'When I worked at the bank in Bideford, I got into trouble for writing verses instead of attending to my work! Have you ever tried your hand at writing? In imitation, perhaps, of the great writers you admire?'

Edward had never admitted it before, but he had written some verses for Jane.

'Well, I have Sir, a little, they're not good of course...'

'Good man! Never mind the quality for now, your efforts will increase your appreciation of the great writers. Study their style, their choice of words! One day you must show me your attempts.'

Mr Rock went on to ask him about employment, and was sympathetic about the difficulties he had encountered, saying that these were hard times in which to live. Then he talked of the importance of temperance.

'Gentlemen may take the occasional glass of port but alcohol has no place in the life of a poor working man. I am sure you are aware of the devastation it can cause.'

Edward had been in an inn on a few occasions but decided it was best not to mention this.

'I am, Sir. I know it can ruin a family, Sir.'

Mr Rock then told him that he was accepted as a member and was to have free access to the Second-Class Reading Room where he could read any of the books from the library, and also the newspapers and journals which were passed on after three days in the First-Class Reading Room. After years of craving reading material, he could hardly believe he was to have access to the twelve hundred volumes in the library, but it was so. He was shown around the building, and Mr Rock selected a book for him before showing him to a free seat. Edward grasped Mr Rock's hand:

'Thank you, thank you so much, Sir! You'll never regret the opportunity you've given me!'

When Mr Rock had departed, Edward, pretending to read but too excited to concentrate, observed his surroundings through surreptitious glances. The atmosphere of the room was hushed and serious. There were three long tables with chairs set out for study, about half of them occupied. A few men whom he recognised had nodded to him but others seemed too engrossed in their reading to notice him. Two gentlemen with disapproving expressions stared down at him from frames on the walls.

He turned back to the book: *The Seasons: A Poem by James Thomson.* Mr Rock had told him that it had been written a hundred years ago.

'As you say you like to walk in the countryside, I think you will appreciate it.'

He turned the pages until he reached the section entitled *Autumn.*

> 'Crowned with the sickle and the wheaten sheaf
> While Autumn, nodding o'er the yellow plain,
> Comes jovial on.'

The room receded and he saw the God of Harvest looking on with benevolence as the lovers, Palemon and Lavinia, (himself and Jane, surely) walked hand-in-hand through golden fields. Edward felt he was coming up from the bottom of the ocean and seeing the universe afresh.

A few days later he called in to see Jane after breakfast. She was sewing at the table with her grandmother, alongside in the rocking-chair, scrutinising the work and making suggestions. Every time he saw Jane he experienced a little shock of pleasure and found for a moment he could not quite breathe or find the words to answer her greeting; her eyes were brighter, her hair a little darker and more lustrous than in the picture of her he carried always in his head, and each time she met his eyes the connection between them strengthened.

He bent to kiss her.

'Careful!' She held him back, laughing, until she had removed the pins she held between her lips.

'Be 'ee certain there's no more in there? Am I safe?'

Jane's grandmother peered at them short-sightedly. 'Get away the two of 'ee, that's enough, you'm not wed yet!'

'Grandma, will 'ee make sure she has pins in her mouth if any other man comes calling? They'm only to be removed for me, see!'

He had a plan to share with Jane. He was sure that the way to make money was to go to those who had plenty – there was nothing to be gained from scrabbling about in the town where few people could afford to employ anyone; the answer lay with the gentlemen who lived in big houses in the country.

''Tis their duty to support those in need and drive out want. And I'm going to offer something no one else can!'

She gazed up at him with her lips parted in surprise, and he kissed her again quickly before grandma noticed.

'What? What will 'ee do?'

'Portrait painting! Or drawing at least, first off. 'Tis them paintings in the Reading Room that gave me the idea. I can't do 'em good as that of course, not yet, but I'll practise. I'll draw you! Give me reason to sit here with you!'

He could see she looked doubtful. 'Where will you get the paper? 'Twill need to be special, won't it?'

'Oh, it'll cost a fraction of what I'll sell it for when I'm done. Artists can earn a lot of money, pounds and pounds for each picture! I plan to ask some of the men in the Library to let me draw 'em before I visit people I don't know. Look, tell me, who is this then?'

Jane scrutinised the paper. 'Well, 'tis your mother of course, I can tell because you wouldn't be drawing any other person in bed.' She held it to the light. 'There is perhaps something of her in it. You'm very clever, Edward. Her hands is a bit big though, bain't they?'

He looked at the drawing again. The hands did look rather strange; the eye was drawn to them rather than to the face.

'You may be right. I'll try 'em again; I can rub out the marks with a piece of bread, that's a trick I've learned.'

His colleagues in the Library were not very encouraging about his chances of success when Edward told them of the plan. One warned that he must continue to pursue opportunities for manual work, but felt, however, that the fresh air and exercise would be valuable. Edward decided to combine his efforts as an artist with attempts to carry out shoe repairs and set off with materials for both occupations.

As he followed the river out of the town he felt like Christian from *Pilgrim's Progress* embarking on a journey that would perhaps enable him and Jane to marry at last. There was no doubt that he would be the only portrait painter in the area.

He was going first to Rose Hill. Jane had been praised by Mrs Horden for a bonnet she had made and had come to know the servant, Prudence, so he knew for whom he should ask. He was glad to leave the town behind. A flock of gulls wheeled and cried as they followed a plough on the far side of the field, and the low autumn sun picked out the pink-and-white flowers and glossy black fruit of the brambles; he would pick some on his way home for Elizabeth. The household chores and his mother's increasing need for care were wearing her down; he knew she would be grateful for a small reminder of autumn. As he strode along the rutted lane, the delight he took in his surroundings melded with the pleasure he had found in reading *The Seasons*; some phrases he had mulled over came back to him – how true they were! Reading taught him how to find words for impressions, for feelings and thoughts; it appealed to his imagination and his sense of reason. As he started to sing the harvest hymn learned in chapel, he considered the words as he sang them and seemed to understand them for the first time, while his boots beat out the rhythm on the stony ground.

Prudence, a fair-haired girl with a welcoming smile, invited him into the kitchen and allowed him to reheel her boots. Being the only servant, she seemed glad of the company and laughed when he teasingly offered to kneel at her feet and lace them for her. However, he had a less favourable reaction from Mr Horden who, after listening to his carefully worded introduction, waved away the sketch of Jane.

'If I ever wanted my portrait painted, I would go to an experienced artist. Besides, have you not heard that there is a visitor in town offering photographic portraiture? Painting will be obsolete before long.'

As he left the room, Edward heard him telling Prudence that she was never again to bring in any itinerants. He retraced his steps back to the road, consoling himself with the memory of Prudence's gratitude when he refused to charge her for the new heels.

He walked on to Bishop's Tawton and called at four more houses. At Hall he was rewarded with sixpence when he did a sketch of the cook; and he earned a shilling for two repairs at the Vicarage, but was rebuffed by his intended audience. He was interrupted before finishing his introduction in one house and in another was told to stick with cobbling. 'You should leave artistic endeavours to educated professionals since it is obvious you have neither natural talent nor training.'

He paced back to Barnstaple with his eyes cast down on the stony road, lacking the will to pick any blackberries for Elizabeth.

As he passed the Lamb Inn on Boutport Street he saw John Pugsley with whom he had worked at the lace factory. John was now married to a thin, melancholy girl and had two small children.

'Edward! How be 'ee, boy!' The man staggered a little and Edward realised he had been drinking. The door of the inn was open; a man among the crowd at the bar turned and waved to him.

'Edward! Come on and have a jar with us!'

He thought of home with its dreary kitchen, Elizabeth's tight-lipped resignation and his father's furious complaints. A warm buzz of conversation and the dark fruity aroma of ale drifted from the inn; he had coins in his pocket. But he remembered Mr Rock's warning before he gave his answer.

'Not now, boy. I'm gwain to the Reading Room.'

1847 – 1854

Marriage

Come, wife, my love, away – away
To mossy cave and bower;
Or let us in our shadows play
With Nature one short hour.

Chapter Four

Edward and Jane were talking and laughing as they walked along arm-in-arm. Their path had taken them to the uplands above the river and when they turned to look back at Barnstaple, the houses appeared as small as matchboxes. They stood and stared for several minutes, pointing out streets they knew and buildings that had been important to them, then they turned their backs on the town. The road led them on into the hills, winding through fields and woodlands, past whitewashed farmhouses and isolated cottages.

They had chosen to walk to save the fare. The carrier's cart bringing their few possessions was expensive; besides, the three or four hour walk to Bideford, being longer than they were used to spending in each other's company, was pure pleasure, especially as they knew that in just a few days they would be man and wife, and would never again have to be separated.

Jane paused to adjust her bonnet. She hoped that the surprisingly warm October sunshine would not fade the cloth roses decorating one side. Edward did not like her to hide her face in a poke bonnet, so the brim was narrow and trimmed with dusky pink lace to match the wide pink ribbons, and she had pleated the cream cotton instead of simply gathering it at the crown. She had made it especially for their wedding and did not trust the carrier to deliver it without damage. Edward took advantage of her raised arms to kiss her again.

'Look, no one's coming. Climb over the stile with me - the long grass'll make a soft bed!'

'No! Us have waited eight years, few more days don't matter!'

'They matter to me.' He pulled her close to him and ran his hands right down her back; she let herself melt into him for a few wonderful moments before breaking away. All those years had been hard for her too, but she had been determined that she was not going to be one of the young women who gave birth to babies in the Workhouse. 'No! Edward, you'm wicked trying to lead me on like that, you won't catch me!'

And she ran ahead laughing until he did catch her. It was only the appearance around the next corner of an old man on a donkey that prevented her from falling into danger again.

They resumed their journey while Edward sang quietly to himself. She squeezed his hand, leaning in closer as they walked. She was pleased to see him in a more jovial mood.

During the past two years, he had experienced bouts of sadness that lasted for days on end. He had sat with his mother as she stopped trying to talk and, with closed eyes, gradually sank further into the bedclothes until the morning came when they realised she had gone. He still did not want to leave her bedside.

Elizabeth found employment a few weeks after her mother's death. His father took on a servant to cook and clean, and married her only a year after losing his wife. Edward found living with his mother's replacement intolerable but did not want to spend money on lodging elsewhere when he was trying to save enough to allow him to marry. He had found work as a French polisher, so when he heard of possible employment in the same trade in Bideford, he suggested to Jane that they might be able to marry and move to the town. Although the famine had continued to worsen in Barnstaple, conditions were better in Bideford. Cheap American flour and pork was bought by the Mayor and other benefactors and sold at cost price; along with less stringent application of the Poor Law this eased the crisis and there was increasing prosperity in the town. There might be greater opportunities for them both. Mr Rock had also set up a Literary and Scientific Institution, smaller than that in Barnstaple it was true, but without it Edward could not have countenanced moving.

He had been lodging in the town for the last two months while working at his new trade, and had eventually found a small house in Mill Street they might be able to rent. It could also be used as a milliner's shop which they hoped would be an insurance against future illness or unemployment. But when he walked back to Barnstaple one Sunday to tell Jane about the house and work out the costs, it was clear that Edward did not have enough to set up a home. He was still not in full-time work.

Jane watched him sitting with his head in his hands. Should she tell him? Would he mind that he could not provide for her himself?

'I have a little money.'

He looked at her, startled. 'You?'

'I've five pounds, nearly. £4 17s 10d.'

'Five pounds? Where did you get it?'

His face was such a picture, she had to laugh. 'Where do you think? I worked for it, of course!'

It had not been easy, but she managed to put a little aside each week. She had a good reputation now as a milliner because she made attractive bonnets in the latest designs. Her trick was to go into town when the coach arrived from London to watch as the passengers descended and walked over to the carriages waiting to take them on to country houses around Barnstaple. She might have appeared to be watching from idle curiosity but in fact she was staring at the hats, gauging the width of brims and ribbons, scrutinising the fruit or flowers that decorated them, and memorising the shade of pink or green that she knew would be the latest London fashion. Then she returned home to create an example to show to customers. Jane was skilled at knowing which colour would flatter a sallow or rosy complexion so when customers looked in the mirror, they were rarely able to resist buying. But she had to keep her prices low because, living where she did, she could not attract the wealthiest customers. Edward said the house in Bideford was in a much better situation.

Her savings enabled them to make his ideas a reality. There had been the problem of her grandmother, but the cousins in Well Street offered to take her in. At last, they could plan their future.

'I hope Grandma's all right. Do 'ee think Ann'll remember she needs her food cut up small?'

Edward caressed Jane's hand. 'Oh, her'll be just fine. Her wanted us to be wed, didn' 'er. Us'll go back and see her one Sunday.

Hello there! Have 'ee been to market?' Edward spoke to the woman who was walking towards them, sweeping off his hat with a flourish as he had to everyone they met. 'Us is getting wed! Do you envy us? What could be finer!'

He greeted a farmer driving a cart and a woman with a flock of geese, and even a gentleman's carriage; the latter did not stop, of course, but everyone else wished them well. It seemed the whole world was celebrating with them, making Jane feel quite giddy with excitement. Edward said they were all envious of him marrying such a beautiful girl.

They climbed over a stile into a field for lunch. The weather had been settled and warm for over a week, a real Indian summer, so the ground was quite dry but Edward put down his coat for her to sit on. She warned him that if he tried to do anything but eat, she would run straight back to Barnstaple. When they had finished the bread and ham and apples, Edward lay back and closed his eyes for a while. She was safe to observe him now. She had often tried to conjure his physical presence when she was alone; his broad, strong chest rising and falling with every breath, the slight smile softening his face, the reddish beard and the hair on his forearms and the large hands folded across his belly.

As she looked at him, she tried to imagine their wedding night and the powerful longing that came over her persuaded her to lie down beside him and press herself against his side, but she held both his hands imprisoned so that he could not tempt her any further. When they were together in her house she had allowed him to be more familiar with her, because the sound of her grandmother moving about in the room above and the occasional shouted reminder that it was time for Edward to go home prevented them going too far; but now she had to be in control if she wanted to wait until they were married. She did not mind. Soon she would be with him every day and every night.

She cuddled up to him and rested her head on his chest. 'I love you, Edward.'

When he spoke, his voice seemed to reverberate from his chest straight into her ear, as if she were part of him.

'I love you too, more than the whole world.' As best he could, he stroked the hands that were restraining him.

'Can 'ee hear the skylark?'

She had been listening to his breathing and to the whisper of leaves in the breeze, but there it was: a fast, rich outpouring of joy way up above them. She opened her eyes and squinted up at the sky.

'Is that it? That little thing?'

'Yes. Such a small bird but its song is the most beautiful I know. Heavenly bird. No:

> Bird of Heaven, I love that song,
> Trilling from thy merry tongue.
> Here upon the grass I lie,
> Drinking in thy ecstasy.'

Jane looked up at him. 'What's that? A poem?' He had that faraway look in his eyes and she kissed him to bring him back to her. 'Is it from one of they books in the Library?'

'No, it's from my head! If us had some paper, could write it down. Is it good, d'you think? I could make it longer. Mr Rock liked the last one I sent him.'

'You've such things going on in your head! Fancy thinking up all they words. Make one about me, then.'

He rolled over on top of her so that he could look into her face, but she kept her hands against his chest to hold him off.

> 'Down upon the grassy bank
> Pretty Janie lay,'

He paused to think for a moment.

'And when her Edward saw her
She took his breath away.'
'Oh, Edward.' She let her hands slide around his back and she drank in his warm smell and the wonderful weight of him, the familiar words whispered again in her ear and his hand running down her side. She held his hand still and thought she would remember this day for the rest of her life.

After a few minutes of lying together with the skylark rejoicing above them, she realised he was laughing silently.

'What be 'ee laughing at? What's funny?'
'Down upon the grassy bank
Pretty Janie lay,
She was lying there a-hoping
He would lead her all astray.'
She squealed in protest and struggled from under him, giggling. 'I am *not* hoping for any more of your wickedness, let me up, *now!*' She leapt to her feet but allowed him one more embrace before they continued on their way.

They asked for a drink of water at a cottage in Eastleigh, then the road wound slowly down into a valley and on until, suddenly, there was Bideford before them.

'Oh!' Jane stared.

The broad river running bright and majestic below them was crossed by the numerous arches of the bridge, and adorned on its far side with tall-masted ships moored by a long quay from which the old town rose steeply, its houses piled one above the other like a pack of cards, dazzling in the late afternoon sunshine. The sounds of a busy town came drifting across the water: the shouting and hammering of men at work, the neighing and clatter of trotting horses, and the mewing of gulls wheeling above the fishing boats.

'Is that where us is going to live?'

She thought it seemed a more attractive town than Barnstaple – and it was healthier, surely, to live on a hill than on a flat plain with poor drainage.

'Yes, look! See that big building over there on the right? That's the Mansion House where the library is! And that handsome barque with the tall masts? That's Mr Richard Heard's *Devonia* that takes people off to Canada. I've met a heap of people who are thinking of taking a passage. But us won't go, will us? And if you go up the river that way, that gets you to Torrington but I've not been there yet, and the other way, that's Appledore.'

'And where's our house? Is it there on the Quay?'

'No, it's behind they big houses.' He turned to her. 'Our house!'

He looked so happy that she pulled him to her and they hugged until she had to protest that he would squeeze all the breath out of her.

There were many new things to see as they walked across the bridge and along the Quay. Barnstaple was the only town Jane knew and she had been unable to imagine Bideford. Even the smells were distinctive. Edward said it was the smell of the sea, but she had never seen the sea except from a great distance.

They turned up a wide street lined with large houses where Edward said important people lived. When they reached the end, he stopped and pointed.

'There it is!'

Just across the road, a little three-storey house huddled between a cottage and a larger dwelling. There were small bay windows on the ground floor and the first floor, and she could see straightaway that she would be able to display her hats there. As the wealthy people came from their grand houses and turned into Mill Street, the first thing they would see would be her hats!

He pointed across the road. 'And that's where my workshop's to, just in there behind the Swan Inn. And up that way, Potter's Lane, my lodging's there. I won't be far away!'

He unlocked the door of the house. The room they entered was spacious with a low ceiling; the walls were dark and grimy but the bay window let in plenty of light.

Edward was looking at her to see her reaction. 'I've been worried you might say 'tis too dark.'

'No, I don't think 'tis, a coat of whitewash will change it. I can soon do that. 'Tis big for the sort of shop I've pictured, I'll be seeking for summat to put in it! But us could put a screen across here. And there's plenty of space for a work table.'

A door led through to a back kitchen with a large fireplace and beyond was a tiny yard with an earth closet shared with two other cottages. Edward ran up the stairs to the first floor.

'Wait 'til you see up here!'

There was a good-sized room with a window looking out on to the street and a smaller back one, then more steep stairs led them up again to reach a large attic room with a ceiling that curved right up into the roof.

'Oh my! Edward, what shall us do with all these rooms!' She could hardly believe that the whole house was theirs. Each room needed whitewashing and the windows were badly fitted but she knew she could push rags into the gaps beside the frames to make them draught-proof. 'There's work to do, but I'll soon have it looking nice.'

'You like it then! Have I made a good choice? I thought I could use this room for reading for the time being. Later us'll need to fill it and the small room below with beds for all the children us'll have!'

The images of intimacy conjured by his words made her blush, but his vision of the future secretly thrilled her.

That night Jane slept alone for the first time in her life. After lying awake for the first half an hour, listening to the creakings and rustlings of the unfamiliar house but too excited to be afraid, she slept soundly, only waking when she heard Edward's rich, musical voice calling to her from the bottom of the stairs on his way to work.

Their wedding three days later was a simple affair with two witnesses. They were to marry in the Register Office on the Quay because, being Methodists, they would not marry in the church. Edward had two hours' leave from work so after the ceremony they returned arm-in-arm to the house for a while, laughing with relief that she had only stumbled over the words once and telling each other how fine they looked. While they fed each other morsels from the special tea she had prepared, she allowed him to stroke her thigh and she felt her long-held reserve melting away.

When at last they were able to climb the steep stairs to the newly-whitewashed bedroom, and saw and held each other for the first time, she wondered at the hair which grew on his belly and legs where hers were smooth, and at the strength of his body. She had never seen a man naked before; but she knew what to expect from their first time together so what followed was as natural as a fledgling taking wing, and as gentle as a flower breaking free from its bud.

The night time became the best part of each day. She went about her work smiling at the memories of their love-making and looking bright-eyed with anticipation of the night to come, so that the neighbours remarked on her happy nature.

'You'm always smiling, maid, what is it you know about?'

Her joy seemed to give her extra vitality, enabling her to accomplish far more work than before and still have energy to spare. And when the supper things were cleared away, they curled up in bed together, telling amusing stories of the hours spent apart until their caresses shut out all thought of daytime concerns.

By the sixth day following their marriage, Jane had cleaned and whitewashed the whole house. When she woke, the rising sun cast beams of yellow light on the white bedroom walls. The room was quite bare, containing only the bed and a chair piled with clothes, but it was perfect in its bright cleanliness. The bay window curving out above the street needed curtains and she had a fancy to make blue ones when they could afford them. She would line them with heavy fabric to keep out the early morning light and noise; it was probably the sound of two women talking below the window that had woken her this morning, and now she could hear a passing horse, the extra clip from its hoofs suggesting a loose shoe.

She leaned over Edward, who was snoring gently, and inhaled his familiar smell. Sharing a bed with a man was very different from sharing with her grandmother, who had been a soft, sighing presence with a sweet mustiness around her. She wanted to cuddle up to him again but decided to let him sleep on for a while. On Sunday they had stayed in bed so long that it had been too late to go to chapel. Edward said it did not matter as being here together was enough of a blessing. They laughed together rather guiltily, until he grew serious.

'It's true, I don't need to go to chapel.' He took her in his arms again. 'With my body I thee worship.' It was another hour before they got up.

She crept down the steep stairs, knowing already which ones creaked a little, and went into the kitchen. Edward had brought in wood and coal and had fetched water the night before. She lit the fire, then washed quickly in the plain earthenware bowl, and swept the kitchen floor. Edward liked to drink a cup of hot tea every morning which she thought rather extravagant, but she liked to indulge him even if it did mean lighting the fire as soon as she got up.

The kettle was boiling by the time she heard his footsteps on the stairs and when she turned with a smile, he lifted her up and sat her, giggling, on the table.

'There, you'm on a plinth and as pretty as a Greek goddess.'

It was sometimes difficult to know what he meant, but he made her laugh.

When he left for work she made the first trip of the day to fetch water from the pump, a minute's walk away in Chingswell Street. She felt a little shy as she approached the group of people waiting their turn but she recognised the woman with whom she had spoken the previous day. Eliza Elliott, at twenty-eight, was only a year older than Jane but already had five children. She had given birth only four weeks before and really should have not been carrying heavy weights, so Jane carried one of her buckets back to the house in Cock Street, just around the corner from Jane's home. Eliza shouted at the little ones that had toddled out of the door while she was away, then slapped a little girl for weeing on the floor. Jane helped her by tipping the water into a pot over the fire to heat for the washing and made a silent resolution to see if she could help in other ways, at least until Eliza was strong again. She was sure she would manage things better when *she* had children.

She went home and put on her second-best bonnet and a warm shawl. Edward had told her that today, being Tuesday, was market day so she had made up her mind to investigate.

She had twice walked along Mill Street with Edward, but now that she was alone she looked more carefully. It was a long, narrow street lined with terraces of cottages and a few larger houses, with here and there a passageway giving access to the rear yards and gardens. She could hear the grunting of pigs from some yards and a couple of chickens, which had wandered out from another, were chased back with much flapping and squawking. There was a butcher, a greengrocer and a baker, so she did not have to go far for her everyday requirements. Most of the houses were simple dwellings but some utilised their front rooms as workshops. Looking in the windows as she passed, she saw a shoemaker, a basketmaker, a tailor, and a man carrying out some very fine work who might be a watchmaker. She didn't like to peer in too closely when she saw women sewing inside; she guessed that many had already heard that she was starting a milliner's shop and she did not want to appear too curious. She had already decided to concentrate on hats for the time being because when she said she was a dressmaker and milliner, several people had said,

'You'll be fighting for work then, maid!'

It appeared that there were many dressmakers in the town, but she had seen only three milliners' signs in High Street and Mill Street when she was with Edward, and the hats on display were of indifferent quality.

She saw that the shops in High Street were bigger but none yet had the large plate-glass windows that had started to appear in Barnstaple. It was busier too, with several farmers' carts and two carriages drawn up and the pavements quite crowded. She looked in the windows of the drapers' shops, trying to decide which one was the best, and also at a large ironmonger's. There were several things she needed for the house when she had enough money. She needed to buy a tin bath because Edward liked to immerse himself once a week, something she had never done.

She followed the directions Edward had given her, turning up another steep street which took her to the market square. There were several long low sheds housing butchers' shops, and stalls set up in the open air by farmers' wives using the large panniers in which their goods were transported. Some were sheltered by canvas erections. There had been a heavy shower earlier and the stallholders looked rather miserable and bedraggled. A farmer's wife with a round, pleasant face greeted her in a gentle voice, so she stopped at her stall and bought potatoes, onions, carrots and cabbage.

'There you are, my lover. And where be 'ee from?'

'Barnstaple. I've come to live here with my husband.' It made her blush with pleasure to say the word and the woman smiled sympathetically.

'Just wed, are you? And what does he do for a living?'

'He's a French polisher. And I make bonnets. I'm starting a shop down Mill Street.'

The woman was impressed. 'Well, chiel, if you could dress me a bonnet that makes me as pretty as you be, I'd come to you straight off, except when I *do* need a bonnet, I go to Mrs Mary Carter.'

Jane felt reassured as she walked back down the hill. She was sure she would be able to win customers when they saw what she could do. She stopped again to look through the window of Vellacott's draper's. She needed to build up her stock of ribbons and fabric and had carefully counted their money again to work out how much she could spend. She gathered her courage and walked in. There were bolts of cloth stored on shelves reaching right to the ceiling, and a whole wall of shallow drawers containing the haberdashery. She asked to see the offcuts of fabric and chose a length of chocolate-brown velvet and some dark-green silk; then, after deliberating for a long time over the cottons, she selected a length each of dusky pink and a cream print. Next she asked for some ribbons in toning colours and the assistant, a friendly and helpful young man, offered her a bag of colourful cotton scraps which could be used for making flowers. The bill came to 2s 9d; she turned down the offer of credit and carefully counted out the coins. She felt she had chosen well: she would be able to use the lengths of fabric to show the effects that could be created with different colours. Edward had made her a sign which he would put up as soon as she had the shop ready, and she had read the delightful words at least twenty times: *Mrs Capern, Milliner*.

As she walked along Mill Street she saw a familiar figure, but for a second didn't recognise Edward in his work clothes. They walked towards each other, smiling broadly, stopping just a few inches apart, a much greater distance than they desired, but both were aware of the glances of passers-by.

She spoke first. 'What be 'ee doing out, then? You should be at work!'

It was thrilling to see him in his long work apron; he seemed a different person yet, at the same time, wonderfully well-known to her. He caressed her hand with one finger, in a way that people would not notice.

'I'm on an errand for Mr Lock, buying some nails from Tardrew's. I might be home this afternoon.' His eyes shone, teasing her.

'This afternoon! Why?'

'Well…' He held her gaze and they both laughed. She longed to put her arms around him.

'Edward! You've got work to do!'

'When this present job's finished, there's no more polishing for the time being, but maybe I could use the workshop to make your new hat-stands.'

'Then that's what you must do! Coming home in the afternoon – how can 'ee think of it!'

'I can think of nothing else.'

She went on her way, smiling. In truth, she was a little concerned about his ability to make good hat-stands, but she kept her worries to herself.

Back home, she stoked the fire, put the vegetables and bacon on to cook for dinner, and walked through to the shop. She had a good table with a drawer and she covered this with a clean white cloth, folded several times, positioning her chair so that light would fall over her left shoulder. There was a looking-glass on the wall and a chair for customers for which she was embroidering a cushion cover. Then she unpacked the rack which held spools of thread, the pin-tray, the paper containing her millinery needles, her measuring tape, the brace-wire and stay-wire and scissors. From another box she took her ribbons and fabric then arranged them on the shelves that Edward had put up, and on the top shelf she put the jar of foliage and berries they had picked on their Sunday afternoon walk. She had refreshed and pressed her wedding bonnet, and had re-dressed another in colours which would suit an older woman; these she placed on stands and displayed in the window, then stood back to admire her work. Mrs Capern, Milliner, was ready to open her shop.

Chapter Five

Edward leaned over the coffin he was polishing and tried to maintain a steady rhythm of circular movements. When his mind wandered on to more interesting subjects, five or ten minutes could pass before he realised that he had over-polished an area or missed a bit altogether and the resulting smears were difficult to eradicate. Mr Lock's attention never wavered. He was planing a table leg on the other side of the workshop and his movements were as balanced and fluid as the pieces he created; he could work all day without uttering a word and his features were never stirred by emotion. He was the best cabinet-maker in the town.

Mr Lock had his back turned and in any case his view was partly obscured by stacks of oak and elm timber. They could not work alongside each other in case any dust settled on the polished furniture. Edward patted his pocket. Whenever an acquaintance lent him a book, he brought it to work in case there were a few spare moments when he could read. Today he had *Wise Saws and Modern Instances* and he was enjoying the stories in it; but most of all he was impressed by the knowledge that Thomas Cooper had written the book while confined in Stafford Gaol for sedition, having organised riots in support of Chartism. The working men of Bideford had little awareness of their rights. Should someone step forward to be their leader? Perhaps he, Edward, should be prepared to go to gaol for his belief that every man, however poor, should have the right to vote. But if such a fate should befall him – and some Chartists had even been transported – what would become of Jane? She was even more precious to him now that she was carrying their child; this knowledge thrilled him to the depths of his being and to think of her suffering in any way brought tears to his eyes.

A young shoemaker called John Gregory had lent him the book, having borrowed it from his master. He liked John from their first meeting; he had a thirst for knowledge that was rare among the people Edward met and he believed fervently in the rights of the working man. He showed Edward his attempts at writing, in which he asked why man should be given intelligence if he was not meant to use it, and whether the government should take responsibility for educating children. John was full of ideas but had little access to books and no knowledge of poetry. He could not afford to pay the membership of the Literary and Scientific Institution and Edward did not want to presume on Mr Rock's kindness by asking for sponsorship.

Edward wanted to introduce John to the work of John Keats. Mr Rock had sent a volume of the poems to the Library with the express instruction that Edward should be the first to read it. What a revelation it had been that mere marks on a page could reveal the mysteries of the heart and its sensuous response to nature! He had sat in the Reading Room stroking the green embossed leather cover, running his finger along the page edges, and marvelling that he held Isabella's sorrow and the miracle of the Grecian Urn between his palms. He could not, of course, take the book out of the Library but Jane saved and smoothed the scraps of paper that wrapped pennyworths of tea and sugar, so that he could copy a few lines to bring home and study. To think that the poems were written while the poet was so young, and how tragic that he should die soon after! Edward stood up straight, sighing at the thought, and was brought back to his current situation. He had again been distracted from his task; it was as well that the future occupant of the coffin would not be able to see it.

The workshop door opened and young John Gregory looked in, his eyes alight with excitement. He had never come to Edward's place of work before. He addressed himself to the cabinet maker;

'Excuse me Mr Lock, I'd like a word with Mr Capern, if I may.'

Mr Lock nodded, barely looking up. John was wearing a shoemaker's apron which reached almost to the ground but his wrists and ankles thrust out beyond his clothes because, although seventeen years old and already tall, he was still growing. John spoke in a low whisper.

''Ave 'ee heard anything about the goings-on in Paris? Mr Lerwill told me of it, but 'ee didn't know a lot.'

There had been revolutions all over Europe as the poor rose up in protest at their unjust treatment. There were a few men in Bideford who followed the news with excitement but Edward did not know the latest as it was several days since he had been to the Reading Room to read the newspapers.

'The workers have been rioting and have barricaded themselves in part of the city. Do 'ee think same could happen in London? 'Cos it's been shown petitions don't make 'em listen. You should write one of your poems about it! Send it to Parliament!'

'I'll read the papers tonight and call in afterwards, tell you what I've found.' Edward saw Mr Lock glance over at them from under his bushy eyebrows. 'Back to your work now, I'll see 'ee later.'

After John had gone, the two men worked on in silence until Mr Lock put down his plane, walked over to Edward's bench and looked down at the smear on the lid of the coffin. He was a mild man; Edward had never seen him roused, and he spoke quietly now.

'This won't do, Edward. Your head is full of your strange ideas and your books instead of your work, I suppose. Bookish men aren't favoured by customers you know. If the word gets around that you've always got your nose in a book and are interested in troublemakers, us'll lose custom.'

He regarded Edward calmly.

'You should watch out for shoemakers. The better their shoes, the more dangerous their ideas. I've often heard that said.'

He turned and walked back to his bench. Edward was raging inside but at a loss to know how to reply. He should be more careful with his work, he knew that, but to turn his back on books and learning was impossible. It was unjust to expect him to do so! And young John – dangerous? It was absurd. But he knew he could not walk out as he was tempted to do – what would he say to Jane? He took a deep breath.

'I'm sorry, Mr Lock. I'll give the work my full attention in future.'

He could not afford to upset Mr Lock; as it was, there was no work for this evening. The cupboard he would be working on tomorrow would only take a few hours. A small deal coffin stood on the workbench but the grieving parents could not afford polished wood for their child. Jane's shop was slow to flourish and she was beginning to feel downhearted, but he was confident that their fortunes would soon change. Something would turn up.

A few weeks later Edward strode along Mill Street, dodging two women and almost colliding with a pony and trap that was coming round the corner from Lower Gunstone. The driver swore at him.

'Beg pardon, Sir, in a hurry, see! I've some good news!'

He had heard the news while polishing at the busy upholstery business on the corner of High Street and Mill Street which Mr John Lee combined with Bideford's postal office. He could not wait to tell Jane.

Mr Lock was coming out of his workshop and, seeing Edward almost running along the street, raised his eyebrows questioningly but Edward didn't stop.

'Be in to see 'ee later Mr Lock! Got summat to tell 'ee!'

He reached his own front door and burst into the hushed atmosphere of the shop where Jane was talking to a rather large lady in black; she gave him a sharp look, so he went through to the kitchen where he paced up and down, feeling he would burst if she did not come soon. Finally he heard the door close and Jane appeared, looking concerned.

'Whatever's wrong?'

'Wrong? Nothing, my sweet, everything's right! Come here! I've heard news of a job – exactly the job for me! The pay isn't high but us'll manage! I'm sure to get it!'

'What is it?' He saw the doubt in her eyes; he had come home with news of work before but this was different.

'Letter carrier! For the Post Office! 'Tis ideal for me; you have to read well, see, read all sorts of writings by important folk and by others who aren't that handy with the pen, and then work out where the letters should go. And it's very serious because you'm working for Her Majesty and you have to get someone of high standing to say you'm a suitable person – I hope I can do that! Mr Rock will help, I'm certain. I'll write to him today!'

'A letter carrier!' She was looking more impressed now. 'Where to, where would you carry them to?'

'From the Post Office here to Northam and Appledore, then bringing locked bags of letters back to Bideford. If I can get the recommendation fast, I can start next week!'

When he imagined himself walking the country lanes every day on such an important mission, he felt quite overwhelmed with excitement. It would combine his two favourite activities, walking and reading! What could be better?

'But what's the pay? Will it be good pay?'

'Seven shillings a week, but 'tisn't long days, you see, because it's a second post them is starting up. So I leave at eleven and must be back by four for the letters to be sorted and dispatched.'

'Seven shillings! Edward, it's not a lot. We spend four shillings a week on bread alone. Wouldn't you be better to stick with your trade? You can earn fifteen shillings as a polisher!'

'But only when I've a full week's work, my flower, and when does that happen? This is regular,' he took her in his arms, 'and I can do my polishing as well, mornings and evenings. Us'll know us always has seven shillings, and whatever else on top. That'll be a comfort, won't it, with this little one that's coming along.'

A few days later Edward walked to Barnstaple to see the Honourable John Fortescue M.P. Jane had brushed his Sunday clothes thoroughly, but the road was muddy after overnight rain and he was afraid of making a bad impression by arriving with mud-spattered trousers. He stopped to roll his trouser legs up, but he could not protect his boots. He would just have to wipe the mud off with some grass before he entered the town.

The meeting, arranged by Mr Rock so that Edward could ask for a recommendation for the position at the Post Office, was to take place at the Guildhall where the M.P. had a prior meeting with the Mayor. He walked fast because whatever happened, he must not be late – a letter carrier must always be prompt – and as he walked he rehearsed what he wanted to say, enunciating clearly to the startled birds that flew from the hedgerow.

'I'm an educated man, Sir, and I have read many books.'

Would Mr Fortescue ask him where he went to school? If he did, all might be lost!

'The poems of Mr Coleridge and Mr Keats, Sir, and many others.'

He must not mention his interest in Chartism.

'I am honest and trustworthy, Sir, and I never partake of strong drink. I have a wife, and a child on the way.'

Suppose he was asked about his previous employment? Would his changes in trade count against him?

It was only ten o'clock when he arrived in the town so he had an hour to spare. He was to visit Jane's grandmother to give her a shawl that Jane had knitted; but he felt too preoccupied to go there first, so he kept the shawl hidden under his jacket while he wandered along the High Street, where meetings with old friends distracted him from his feelings of trepidation.

Finally the clock told him that the time was near and he knocked at the door of the Guildhall. A clerk told him to wait in the entrance. After a few nerve-wracking minutes a gentleman came down the stairs and would have left the building if the clerk had not addressed him.

'What's that? This chap to see me? What's your business, my man?'

For a moment Edward was tongue-tied; he thought the M.P. would be expecting him.

'Sir, excuse me, I don't want to be wasting your time, Sir, but I believe Mr Rock asked if you would see me, Sir, concerning a position at the Post Office.'

'Post Office? What Post Office?'

'Bideford, Sir. I wish to apply for a position as a letter carrier, Sir.' How had he ever imagined he could be a letter carrier?

'Ah yes, I seem to remember! It's a very responsible position, you know, carrying private and sometimes valuable letters. Only a loyal and trustworthy man can be considered – are you that man?'

He was tall and he peered down at Edward as if he was a child.

'Yes Sir, I –'

'It used to be that the postman was paid by the recipient of the letter, so naturally he ensured that it arrived at the correct destination, but now with the pre-payment of stamps it is essential that he is entirely honest. Does that description befit you?'

Every time Edward opened his mouth to attempt an answer, the M.P. asked another question.

'Can you read sufficiently well? You do not take strong liquor, I hope? I believe Mr Rock told me you do not. Well, he is a good judge of character so I will take him at his word and will write to the Post Office to recommend you. Capern, wasn't it? Good day to you!'

And he was gone.

He walked back to Bideford in a daze, still unsure whether he would obtain the position. Would the Honourable John Fortescue remember to write the letter? If he did not, someone else might be appointed before Edward could write to Mr Rock again.

Every day Edward went to Mr Lee's shop hoping for news, walking through the displays of chairs and chaises-longues to reach the post-room at the back, until at last Mr Lee greeted him with a smile and waved a sheet of paper.

'It's arrived! The Post Office has approved your appointment and you are to start on Monday!'

Jane was as pleased as he was. As they sat eating dinner together, she admitted that she was relieved to know that there would be a regular wage coming in every week, even if it was a small amount, because she had feared that the day might come when there was no money at all. She gazed at him.

'Just think, you, a letter carrier! Oh, but with it being such an important position, will 'ee have to wear Sunday clothes?'

Mr Lee had told him that, in London, the postmen wore smart red uniforms like soldiers, but that it was not necessary in rural areas. Jane looked disappointed.

'Still, you should look smart, you can't wear your old work clothes. I think you should wear your Sunday coat and I can make you a heavier one for when the weather gets colder. You'll be out in all weathers. But then, the hat I made will help keep you dry as I've felted the wool. Pity though, I could fancy you in red like a soldier!'

Edward loved her more than ever when she smiled so mischievously at him.

He hardly needed a coat at all when he set off for Appledore for the first time. It was a beautiful May morning and, although his mind was much exercised with remembering Mr Lee's instructions, his heart lifted as he walked through Potter's Lane and out of the town. He carried two locked bags of letters strapped across his chest, one to be delivered to the

Northam office and the other to Appledore, after which they would be delivered house to house by a postman in each village. He also carried a small bag of letters to deliver to outlying houses along the way. On the way back he would carry two locked bags and all the letters that were proffered to him together with the pennies for their postage. He had been given a bell to alert people to his approach so that they might bring out their letters, but for the time being he had wedged it upside down in the pocket of his Sunday coat so that he did not ring it inadvertently. Edward had been issued with a book of instructions and knew that he must not make mistakes of any kind; the messenger who had walked the round for many years had recently been charged with embezzling a penny and, although after a lengthy trial he was found not guilty, he was dismissed from the Post Office.

He strode out along the causeway that ran across the marsh. At his approach a flock of small wading birds wheeled up into the sky emitting a chorus of high-pitched calls, and coming to rest on the far side of a reedy pond. A gentleman riding a large cob towards Bideford greeted him cheerily – that would never happen if he was not recognised as a messenger working for the Queen! He started to whistle, marvelling that he could be paid for taking a walk on such a fine day.

Mr Lee had sorted the letters for him, but when he came across a labourer clearing a ditch, Edward hailed him to check that the next turning was indeed Orchard Hill. After passing several sizeable villas on a pleasant lane, which was well-maintained for the carriages that travelled along it, he came to the young ladies' school run by Mrs Frederica Hake, the house next-door being a boys' school headed by her son. There was a newspaper, and letters bearing unfamiliar stamps which came from the East Indies; it was extraordinary to think of their journey beginning in such an exotic place, and of all the hands, both brown and white, through which they had passed. He hesitated for a moment on the drive of the imposing house; should he walk right up to the front door or go around to the servants' entrance? But no, these letters were not for the servants – besides, why should he even think of going to the back door when he was on such an important mission? Boldly he lifted the large brass knocker then handed the letters to a housemaid, who gave him an arch look when he winked at her and addressed her as 'my lover'.

The road took him down to a part of the riverbank he had not visited before and he followed the shore past a smoking lime kiln and a boat builder's yard to deliver a letter to a house with beautiful gardens sloping down towards the water. He thought the cottages at Cleave would be grand to live in, with their outlook on the river in all its moods. He returned to the tree lined main road to deliver a newspaper and a letter to Mr Ley at Durrant, whom he believed to be the magistrate he had seen occasionally in the Reading Room. He was trying to glance past the housemaid who came to the door when Mr Ley himself came down the elegant staircase and took the letter.

'Ah, excellent, a second post at last! Please be sure to call on your way back, I need to reply to this.'

Edward answered in a manner he felt befitted an employee of Her Majesty, but Mr Ley did not appear to recognise him.

He thought Northam a compact and well-built village. The postal office was situated in a neat cottage in Cross Street. He gave the postbag and his time ticket to the postmaster, Mr Yeoland, then continued on a winding road towards Appledore. Turning into Bidna Lane, he walked between vivid green oak and ash hedges resplendent with red campion and white stitchwort; when he saw a bullfinch fly quietly out, he parted the foliage and was thrilled to see a clutch of five blue eggs in a twiggy nest. He walked on until he came to the modest dwelling of an old, toothless labourer for whom he had a letter. Edward read the letter for him and, although it contained nothing but good wishes from his son and reassurances of good health, the man insisted on showing his gratitude by giving Edward a small jar of honey which he placed carefully in an inside pocket.

Back on the main road, a vista opened on his left over a large plain which he realised must be the common grazing land known as Northam Burrows; beyond, a wide barrier of pebbles about two miles in length prevented the ocean and river estuary flooding the land. He had wanted for a long time to see the famous Pebble Ridge! He stood for several minutes with the fresh salty air caressing his face, while his gaze travelled slowly over the wide expanse which was almost a wilderness, the only signs of humanity being a labourer clearing a ditch and three ships in full sail out in the bay. He must, one day, bring Jane here. Perhaps they could walk together to the water's edge.

He turned quickly to descend the hill to Appledore, having almost forgotten the time. It was unfortunate that the Post Office did not supply their letter carriers with a timepiece to ensure they arrived promptly, because he would like to have a watch which he could take from his waistcoat pocket to consult as a gentleman did.

The view across the broad River Torridge to Instow on the far bank was equally romantic. On the Quay fishing boats were being unloaded on to donkey carts, nets being mended and barefoot children running here and there. A group of fishermen staring out over the Bar looked at him curiously when he asked for the postal office, but pointed him pleasantly enough back past the fine large dwellings on the Quay to a more modest terrace of houses. Turning that way, he saw how smaller cottages were ranged in tight rows on the hill above. The postmistress, Mrs Sarah, was not at home because she combined her role with that of schoolmistress, her husband being away at sea, but her daughter greeted him and explained that she was the letter carrier for the village. She took the letters from his bag and replenished it with post to be taken to Bideford; before he knew where he was, he was climbing the hill out of the village again.

As he neared the first houses on the Northam road, he paused and took out his bell. Should one ring it loud and long or give just a brief ding-dong? He swung the bell once. To his surprise a young girl appeared almost immediately from a lane on his left and ran up to him, holding out a carefully folded letter.

'Please Sir, Ma says will 'ee take this to my brother? Her heard there's an extra post today and 'tis to say that father's bad.'

He saw the letter was addressed to a farm near Torrington.

'Don't 'ee worry chiel, 'twill arrive tomorrow.' He patted the child on the head, took her penny, and marked the letter with his initials and the number of his bag.

As his journey progressed he grew braver, swinging the bell three or four times as he neared houses and even shouting out to inform people of the extra collection. He was fascinated to see the confident, authoritative handwriting on the envelopes from the large houses, and the laboriously formed letters and wildly inaccurate spellings that issued from cottages; but whether they came from cottage or castle, all the letters jostled together in his bag without discrimination. He was asked if he would write a letter on someone's behalf the following day, and to read a letter that he had delivered that very morning. By the time he was striding down the hill towards Bideford, he felt enamoured of his new job.

What a great invention was the penny post! Just a few years ago, not many of these people could have afforded to receive a letter, but now thousands of letters were carried to the most remote regions of the kingdom by mail coach, by railway and by foot, the volume of post multiplying daily as if written communication was being discovered for the first time. Letters of love and compassion, of urgent business, advice and exchanges of ideas. And what a clever idea was the postage stamp costing just one penny and bearing the image of the Queen! Sir Rowland Hill was indeed a great man to have brought such reforms into being – not least because he had created employment here in North Devon for Mr Edward Capern, who was an integral part of the great web that was the Post Office, one of thousands of postmen at this moment walking the streets and lanes of England.

Chapter Six

Jane heaved the basket of wet washing along Cock Street to the piece of waste ground next to the pigsties. Eliza Elliott was already there with the smallest children around her feet on the scuffed, rocky ground while an older boy was climbing the tree to which the washing lines were attached. She propped up one line with a pole, and the breeze caught the clothes making them flap and crack like whips in the sun.

'Here, maid, let me help you, that's heavy for you with the way you'm in. 'Tis good dryth today with this wind.'

Jane put her basket down with a sigh. She didn't have a mangle, so the clothes were very wet and heavy even though she was good at wringing them tightly.

'He's kicking so much today, I'll be black and blue inside I think. Feel this!'

Eliza put her hand to Jane's belly and their eyes met in amusement.

''Tis a boy then, for sure. My boys never kept still.'

Together they started to peg out the washing. It was good to be outside after two hours bent over the washtub. The air felt fresh and dry after the steamy gloom of the kitchen and a blackbird sang from the straggly hedge at the top of the plot, reminding her of the garden at Ashford that she had left so long ago. Eliza pushed the washing up with another pole, and Jane glanced down towards Mill Street. It was always a worry being away from the shop in case she missed a customer, although it wasn't unusual to see no one at all on a Monday, it being washday.

'Eliza, how soon will I be able to go back to the shop, do 'ee think, after the child's born?'

She had so many questions she would like to have asked her grandmother or, better still, her mother. She had tried hard to conjure memories of her mother, but although she could remember closeness and warmth and a soft voice, she could not picture her face. Eliza was lucky; her mother always came from Weare Giffard to stay for a couple of weeks when a baby was due.

'Oh, a few days, I don't doubt. You'm strong and healthy. Though you'm small.' She appraised Jane's figure. 'You'm narrow in the hips, rather, and it generally goes better when you'm big like me.' She laughed. 'But as long as you and the chiel both live, that's all us can hope for, amn't it? Anyways, I don't mind taking the little one in so you can be in the shop.'

Jane thanked her, but secretly thought that neither she nor Edward would be happy with that. Eliza had become a good friend but was rather rough with her children.

An elderly woman tottered up the path towards them. She was bent almost double and could see only a few inches ahead, but she seemed aware of their presence.

'I said her's not in! I told 'em! Her's gone away!'

Jane and Eliza looked at each other. Poor old Hannah Hookway never made much sense. Sometimes she thought she was talking to her mother who must have died years ago, and once she thought Eliza was her sister. She lived in a tiny cottage further down Cock Street with an elderly pauper couple, Mr and Mrs Croscombe.

'Who bain't in, Miss Hookway?'

'"Hello! Hello!" But her's not in!'

'Oh!' Jane had a sudden thought. 'P'raps it's the shop!'

She took off her apron and hurried down the path while smoothing her hair which had turned frizzy with the steam from the washtub. As she turned the corner into Mill Street, a woman was coming out of the shop; Jane quickly apologised and invited her back in. She only wanted her bonnet to be dressed with some new face trimming and ribbons, but it was pleasing to have another customer.

There had been far fewer customers than she had hoped. She had taken to decorating her own bonnet in a different style each week and walking through the town; women sometimes stopped to admire her work but when she invited them to visit her shop she rarely received a positive response.

''Tis wonderful what you can do, my dear, but I always go to Mrs Webber. I couldn't change.'

And sometimes, 'Well, I'd like to come to you, but you'm Chapel, bain't you, and I have to support Church, you see.'

Jane could only hope that orders would eventually build up through recommendations from the few customers she had, and that she wouldn't miss too much work when the baby came. Edward was very good at telling people about her, especially now that he was out delivering letters for much of the day. He had made many friends through the Library and also through his habit of stopping to talk to anyone on the street; every time he came home, he had stories to tell of the people he had met. He was becoming known for his skill in reading and writing and it wasn't unusual for there to be a knock on the door in the evening from someone needing his help.

'The carrier here in Bideford has brought a letter, Mr Capern, and I do think it's from my brother who went to the Canadas. I've been that worried about him – can 'ee read the letter so I can hear his news?'

Or it might be someone needing a letter written to a landlord who wanted to put up the rent. Usually Edward was given something for his trouble – a small piece of bacon or a bag of apples, and once they were given a rabbit. The gifts helped ease the strain on the housekeeping money and Jane felt very proud that her husband could do such clever things. When she told Eliza that he sometimes read to her in the evenings, Eliza stared at her in wonder.

'My William barely says a word to me when he's home.'

Yesterday evening Edward had not gone to the Reading Room, so they sat at the top of the house and he read to her from a weekly magazine he bought for 1½ pence. Jane had lit a fire; the reflections from the flames and from their candle flickered on the walls and on the arched ceiling of the room which, to the sound of Edward's rich, mellow voice, was suffused with warmth. She sat on his lap so that she could make use of the candlelight to continue a tiny flannel coat she was sewing for their baby, while he stretched his arm around her, enabling him to embrace her and hold the book at the same time. She was cocooned in warmth and safety, and she just had to kiss him from time to time. He accepted the interruptions without complaint.

The article he was reading told of the lives of women similar to herself who lived in Holland. She preferred it to the poems, some of which she secretly found rather dull, although she admired the way he read them. Dutch women, it seemed, kept their houses excessively clean, a habit developed to keep away the diseases which were prevalent in the low, damp places where they lived. They even hung the pillows out of the bedroom window each morning to air, which seemed to her an odd thing to do in a damp climate. Edward had suggested that Jane might want to read the journal herself when he was out, and she did try because the writer, Eliza Cook, seemed a sensible woman who could write about lots of different subjects. But many of the words were long and difficult, so she decided that it was dull work without Edward's voice to bring the story to life. And besides, she could not read and sew at the same time.

One Sunday in September, Edward walked arm-in-arm with Jane along the narrow cobbled path that led from Allhalland Street to the Wesleyan chapel, then nodded to members of the congregation as he removed his hat and they took their seats in a pew near the back.

He found it hard to concentrate on the service. The minister's voice was powerful and warm with emotion; it rose and fell and paused dramatically to lend weight to the words but the meaning did not engage Edward and the plain whitewashed walls held nothing to distract him. He glanced at Jane, as he had been doing every few yards since they left home. As her pregnancy advanced, it seemed to him that she grew more radiant every day and he loved to remind himself that he had played a part in producing her voluptuous figure. She saw that he was looking at her and gave him a little nudge; she was trying not to smile which made it even harder for him to focus on the minister.

It was a beautiful autumn day so, after dinner, he suggested they should have a walk. He took her gently in his arms, unable to crush her in one of his exuberant hugs because her stomach swelled between them in a way that he found both adorable and deeply moving.

'In a few weeks you may be too tired to go out – us should make the most of this weather while us can.'

As they went down Bridgeland Street Edward pointed out the grand houses belonging to Mr Maxwell who was president of the Literary and Scientific Institution, and Mr Robert Whale, the famous artist with whom he had exchanged a few words. Then as they passed the Manor House on the Quay he looked up.

'See that window up there? That's the Reading Room; I can sit there and look right out on the river.'

The Quay was tranquil in the Sunday afternoon sunshine. Five or six people sauntered along past the shuttered inns, and a single horse was tethered where, during the working week, a dozen or more carts vied for position. They walked along the river's edge where fishing boats rocked and bumped gently against the Quay wall, and two small boys dangled crab lines.

He looked down at them affectionately and squeezed Jane's hand. 'Shall us let our son come here, do 'ee think? I'd have a mind to go with him, 'tis years since I fished for crabs. I want him to be easy in my company, different from the way I was with my father. But I shall want him to have an education too; after good health that's the major thing.'

'Us may have a maid, you know!' She smiled up at him, and he thought he wouldn't mind at all having a girl if she was as pretty as her mother.

'Well, in that case, education wouldn't be so important, but I'd like her to read and write. Whichever us has, 'twill be your gentle influence which'll make our child loving and confident. I don't know where I'd be if I hadn't had my mother's encouragement.'

Jane looked doubtful. 'You'd be better at teaching it to read and write, don't 'ee think?'

'Yes, but I would like it to go to school if it's a boy. I hope us'll be able to afford the fee.'

'None of Eliza's children have been to school. But ours will be different, won't 'em.'

They walked across the bridge, feeling the breeze freshen as they reached the middle of the river, and he suggested that one day they should go out with a boatman and let themselves be rowed to Appledore or Weare Giffard. He wanted to take her to Northam too to see the great wall of pebbles. But Edward knew he should not wish for more than he had at this moment; his Janie on his arm, glowing with wellbeing and carrying their baby, and he could only pray that mother and child should live and be healthy.

She insisted that she could go on for a long time without getting tired so they left behind the cottages, warehouses and shipbuilders' sheds that clung to the river's edge and climbed the hill that led them away from the town. The wayside trees were stirred only occasionally by a passing breeze, and the hedgerow birds were silent except for a robin that led them on with its mellow warbling as it flitted from twig to twig. Edward drank in the serenity of the landscape basking in the gentle September light and gently caressed Jane's hand as they walked. The branches of cottage apple trees were pulled almost to the ground with the weight of their fruit, scarlet rosehips glowed like jewels in the lush hedges and hawthorn trees thrust their dark red berries towards the azure sky.

'It puts me in mind of a poem to Autumn by Mr Keats:
  Season of mists and mellow fruitfulness,
  Close bosom friend of the maturing sun.
I must see if I can't learn it all when I go to the Reading Room next, so's I can say it for you.'

They went on up the hill, standing on tiptoe every now and then to see over the high hedgebanks to the view of distant hills until, looking back the way they had come, they saw a flat-topped headland reaching out into an expanse of glistening blue water below the far horizon.

Edward pointed. 'Look, the sea! And that must be Baggy Point, though you'd hardly believe it, because don't it look small from here!'

A few late swallows skimmed the surface of the lane, darting over the hedge to avoid the lovers, and a buzzard soared overhead, mewing for its mate. A dark-bay carthorse grazing in a field lifted its head to stare, then trotted over to the gate to greet them, its massive feet clomping heavily on the soft turf, making the ground shake. The horse allowed itself to be stroked and patted. Jane marvelled at the velvety softness of its nose; she reached up to push back the long mane that hung over the horse's eyes, while it contentedly blew warm breath at them. Edward patted its strong muscular neck.

''Tis Sunday for him as well today. Not even horses work on a Sunday. In fact, the only people who work Sundays are preachers and postmen; 'tis fortunate there's only one delivery or I'd be working too.'

They wandered up past a newly-ploughed field where rooks hopped and pecked among the dark red furrows and gulls wheeled and cried overhead, until they came to a gateway where a track led steeply down to a farm, the roofs just visible below them. The view from here was sudden and breath-taking, stretching for many miles in almost every direction. Edward turned a full circle: hills, fields, woodlands and barely a house in sight. He felt he was on the very top of the world. To the south, beyond the farm, the land fell so steeply that the River Torridge was obscured from view, but the eye was drawn irresistibly to another valley at right-angles to the Torridge, a little valley enclosed by gently sloping woodland, home to a winding river glinting in the afternoon sunlight with white cottages here and there along its banks.

At the end of the valley, in the far distance, a church tower could just be seen high on the horizon.

He pointed it out to Jane. 'That looks an enchanted place! Shall us walk there another day? When the baby comes, us can carry him in our arms!'

A working man in Sunday clothes was walking along the lane towards them so Edward called out to him. 'Can 'ee tell us what is that little vale down there?'

The man stared. 'You'm strangers then. That's the River Yeo, runs down into the Torridge.'

'And the church tower beyond?'

The man shaded his eyes to look. 'I haven't rightly considered of that afore. But I'd say that must be Buckland church, Buckland Brewer, right along the valley then up a master long hill. I went there one time and it's a sizeable place.'

Edward gazed at the valley again. There was something most inviting about it. He would go there one day, he was sure, and climb to the village high on the hill.

They followed the lane as it wound and dipped alongside a spring of clear water where watercress grew, and he watched as Jane stopped to pick some late-flowering herb robert.

'I could make some little flowers like this to decorate a bonnet,' she said, examining them carefully, 'I've some cotton just the right colour.'

The hedgerow bore a profusion of black and red blackberries and late bramble flowers where bees were searching for yet more pollen. Jane had brought a muslin bag so they stopped to gather the ripe fruit, carefully avoiding the thorns as they reached deep into hedge; but they fed as many to each other as they placed in the bag, until eventually their fingers and lips were stained dark-red from the juice and he had to suck her fingers to clean them. When she laughed, her eyes shone as dark as the ripest blackberry and he felt almost overwhelmed by the love he felt for her. As they wandered on, Edward fumbled for the words he needed. He was under her spell, that was it, he was bewitched. He turned to her.

'My Janie has bewitching eyes,
So black and bright with lustre,
And such a cheek and rosy mouth…'
'You! What be 'ee saying now about me? But 'tis clever;
I don't know how 'ee think of such things, Edward.'

She put her arms around his neck and as they embraced there in the lane, he felt the miracle of their child pushing against him.

If only every day could be like this! If only there weren't the petty concerns about where the next shilling would come from, concerns that distracted him from his love for Jane and for poetry and learning. He sometimes wondered whether, if he had the time to concentrate on it, he could one day write a poem to be published in the newspaper. He only ever wrote three or four lines, and the poems that were published were often twenty lines or more. But what a thing it would be to accomplish, a poem in the newspaper!

As they walked Jane's thoughts returned to the forthcoming addition to their family and she described all the little garments she had sewn; they seemed to him to be very numerous for one small child but she thought that there might not be enough when drying clothes was difficult. He explained to her about the crib he was making and the joints that Mr Lock had shown him how to construct. He was very pleased with the work he had done.

'I'm getting good at carpentry, I think. I've a mind to take it up alongside the polishing. There's more to think of and study; a man's brain can get weary having to think just about polishing.'

At last they turned to retrace their steps, although Jane insisted she was still not tired, and Edward wished they could walk for ever amongst the green hills. He put his arm around her waist and held her close as they walked towards the setting sun. He was with the woman he loved and he had so much to look forward to – not least a blackberry pie.

Chapter Seven

Jane woke suddenly on her first wedding anniversary. The room was dark and the street outside was silent. She had been having the strangest dream. A woman was standing behind her to lace her stays, pulling the laces so tight Jane could hardly breathe, but before she could call out the laces were loosened again. What an odd dream. She did not even know who the woman was, and it was months since she had worn a corset.

She turned over carefully. The last two weeks had been really uncomfortable; when she was lying down she wanted to stand and when she was standing she wanted to sit. Eliza said this meant her time was near.

Everything was ready. The clothes and shawls were laid out in the chest and the crib stood by the bed. Mrs Bowden from Meddon Street had promised to come as soon as she was needed but Jane still felt nervous. When she tried to picture what the future might hold, she sometimes saw herself and Edward sitting in silence beside an empty crib, or the child left motherless and Edward being forced to remarry.

Suddenly her abdomen began to tighten. She gasped and cried out in surprise and recognition that it was this that had caused the dream. Her time had come.

All day she laboured. Sometimes, in a desperate attempt to be comfortable, she walked around the bedroom, no longer the comforting place she loved because Mrs Bowden had drawn the curtains against the daylight as if someone had died, and she had placed a bowl at the end of the bed alongside a mound of cloths and a large pair of scissors from which Jane averted her eyes. During the pain-free times between contractions, when she would have liked to lie quietly and perhaps doze a little, Mrs Bowden made her get up and kneel at the bedside to ask for forgiveness for her sins so that she would be prepared if the Lord decided to take her. As the day wore on the contractions came faster and stronger with hardly a moment between, so that she wished that he *would* take her, although the nurse soothed her and told her that her child would soon be born. At last the intensity of her body's resolve blocked out all else; although she heard Mrs Bowden beseeching her to slow down, to wait, she could not and with one final supreme effort it was over. As she panted and cried, her voice merged with another – a small, scratchy voice which astonished her, then Mrs Bowden held up her son, flailing and protesting, and alive.

She was still crying when he was clean and nestled on her breast, although she scarcely knew why.

'Is he strong? Is he healthy? He looks healthy!'

The nurse was busy at the end of the bed. 'He's a good, strong boy, a big child. He was big for you.' She busied herself again.

'But I'm well? I'll live? I feel well now it's over!'

Mrs Bowden hesitated. 'Would Mr Capern pay for a doctor, do 'ee think? 'Twould be good for you to see one.'

Jane was shocked; she had never needed such a thing before. 'But that would cost a lot of money, wouldn't it? How much would it cost? Why do I need a doctor?'

She averted her gaze. 'The baby is big and came very fast. You have a tear and a doctor could stitch it up. He would charge seven or eight shillings, I think.'

They could not possibly afford eight shillings. After paying Mrs Bowden 1s 6d there would only just be enough left to pay the rent; it was out of the question.

'Please, don't mention the doctor to Mr Capern. I'll mend, won't I? He needn't know.'

The nurse looked at her straight. 'Mrs Capern, a husband can't help but know these things.'

Jane put Mrs Bowden's words out of her mind. When Edward came home from work, he was overjoyed with his son and wept openly as he cradled him in his arms. He had already decided that if their child was a boy it should be called Charles, but now he presented the baby with a whole string of additional names: Henry after his two little brothers who had died in infancy, Newton after a clever man who had been the subject of a lecture, and Wood after his mother's family. Jane called him Charlie and Edward soon followed suit.

Their son proved his vigour by protesting loudly at all times of the day and night. She did not mind at first; she was in any case too excited to sleep for long and she was proud of his strong lungs and his determination when he suckled. Eliza and other kind neighbours brought in food and lit the fire. Edward carried up a cup of tea and some morsels to eat. She was hungry and ate well, despite being in pain. She thought it must, surely, be normal to have pain after a birth.

Charlie sucked greedily at her breast then turned away and yelled as if furious with her. She stood up to walk painfully up and down the kitchen, rocking him and trying to give her voice a soothing quality, because that was surely how mothers ought to talk to their babies. Eliza had told her that once babies fell into a routine after a couple of months, they needed feeding less often, but instead his screaming had increased and went on for hour after hour. Nothing Jane did made any difference, and she longed for silence. She was tired; so tired.

'Charlie, hush, hush; mama's here. Come on, Charlie, you should be happy when you're with mama. I was happy with my mama, Charlie.'

Her voice wavered a little. His head bobbed down on to her shoulder as if exhausted, then with renewed effort he arched his back and screamed again. She wondered sometimes whether he knew she was in pain. When she sat down with him, the pressure made her feel she was on fire. When she walked around the room, it was as if a fish hook caught deep down inside her was being drawn out by an invisible line.

Jane sat in the chair and offered him the breast again but he turned away as if she were giving him poison. She knew he was not hungry. He fed well between his bouts of crying and was growing steadily. Eliza said he was a good, solid baby,

'He'll settle soon, maid, you'll see.'

She hadn't told Eliza about her pain.

She laid him across her lap and tried to jiggle her legs to rock him but the movement made her tense up and gasp, so she tried walking again. His little knees were drawn up against her chest as if he were trying to push her away, and his screaming so close to her ear was becoming unendurable.

'Charlie, stop, please!'

She hadn't even swept the shop or the kitchen yet, or put the water on to heat over the fire for washing his napkins, and she was barely respectable if a customer came. She had never dreamed that having a baby would be like this.

Suddenly, she had had enough. She couldn't help him. He didn't want her. She put him down in his crib and stared for a moment at the tiny being with his red, contorted face and clenched fists then she went up to the bedroom and lay on the bed. It was only when she was lying down that the pain eased.

She heard a customer come into the shop downstairs and call out, 'Mrs Capern? Mrs Capern?'

She could not rouse herself. She was exhausted and utterly miserable. When she heard the door close she put her head under the pillow to shut out the sound of any more demands, from customers or from her baby.

When Jane woke, she was appalled by what she had done. She ran down and picked Charlie up, although he was now asleep, and took him upstairs to lie on the bed beside her. He could have choked to death and she would not have known! And she had turned away a customer although she desperately needed to make more money. She stroked the soft dome of his head. His eyelids formed perfect half-moons fringed with dark lashes. He had two fingers in his mouth and sucked them periodically, his little mouth moving as if by design.

She slid down on to her knees beside the bed and asked the Lord to help her. She had to become a better wife and mother.

When Edward came in that evening, Charlie was crying but he was clean, fed, and in his crib and the meal was ready. Eventually he fell asleep and after supper they went upstairs and she sat on Edward's lap, relaxing into his affectionate embrace while he read to her from Eliza Cook's Journal for half an hour before bed. It was a poem called *The Sea Child* and told the story of a boy who grew up on the seashore. Edward greatly admired the writing.

'A man like Mr Keats, his poetry is sublime and it fills me with wonder, but I could never attempt anything like it. But when I read Eliza Cook's work I feel I could try to write something similar. She understands ordinary working people. You know that I cannot read her poem *The Old Armchair* without weeping tears of regret for my mother.'

Jane cuddled in closer. 'This one makes me feel even more that I'd like to see the sea one day and walk along close to it and see the things that are in the poem. Could us do that?'

She laid her head on his shoulder and he stroked her hair, then ran his hand down her dress and caressed her thigh and gently moved his hand up, pressing her legs apart. As soon as she realised his intentions, she grew tense, feeling again the hook of pain deep within.

'Look, the fire needs attention.' She jumped up, fussed a little with the fire, then went to sit on the other chair and busied herself with her sewing.

'Janie?' She couldn't meet his eyes. He came and knelt beside her. 'You still love me, don't you, maid?'

She felt close to tears. 'Edward, of course I do, you'm everything to me.'

'Then, in time things'll be like they were, won't they? You'd tell me if you weren't well.'

'Of course I'm well.' She spoke quickly. 'It's just a bit too soon, that's all.'

How could she tell him that she was different? She held back her tears and picked up her sewing again.

'As long as that's all, then.' He returned to his chair, and after a few minutes he picked up the Journal and began to read silently.

Edward walked up and down the darkened shop, singing in a low, soft voice.

'Rock-a-bye, baby, thy cradle is green,
Father's a nobleman, mother's a queen...'

Charlie was wrapped in a shawl at his shoulder, and was crying as usual. In the shop a swathe of shadowy fabric lay abandoned on Jane's work table and the silhouettes of two bonnets on hat-stands in the window gazed out on to the street. He paced steadily back and forth. He was trying to give Jane a chance to finish preparing the supper in peace. He sensed that she was still secretly suffering from melancholy, although she was determined to get through the day without fuss. Their little house, that had been so full of warmth and love, now seemed subdued. He wished she would tell him what was wrong, and he wished that his mother was still alive to give advice. She would have known what the problem was.

He counted his paces as he sang; six paces towards the shop door, turn, six paces back, turn. He hoped there would be time after supper for an hour in the Reading Room. As Jane was so often preoccupied in the evenings, he had been spending more time there. Why sit upstairs with only five books for company, books he knew almost by heart, when there were five hundred to read in the Library? He might not have the chance for much longer because so few men used the Library and attended the lectures that the Institution was threatened with closure. Sometimes he was the only person reading there. There was so much that he wanted to know and each book held a key which could open a door to greater understanding.

He paused in his pacing and shifted the baby on to his left side. The little bunched-up body relaxed for a moment and his head rested sideways on Edward's shoulder, but then he arched his back, drew up his knees and wailed again, a rhythmic, vibrating cry. Edward sighed and started to sing again.

> 'Little dotty derrymouse,
> Sleeping in your tiny house,
> Rounded like a ball...'

Knowledge was even more important now. He had a son, and all the knowledge he gained could be passed on. He must also work with others to make the world a better place for Charles. If in his son's lifetime all men had a warm, dry home and sufficient to eat, if education could be freely available, if all men could win the vote – what a great achievement that would be! And it was essential that Charles should go to school. Edward had stood outside the British School in Higher Gunstone listening to the rise and fall of the master's voice and the chanted replies of the young children, imagining Charles taking his place among them. He went to Bridgeland Street where he peered through the windows of the Grammar School at the rows of boys engaged in quiet study. If Charles was to go there when he was older, not only would they have to find the fee, which might be as much as sixpence a week, they would have to forego the wage that Charles could earn by going to work. How many more children might they have by then? Would he be able to support them?

He changed direction and paced from the fireplace to the staircase. Since his son was born, the pauper children of the town held a morbid fascination for him. There was a tousle-haired boy of eight or nine frequently to be seen on the Quay who had a wretched, beaten look as if he had never heard a kind word. His feet were bare and he wore a man's coat from which the sleeves had been ripped, over a ragged dress which had perhaps been passed down from an older sister. There were several large boils on his neck. The boy approached loiterers on the Quay with his gaze on the ground, offering matches or a few wrinkled vegetables for sale before shuffling away, never hopeful of a sale.

What had brought him to this sad existence? As like as not an errant mother or heavy-drinking father was the cause, but it could just as well be repeated illness in the family or a blameless parent thrown out of work. The poor child would almost be better off in the Workhouse.

He had to ensure a secure position in society for his son. With an education, you could hold your head high. With a wealth of knowledge you could increase your social standing, converse with gentlemen, make an impression.

Through the bay window, he saw a tall, gentle-featured man in a rough, brown, ankle-length overcoat. It was the lamplighter, Hezekiah Branch. He stopped on the corner of Mill Street and reached up with his long pole to carefully hook open the glass door of the streetlight and light the gas. The flame flickered and steadied, spilling a soft pool of gold on to the pavement. The warmth of the light was inviting; Edward stepped outside. Mr Branch wished him a good evening then walked on down Bridgeland Street to bring more lamps to life.

Perhaps it was the shock of the colder air that stopped Charlie's crying but the sudden silence made the street a wonderful place to be; quiet and cool and empty. Edward stood under the lamp and moved the baby round to cradle him in his arms.

'There, little man, that's better. Us can see 'ee properly now.'

The baby seemed to listen to him and his little head wobbled with the effort of finding his father's face, until he focussed suddenly as their eyes met.

'There, you can see your papa now!' Edward was entranced with the sudden connection. Father and son stared at each other intently, then Charlie's mouth opened and his eyes shone and there it was, a smile, the first Edward had seen! And then, it might have been a hiccough – but no, it was unmistakable – a chuckle! Edward laughed out loud and the baby joined in, a curious, half-formed chortle which he seemed to forget as the effort to focus his gaze became too great; then after a wobble and another fierce, intent stare, the laughter came again, as if his father's face was the most amusing thing he had seen in his short life.

'Look, there's more lights down here!'

Edward turned into Bridgeland Street. Hezekiah Branch's tall, shadowy figure was striding in a leisurely manner across the road, leaving another lamp burning bravely in the dark. He followed in the lamplighter's footsteps and held his son up in the next circle of light, waited for his gaze to settle and the laugh to come; then on to the next until they had laughed their way down to the Quay, where the lamplighter was illuminating the river.

'See, my son, there is light and laughter in the world! I hope soon there'll be more in your mother's life.'

He walked home with Charlie falling asleep on his shoulder. He was here, in a town that he had come to love, and was returning with his baby in his arms to his beloved wife. Surely he and Jane would find again the joy they had known together.

Chapter Eight

Edward whistled as he walked up the drive to Port Hill House. In the sixteen months since he started working for the Post Office, he had become almost friendly with Captain Keats, who passed on the newspaper to him when it was three days old if they happened to meet. This was very welcome because the Reading Room was now so poorly attended, it did not open every evening. Edward always rang his bell loudly as he went up the drive in the hope that he would be able to see Captain Keats himself rather than just the pretty housemaid. Today the Captain was standing on a grass bank flinging his arms about in a dramatic but controlled manner while holding a small blue-and-white flag in each hand. He stood next to a strange device. Whatever was he doing? Edward watched him for a few minutes, then coughed loudly when the Captain paused in his gesturing.

'Ah, Capern, I have a letter for you but first, come here, my friend!'

He explained that the device was a powerful telescope which gave him a clear view to Cross House in Little Torrington, nine miles away, where his friend Major Wheeler lived; they were exchanging messages in the manner that was used to communicate at sea.

'Here, have a look.'

Edward was amazed to see a small figure also holding two flags, yet when he took his eye away from the telescope and looked in that direction, he could only see distant hills.

'Quick now, take this paper and pen and I will tell you the letters he is communicating. He has just told me that his breakfast was burnt this morning.'

Edward did as he was told and gradually the message was spelled out: *Farewell Rain Has Arrived.*

'There! He will go inside for a brandy now because the view will not be sufficiently clear for signalling, but I think the rain may pass to the east of us. Come, and I will give you my letter and the newspaper.'

He looked forward to telling the postmaster, Mr Lee, about the telescope; he was always interested in what was going on. As he walked down the drive he picked up a windfall apple, and from the hedgerow some scabious, herb robert and daisies, forming them into a little posy and tucking the stems into his breast pocket to take home for Jane. He would give one of the daisies to Charlie who could hold things between his finger and thumb now. He would look at it intently, then probably try to eat it. Edward chuckled to himself. Jane would chide him for giving the baby such a thing, but it would do him no harm. He would have liked to go out into the fields on a Sunday so that Charlie could crawl amongst the flowers, but Jane usually said she was too busy or did not feel well enough. They had fallen out over it once; he had tried so hard to persuade her to come out for a walk with him, but she had crossly listed all the chores she had to complete. He worried for her health, shut up in the house all the time as she was. They used to have such happy times together in the lanes and fields. He had written a poem for her about their quarrel and left it on the table, but she had made no comment on it.

A party of swallows perching on a dead branch took off as he approached, wheeling and twittering overhead before coming back down to rest when he had passed. Soon they would be gone, taking the long warm days with them; he would again be walking through rainstorms and hail and ice, and sometimes wading over the causeway when it flooded, but the prospect did not daunt him. His daily walk to Appledore had made him strong and healthy. And he was well-known now; even men such as Captain Keats welcomed him and shared their outlook on the world with him.

He called out a greeting to young Dr Ackland who was riding in the direction of Northam, then rang his bell as he turned into Orchard Hill. As the bell's reverberation died away, the silence of the lane flooded back. That was how it was in September; the birds stopped singing, harvest was complete and the fields lay golden and empty, the air was still and hushed as if it was the Sabbath. He was thinking of writing a poem for each month; he had been thinking of it for some time but no sooner did a line occur to him than a passer-by stopped to speak, or he had to knock on a door to deliver a letter. Never mind; one day he would do it.

'It is the Sabbath month, the resting time,
When Nature pauses 'mid her busy toil.'

There, that was a start.

He collected a bundle of letters and a large fee from Mrs Hake's school. He glanced at the letters as he dropped them into his bag, admiring the careful, beautifully formed writing. They were addressed to distant towns and two to the East Indies. Mr Lang at The Retreat had a letter for his lawyer, and a cottager needed help with an address. Then it was time to head back over the causeway to the town.

He thought to take the flowers to Jane as he passed but saw that she was with a customer, so he went straight to Mr Lee's shop.

Mr Lee was busy at the post office desk when Edward came in and did not reply to his greeting, which was unlike him. Edward waited a minute but soon lost patience.

'Is all well, Mr Lee, Sir? I have quite a bundle here to be sorted before the post goes out.'

Slowly, Mr Lee put aside the letter he was reading and stood up. 'No, Mr Capern, all is not well, I am sorry to say.' He came out from behind his desk and put his hand on Edward's shoulder. 'There is to be an alteration in the post.'

Edward was bemused. 'An alteration? What sort of alteration? Am I to work different hours? That will be no problem; you know that my other work, such as it is, can be done at any time.' Why did Mr Lee look so serious?

'I'm sorry, Mr Capern, but it is not that. I have had a letter from the surveyor,' he indicated the paper on the desk, 'and he informs me that in future the post for Appledore will not come through Bideford. It is to come from Barnstaple and be conveyed by boat from Instow.'

'Well, then,' Edward tried to take in the information, 'will I have to walk to Appledore and carry the letters to Northam? Yes, and take them all back to Appledore, is that it?'

Mr Lee shook his head and patted him on the shoulder again. 'No, the carriers already resident in those villages will do that. I'm sorry; there will be no work for you after this week.'

He couldn't believe it. Mr Lee told him that as he had not been dismissed through any fault of his own, he would be entitled to be appointed for the next vacancy that occurred. But when would that be? There had been no new positions during the eighteen months he had worked for the Post Office.

He walked slowly back along Mill Street. How was he going to tell Jane? She would be so disappointed; he hated to disappoint her. Slowly he opened the door to the shop, the little posy of flowers in his hand.

Two months later Edward stood at the upstairs window looking down on to the street below. Everything was grey; the dreary sky, the roofs, the passers-by with faces downcast and arms folded to ward off the cold dampness. He watched an old woman shuffle along the street, her face and hands red and chapped, the cold penetrating further into her bones the longer she was out in the chill air. Would she return to a comforting fire or to a bleak, bare room? November brought death to the poor and the sick; he felt he would hear the wails of despair if he attuned his ear more closely to the dreary season. He could go out, but to what purpose? No birds sang; no leaves or fruit remained on the trees after the bitter winds; no sunlight gleamed on the river as it surged past its sodden banks in a brown and angry torrent, and the sky would soon grow dark. The days were short now, and the nights excessively long.

He turned from the window. The weak light that managed to find its way through the thick cloud outside did little to brighten the aspect of the room, and there was no fire. How could he ask Jane to light a fire when they could barely afford to keep one burning in the kitchen? His chair had been thrown on to its side and scraps of paper were scattered on the table. Jane would tell him he shouldn't have torn up them up; the reverse side was blank and could have been used. There would be no more paper because they could not afford to buy the tea or sugar that was contained in it. But it was no matter; what need had he of paper? No one would want to read his poems. He picked up one of the shreds.

'O cruel November! Thy lifetime is drear –
Thou'rt death on his pale horse to me.'

Poetry should be uplifting, inspirational. Nobody wanted to read gloomy thoughts, least of all his, which were unoriginal and banal. John Clare had written moving lines about the month of November, but he could not. He should give up all thoughts of poetry. And reading. What good had reading books ever done him? Now that the Literary and Scientific Institution was likely to close, he would not in any case have the chance to read new books. He would never be able to afford to buy books. He returned to the window.

He had spent the morning searching for work. Mr Lee had neither polishing to be done nor news of further work for the Post Office; Mr Lock had no work for him this week; the carpenter who gave him occasional employment expected to need help with some windows next month. Next month! He had enquired at the shipyards, the culm mine, the potteries and the brewery but there was nothing, not even for a common labourer. He had then stood on the Quay and watched as emigrants boarded Mr Richard Heard's *Devonia*, leaving behind all that was familiar for the chance of greater prosperity. Perhaps he should be taking his little family to Canada. Although he had no wish to leave Devon, it galled him to think that he did not now have the chance to do so, because he could not afford the fare.

It was no wonder that Jane turned away when he tried to embrace her – what use was a husband who could not even provide for his family?

He heard Charlie start to whimper and then to cry on the floor below. He had been unwell for several days; just a cold, Jane said, but he had woken and cried several times in the night. There was no purpose in him trying to soothe the child. Charlie would want his mother. He was no use even to his own son.

When Jane heard Charlie starting to cry upstairs, she drew in a long, slow breath. Would Edward go to him? She couldn't leave this customer, not now.

The woman was a farmer's wife and was not short of money, that was certain. There were several petticoats under her skirt and she wore a good woollen cape. Yet when she had come in and asked the cost of the bonnet in the window, her response was, 'Oh, my dear soul! What a price!'

''Tis considered to be very reasonable for the times, Ma'am,' Jane had replied evenly.

'Reasonable! I've never heard of reason in the prices of a milliner!'

Jane took a deep breath. 'I've heard, Ma'am, that prices of materials will get even higher. 'Tis a bonnet that a lot of folk have admired. And well suited to your style and complexion.'

The woman had grunted and was now walking around the shop, examining everything. She even pulled open the drawer in the table. Jane stood motionless with her arms folded; a customer like this was the last straw today, but she must be careful. If she said what she wanted to say, the word would soon get around the town that she was rude to customers; Bideford was like that. The woman's boots creaked with every step as she paced around the shop, making Jane shiver all over. Charlie's intermittent cries were becoming more regular.

The woman peered at herself in the mirror. 'I think I'll have this bonnet made over. I like your styles, but not your prices. I expect I'll need to go to Mrs Carter.'

Charlie started to wail. Jane was close to losing patience, but she made her voice sound sympathetic.

'Oh! I see now that you'm poor. I can't turn my back on the needy. If you can't afford to make yourself tidy for church, I'll trim your bonnet for cost, or for nothing if need be.'

The woman turned on her, her face reddening. 'I am not an object of charity!'

Jane gave her a straight look and was careful not to smile. 'I'm sorry; I understood you wouldn't be able to pay to have it made over.'

'Well, you'm wrong. My husband lets me spend what I like on clothing! I'll have it trimmed with velvet and lace and in your best style.'

'I'm glad, Ma'am; that's a wise choice as I can see your bonnet is a good one. Wait one minute now while I fetch my tape measure.'

The woman wouldn't know that the tape measure was in her pocket; that was one place she hadn't been able to look during her examination of the shop. Jane ran up the stairs and found Charlie had managed to clamber out of his crib. He was crawling across the floor, sobbing. She picked him up and cuddled him while she ran up the next flight. Edward was standing at the window; she thrust Charlie into his arms.

'Sorry to disturb your writing but I've a customer; you must take him.' Edward wrapped his arms lovingly around the baby; he didn't seem to be very busy. She ran back downstairs and took a deep breath.

'Now then, I've some midnight blue velvet which would suit you very well, or might you prefer brown? I can see you've got good taste; you won't be wanting anything too bright.'

By the time the woman left, having happily accepted the high price Jane asked, they were on good terms. She sighed and sat down. The work would earn her one shilling and ninepence. After a good week, when Edward had some polishing and carpentry, he might bring home twelve shillings, but it looked as if he would not earn anything at all this week. Their rent was three shillings a week and they usually spent four shillings a week on bread alone – in the lean weeks, it was difficult to manage. She could never afford to buy meat now, but could get bones from the butcher for a penny to give the vegetables some flavour. If the day ever came when they were unable to pay the rent – that thought kept her awake at night.

She didn't always tell Edward when things were especially hard; he had enough to worry about. He had taken it very badly when he was laid off from the Post Office and now it seemed that the Reading Room might close because so few men used it. He was so clever with reading and with writing things down; but his cleverness didn't pay the baker, and there weren't any jobs for him that made use of his talents. They were kept for people from the better classes.

There were plenty of others who were poorer than themselves. She would manage, because she had had a lifetime of managing. There were worse things than poverty. Poor health, for one.

She stood up and walked through to the kitchen. The weather had been cold and drizzly for two days so she had not been able to hang out the washing. She moved the clothes-horse closer to the fire and turned over the baby's napkins that were draped over the backs of the chairs. There was water to fetch, coal to bring in, the privy to clean. At least she would be able to get on with it and uninterrupted, because Edward seemed happy to look after Charlie. She stared out of the window at the colourless sky, then set to work.

The months became a year and Edward's employment was still irregular. Jane had almost given up hope of him obtaining another postal round.

She raised her eyes from the black lining she was sewing into a mourning bonnet and peeped over at Charlie. She was careful not to turn her head because if he saw her looking at him, he would lose interest in his play and demand her attention. He was pretending that his three empty cotton reels were a horse, a cart and a driver. He pushed them along, clicking his tongue and calling out in his high, imperious voice.

'Whoa, there! 'top, Cha-cha say!'

The horse stopped obediently and the driver jumped down from his cart. Charlie looked up at Jane but she quickly averted her eyes and continued with her sewing. Mrs Croscombe's husband had just died and she oughtn't to go out until her bonnet was dressed in black. It was late to be working on a Saturday but she wanted to get it finished so she could start on some dress alterations on Monday. She had to take in whatever work she could get to make ends meet.

The driver was back on his cart: 'Go, horsie! Go, Cha-cha say!' Jane stifled a giggle. His commanding voice was at odds with the soft curls that fell to his shoulders and the warm shawl wrapped over his dress and knotted at the back. The horse and cart couldn't go very far because Jane had tethered Charlie to the table leg with a long string that was tied around his waist. It was the only way she could get any sewing done. He could run now, with a stumbling gait that threatened to pitch him forward at any moment. If a customer came in, he could be out of the door in seconds and he didn't turn to see if she was following as he sped off along the street. Other favourite destinations were up the steep stairs or, even more worryingly, into the fireplace. He was very determined.

'No, Charlie! It's hot!' Jane would tell him. He regarded her seriously. 'Hot! Cha-cha like hot.'

She glanced up at the shop window as a middle-aged couple walked past arm-in-arm. She was waiting for Thomazine and her husband Lewis to arrive, and hoped that Edward would be in a more talkative mood when they all had supper together. He had been upstairs for the last hour or two.

Since the Literary and Scientific Institution closed he spent his time leafing despondently through his small collection of books or pacing the streets in frustration. He never tried to write poems anymore. She did her best to keep him interested in the affairs of the town and to provide him with cheerful company, but there were times when he was so downhearted, even Charlie's antics failed to rouse him.

She tied off the thread and began to sew in the ribbons. The bonnet was very plain and would have looked better in silk, but she was using scraps because she could not be sure that Mrs Croscombe would be able to pay her. Her memory had got so bad, she might well forget that her husband was gone; but Jane didn't like to think of the elderly woman having the added indignity of not being able to dress appropriately.

She had gradually acquired some good customers but they did not need new bonnets very often. It had been an exciting day when Mrs Maxwell from Bridgeland Street came in the shop. Jane made her a new bonnet in brown silk lined in finely pleated cream silk and decorated with dark-red and cream flowers around the right side of the crown and the left side of the interior. It took a whole week to make and Mrs Maxwell was so pleased with it that she ordered one for her oldest daughter, Miss Harriet, in different colours. It was a pity that most of her ten children were boys.

A sudden knock on the shop window made her jump. The door opened and Lewis came in beaming followed by Thomazine, so like Edward she could have been his twin. Their complexions were glowing from the cold evening air. Since their marriage a year ago, they had been lodging with Mr Hockridge, a farmer in Orchard Hill, close to where Lewis worked as a shipwright. Thomazine had found a little dressmaking work.

Charlie was looking with interest at the visitors.

'Let's take this tether off you, boy! There! Up you go!' Lewis threw him up in the air and Charlie screamed with excitement.

The visit from his sister seemed to raise Edward's spirits; it was a relief to hear him laugh again. When they had eaten supper, and Charlie had been put to bed by his aunt, Edward and Lewis went for a walk around the town. Jane was pleased to have time alone with her sister-in-law. She passed her another plate to dry.

'You'm looking very well. You'm not expecting, I suppose?'

Thomazine sighed. 'No. No, I'm not. 'Tis a year now since we were wed.'

She looked despondent and Jane gave her hand a squeeze.

'Don't 'ee worry, 'twill happen in good time. You should be glad they don't come along too quick. My friend Eliza over the road has had two more girls since I was carrying Charlie, seven children now. You wouldn't want a long family like that. And she was none too well with the last; you remember I took in the two youngest for a few weeks so's she could rest.'

'What about you though, Jane?' Thomazine asked. 'When be 'ee going to have another? Charlie came along pretty quick.'

Jane scraped more soap from the bar to dissolve in the hot water, and added a greasy pan. She wished she had not brought up the subject of children. 'I don't know. One day I suppose.'

Thomazine was looking at her curiously. 'But you'm well now, aren't you?'

Jane swilled the water off the pan and handed it to Thomazine.

'Oh, I suppose I'm well. After a fashion.'

She lifted the heavy ceramic bowl and carried it out of the kitchen to empty the dirty water into the street drain. The street was deserted, but she could hear shouts and loud laughter coming from the Swan across the road. She stood and listened for a few moments, breathing the cold night air.

Thomazine was still leaning on the kitchen table and gave her a straight look.

'You *are* well, aren't you? No more pain?'

Jane had not talked to anyone but Thomazine about her troubles, and had not mentioned it to her for a long time.

'Not pain exactly. But, I'm different, that's all.' She sighed. 'Not like I used to be.'

Jane turned away. She felt unable to speak. She poured some more hot water from the kettle into the bowl, added some soap and washed out the dishcloth.

'Edward does know, doesn't he? How you feel?'

'Oh yes, he knows. He's very good really.' She didn't tell Thomazine that when it was time for bed, she sometimes busied herself with some task or another, knowing that he'd be asleep by the time she climbed carefully under the blankets.

'It isn't pain exactly, you know, not now, or not all the time. It's more like someone has tied a knot too tight inside me. I feel it when I walk too. I can't walk any distance.' She took Thomazine's hand. 'Now, don't think 'ee any more about it. I'm well enough, I was just a bit unlucky, that's all, but most have no problems. You'll be all right, you'll see.'

There was another reason she did not want any more children for the time being. Their income was so irregular that she was afraid they would not be able to feed another child. Suppose there were more babies and Edward's work fell away even more? Suppose she was too ill to work after the birth? Once, when Edward pleaded with her for another child, she broke down. 'I can't have a child just to see it starve!'

She didn't often worry him with the seriousness of the situation because he was a good man and always brought his wages home, unlike Mr Prust next door who spent most evenings in the Barley Mow. But money was very tight, some weeks. She even told untruths sometimes. If Edward had an early supper before a lecture, she told him that she would eat later, but then missed the meal to save money.

Thomazine knew about their difficulties with money of course, but Jane did not want to spoil the evening by talking about it now. She wiped her hands on her apron.

'Come on, let's sit by the fire and you can tell me about the last time you went to Barnstaple, and how my grandmother was.'

When Edward and Lewis returned, they were both in high spirits. They had seen Mr Maxwell return on the coach from London, where he had been for a director's meeting about the Taw Vale Railway. Everyone seemed very excited about the prospect of the railway coming to Barnstaple, and eventually on to Bideford.

Edward said there were several hundred people waiting to see the London coach arrive at the New Inn and Mr Maxwell was able to tell them that work on the railway was to start at once.

'You should have come!' he told Jane. 'Quick as anything a band was formed and went marching down the street in front of Mr Maxwell, and all the people following on behind all the way to Bridgeland Street! And the church bells ringing! Then someone fired the cannon on the Quay!'

'Oh, I heard that, I wondered what it was!'

'Mr Maxwell looked out from an upstairs window of his house to give a speech. He thinks us'll soon see work starting on the railway to Bideford as well. 'Tis a great day for the town!'

Edward had heard that the man who usually wrote the Bideford news for the *North Devon Journal* had not been present at the gathering, so he intended to write an account himself and send it in with the hope of publication.

'I'll make sure I write everything – conjure the importance and excitement of the occasion for folk who weren't there. I really think I might have a chance of getting it in the paper!'

Perhaps that would raise his spirits, at last.

Chapter Nine

Jane and Edward sat in the upstairs room, one each side of a candle that she had only recently lit. The August evenings were generously light; she had calculated that they could save sixpence a week on candles in the summer. She was mending Charlie's dress, which he had torn trying to climb into a tree while she was hanging out the washing.

'Look!' She held up the torn garment. ''Twas lucky he only had a scratch. I only turned my back for a moment.'

Edward glanced up from his writing. ''P'raps it's time he had trousers. Skirts was never meant for climbing trees.'

Jane was taken aback. 'Trousers? But he's not even three yet! Besides, 'tis easier for me to find fabric for dresses, and they'm more practical for growing into and altering. Maybe when your trousers are wearing out and could be cut down, us could think about it then. When they'm going at the knees.'

'I'd better go to chapel twice on a Sunday, then!' Their eyes met affectionately. She selected a piece of material to patch the dress; it was a close match.

'Eliza said I should have slapped him, but I think he was only trying to do what the big boys do. But 'tis true he is headstrong, so maybe us should be firmer with him.' She knew that Edward wouldn't agree to physical chastisement; he was against it on principle and, in any case, doted on his son.

'He's a grand little boy; he's got character, that's all.' He leaned back in his chair. 'What do 'ee think of this? I've written about how the railway would benefit Bideford, both for folks travelling away and for the visitors it would bring. Listen, this is how I describe the town.' He flung out his arm for emphasis as he read.

'*Bideford, seated on her hills crowned with terraces commanding extensive views of unrivalled loveliness;*

Bideford with her broad and spacious Tor, her Geneva-like scenery.' He looked at her over the top of the paper. 'Geneva is a town in Switzerland that I've heard is very charming. *Bracing sea breezes, beautiful promenades, corn-clad hills, luxuriant valleys, smiling villas, and picturesque grandeur, will, by medium of Railway communication, be soon seen and duly appreciated.* What do 'ee think? I think folk'll realise what a grand town it is, won't 'em? So of course us needs the railway.'

It was a relief to see him enjoying himself so much. ''Tis wonderful, Edward! You've such a way of making people see things.'

He had been very excited last month when he read in the *North Devon Journal* that the newspaper needed a correspondent for the Bideford area. Because his article had been published the previous year, his offer was readily accepted and, what was more, he was told he would be paid one shilling and sixpence for a half-column. He had not expected that he would be paid for the privilege of writing for the paper; although Jane did not see why he should do it for nothing, especially as he was spending many hours looking for stories, and had to buy paper and a penny stamp each week. At least he was sent a free copy of the newspaper.

As if he could read her thoughts, he said, 'This'll run to a whole column but naturally I won't be paid for the extra space. But I think I'm making the news more interesting. 'Tis very dull when all there is to read is a list of people who've appeared in court. I want to make folk look forward to reading the Bideford news.'

'Mrs White told me her husband has been reading it aloud to her, he likes it so much.'

Jane finished the mending and picked up the stockings she was knitting for Edward. She had been able to buy some black wool quite cheaply and aimed to make several pairs using smaller needles than usual in the hope that they would wear for longer. His old socks had been darned over and over. The click of her needles and the scratch of his pen came together in a gentle rhythm. She glanced up at him after every few stitches. The candle flame burnt steadily, illuminating his high forehead and sensitive mouth, and accentuating the reddish tinge to his beard and wavy hair. His face was animated as he stared into the distance and then commenced writing again, and she saw that his lips moved now and then as the words came into being. It amazed her to think of the ideas that were coming into his head, forming themselves into words, and flowing out with the ink on to the paper. She would like him to read to her again but he was completely absorbed in his work.

She finished the stocking, and yawned. ''Tis getting late, Edward. Will 'ee come now or shall I light another candle to take down?'

He looked up at her and she saw that it was a few moments before he took in what she had said.

'You'd better take another. But I won't be long.'

She went downstairs and quietly opened the door to Charlie's room. The moonlight shone through the front bedroom and on to his bed; she didn't need to waste money on a candle. He was lying on his tummy with his knees pulled up to make a soft, compact little bundle. His mouth was gently puckered as he breathed deeply and regularly. She stroked his curly hair back from his face and pulled the coverlet up a little, then she quietly closed the door.

She undressed and slipped between the cool sheets. She lay with her eyes open, listening to the faint movements from above and longing for the comfort and warmth of Edward's arms around her, and the whispered endearments which would follow. She knew that when she heard him descend the stairs she would feign sleep. How could she do otherwise? The caresses for which she yearned would naturally lead to greater desire and she would experience pain, despite his care and tenderness.

She lay for a long time, staring up at the ceiling as clouds passed across the moon and sent silver shadows coursing through the room. Edward was in no hurry to join her in bed.

Jane found that knowledge hard to bear, but she did not know how to make things better.

Edward sighed with satisfaction as he finished writing the article. He felt he had found words which would move people and might even be read aloud and shared, not just in Bideford but throughout North Devon. He stood up and walked to the window.

A full moon hung as if suspended on a string above Bideford's shadowy roofs, so huge and bright and peaceful that it seemed just a few spans away. Edward stared, overcome by the mystery of the scene. Slowly, one of the scattered clouds that drifted like thistledown through the ink-blue sky obscured the moon, then the edges of the cloud grew bright and, by degrees, the tranquil moon reappeared and its brilliance again filled the room. As the silver light flooded over him, he felt himself gathered into the moon's majestic embrace. The moon chose to find *him* amongst all the other men who might be looking out at this time, and he knew that Nature was speaking to him.

Through poetry, he could make others aware of the beauty and majesty of nature; he could move others as he was moved.

'While the thought thrills thy brain, take up thy poet's pen.'
Already he had found a line, perhaps the first line of the poem. Why had he not tried to write any poems throughout these long months? Why had he not made better use of his time while he struggled to find work? He returned to the table and looked down at his seven treasured books that he had acquired with such difficulty and hard toil; he ran his hand along their spines and then he reached for his pen.

As the *Water Witch* drew away from the Quay, she let out two low, long blasts from her horn and steam shot from her funnel. Edward stood with the other well-wishers on the Quay waving and shouting to the passengers on deck.

'Good luck! Bon voyage!'

He watched as the steamer turned and made its way downriver with its flags fluttering and sunlight reflecting from its bright paintwork. To travel on a steamship to Bristol and then on a railway train to London would be utterly thrilling, and to visit the Great Exhibition in the splendid Crystal Palace in Hyde Park and see the products of the world on show – the thought made him feel quite weak with excitement. But such an adventure was not for him. The fare for the *Water Witch* alone was six shillings, and although that was a generous offer with a free return trip, he would never be able to afford such a sum. He had established that the majority of the *Water Witch*'s passengers were going to the Great Exhibition and it amazed him that so many people were travelling from Bideford.

He turned away and walked along the Quay. He could not be downhearted for long; he might not be able to see the sights of London but there was always plenty to admire in Bideford. He paused to watch a brigantine sail from the Quay, bound for Wales with a cargo of culm. He had been spending more time than usual on the Quay so that he could include shipping news in his column. He had been ignorant of the functions of the various vessels, but he found that the crew and bystanders were only too willing to share their knowledge. As the weeks turned to months, his early enthusiasm at writing for the newspaper had given way to anxiety; he realised he could not merely extol the beauties of Bideford week after week – he had to record faithfully all the activities of a busy town. It was easy to find out about fires, robberies, accidents and ship launches; he simply had to listen to the gossip on the street and verify the facts.

But he had been mortified when Mr Lee mentioned that there had been no reports of Town Council or borough magistrates' meetings. He had not thought to write about such things! He could not believe he had been so foolish but he was at a loss to discover how he could find the information he needed. If he was to attend all the meetings himself, there would not be time to earn money. When he admitted his ignorance, Mr Lee suggested he ask for minutes of the meetings and had spoken to the clerk to the magistrates on his behalf. Edward now had to visit the town clerk, Mr Charles Carter, who was a retired solicitor and a magistrate – but would such an important man trust Edward with the Town Council minutes?

He turned into the High Street and paused outside Mr Lee's shop. There would be a table for him to polish and he could go in now to see whether it was ready; but he knew he was really only looking for reasons to postpone the work. He continued along Mill Street and lifted the brass lion's head to knock on Mr Carter's imposing door. He gave his name as Mr Capern, Bideford correspondent to the *North Devon Journal*, hoping he would not be thought presumptuous. He was shown into a small study and his eyes were immediately drawn to the leather-bound books which lined the walls from floor to ceiling. There must be hundreds, maybe over a thousand books! The room also contained a large soft chair, a desk with a thick writing-pad and assortment of pens. A tall, elderly man rose and shook his hand.

'So, I meet our new reporter at last! I have been curious to learn who it is that brings such a poetic flavour to our Bideford column. Sit down.'

Edward felt heartened. 'Thank you Sir, thank you. I try to employ language that may educate and uplift. Did you read my article last week, Sir, when I described the great storm that affected the town? "*The mighty voice of Jehovah thundered along the Heavens, and the searchlight of his omnipotence threatened immediate destruction to the puny inhabitants of earth.*" I felt my words did justice to the power of the storm, don't you agree, Sir?'

Mr Carter sighed, removed his spectacles and pinched the bridge of his nose. Then he looked at Edward.

'No, you mistake me. If I desire poetic language, I turn to the works of Mr Wordsworth or Mr Tennyson; I do not expect to find it in the news section. I have been concerned that there is insufficient substance in the news, although I admit that there has been an improvement in the last week or so. I hope that will be maintained. Do you propose to attend Town Council meetings?'

Edward was taken aback. It wasn't the response he was expecting.

'I'm sorry, Sir, I... I'm still learning, Sir, and I aim to be more particular in including the relevant information. I can't attend meetings because I'm a working man, but I was going to ask you, Sir, if I might use the minutes of the meetings so that the account might be accurate.'

Mr Carter scrutinised him from head to toe. He wished he was not wearing his working clothes.

'I pride myself on being a good judge of character and I have heard that you are trustworthy. Do you live close by?'

Edward explained that his house was but a short distance away. Mr Carter told him that he would drop the minutes in after each meeting and would want to have them returned the following day.

'But I expect you to be accurate in your transcription. You may omit extraneous information if there is insufficient space but there are to be no whimsical additions.'

Edward backed out of the study, thanking Mr Carter and assuring him that he would do as he was asked.

He walked slowly back to Mr Lee's shop. Being a correspondent was proving more difficult than he had expected, but surely it would be acceptable to retain a poetic element providing he covered the news in sufficient detail. There was no doubt there were benefits to the position despite the very low pay. Just last week he had been sent a ticket to a concert at the Mansion House which he would never have been able to afford. The concert consisted of a variety of music played on large brass instruments by members of an apparently nationally-known family by the name of Distin. He was unsure whether he had enjoyed it, but certainly he had never before heard anything so loud. His ears were ringing by the end of the concert. He had been at somewhat of a loss to know how to write about it, but eventually said, '*It is rarely that we listen to such a performance and it would appear invidious for us to criticise the merits of any particular piece.*' He was rather pleased with that.

He was also working on another project. A Mutual Improvement Society had been started in the town earlier in the year, the aim being for tradesmen, gentlemen and artisans to mix freely and share knowledge for their common enrichment. He had made many friends there and helped several men with their reading and writing. A talk was given at each meeting by one of the members; the subjects had included Peace and War, England's Greatness, Phrenology, and Is the Moon Inhabited? And he had volunteered to speak on Poetry. He had sent one of his poems to Eliza Cook and had received a most encouraging reply – he had been so thrilled the day her letter arrived that he had immediately volunteered to give the talk. Now, when he thought of standing to speak before an audience, he experienced a cold rush of fear, yet he knew that he was more able than most to speak on the subject. He was reading a borrowed copy of Mr Shelley's *Defence of Poetry* to help him organise his thoughts, and he had practised speaking loudly and clearly from the shop door while Jane listened in the kitchen.

He found Mr Lee putting the finishing touches to the table.

'Any news of new postal rounds, Mr Lee?'

Once an area was in receipt of one hundred letters per week, a new postal walk could be established and there were hopes that this level might soon be reached in the Westleigh and Buckland Brewer areas. Edward felt he would be tempted to send some letters himself to increase the numbers. Mr Lee looked up from his work, and he was smiling.

'Ah, Mr Capern, here you are! The situation has improved a little; 87 letters for Westleigh and Horwood this week and 91 for Buckland Brewer. But meanwhile, I've even better news for you. The number of letters for Bideford has increased so much recently that it's no longer viable for the carriers to cover the outlying areas, so I need someone to cover Orchard Hill, Cleave, Durrant and Port Hill. The pay will only be four shillings a week and will include Sundays, but it might tide you over until one of the longer rounds is confirmed. You can start on Monday.'

Edward felt quite weak with relief. It was nearly two years since he had been laid off.

There was time to hurry home and tell Jane the good news before starting work on the table. It really seemed as though their luck was about to turn.

A week later Jane went through to the shop where Charlie was playing with a small wooden boat that she had made for him. She sat down at the table and smoothed out a scrap of paper. She wanted to have the figures all laid out by the time Edward came back from work, because he seemed to find things easier to understand when they were written down. She could picture things in her head – the coins in one hand and the bread and soap and candles that they would buy in the other hand, and she knew exactly how they would balance. It was much harder to write things down.

Although she was pleased to see him so happy, she had been rather worried by Edward's appointment. The pay was very low and, as she feared, when he started working for the Post Office again his income from polishing fell still further. The part of the day that was not taken up with delivering letters was spent finding stories for the newspaper and talking to people about the goings-on in the town. He was also spending many hours preparing a talk on Poetry for which he would not be paid. They could not live on any less. If Charlie was sick and needed a doctor, if Edward had an accident and was out of work for a week, or even two – she had pictured all the things that could go wrong as she lay awake.

And suppose she was to have another child? For some
months now she had been drawn irresistibly to the cradles of
her friends and neighbours and had dreamt of holding her own
little baby again, of searching the tiny face for Edward's and
her own familiar features. She frequently reminded herself of
all the difficulties she had experienced when Charlie was
small but it did not stop her longing for another baby.
However, she had a plan that might make their precarious
finances more secure.

On the left side of the paper she wrote their weekly
income: 1s 6d from the *North Devon Journal*, 4s from the
Post Office. If Edward was eventually given a longer round,
which was by no means certain, that would increase to about
8s. She chewed the end of the pencil. 5s from polishing and
carpentry and 5s from millinery. The amounts varied from
week to week. Edward had once written numbers all over a
sheet of paper, then told her 5s was the 'average' amount, but
she already knew that. She drew a line under the figures the
way he had shown her: their typical income was 15s 6d, but
the earnings from polishing were falling. On the right-hand
side of the paper she wrote down what she spent. If she
bought bacon just twice a week to eke out the bread and
vegetables, and if no shoe leather was needed, and if the
weather wasn't so cold that extra coal was needed, they spent
14s 3d a week. That didn't include Edward's penny stamps
which he seemed to need quite often for letters to writers he
admired, or the occasional book or journal, or the extra
pennies they would need for Charlie to attend the school in
Gunstone. He was only three, but Edward said he ought to
start school soon.

She sat back in the chair.

'Mummy, anchor come off!' Charlie held up his little boat
in consternation.

'Give it here and Mummy'll tie it on for you. There; now,
don't be rough with it.'

'I not rough, sea did it. Might go wrecked!'

114

She laughed. 'Don't 'ee let it get wrecked!' She was frequently amazed by the words he came out with. Edward was always teaching him something new.

From the street came raised voices and then a scream. She jumped up. Thomas Harwood, the greengrocer from across the road, was shouting at old Mrs Croscombe and Miss Hookway while they held on to each other and cowered away from him.

'Wait here, Charlie.' She dashed out into the street just as Edward came along and people appeared from neighbouring houses.

'Keep right away from my house, the two of you!' Mr Harwood would have struck them but Edward was there in an instant and restrained him, shouting and struggling, with the help of another man.

''Tis due to them my pigs is dead! They'm o'erlooked and 'tis plain it's them as did it! Bloody witches they be and always poking round where they'm not wanted!'

Miss Hookway was wringing her hands and screaming 'Get out! Get out!' while Mrs Croscombe sobbed and clung on to her. Jane hurried over to them and put herself between Mr Harwood and the two old women, so that their view of him was obscured.

'Come on now, both of 'ee, come on home. Mrs Croscombe, you take my arm, that's it, and Miss Hookway t'other side. Come on, back home in the warm.'

She led them back to their cottage in Cock Street, glancing in the shop window as she went to make sure that Charlie was safe. Once they were back home, neither of the women referred to what had happened and Jane hoped they had already forgotten; but Miss Hookway kept up a thin high moan as she sat in her rocking-chair. Jane held her hand and talked to her quietly until she settled, then made up the fire for her although there was little coal left. She looked in the pot where they kept their money.

'I'll order a bit of coal for you, shall I, Mrs Croscombe?'

The old woman was picking up pans and putting them down again as if she was looking for something. 'Thomas gets the coal, always, he'll get the coal, chiel,' she said vaguely.

Jane sighed. It was best not to remind Mrs Croscombe that her husband was dead; it would only upset her again. The house was very dirty. She resolved to come in the next day to have a clean-up and take some of their clothes home to wash; they would have to be boiled.

She took the old woman's cold, thin hand. 'Now don't 'ee go out again, will 'ee? 'Twill be time for bed soon.'

She wasn't even sure that Mrs Croscombe remembered who she was. At least they were in familiar surroundings here and could just about manage with the help of neighbours. It had to be better than the Workhouse.

Edward was on the floor playing with Charlie. She closed the door on the cold outside air, glad to be back in her clean, tidy house.

'Witches! He'd have hit them, wouldn't 'e, if us hadn't come along? Two poor, weak old women; he should be ashamed of himself. What did you say to him?'

Edward explained that John Gregory, the young shoemaker who lodged with Mr and Mrs Harwood, had warned that there was trouble brewing. It was Mrs Harwood who had first got it into her head that the pigs had died through witchcraft.

'I know some of the old folk still believe in it, but a young couple like that ought to know better. No education, see! He should teach his wife fresh ways of thinking, but he wouldn't come to the Reading Room when it was open and he won't come to the Mutual Improvement Society. I asked him enough times! We heard a talk last month on Animal Chemistry and certainly witchcraft played no part in it. I told him what I thought of him today, so he's not best pleased with me.'

'You haven't upset him, have you?' She hoped there wouldn't be any more trouble.

'I've made it clear that he's to leave those two alone. I'll put it into the paper too. *Allegations of Witchcraft in Cock Street*. You'd never credit it, would you?'

After they had eaten their soup, she showed him the figures she had written down. Thinking of the two pauper women had increased her resolve still further; she was not going to let her family come to such a pass.

He tried to brush away her concerns, as she knew he would. ''Twill be well now I'm back with the Post Office, my flower.'

'But wait; listen,' she told him. 'I've a plan which'd mean you don't have to go out polishing anymore, and would make us more money.'

She explained that the shop was bigger than she really needed. If he were to make a screen – she had already made a sketch of how she wanted it and it would not be too difficult – they could divide it and set up another business alongside the millinery.

'There's no grocer this end of Mill Street, so us could start out with a little tea and sugar and build up when us can afford to buy in more stock. You can be in there at the start and finish of the day and your friends can visit you to talk and tell you news, and you can call me if someone needs millinery. Us'd have to stay open longer than for the millinery of course, until ten I suppose, but us could have a bell for folks to ring if us weren't there.'

'The early closing movement is growing in strength, so after a while perhaps us could close at eight.'

She could see he was impressed with the idea of being a shopkeeper. They walked through to the shop and she showed him what she planned.

'Us could have a counter here, on the left as you come in the door, and shelves behind. Then behind the screen my table and millinery things. And I've another idea for what I could do.'

She felt sufficiently encouraged by his response to tell him the second part of her plan. When Mrs Maxwell was having her bonnet made, she had asked Jane to recommend a good kitchen maid.

'In Barnstaple there was a registry office for servants and they charged a fee for setting people up. So I thought I could do that! You can ask around, those that need work and those that need servants, and send them to me and I can match them up! Us wouldn't make our fortune, but 'twould be money coming in without too many hours of work. Something I could still do if I... well, if I was...' She felt herself blush when she saw the way he was looking at her.

'Janie?' He took her hands in his but she couldn't meet his eyes. 'Do 'ee mean if us should have another child?'

He put his arms around her and the tension of the last few years lessened as she spoke. 'It's not that I don't love you; I do, so much, Edward, and you'm always so gentle and kind and try to make it easy for me. Anyway, I do feel braver now; it can't be so bad a second time.'

'If we're blessed, it'll go well this time, I'm sure.' He was looking at her with so much love in his eyes, just like the old days. 'And with the plans you've made, my flower, the money will be a bit easier. Us'll set them going at once!' Gently, he turned her face towards him. 'And Christmas is almost here – I shall have a whole day with you and Charlie! All'll be well with us again! I shall write a poem and fill it with our happiness!'

Jane lowered the heavy buckets of water to the ground outside the shop door. One was for herself and one for Mrs Croscombe who was no longer strong enough to fetch water.

'Charlie, come on, time to come in now.'

She didn't really like him playing out in the street because some of the carts came along very fast, but she had allowed him a few minutes with Eliza's children while she went to the pump. Charlie was chasing Mary around the legs of passers-by and both children were squealing with pleasure. She could allow him another few minutes' play.

Christmas was now only two days away. Mr Harwood across the road had placed sprigs of holly amongst the apples and oranges displayed in his cottage window while Mr Davies, the draper, had hung a string of cut-out letters which read 'Here's a Merry Christmas'.

As she leaned contentedly against the door, she heard a rhythmic thumping and some shriller notes from further down the street. People emerged from their houses in bewilderment.

'What's that noise?'

Mr Davies knew the answer. ''Tis the German strolling musicians! I heard last night they'd arrived in town.'

Charlie ran to her and pressed close to her skirt as he gazed wide-eyed up the street, then covered his ears as the musicians appeared, the first pounding a huge red-and-white drum to produce a deafening cacophony, and his companions capering along behind playing a jolly tune on brass instruments. Along with the other delighted onlookers Jane found herself clapping in time as they passed; she was too shy to dance along behind them as Mrs West did, but she put a penny in the hat proffered by a young boy who pranced beside them.

'Clap, Charlie, clap to the music!' But he hid his face in her apron, quite overcome by the unfamiliar uproar. Eliza's children had run up Cock Street as soon as the musicians appeared and were watching from a safe distance.

The band turned into Bridgeland Street and gradually the music grew more distant and died away; but the onlookers lingered a while, laughing and talking, before wishing each other a 'Merry Christmas' and going on their way.

Jane wished Edward could have shared in the fun but perhaps he would see the musicians elsewhere in the town. Charlie was now marching along the middle of the street with several other small children, pretending to bang a drum and shouting 'Boom! Boom! Boom!' at the top of his voice. She opened the door and picked up the buckets.

'Charlie, come on, help me tip the water in the bowl!'

He came running in, still laughing. The house looked particularly welcoming. The yule log lay ready on the hearth, and Edward had strung arches of holly and ivy over the door and the fireplace, having seen similar arrangements in Mr Ley's hall at Durrant, where even the antlers that hung on the wall were decorated.

'Charlie pour water! Charlie do it!' He climbed on to a chair and tried to help her lift the bucket.

'You can help! There, in it goes! Us must get Daddy's trousers clean, that's the way.'

She straightened up and let him play with the water for a few minutes. Just two days until Christmas! She and Edward would have the whole day together – something they had missed since he had been delivering letters seven days a week. She had managed to put by a shilling which should be enough to buy a small piece of beef, the first they had had all year. Thomazine and Lewis would come in later and bring some cake to eat and there would be time for talk and laughter. And when they had gone, and Charlie was in bed, then she and Edward would be alone together. The thought gave her a warm glow inside.

Suddenly the shop door flew open and Edward strode into the kitchen, grinning and waving a copy of the *North Devon Journal*.

'It's in! My poem's in the paper!' He picked her up and she found herself being whirled around the room while Charlie gazed in astonishment. 'It's here on page six, look!'

She was feeling rather giddy. 'Edward! Is your name there too?' Imagine, her husband having a poem in the newspaper!

He smoothed the paper out on the table, carefully avoiding the wash-tub. '"Original Poetry" it says at the top and mine's the first one! And there, look, there's my name, "E. Capern, Mill Street, Bideford." I intended the words to be sung but folks won't know the tune – never mind!'

She ran her finger under the words and read them carefully. '*The Good Times Are Come Again: A Christmas Song.*'

'Here:' he said, 'I'll sing you the first verse:
>   The good old times are come again;
>   The laughing days of yore,
>   When Mirth leaps forth to entertain
>   Old Christmas at the door,
>   And Joy with music welcome him
>   To each ancestral hall,
>   While holly boughs becrimson'd gleam
>   On every cottar's wall.'

His deep, well-modulated voice seemed to reverberate right through her, and the words that so cleverly described their happiness filled her with pride. What a Christmas Day they would have!

Chapter Ten

Right from the start, Milly was a happy child. The first time Edward saw her lying in Jane's arms he saw that she was contented, as if she had arrived exactly where she wanted to be. The morning after her birth, as he strode along beside the river carrying letters for the villages up in the hills, he pictured again and again the calm little face with its halo of dark hair, and the dark eyes like little reflections of her mother's eyes which shone with tears of joy.

He had only been asleep for an hour when Jane woke him to tell him that her time had come. He had pulled on some clothes and rushed out to fetch Mrs Bowden, then bade Jane a loving and fearful farewell before gently lifting Charlie from his bed. They were to spend the night at Eliza Elliott's house, in order to leave his own home to the business of women. Charlie soon went back to sleep, wrapped in a blanket on the floor; but Edward was disturbed by anxieties for his wife and by the discomfort of the hard chair and the table on which he tried to rest his head. When Mrs Bowden finally knocked on the door and he hurried down the street, he saw that light was just beginning to glow in the east, making visible a damp, penetrating mist which drifted up from the river.

Now, as his footfalls beat out a steady rhythm on the road, he felt he could almost have dozed as he walked, so tired was he after the sleepless night and the excitement of spreading the news that he was once again a father. A daughter! A tiny maid the image of his beautiful Janie! Would he ever be able to sleep again after such a momentous event? She was to be called Amelia, dear little Milly, but he would also name her Eliza Cook after the poet whose work he so admired.

At his approach, a flock of curlew rose from the glistening mudflats that lay between his road and the river, wheeling in a chorus of rich, bubbling calls before coming to land again behind him and resume their probing of the mud with long, skewer-like bills. Despite the leaden October sky and the chill breeze that whipped a flurry of rustling leaves from the trees on the hill, despite the approaching dark days of winter, safe in his home in Bideford was a precious bud of new life! He turned to look back at the little white town with its old stone bridge spanning the broad river, and he tried to make out the pattern of streets on the hill and to seek out the spot where his dear ones lay. Just as new life rose in the spring from the decay of winter, so he and Jane had created hope where before there had been only sorrow. He would write a poem in celebration! But not now. His head ached with tiredness, and the well from which he drew the words of inspiration was dry for the time being.

Four times this year his poems had been published in the *North Devon Journal* and perhaps he would soon finish more that the editor would consider worthy of inclusion. Since starting the new nine-mile Westleigh and Horwood round in April, he had time for composing while he walked the route and had a collection of two dozen poems on which to work during the long evenings in the shop.

He waved to the woman at the window of the tollhouse as the road led him away from the river. He crossed the marsh where a stalking heron straightened its neck, staring at him until he approached the turning to Southcott; but his thoughts were not on his surroundings today. Last night there had been times when he feared that Jane's labouring would bring forth only death. As he lay with his head on the hard table, he thought of the young woman who had died in childbirth only the previous week, and he thought of the pain that Jane had suffered following Charlie's birth. He had never fully understood the cause but last night his imagination had conjured distressing details. This morning, he had not liked to ask her about her suffering while she was glowing with love and elation; but after he had held the tiny child and unwrapped the blanket to touch her immaculate little fingers and toes, he held Jane's hand and looked bravely into her eyes.

'Was it very bad for you, this time?'

And she whispered, 'Not so bad. Mrs Bowden says not quite so bad; her's small, you see, little Milly.'

He saw that she too was embarrassed to speak of it and had to look away, but as he gazed at the perfect little child, he felt his fears ebbing away.

As he walked into Westleigh the church bells started to ring, the merry peal sounding out over the river and echoing from the hills beyond. Being so tired, he could not, for a moment, think why they were ringing. Was it Sunday? But no, of course, today was the marriage of Mrs Torr's younger son and Mrs Roberts' daughter from Eastleigh House. How could he have forgotten? As he left the two villages yesterday, cottagers were already picking late-flowering dog roses from the hedgerows and appearing from the woods with evergreen boughs, and now, looking up at the church, he could see flags waving from the top of the tower.

The village was deserted; the ringing of his bell failed to bring forth a single person and his knocking went unanswered, obliging him to open doors and place letters on cottage tables within. As the narrow ways winding between the low thatched cottages echoed to the sound of his footsteps, the unusual situation conspired with his tiredness to make him feel as if he were in the midst of a strange dream. The only inhabitants he saw were a few speckled hens pecking at the scuffed edges of the lane and a solitary dog lying on a doormat, which merely thumped its tail when Edward asked it, 'Where are all the folks, then?'

His answer came when he turned the corner towards the silent church, the bells having now ceased to ring. A triumphal arch of evergreens woven with a profusion of flowers stood over the road. As he passed underneath, he saw a large crowd standing quietly outside the church beside a pair of grey horses harnessed to a pretty carriage.

'There you all are!'

His greeting, although not loud, was shushed by those nearest to him.

'Her's inside now! They'm getting wed! You never saw anything so 'andsome!'

It seemed that the whole village had left their work to watch the bride arrive. William Oliver still wore his blacksmith's apron, labourers in mud-caked clothes and boots had left patient horses hitched to the plough, while Betsy and Fanny Squire continued to sew fine leather gloves as they stood and waited.

Edward whispered rather loudly to those nearest him. 'I've got a daughter! My wife's had a little chiel!'

But the arrival of children was nothing unusual in the village and apart from a couple of pats on the back, he received no great response to his news. He stood for a few minutes gazing along the flower-strewn path towards the church door, wondering whether he might one day make enough money to afford a grand wedding for his daughter.

One of the onlookers leaned confidentially towards him. 'Fancy all them gardeners up at Eastleigh growing all them flowers just to be trod on!'

It was clear that it would be some time before anyone would emerge, so he tipped his hat to the crowd and went on his way to the Vicarage where even the servants were absent, and then on to Bradavin Farm with two letters.

There was more life in the lanes than there had been in the village. After the recent heavy rains, there was a constant trickle of water seeping off the fields to run in little waterfalls down the hedgebanks and into streamlets along the edges of the low-lying lane; a snipe flew suddenly from a ditch with a clatter of wings and small birds chirruped busily among the yellow, gold and bronze fronds of bracken in the hedgerows, able to find food again now that the weather was drier. How busy *he* would need to be, with a wife and two children to feed! *There* was the subject for a poem – the similarities between his life and the lives of the birds. If only his words could earn him money – then he would sing in as carefree a manner as they did!

He paused on a small bridge to look down at the stream which was now a determined grey torrent; in the summer he had watched boys lying on their stomachs on the daisy-strewn banks to reach into the clear, sun-sparkled water and catch trout with their bare hands. The next time he saw such a thing, his little daughter would be able to sit up and to smile when he came into the room, providing she was spared.

As he climbed towards Eastleigh the church bells started to peal again, carried to him on the wind along with the sound of distant cheering, and there was a sudden celebratory burst of cannon fire from the top of a hill where two men stood next to the standard of England.

It seemed the inhabitants of Eastleigh had been determined to outdo their neighbours, for at the entrance to the village there was another evergreen arch which surpassed the other in both size and ambition, this one bearing the legend 'Health And Happiness' on one side and 'Joy And Gladness' on the other, in large coloured letters. He passed underneath in a trance – the celebrations were surely laid on for his benefit! Here the villagers lined the street wearing their best clothes and called out to him happily as he walked between them.

'Have you seen 'em? Be the carriage coming yet?'

'No, but I've got a daughter! A pretty little maid called Amelia!'

Mr Puddicombe cheered him and Mr Edward Garnsey slapped him on the back and asked him if all was well. He handed out the few letters he had for the hamlet before joining the group to wait for the carriage. After a few more minutes of cannon fire, which made everyone laugh, and the joyful ringing of the distant church bells, the grey horses with the carriage carrying the bride and groom trotted into sight. The crowd cheered, then followed the carriage to Eastleigh House where they were all to be treated to a tea.

Edward watched them pass through the gates, and as the carriages of the guests and family turned in, Mrs Roberts leaned out, smiling: 'Come in, postman, and take tea with us!'

He thanked her, but he had to walk deeper into the hills to reach Horwood and was already late, so he continued on his way.

He turned to look back over the gaily decorated hamlet and the sweeping view of fields and hills beyond. Through his tiredness came the sudden realisation of how blessed he was to have found occupations – postman *and* newspaper correspondent – for which he was respected by rich and poor alike. He no longer had to undertake manual work for which he had no real talent. He had a beautiful wife and two healthy children and he was able to write poems – a rare accomplishment even among the wealthy. His desire now was to earn a degree of fame through his writing, and perhaps even fortune.

It was still raining. Water bounced off the street, rushed along the gutters and gushed out of the downpipes. As fast as Jane wiped down the shop window, it misted up again, preventing people seeing the new bonnets she had on display. It had scarcely stopped raining for weeks. She turned away from the window and picked up the bucket and cloths. Mr Willcock, who was deep in conversation with Edward on the other side of the screen, had not seemed to notice as she tidied the grocery shelves and washed the floor around their feet.

'Parliament has refused to grant the Company an Act to authorise the extension from the Fremington terminus to Bryant Ching's pottery yard, unless one third of the capital is raised locally.'

'A third of the capital! But that's sixteen thousand pounds!'

It sounded like bad news. Every week there seemed to be news of the railway, sometimes good and sometimes bad but always difficult to follow. If only it would stop raining. She wanted to go out into the town before Edward went out on his round. She went into the kitchen and leaned over the cradle where Milly lay contentedly, and immediately the baby's dark eyes tried to focus on her own and the ghost of a smile played around her lips.

'Us needs to go shopping, Milly, doesn't us! But not in this rain.'

She kissed her and Milly clasped Jane's hair in her tiny starfish hand.

'I want to come shopping too, Mama.' Charlie, curled up on two chairs pushed together in front of the fire, had a blanket around him and his head on a cushion.

'No, you'm not well enough, my lover, you know that. If you were well, you'd be up at school, wouldn't 'ee.'

'I want to go to school.' He started to cough again.

'You shall go again when you'm better, sweetheart. When it stops raining Mama'll get some medicine for you.'

All the children in that part of town had coughs and thickly running noses and it was said that it was barely worthwhile the British School in Higher Gunstone staying open because so few pupils were well enough to attend. Jane suspected that the damp and draughty building was the cause of the illness.

As soon as Charlie recovered, Edward was to take a day off work – and would have to pay someone to take his place – so that they could all go on the carrier's cart to Barnstaple to visit Edward's father, who was very ill. They had not seen him since March, just before Jane's grandmother died. Edward had never really forgiven him for remarrying so soon and showed little interest in his half-sisters, but they would be able to take the opportunity to see Caroline and Elizabeth.

Jane took Milly's napkins off the boil and rinsed them. She had not seen her grandmother very often since moving to Bideford, but she missed her now that she was gone. There was no one now with knowledge of Jane's early life; no one with whom she could share childhood memories.

She cradled Milly in one arm and wrapped a thick woollen shawl right around herself and the baby and arranged another lighter one over her bonnet and shoulders. She bent down to stroke Charlie's cheek.

'Try to sleep now, sweetheart; Mama won't be long.'

He was too tired even to reply.

The rain had almost stopped but the street ran with water. The drain at the bottom of Cock Street had blocked again and a foul-smelling mud oozed and bubbled from it; she held her shawl right over Milly's face and up over her own mouth until she was well away from it. In the summer the smell was so bad that she had to keep the bedroom window closed, otherwise it would be sure to make them ill.

She walked up towards the market, dodging the little streams that flowed down the rough surface of the High Street. It was usually lively here but today the street was deserted except for a boy rattling a baker's cart down the hill. The sky was heavy and dark, as if dusk were coming. Suddenly five dark-red bullocks careered around the corner of Grenville Street and came skittering and sliding towards her with tails raised, while a man running behind them shouted 'Whoa there! Stand!' She fled into the nearest shop and closed the door quickly behind her, watching in terror as the bullocks hurtled past the window.

'Should never be allowed. It's frightening to be out there whether you'm on foot or on horseback.'

Jane turned to the speaker. She had been too alarmed to notice which shop had sheltered her. Mr Fry, a small man with a round face, was looking at her over the top of his glasses. She had never been in his chemist's shop before.

'Sorry for bursting in like that. I thought they'd run me right down!'

'Do you remember that time when a bullock escaped and rampaged right around the town? It tossed one man and upset a boy's milk pails, then went through the turnpike gate and ended up in a garden in Landcross!'

'I'm glad I wasn't here then!' She looked at the shelves of coloured glass bottles behind the counter. 'My little boy's got a bad cough. Have 'ee got anything that would help?'

Mr Fry asked questions about Charlie's illness. 'I can make up a mixture of hemlock and liquorice which would be helpful to him. The cost would be eightpence.'

'Oh. Thank you, but I don't reckon I will.' He seemed a kind man and did not appear to mind that she was not buying anything.

There were fewer stalls than usual in the pannier market, probably because some of the farmers' wives had not thought it worth coming in, with the roads in such a bad state. Edward had told her that some roads had been ploughed up by the torrents while others were impassable; he had had to take to the fields more than once to get around a flood. She stopped to speak to the pedlar who always set up his wares at the corner of the market. He was a tall, thin man with a long face and sticking-out teeth, and was always smartly dressed in a dark suit. He had been in Barnstaple Market too for as long as she could remember. She sometimes bought thread from him because it was cheaper than in the shops; he also sold bootlaces, garters, pincushions, combs, cakes of blacking, nutmeg graters and an assortment of pills in little packets. He always greeted her pleasantly, and although he extolled the virtues of his wares, he did not try to shame his customers into buying as others did.

'Do you require anything in my way today, Ma'am? I know you always like to have the best and I've some very fine pins today – here, you can test them – for I know what it is with milliners, you can never have too many pins. And where's the little boy today then?' His eyes were sharp, but he didn't seem to have noticed Milly under the shawl.

'He's at home with a bad cough.'

'Then I've the very thing for him! These pills here are very specific for bad coughs, give him two today and he'll be fit and well tomorrow.'

She thought how wonderful that would be if it were true and hesitated for a moment. But Edward was scathing about such cures; she did not want to have to admit to him that she had bought pills from the pedlar.

'No thank you, but I'll take some of this thread.' She had been testing it for strength while they spoke.

She knew what she wanted for Charlie. Her grandmother had been very clever with old-fashioned remedies; women in Ashford knew to come to her when anyone in the family was unwell. Jane regretted the lack of a garden where she could grow some of the herbs her grandmother had used. What she needed now was sage. She wandered along the rows of stalls until she found a woman who had some alongside bunches of parsley and rosemary; the sage was rather shrivelled but it would have enough strength to make a good tea with a little honey. The cost for a sizeable bunch was only a halfpenny.

She bought vegetables and a small piece of bacon and walked wearily back along Mill Street. She was not yet fully recovered, but at least she was not suffering as badly as she had after Charlie's birth.

Just before she reached the shop, she was startled to see a new sign in Mr Harwood's window. *Pies! Pies! Pies!*

What was he up to now? Ever since she and Edward had set up the grocery business, there had been an undeclared feud with Mr Harwood. He was a greengrocer so they were not taking any of his trade, but as soon as they started selling tea and sugar, he did the same, and when they added rice, he did likewise. He was not particularly popular amongst customers due to his irascible nature, so their trade, whilst small, was not greatly affected by the changes he made, except that he insisted on breaking the early-closing agreement by continuing to stay open until ten o'clock every night. Edward was glad that the eight-o'clock closures had resulted in more young men attending the Mutual Improvement Society; he liked to offer advice and direction in the same way as he had been helped when he was young. He was infuriated that Mr Harwood continued to open late, because now other traders were wavering. He would not be pleased at this latest development.

The rain had started again soon after Jane's return. By the time Edward came home he was soaked right through to his skin. His boots were caked with mud; more work for her.

'The wind up at Eastleigh is blowing right off the estuary; bitterly cold, and driving rain with it. My bag of return mail was wet through; 'twas fortunate I memorised the addresses to give to Mr Lee because the ink is nearly all washed off.'

He stripped off the layers of sodden clothes and soon Charlie, who was a little livelier, was sitting up laughing. 'Daddy's in his birthday suit! Daddy's in his birthday suit!'

Jane covered her mouth and tried not to laugh.

'Edward, for shame! Quick, wrap this sheet around yourself and get dry.'

She moved the baby's damp napkins from the clothes-horse by the fire to make room for his wet things. The drying of clothes was becoming a real problem; these would barely be dry for him to put on in the morning, even if she kept the fire in all night, and the cost of all the coal they were using was beginning to frighten her.

'I really need to make you some more clothes, a new coat and trousers at least. You'll catch your death if you keep putting on damp clothes in the morning.'

The heavy material would be expensive to buy. Edward hoped to be given some Christmas boxes; he was going to write a paragraph for the newspaper reminding everyone that their 'most faithful and obliging public servants' deserved a Christmas tip. He was still only earning nine shillings from the Post Office, and although the income from the shop had replaced the money from polishing, it hadn't exceeded it.

The bell rang in the shop. By the time she came back from selling some tea, Edward was dressed and seated by the fire singing to the children, with Milly cradled in one arm and Charlie on his knee.

> 'Up the ash, and down the oak,
> And through the hazel bushes...'

His face was a picture, glowing with health and vitality despite his soaking, and completely entranced by his children;

Milly was kicking excitedly and making little noises while she gazed up at her father and brother.

He looked up at Jane in delight. 'See, she's singing too!'

While Jane was feeding Milly, she told him about the new sign in Mr Harcourt's shop. As she had expected, Edward was not pleased.

'I know what he's up to, he's hoping to catch those who finish work late and want something quick for their supper, and he'll be the only shop open at that hour. And then they'll buy tea and whatever else while they're in there! Well, I'm not going back to late opening whatever he does, but there may be others who do.'

'Is there anything us can do, anything else us can sell to bring in a bit more money?'

He sat Charlie astride his knee and pulled a face to make him laugh.

'Well, 'tis strange, but just today Mr Lemon, the butcher in Westleigh, asked if I'd like some of his cured bacon and hams to sell. So us could give that a try.'

Jane lifted Milly up to her shoulder, where she hiccoughed happily. Bacon and ham! She had not thought of selling that. It could be successful, and even if it were not, they would themselves have the advantage of meat at wholesale prices. And the servant registry was making an occasional few shillings; Mr Harcourt hadn't thought to copy that idea yet.

Chapter Eleven

Edward and the six other men talked and laughed together as they walked quickly through the darkness on the otherwise empty road between Appledore and Bideford; past shadowy houses where pale candlelight made visible the outlines of windows and along winding stretches of road where high hedges shut out the little light afforded by a low half-moon. Mr Lamerton, whose coat was of the thinnest material and who had omitted to wear a scarf, exclaimed on the coldness of the night, while the long-limbed Mr Sweet swung his arms rhythmically across his chest in an effort to create some heat. Edward gazed at the sky and the coldly glittering stars as he walked: up there, the measureless extent of the welkin and here, beneath his feet, the hard ground. He felt himself to be an ant crawling along the surface of the earth.

He turned to William Pearce, striding along beside him, and gestured at the moon.

'So, is there life up there, looking down at us as we look up at them? Us never did decide, did us, in our discussion.'

'No. 'Tis beyond our knowing I think, but perhaps one day science will find the answer. Wait, lads! Us is walking too fast.'

They paused to allow William Griffy to catch up. He was by far the oldest of the group and had the added disadvantage of the shortest legs.

They were returning from the Wesleyan Chapel in Appledore where they had given testimonies at a meeting on teetotalism on the invitation of Reverend Jerome Clapp. Each had spoken in turn about the journey that led them to total abstinence and the benefits it had brought to them. Edward described to the large audience his devotion to self-education, the advantages of having the time for reading and being able to buy an occasional book, and his resultant success in becoming a newspaper correspondent and having poems published. Mr Thorogood had displayed the handsome watch he had been able to purchase by saving for eighteen months the cost of a pint of beer a day; another described the misery and destitution of his former life and the transformation in his family fortunes since renouncing alcohol. The audience were then urged to take the pledge, but Edward suspected there were few drinkers present anyway, and wished that his neighbour Mr Prust would attend such a meeting. His wife had confided to Jane that he was less than kind to her when he returned from the public house.

They fell into small groups as they walked down the road that wound from Northam beneath arching trees, and William Pearce gestured to the moon again.

'Strange to think that the same moon shines alike on Devon and on Canada.'

Edward looked at him sharply. 'You still think of making that journey, then?'

William lowered his voice a little. 'I do, and I wanted you to be one of the first I tell. You know that I've written letters to enquire as to the health of the basket-making trade in Canada and America. Well, I've received encouraging news. I've decided us shall go, all of us; my brother Josiah is very keen to accompany us now that he's finished his apprenticeship.'

He turned confidingly towards Edward. 'I'm so weary of working day and night and gaining so little by it! 'Tis such a struggle now with one child that I don't know how we'd feed 'em if more came along. It'd be too late then to think of going. What sort of future can I give my children if us stays here? You should think of going too, Edward. Us can all leave together!'

Edward remained silent. Their footsteps rang, out of rhythm on the stony road. William was right; what future did he have? But to leave Devon and the countryside he loved, to leave his sisters, his friends? Especially now that he was having some success and his poems had been praised by Eliza Cook and by Mr Rock.

'I can't do it, William! And besides, you have a trade and I failed on all the trades I attempted; what call is there for postmen in Canada?'

'You know what my brother, John, and others have said. Even labourers can earn 7s 6d a day – a *day*, Edward, that's nearly as much as you earn in a week. And food cheaper than here!'

He had heard it all before. 'But I don't want to spend my days labouring! Even if there were openings for writers, men of letters, I wouldn't want to leave the place of my birth.'

He spoke vehemently but he was full of doubt. Should he take his family across the sea, for their sake? Charlie was five now and Milly one and a half; they would have more opportunities in Canada. 'And anyway you'm ten years younger than me; 'tis easier for you.'

'I knew these would be your thoughts. And that's why I'm telling you now, because you may have the opportunity of taking on my round when I go; I'm certain Mr Lee'll let you have it. I'll put your name forward, if you want.'

Edward had not considered this. William was unable to make a living from basket-making alone so he combined his trade with letter carrying between Bideford and Buckland Brewer, a round that paid 1s 6d more than Edward earned. This was indeed an opportunity – he had hoped to be given that round when it was first set up! He turned to William and shook his hand.

'You'm a true friend! I wish you weren't going but, if you'm determined to, I'll gladly step into your shoes.'

The thought of the new postal walk, and the secrets the landscape might reveal to him, strengthened still further his allegiance to Devon.

'Now,' he turned and addressed himself to the rest of the group, 'us is feeling the cold and 'tis time we raised our voices to warm ourselves! I propose my *Song of the*

Devonian, but we'll leave out the last verse with its references to wine, given where we've come from!'

As they walked over the causeway and into the town, Edward took the bass part, Mr Lamerton and Mr Sweet the baritone, and the remaining four the tenor part, their voices ringing out over the marshes and as far as the mill in the Westcombe valley:

'Home of the beautiful, home of the brave,
Where the bright seagull troops whiten the wave...'

Edward's voice faltered with emotion several times but the sentiments of the song also gave him confidence – he was surely making the right decision!

They reached the end of the song and refrained from a follow-up in case they disturbed Dr Pridham in his big house at the entrance to the town; then, wishing each other goodnight, they went their separate ways.

Edward walked in through the dark empty shop to the kitchen, where Jane was sewing in the circle of light from a single candle on the kitchen table. His resolution melted away when he saw her working at this late hour, and he sighed as he sat down.

'Janie, what sort of husband and provider am I, that you have to work almost until you drop?'

She looked surprised. 'But I always work in the evening!'

'You shouldn't have to. You deserve better.' He told her William Pearce's news. 'We've heard stories from my brother, too, of how good the living is out there.'

She put her sewing down. 'I know; and Mr Cutcliffe's wife, the dressmaker, now employing nine assistants. And flour only a shilling for seven pounds.'

'You think us should go then?' He felt utterly miserable. 'Imagine if you could employ nine assistants.'

'I wouldn't want to! I'd be forever checking the quality of their work and I'd never be happy with it. And they'd be gossiping instead of working and I'd have to pull them up for that. No, Edward, I wouldn't like it at all!'

She put her hand on his. 'You don't want to go to Canada, so I don't either. Of course I'd like an easier life, but not there! Not in a place us can't call home! And imagine that awful six-week journey with the children feeling ill all the time, and us as well, I don't doubt. Six weeks on a boat! That wouldn't suit me at all – I've never even been near the sea.'

'I don't think I could write my poems if I were anywhere but Devon.'

'There you are then. Us is staying here.'

Relief swept over him and he watched affectionately as Jane took up her sewing again.

'Still, you shouldn't have to work so late. You should come out for a walk with me sometimes – I'm always asking you! And if you had more leisure time you could read. I left Eliza Cook's latest journal for you, you like that.'

She was quiet for a while. 'I used to like you reading it to me while I sewed. That was my favourite thing, upstairs with a good fire burning. I enjoyed that.'

'Yes, but I've so many meetings to go to now!'

'I know. But the evenings is long, sometimes.' She carried on with her sewing, and wouldn't meet his eyes, even when he put his hand on her knee.

He felt he needed to cheer her up – *he* was feeling more cheerful again – so he told her the news of the Buckland Brewer round.

''Twould be wonderful if I could get it. Do you remember when us walked along east of the river and looked down and saw a little valley, that magical place? Us have never been there. That's the way I'd walk – right along that valley and up to the village on the hill! And I'd earn 10s 6d a week.'

He didn't care that he could earn that in a day in Canada. Devon was where he belonged.

Chapter Twelve

Two months later he walked through the turnpike gate on the road to Torrington and set off in good spirits for his first journey to Buckland Brewer. There was a hint of warmth in the light breeze; high in the bright blue April sky a lark poured forth its liquid song where, until a few days ago, an easterly wind had pursued sullen, grey clouds. The most sheltered growth of the elm in the roadside hedge was in tiny leaf, while the bare boughs of the trees growing on the steep bank above the road bore a fine green haze that he saw to be clusters of buds tipped with emerald – heralds of spring which, together with a chorus of birdsong and the distant drumming of a woodpecker, made his heart sing.

He had been waiting at the Post Office when the London mail coach arrived at five minutes past eight, ready to sort the mail on the benches set out for the purpose, alongside the other letter carriers. He needed little direction because William Pearce had described the route to him several times. His outward journey would take him on good, sheltered turnpike roads alongside the River Torridge and the River Yeo, then up the long, two-mile hill to Buckland Brewer. His return, once he was again at river level, would branch off to Littleham through deep, damp lanes running up the steep sides of hills and down into narrow valleys. The thought of the path ahead led him enticingly on into dreams of the places he would see, the people he would meet and the poems he might write.

His bag was not too heavy on his shoulder, so he did not feel daunted by the thirteen-mile walk ahead of him and settled into a fast, easy stride along the centre of the road. The broad, smooth water of the River Torridge on his left was skimmed by swallows newly-arrived from Africa; they wheeled away as two barges moved slowly into sight accompanied by the faint measured plash of their oars. Edward called out a greeting and was rewarded with an answering shout and wave from the bargemen.

He followed a long gravelled driveway up to Hallsannery, one of only two grand houses on his round. Here he handed a bundle of letters to a fair-haired housemaid who, in answer to his enquiry, gave him a little curtsey and told him shyly that her name was Amelia.

'You have the same name as my little daughter and you'm equally pretty!' he told her. She giggled and quickly shut the door.

At Landcross he stopped to speak to some workmen who were painting the windows of a newly-built Wesleyan chapel which, they informed him, would be open in time for Easter services. He asked for directions to his next delivery, a letter addressed amusingly to Mr Part Rich at Wortertown; he was sent over the bridge that crossed the Yeo near its confluence with the Torridge and down a sunken lane where a profusion of primroses grew. So intent was he on admiring his favourite flowers that he nearly missed the entrance to the farm, until reminded by the nasal honking and hissing of half a dozen geese waddling purposefully towards him with necks aggressively outstretched. He backed away from the open gate but a woman, whom he guessed to be Mrs Partridge, ran from the door scolding and flapping her apron at the geese.

They crowded in a wary group in the corner of the yard while she apologised to him profusely. 'They'm beggars, they really are, but they'll soon get used to 'ee.' The geese edged forward, fixing him with their cold, hard stares, but she flapped her apron at them again. 'Get out! Get back! 'Tis Mr Capern, i'n't it, Mr Pearce told us all about 'ee, didn'em, so come on in now and have a drop of milk.'

The good, comfortable-looking farmhouse, surrounded by tidy outbuildings of various kinds, had a low thatched roof and a white front festooned with roses that would, no doubt, bloom early in this sheltered spot. He was ushered into the kitchen where he refused a chair, explaining that he was as yet unsure of the timing of his walk, so he remained on the mat while he drank a cup of warm milk, Mrs Partridge assuring him that it was fresh from one of their cows. She was a woman of middle age with a rosy, good-natured face and a friendly manner; within a few minutes she had enumerated the members of the family and the farm servants who kept the 160 acre farm and lime-burning business running smoothly, and found out about his own family.

'A little maid too! I never did have a little maid, just the four boys and three of 'em living. Take this for her now; I make them sometimes for my brother's maids.' And she gave him a little doll made from a clothes peg clothed in a scarlet dress.

He smiled to himself as he walked back along the lane, having successfully circumnavigated the geese. How could he even have considered that he should leave Devon? He was certain he should never receive such a welcome amongst strangers in Canada.

He carried some letters to Landcross Rectory, stood for a moment to admire the tiny church with its wooden belfry, and after a few deliveries to humble but welcoming cottages, he re-crossed the Yeo and followed the turnpike road which kept a straight course alongside the meandering river, leading him irresistibly into the steep-sided valley. Big yellow-striped bumble bees droned around the banks searching for a hole fit for a nest, their familiar burr-rr pleasing to him after the silence of winter, and indeed the valley was alive with music; thrushes sang from the wooded hills, the river murmured and children's voices rang from the white cottages dotted close to its banks. There was little wheeled traffic; he had heard that many of the farmers preferred to take their carts over the hilly routes to avoid paying the toll.

After he had walked for a short distance, the sounds of nature were joined by the busy clatter and creaking of mill machinery and then the rushing of water from the mill wheel as he approached the buildings over an old stone bridge. Mr Henry Guard, the master of the flour mill appeared and shook his hand, leaving a white floury imprint. He pointed out an old packhorse trail winding pleasantly down into the valley that would be a shorter way from Landcross if there were no letters for the first few cottages on the turnpike road. After wishing him a 'good morning', Edward paused for a moment on the bridge and saw the iridescent blue flash of a kingfisher pass beneath him and shoot as fast as an arrow around the next bend in the river.

The river was his constant companion as he continued on the road, sometimes flowing along in the sunlight beside him and sometimes wandering on the far side of the meadow, its low placid murmur always discernible to the ear. He paused to watch as a young woman kneeling at its edge repeatedly dipped and lifted bed-sheets to let the sparkling water run through them, while across the road the already clean washing strung between a tree and the cottage wall rippled and dripped gently in the breeze. Drawn by the booming and rush of water from another mill, he followed a short track running off the road, and came to an agreeable house where white ducks sat contentedly on a bright green lawn sloping down to the river's bank. A clutch of children ran towards him but came to an abrupt halt at the sight of his unfamiliar face.

'Wass your name?' asked the oldest girl, who carried a baby wrapped in a shawl. She had to shout to make herself heard above the swish of the great wheel turning in the water. He crouched down to them and the smallest child backed away a little, his finger in his mouth.

'Mr Capern, your new postman, and who are you?'

'I'm Ann Davey. And this be my baby sister, Mary, and these three toads be my brothers and I got big brothers and sisters too but they'm working.' She looked at him challengingly, as if he might contradict her.

'Well, Ann, and why be 'em toads?'

''Cos they'm all for runnin' off and I has to see they don't get drownded in the river or caught up in the wheel. 'Tis a fine old job, sometimes.' She sighed resignedly.

He patted her on the head. 'Can one of they toads tell their father there's a letter for him?'

He moved his bag on to his other shoulder and marched on. There were letters to deliver at two more watermills, but first he passed a field where workers were stacking poles at intervals in conical heaps.

'What be 'ee doing there then?' he shouted.

A young man in rough working clothes turned and waved to him. 'Setting the hop poles! Hops for the brewery up Littleham!'

He had never seen hops growing before, but he would be passing this way every day so would see them develop through spring and summer and into autumn.

'May they do well and flourish!' he shouted back, smiling to himself as he added in an undertone, 'even if they are to be made into the ale that causes such misery.'

As he continued along the road, the valley opened out like the pages of a book, its steep wooded sides giving way to gently sloping fields and exposing a wider arch of clear blue sky. When a spring cart containing a farmer, his wife and his man came up behind and gradually overtook him, its driver shouted out a greeting in a gruff voice, and for a while he walked behind them as they jogged along. He noticed with amusement that the broad-hipped farmer's wife was squeezed between the two stout men, who bulged beyond each end of the seat so that they seemed almost in danger of toppling out on to the wheels. The cart slowly drew away from him and disappeared around the next bend, leaving him chuckling as he walked.

He kept pace for a short distance with a pair of dark-bay horses ploughing in the adjacent field, their huge shaggy feet clomping through the dark soil and their strong shoulders rippling as they threw their weight into the heavy collars. When they reached the headland the ploughman stopped them and turned to shout to Edward.

'Up to Buckland then, be 'ee? First day?'

'That's right! That's a fine team you've got there.'

The man laid his hand on the neck of the nearest horse. It turned and nuzzled at his pocket, while the second nodded its head, as if in agreement.

'You won't find better in this parish, nor a straighter furrow. They'm good beasts, these two.'

Edward looked back across the field, which resembled a length of dark brown corduroy, each furrow perfectly parallel to its neighbour.

'That's a skill you have there! Took you a good many years to perfect that, I reckon!'

'It did that, me and the 'osses together. You won't see as good on Buckland farms, I know 'cos I walk up to look at their work! Littleham men be the better ploughmen. You'd better get on now; you've a fair old walk still!'

Edward watched while the horses responded to their master's gentle commands, turning in a tight circle to pull the creaking plough steadily back along the field, while the ploughman walking behind pressed with all his weight on the handles, then seemed to be carried along by the strength of the horses. Edward felt he had walked into a happier, more innocent place, far away from Bideford's grimy backstreets with its avaricious shopkeepers and hard-hearted officials. There was poverty here too, of course, but also riches – such as those Lenten lilies beneath the trees, so bright against the bare dark loam. He crouched and lifted their faces, so that he might see them more clearly. Daffodils, the lecturer in botany at the Mutual Improvement Society called them, but he preferred the old Devon name. Many in this area believed that the presence of the flowers would cause eggs to become addled.

Ah, life was such a puzzle! He had embraced the new world of steam with the advantages the railway would bring but how he would hate to see a steam plough roaring through this valley, and the ploughmen and their placid horses thrown out of work! The horse had served man for countless generations; the men who worked with them were amongst the best in the land, their lives as straight as their furrows. The railway would hasten progress into the modern world bringing many improvements, there was no doubt about that, and much would be gained – but there would also be losses. And by delivering letters Edward was bringing new ideas to an area where knowledge had been based on tradition passed down through the generations, so he was as much a part of the drive towards modernisation as was the train. But for now, the modern world was distant from this place. He would write a song for the old-fashioned plough, one that the teams-men of the whole area would like to sing!

Before long the road crossed the river and he saw the turning that must lead up to the village. It was a steady climb of almost two miles broken only by a walk along a coach drive to Orleigh. William had told him about the grand old house but he was still unprepared for the size of it. It seemed to be the length of a street, higher even than the grand houses in Bridgeland Street, and all for just two people and their servants. As he walked back to the road he mused on the strangeness of life, that some should have more rooms than they could visit in a day and others have to sleep four to a bed.

He rang his bell at intervals as he climbed the hill so that people could walk from the farms to meet him, saving him a trudge down muddy, deeply-rutted farm lanes. It pleased him to see a young woman in a white apron hurrying along the track towards him and along another, a young boy on a cantering pony. When he paused for breath, turning to see the wide view over the now distant valley, the undulating hills beyond speckled with white farmhouses and clusters of cottages, with the high moors beyond, he wished very much that Jane was at his side to share it with him.

Sometimes the road levelled, even dipped a little, then climbed steeply again until he thought the village of Buckland Brewer must surely be around the next corner, or the next. Finally the church tower came into view and he climbed a stile, as William had instructed him, to follow a field path and avoid a loop in the road; he passed through a flock of grazing sheep and then a field of turnips, until he emerged on the village street. The wind was noticeably colder here than down in the valley. He counted the cob-and-thatch cottages until he reached the ancient house he had been told was the postal office, where he knocked on the door. A man a little older than himself appeared from a workshop at the side of the house, looked him up and down without a word, then took a pocket-watch from under the bib of his long apron and scrutinised its face.

Eventually he looked up again and broke into a smile. 'Well, Mr Capern, not yet midday, you'm early!'

They shook hands and the man introduced himself as Mr William Withecombe, carpenter and postmaster. 'You'll be wanting to do your village deliveries now, but if you give me the others, my daughter Martha will run around to Tythecott and Bilsford and the outlying farms. Where will you be eating your dinner?'

This was something that had concerned Edward. There was a two-hour wait before his return journey, to give people time to write replies for him to carry back to Bideford. William Pearce had had the loan of a small workshop where he made baskets to sell to local people, thus making use of his otherwise idle time. Jane had pointed out that the post round, with its late start and early finish, was only a part-time occupation, and had suggested that there might be houses where there was furniture in need of polishing. Edward was not too interested in this idea, but he would need somewhere to sit and eat his dinner.

'As the weather is so fine, I'll find myself a sheltered spot outside to sit.'

Mr Withecombe pointed him in the right direction for his first delivery, a letter from Canada for a woman who ran a bakery from her cottage. In turn, she sent him down a narrow lane with primrose-starred hedgerows for his next delivery to a shoemaker, then on to a tiny grocer's shop in an old cottage where sparrows nested in the thatch. His next deliveries took him along the road to the vicarage where an open gateway gave him a panoramic view over the countryside to the south; then past rows of cob-and-thatch houses and a substantial chapel to an old inn, where two labourers were enjoying half-pints of ale. Women standing in clusters outside their cottages ceased gossiping to watch him go by while craftsmen at the doors of their workshops regarded him curiously, but all replied cheerfully enough to his greetings.

Finally he sat thankfully on the grass outside the church gate, with the village pump and a tethered goat for company, and took from his pocket the loaf, piece of cheese and slice of onion that Jane had wrapped in a cloth for him. He had barely started on his dinner when he heard a door open a short distance away. A middle-aged man appeared from behind two outbuildings and beckoned to him.

'Us don't like to see 'ee having to rucky down on the damp old grass like that, Sir. I be gwain back to work now and the boys to school, but you come in and sit yourself down with the wife and the maids. No, come on now, I won't take "no" for an answer!'

Edward thanked him and went down an alleyway to the cottage door that was being held open for him. He found himself in a low-ceilinged kitchen with a broad, deep fireplace on one wall and a long deal table taking up much of the room. Three women were watching him a little nervously from behind the table; he hesitated for a moment, unsure how to greet them, but the oldest, a woman who was perhaps in her forties and had a broad, kind face, rose from her chair and stepped forward timidly.

'Come in, Sir, come in and rest yourself! Us have finished our dinner but you'm welcome to sit here with us. Polly, get Mr Capern a cup of water. Here, Sir.'

She drew out a chair for him, and he looked up at her enquiringly. 'You know my name?'

She answered shyly. 'Oh yes, Sir, us have heard all about 'ee, that you'm the new postman and you'm clever with writing and rhyming and suchlike.'

He sat down. He saw that the two girls – for they were just girls – had the same intelligence about the eyes and were clearly sisters, although one was dark and one fair; each had her wavy hair tied back from her face to fall in a coil down her back. The older one, Polly, brought him a cup of water, telling him shyly that it was fresh from the pump, then both resumed sewing the gloves they were making while their mother washed the dinner plates in a bowl of water. He ate his bread but glanced up now and then and invariably caught all three scrutinising him, whereupon they quickly looked down. The youngest girl stifled a giggle and Polly gave her a nudge. The only sounds were the crackling of the fire and the faint splash of washing-up water. He chewed his bread as quietly as he could.

When he had finished, the mother spoke again. 'Would 'ee like an apple, Sir? I'm sorry I can't offer you a dish of tea; I don't keep it generally, but I'll get some in for tomorrow if you'd fancy it.'

He was quite taken aback by her kindness. 'But I mustn't intrude on you again!'

She insisted, saying that he was welcome to come in and eat his dinner every day. She wouldn't hear of him sitting outside on the grass. 'There's others that would ask you in, Sir, but they'm not all as clean as they might be, if you take my meaning.'

He liked her gentle, apologetic manner, and felt fortunate to have found such a welcoming and comfortable home to spend his spare hours.

'Then thank you, I will come again tomorrow and I'll bring a twist of tea and hope you'll all share it with me. 'Tis true I do like a cup of tea with my dinner.'

He asked about the family. Mr Ley was a thatcher who was working at present in the village but did not return for his dinner when he was working in one of the outlying hamlets;

148

one son worked with him, the oldest was a servant at Orleigh and the two youngest boys were in school. Polly and Ann were eighteen and thirteen.

He smiled at the two girls, who were looking pleased that they had eventually been mentioned. 'And have 'ee been to school?'

Ann looked at Polly, daring her to answer, which she did in a very quiet voice. 'Yes, for a year or so, Sir. Us can read, but us was never taught to write.'

'Please don't call me "Sir"! I'd like "Mr Capern" better. and if us becomes friends you can call me Edward. And do you like to read, Polly?'

She looked as if she had never considered such a thing before. 'Well, I read the Bible on a Sunday, sometimes.'

'Then maybe I'll bring you something that you'll like to read better.'

He asked her about the glove-making, and all three lost a little of their shyness as they told him about the packwoman who brought the materials from Torrington and collected the finished gloves, and how these gloves they were sewing now were fairly easy but some were 'dreadful finicky'. In turn he told them about Jane, how clever she was with her needle, and about Charlie and Milly. When he had finished, an easy silence fell while the girls continued with their sewing. Mrs Ley, after putting two irons to heat in the fire, took some linen from a basket and smoothed it out on the table.

He could sit back in a relaxed fashion, looking around at the cottage room with its dresser of blue-and-white china, its colourful rugs and welcoming fire. He did not feel he had to make conversation. There was time to think. He had entertained a faint hope that he might find such a place, and now the germ of an idea was beginning to grow.

'Would 'ee mind', he asked, and three interested faces looked up at him, 'if, while I sit here, I was sometimes to do some writing? Work on some verses perhaps, that I've thought up while I'm walking?'

The two girls looked at him in wonder.

149

'Why, of course not,' Mrs Ley replied, 'why ever should us mind that?'

When he judged that it was time to start on his return journey, he thanked the women and went out into the village street. It had clouded over somewhat and the breeze was a little cooler, but a glance at the sky told him that he was unlikely to get wet. Knocking at the door of the postal office, he entered a small room where Mr Withecombe was sitting behind a desk sorting through some papers.

'I've several letters here already been brought in but, if I were you, I'd give a blast or two so folks know you'm about to go.'

Edward went to the door and blew the little post-horn he had been given. The fruity, musical notes echoed down the village street. A couple of dogs with wagging tails came to see what the noise was about, and a young girl ran out from a cottage with a letter and a penny for the stamp.

The return journey was pure pleasure. He blew the horn at intervals and collected a few letters and pennies along the way, then found his way over the hills to the hamlet of Littleham where he had a few deliveries to make before walking back along steep sunken lanes to Bideford. The walk took him a little over two hours; his mind was free to admire the wonders of the spring day and to work on some ideas. He had a melody in his head that he could use for a song about ploughing; he also wanted to write a poem about April.

He had been involved in a recent correspondence with Mr Rock in which he had been advised to try more ambitious rhyming schemes. Edward had not, at first, understood what was meant, until Mr Rock explained a way of using letters to describe the pattern of rhymes at the end of each line of a poem, and he realised that he had already instinctively been using a very simple rhyming scheme. Once he understood how to study poems in this way, he started looking back at poems he had read and was enthralled to see how they worked; he desperately wished he still had access to a library so that he could revisit all the poems he only half-remembered. Mr Hayman's bookshop in Grenville Street had a copy of Coleridge's *The Rime of the Ancient Mariner* which he hoped to buy next week for sixpence. The more he read, the more he realised what complex things poems were, not only in the choice of words but also in their rhyme and rhythm and length of lines. He had been writing in the darkness of ignorance but now he had so many ideas!

He strode along the lanes while allowing his gaze to pass over the unfurling leaves and opening flower buds, listening to the rhythm of his footsteps and murmuring '*proud, April sky, cloud, on high, maiden's eye,*' – only half-aware that he was talking to himself, but aware enough to know he must keep quiet when passing a labourer clearing a ditch or a girl on a donkey. It would not do for people to say that the new postman was mad. He would write such poems and sing such songs, the world was sure to listen! And now, at last, he had more time in which to do it.

1854 – 1856

Poetry

Foster Genius, e'en the humblest;
'Tis a little jewel rare:
Purest gold, and gems most precious,
Oft the coarsest covering wear.

Chapter Thirteen

Edward sat in a deep leather armchair in the elegant surroundings of the Barnstaple Literary and Scientific Institution. He felt almost as nervous as he had on his very first visit nearly ten years ago, despite being welcomed this time as a special guest of its founder Mr Rock, whom he now awaited.

He opened his canvas bag and leafed through the sheets of paper again. Mr Rock had asked to see all the new poems. He wished there had been more time to work on them. He heard voices in the entrance hall so he crossed his legs and tried to look nonchalant. Finally the door opened and Mr Rock strode in.

'Mr Capern, welcome! I am sorry to keep you waiting. No, please, sit down and let us talk together. Tell me, how is your little family?'

Edward was always happy to talk about Charles and Milly and entertained Mr Rock with tales of their achievements and funny little sayings, until he laughed and held up his hand.

'They are a credit to you and Mrs Capern; I hope to meet them one day. But now we must get down to business. You have some poems to show me I think, but first tell me what you have been reading lately.'

Edward explained that he had mainly been rereading the few books he already possessed. 'I miss the Reading Room dreadfully. I know it was not your fault that it had to close, Sir, but it is a great loss to the town.' He hoped Mr Rock would not be offended at his speaking so.

'I know it; it was most unfortunate, but what can one do? It seems the men of Bideford just weren't interested in reading books and attending lectures. Although I hear the Mutual Improvement Society is more successful in gaining a response.'

'Yes, I think people feel 'tis their own society, one they have created for theirselves. There is also to be a Mechanics' Institute; the Reverend Charles Kingsley who is currently living in Bideford has supported its formation. But 'tis the Library I miss the most, Sir. I'm sure I would write better poems if I could read the work of great men.' He took out the sheaf of poems. 'I'm afraid you will think them poor things.'

Mr Rock gave him a warm look. 'Let me be the judge of that. Give me four or five to start with! And by the by, I will send you an anthology of poetry when I return to London.'

Edward handed him the poems and waited uncomfortably. Mr Rock raised his eyebrows occasionally as he read, and made little noises which could be appreciation or disappointment, it was difficult to tell. Several times Edward started to explain a poem but Mr Rock held up his hand to silence him.

Finally he looked up and smiled. 'This one, *To a Celandine*, appeals to all my senses – I hear the rush of mill water and share your delight in the flower you find. You really have conjured the scene for me – it is full of magic influences!'

His gaze was very direct but kindly.

'Thank 'ee, Sir; I'm sure I don't deserve your praise. I've one here that's rather different and I would like your opinion of it. I wrote it just last week.'

It was a poem of which he was rather proud. Mr Rock read and hummed a few times, smiled, and read it again.

'It conjures perfectly the pleasure you take in your life as a rural postman, and it is an achievement to make it so amusing! How long did this take you to write?'

'Oh, it just came to me as I walked, the words tumbling forth so fast that I had to write them on the backs of people's envelopes in case they were lost to memory. Every time I came to a stile I stopped and wrote, resting my postbag on my knee, and then I had to run like the devil to make up my time, even up the steep hills, and stop again because the ideas were coming so thick and fast – '

Mr Rock was laughing. 'You had no paper? What of the letters you had to deliver?'

'Well, I was careful to write only on those addressed to wealthier people, those who would have some paper in the house and would let me have a sheet so I could copy out my words. People are usually very generous like that.'

'I noticed that some of the paper you use is very thin...'

'Yes, that's the paper we use in the shop to wrap the tea and sugar. I use that sometimes but it does not rest well upon a stile or field gate!'

They laughed together, and Edward began to relax.

'Well, perhaps I can help you there. Being a stationer I am not short of paper!' He reached for his briefcase and searched inside. 'Here we are. Here is a book in which to write your poems. It is only cloth-bound – I don't have any leather-bound books with me I think, but it will suffice, I'm sure. Ah, but you need another to scribble in; here, I have a smaller one that will fit in your pocket so you won't have to write on envelopes anymore! Keep the larger one at home for the fair copies.'

Edward took the proffered books. Page after page of clean, white, thick paper. Perhaps a hundred or more pages! And the smaller notebook, just the right size for his pocket so he could take it out and jot down ideas as he walked, without the woodgrain of gate or stile pressing through! What poems he would write!

'Thank you, Sir! I can't tell you how much your kindness means to me!'

'It's nothing. Now, let me read some more.'

Edward watched Mr Rock's expression as he read the rest of the poems; sometimes he raised his bushy eyebrows; sometimes he inclined his head to one side and pursed his lips; once or twice he frowned. Finally he read the last sheet of paper, put the sheaf down on his lap and smiled at Edward.

'Well, you have indeed worked hard! I have read them quickly and that doesn't do them justice but you have some good work here. Very good work.' He leafed through the poems. '*An April Memory* I think particularly fine; you have used a more complex rhyming scheme as I suggested.'

'Yes. but I found it very hard. The simpler rhymes trip off the tongue with greater ease.'

'Of course, but sometimes the extra work is worthwhile. But there, you must write what comes naturally to you; I must not try to mould you in that way. I like the poems to May, June and September – you will write one for each month I hope? And *The Primrose Voice* is delightful.' He joined his hands as if in prayer and seemed to be deep in thought. Edward was unsure whether or not he should speak.

Finally Mr Rock looked up. 'You have had several poems published in the *North Devon Journal*, have you not?'

'Yes, Mr Avery has been very kind.'

'But no other newspapers?'

'One appeared in the *Exeter Flying Post* last year, Sir, and a friend arranged for one to go in the *Worcester Journal*. I wouldn't know where else to send them. I know no one else.'

'Hmm. I think we can do better than that.' He fell silent again and Edward began to feel restless. 'I think… yes.'

He looked up and smiled encouragingly. 'I would like to help you, Mr Capern, because I think you have real talent. You write in a manner that appeals to me, perhaps the way I would have written if I had chosen to spend more time on the arts and less on commerce. So, we'll see.' He nodded slowly.

Edward was puzzled. Might Mr Rock arrange for some poems to be published in London papers? He seemed to know a great many people. 'What is it you have in mind, Sir?'

'Well, I may as well tell you now. I think we could arrange to have a volume of your poems published.'

Edward stared at him. He did not understand. 'A volume, Sir?'

'Yes, a book of your poems. It is something I could arrange for you.'

Mr Rock was smiling at him but he could not reply. He felt he was tingling all over.

'My poems in a book?'

Mr Rock laughed. 'Yes! Don't look so surprised! I'm sure you know you have considerable talent and you have made wonderful progress with your writing during the last year or so. Because you are as yet unknown I would arrange for them to be published by subscription; interested parties would pay in advance for copies, that way the publisher would know that the cost of production would be covered, and I would hope that you would make a good sum of money from the sales, enough to secure an education for your children and make your life a little easier.'

He had never dreamed such a thing could happen. His poems in a book, a proper book that people could hold in their hands, and open, and read?

'Sir, I don't know what to say.' He was afraid he might break down if he tried to say more. 'I can't thank you enough, Sir.'

'Well, I have helped you from the beginning, have I not? Since you first became a free member of the Literary and Scientific Institution. And of all the members I funded, I think you have made the best use of the opportunity and made the most progress with your education. And I think you are sensible enough that you will not let the idea of being published go to your head. There are too many working-class writers whose small successes have turned them to drink, or if they fail they have been driven mad with it. Look at the Northamptonshire Peasant Poet, John Clare, for example, and the Reedmaker Poet, John Critchley Prince. You must promise me you will keep your feet firmly on the ground, whatever the outcome.'

'I will, Sir!' He jumped up and shook Mr Rock's hand. 'You will never regret this, I promise! But can it really be true? A book with my name on the cover? I can hardly believe it!'

Mr Rock laughed. 'I think you will injure my hand if you shake it any more! Now; I want you to keep writing. Show me more poems so I can make the selection when I am next in Devon; that will probably be in the spring when I will be making plans for the tenth anniversary of the Institution. Perhaps I may visit you in Bideford and meet Mrs Capern and Charles and little Amelia.'

'Mr Rock, I will repay you for your kindness by writing the best poems I have ever written!'

The buckets made a cold, metallic clang as Jane put them down on the rocky ground. The queue for the water pump was even longer than yesterday. At least ten people huddled wearily in shawls and jackets against the chill early morning air, their grumbled complaints almost drowned out by the squeak of the pump and the rhythmic gush of the water. High above the grey walls of the houses forming the sides of the yard a seagull circled, protesting loudly.

Eliza was in front of her in the queue and turned to smile. 'More water! What do 'ee do with it all? I saw Mr Capern here earlier.'

'Yes, he's been twice this morning. I'm going to scrub all the floors, bedrooms as well, just in case.' As soon as Jane spoke, she regretted it because she knew that with eight children to look after, Eliza could not be so particular about cleanliness, even now that there was cholera in the town. She did not add that she was also going to whitewash all the walls again. 'I'm sure 'tisn't necessary though, all this cleaning, not really.'

'Well, I haven't got time for it. My lot'll have to take their chance.' Eliza pursed her lips and turned away, but then Milly's little dancing figure caught her eye. 'Look at that – dear little dot! Did 'ee ever see anything so pretty?'

With a look of intense concentration on her face, Milly was holding up her skirt and hopping from foot to foot with high knees and pointed toes in imitation of a white, high-stepping pony they had just seen pulling a trap, her little black button boots tip-tapping on the stony ground and her dark curls bobbing up and down. Jane watched her indulgently and it wasn't until she looked around that she realised almost everyone in the queue was watching and smiling. At the same time she saw Ellen Lee, her head held low with embarrassment, crossing Chingswell Street and coming into the yard to join the queue.

'Milly, come here, now!'

Surprised at her mother's sharp tone, Milly ran to Jane and clung to her skirt. Jane shifted Milly to stand in front of her and held tight to her hand. The two people who had joined the queue after Jane moved away uneasily as Ellen came to stand behind them.

Eliza whispered to Jane. 'Her shouldn't come while other people are waiting, 'tisn't fair.'

Jane didn't reply at first. She felt sympathetic towards Ellen and was hoping that she hadn't noticed how Milly had been called away. 'There's always folk here. Her's got to get water sometime.'

When Ellen's sister Elizabeth died from cholera two days previously, it was the first death in this part of the town, but it was whispered that there had been others elsewhere. Edward said that the Town Council did not want people to panic, so families were asked not to talk about the cause of death, and he agreed he would not put details in the newspaper; but of course in close neighbourhoods such as this, a death could not be kept secret.

A sudden thought came to Jane. She whispered to Eliza. 'Do you think her needs water to wash her sister's clothes? Edward says those that wash the clothes of the dead are almost certain to catch it!'

Ellen had her head down in the vain hope that she would not be noticed; it was clear that no one else would speak to her. When Eliza had finished at the pump, Jane asked her to hold Milly's hand and when she had filled her own buckets she picked them up and walked bravely towards Ellen, stopping just a few feet away.

'Ellen, I'm so sorry for your loss. But, did 'ee know that you must burn the clothes? You mustn't wash them, do 'ee understand?'

Ellen looked at her wide-eyed, then nodded slowly. 'Thank you.'

Jane wanted to reach out and touch her but knew she must not. She walked away with Eliza, saying little in reply to Eliza's complaints about Ellen. How could they know why Elizabeth caught the cholera? The Lees were a clean, respectable family, no different from others hereabouts, and didn't they all breathe the same air, eat the same food and drink the same water? It was true that Bideford was not suffering as badly as some places; in London hundreds had died in the last few weeks, but the disease was in Cardiff now and it was feared that further infection might be brought from there to Bideford by ship. There had been several deaths in Appledore, where the presence of pigsties amongst the narrow streets was implicated. And there were pigsties right here, at the top of Cock Street!

'Eliza, I think it's just God's will. But drains like that don't help. Make sure you don't breathe in as you pass.' She gestured towards the drain at the bottom of Cock Street which was smelling dreadful again, although someone from the Council had poured disinfectant down it after Edward complained. They all avoided the Quay as far as possible because there was such a stench from the river mud at low tide; it could not help but be damaging to health. Many of the wealthy and those who had family out in the country had already moved out of the town. The shop had been very quiet and she'd had no customers for millinery all week. It worried Jane, but Edward did not seem interested. His thoughts were always with his writing.

He was in the shop talking to Mr Woolacott. Milly threw her arms around his leg and he lifted her up into his arms where her prattling proved sufficient distraction for him to bring an end to the conversation, and he brought her through to the kitchen.

'Janie, are you really still set on doing all that work today?' He kissed and cuddled Milly. 'Mama works too hard, doesn't she, my flower!'

He had read her an article from the newspaper that stressed the importance of cleanliness in the fight against cholera, but he did not feel that their home posed a risk. They had had a slight disagreement about it.

'Yes, of course I'll do it, I have enough water now. I don't mind, I'm glad to do it.'

'Well, don't wear yourself out. Charlie, sit up, you can't write with your head down on your arms like that; that's better, now see that you form the letter *g* the way I showed you. Now, I must go to work, my sweets! Sing me a song before I leave!'

He put Milly on Charlie's lap where she squirmed and giggled while her brother blew raspberries in her hair. Jane placed a pot of water on the trivet over the fire and straightened up to watch the children. They looked so healthy and happy and full of life; she knew she should try not to worry so much – but cholera could take even the strongest within a few days.

'Come now, sing one of Daddy's songs for him before he goes!' she told them.

Charlie put on his helpful, encouraging face. He was never bad-tempered or difficult with his sister. 'Listen, Milly, listen to Charlie! Sing with Charlie!

"Twoot, twoot, twoot,"
The thrush sings in the tree,
"Twoot, twoot, twoot"
And not afraid is he…'

Milly already had as sweet a voice as her brother, but the syllables were difficult and she frowned and pursed her lips as she tried to pronounce them, the effect of which reduced them all to laughter. Then she ran up the stairs like a little cat to wave goodbye to her father and brother from the upstairs window, as she did every morning, while Jane quickly washed the breakfast things and put more water on to heat.

Milly came shuffling down the stairs on her bottom   and danced across the floor, but suddenly stopped and ran to the back door. 'Wee-wee, Mama, Milly need wee-wee.' She tried to reach the door handle.

Jane quickly picked up the china bowl they used upstairs and persuaded Milly that it would be fun to sit on that instead. Since the cholera outbreak, Jane hated using the privy because it was in such a bad state, and seeing Ellen this morning had brought home to her the reality of the threat. It was best if the children did not go out there at all. She did her best to keep it clean by adding ashes from the fire, but the occupants of the other houses who shared it did not seem to care at all about cleanliness. Poor old Miss Hookway and Mrs Croscombe couldn't help themselves of course. The pit badly needed digging out and the job would fall to Edward again. She had asked him several times if he would do it, but he was always so busy.

By the time Edward came home she had scrubbed the floors, stopped up the mouse holes and whitewashed the walls; she had to break off a few times during the morning to serve customers but no one had been in all afternoon. Milly had played happily on the beds and only had a little whitewash in her hair, and Charlie had kept her entertained since he returned from school. There was now just enough time to do the main bedroom before she cooked the supper; she had already heaved the bed to the centre of the room and brushed down the walls to remove any flakiness where insects could hide, and was looking forward to seeing all the work completed and the rooms clean and bright.

Edward called from downstairs. 'Janie?'

'I'm up here! Come on up!'

He appeared, beaming, in the doorway. ''Tis a beautiful autumn day, there's warmth in the sun yet. Come on out! Us'll close the shop and take the children to the woods; the leaves are just beginning to turn colour and I heard a wood lark singing as I came past!'

She had hoped he would praise her hard work. She picked up the brush and dipped it in the bucket of whitewash.

'I can't, Edward. I have to do this before the children go to bed!' She turned away and made long, sweeping strokes up and down the wall.

'Janie! You don't have to do that now, chiel! Do it in the winter when it's dark and raining! Come on, put the brush down and let's go.'

Her stomach clenched with irritation. She held the brush up so it would not drip and turned to face him. 'I really can't, Edward! I'm right in the middle of this and it needs doing! How can I wait for the winter? You know how close the cholera is! And when I'm finished there's supper to cook and a bonnet to trim and sheets to hem.'

'The best way to avoid the cholera is to get out of the town! Go out in the woods where the air is clean and fresh. Come on, pack up a picnic supper and us can go right now. I stood and listened to the wood lark for a minute or two and it sings, *Sweet, of a sweet, of a sweet joy.*' He waved his hand eloquently to illustrate how it sang.

She hated arguing with him. Why could he not see her point of view? It was their health she was concerned for and what could be more important than that? 'Edward, there's the privy to do, too. You promised you'd do it; it's in a terrible state.'

'Damn and blast the privy! Jane, out there the sun is shining! The children need sunshine and country air and so do you, and winter will be with us soon. You'll make yourself ill, working like this! Now, come on, us'll go right away.'

He almost never swore. She dipped the brush in the whitewash again and turned away from him, and she found she was shaking a little. 'I've told you, I can't come.'

His voice, when it came, was so loud it made her jump. 'Then I'll go alone!'

She carried on painting although she hardly knew what she was doing, while he stamped down the stairs and slammed the door. Immediately Milly began to cry downstairs and Charlie came running up with her. 'What's the matter? Why is Daddy cross?'

She couldn't tell them the truth. They would be even more upset if they knew they had missed an outing to the woods. Any pleasure she had taken in her work had gone. She finished the whitewashing and put potatoes on to boil while she fetched more water, feeling almost sick with anger and disappointment.

It was not until the children were in bed and she was washing the supper things that she heard the shop door open. She carried on washing as he appeared in the doorway, but she glanced up quickly and made herself speak as if nothing had happened. 'Did 'ee enjoy your walk then?'

She was aware of him standing very still. She kept on washing and his reply, when it came, was very low. 'No, Janie, I couldn't enjoy it without you.' There was a long pause. 'I'll go and say goodnight to the children.'

She put his supper on the table and went through to the shop to do her sewing. There was just enough light to work without a candle. She worked methodically and without feeling, attaching a dark-brown cotton lining to the inner rim of the bonnet and pleating it into the crown. It was dull work. From time to time she glanced out of the window at the shadows lengthening on the empty street. After a while, she heard him go out of the back door and she realised he was digging out the privy, but it gave her no satisfaction to know that it would be done.

She made up the fire again and put water on to heat so that he could wash when he came in. Then she tidied the kitchen and swept the floor by the light of a single candle on the table. She did not look directly at the small window that gave out on to the yard; but as she worked she glimpsed the glow of his lantern and the shadowy figure that bent and straightened and bent again, and she heard the scrape of the shovel.

She went to bed before he came in and lay very still, feeling utterly miserable. When he lay down next to her, he took her hand in his, and so they lay for a minute or two until she could bear the silence no longer. 'Are you very cross with me?'

She heard him sigh. 'No, Janie, I can't be cross with 'ee. I'm sad, that's all. Sad that you can't share my pleasure. And worrited for 'ee too, working so hard!'

He took her in his arms and kissed her hair, and she could not stop the tears welling up. 'I like to work. I'm only thinking of the children, keeping them safe!'

'I know. But you will come out for a walk with me? One day soon, before the winter comes?'

'I'll try.'

He still had not remarked on the improvements she had made to the house.

Chapter Fourteen

Edward balanced the sack of coal on his shoulder while he opened the shop door. Since the very cold weather had set in, he had to fetch a sack every day but he could not afford to do so much longer. In any case it was said that coal stocks would soon run out because the river was frozen and only the larger boats were getting through.

Charlie was sitting on his little stool by the fire, practising his writing with some difficulty owing to the necessity of wearing gloves, and Milly was bundled into so many layers of woollen garments that she resembled a little fat lamb. Despite the warmth from the fire, the wind found gaps around the windows and doors and chilled the thick stone walls of the cottage, and their breath condensed as they went up the stairs. Charlie's school was closed because it was impossible to get the temperature in the large room above freezing and, in any case, there was insufficient light from the leaden skies and the gas in the lamps was frozen.

'Make way for the coalman! Here's enough to keep my precious ones warm for the day.' He turned to Jane. 'The north-westerly is stronger than ever, I reckon, no sign of a thaw at all. But I hear that a consignment of potatoes has come in, so the price should come down; that's one thing to be thankful of.' Another good thing was the end of the cholera epidemic; the number of cases had been falling and this cold weather had finally brought it to a close.

Jane had a shawl wrapped around her head and shoulders. He looked at her fondly. 'You look like a gypsy queen!'

'Well, it makes me a bit warmer. Look, I've made that piece of blanket into an extra waistcoat for 'ee. Put it on, do, before you go out.'

Mill Street was almost deserted. He walked carefully and had to dodge when the weight of an icicle hanging from a cottage roof caused it to break away, its fall as deadly as that of a sword. Conditions underfoot were even more dangerous in the town than in the country; a heavy fall of sleet the previous week had frozen and the passage of feet and hooves in the town compacted it until it was as slippery as glass. The beauty of the landscape the morning after the sleet had taken his breath away. Every surface was loaded with diamonds which glittered in the sunlight; in the fields every blade of grass bristled with ice and trees stood encased in crystal, their skeleton fingers tinkling at the slightest breeze and creating a tune beyond the scope of mortal musicians. Even the oldest men had rarely seen such a thing before although all knew the name for it, and told Edward, 'Us habn't seen such an ammil since us was boys.'

But the ice proved too much for some; in Buckland Brewer, where the extremity of cold was even greater, many trees in the avenue of limes through the churchyard had been brought down by their heavy burden. Even Edward no longer admired the beauties of the season. As the deadly grip of winter tightened, it brought suffering in its wake.

The mail coach arrived only five minutes late despite the weather, and the driver descended with difficulty, stiff with cold after the long journey from Exeter. He and the horses had eight hours to rest up, during which time the postmen would set off in their various directions and bring back the mail in time for his return journey. Edward sorted the mail quickly and left a few minutes early; it was inevitable that his pace would be slower than usual.

He paused at the bottom of High Street to stare again at the river. The calmly flowing waters had been arrested as if by magic, and the force of the tide had pushed up mounds of ice resembling a mountain landscape. A group of boys cavorted on the shore, daring each other to walk on to the frozen expanse and pass below the arches of the bridge, but jumping back in mock alarm when the loud retort of shifting ice echoed over the Quay.

He walked as fast as was conducive to safety and swung his arms energetically in an effort to keep his blood flowing. He had driven extra hobnails into his boots to increase their grip but there were still times when one of his feet slid alarmingly away and he regained his balance with difficulty. Thirteen miles to walk in these conditions! There would be a warm welcome at the cottage in Buckland Brewer where he now felt so at home, and the embraces of his own little family at the end of his journey. He whistled to keep his spirits up and it rang out across the wide river valley, the only sound in a silent landscape.

The light fall of snow during the night had formed a sheet on which evidence of all who had passed through was displayed; here on the drive to Hallsannery a hare had crossed and run across the field, and here were the prints of a fox and a few spots of blood, a small bird perhaps. The delicate tracery of birds' feet was everywhere.

Mr Harding, wearing a long overcoat with a fur collar turned up around his ears, was out on his doorstep and turned when he heard Edward's footsteps crunching behind him.

'Good morning! Another cold one! Look at this thermometer; fifteen degrees last night and eighteen now – on only three occasions in the last twenty-five years has it been colder and then only very briefly. These continuously low temperatures have no precedent.'

Mr Harding took his letters and shut the door; no hot drink to be had *there*, but never mind, he would be offered one at all the cottages and farmhouses at which he called.

As he walked Edward murmured the lines of a poem he was composing on the wintry weather, and he stopped once or twice to add new lines in his notebook; the silent and immovable barges, the ice-locked waterwheel at the mill, the boys skating on the frozen river. He could include some of these impressions in his newspaper column too. He had been writing poems at every opportunity in readiness for his meeting with Mr Rock, which was to take place next week if the weather improved. He had received a letter in which Mr

Rock told him he was making preliminary enquiries about publication. Edward read the letter and his new poems to Jane; she felt they were the best he had ever written, but she preferred the poems about the seasons to the one about war and patriotism with which he was so pleased.

As he followed the road through the valley, he scanned the ground constantly for victims of the icy weather. Often he saw a bird huddled at the base of the hedge, too weak for flight and sometimes even lacking the strength to hop when it heard his steps. If it were a robin or thrush, he stopped and broke a few crumbs from his loaf in the hope that they might maintain life until the thaw came, but he could do nothing for the redwings and finches for which fear of his presence seemed to hasten death. Once, beyond the hedge, he saw a flash of russet against the snow and recognised a stoat running here and there. Made bold by starvation, it stopped suddenly to stand on its hind legs and stare at him, then it picked up a rabbit's skull and carried it a few yards before dropping it again. He watched helplessly as it made an agile dash towards an exhausted small bird crouching on the frosted grass; a mere pinch of skin, feather and bone, and soon gone. When he walked on, he saw drops of blood amongst a confusion of animal footprints.

Over a field gate, he saw a red deer driven down from the moor by the cold weather, brilliant against the stark white snow. It faced him and stared, one hoof lifted delicately, its ears pricked and its large soft eyes looking directly at him. Neither moved. Then it turned and lifted its feet one by one out of the snow and, placing them again daintily with a little crunch, it walked slowly away.

There were no men working in the frozen fields. The day labourers had received no pay for two weeks and were searching the woodland for firewood; the only sounds were of saws and axes, and voices echoing through the valley. Yesterday, up towards Buckland Brewer, he had seen a man scrabbling on his knees in a field where sheep and lambs were gnawing at frozen roots and he realised that the man was stealing turnips to take home to his hungry family. Edward walked quietly away, knowing that drawing attention to the crime could result in the unfortunate man being sentenced to a month's hard labour.

As Edward came around a bend, he saw a figure crouching by the side of the road and heard the laboured tap, tap of hammer on stone. Surely the old stone-breaker could not be working in these temperatures?

'My dear, what be 'ee doing here? This is no weather for the old; you should be indoors by a warm fire.'

The old man peered up at him short-sightedly. He squatted uncomfortably on the heap of stones, his thin trousers torn at the knee and his gaping boots revealing that he wore no stockings. He was shaking with cold. 'Ah, that'd be a fine thing, a warm fire; a fine thing, eh?'

Edward knelt down beside him. 'But who is it that sets you to work here, Mr Copp? Have they no pity? Tell me, my dear, who it is that makes you work.'

The old man's eyes filled with tears at the unaccustomed sympathy. ''Tis the Board, Mr Capern, the same men I worked for all my long life, those that own the land hereabouts. I went to the Board to beg for money though I never dreamt I would do such a thing. My dear old wife is ill, Sir, I need bread for my Susannah and coal to keep her warm! Though if I was to work all night, I could not get enough. I never dreamt I'd be so old and helpless.'

As he spoke, the old man's toothless gums were revealed and tears ran down his cheeks. Edward's heart went out to him and he took the thin, cold hand between his own gloved ones. 'How much did the Board allow you, my dear?'

'Threepence a day, but not of a Sunday. Do they think us don't have to eat on the Lord's Day? And for this 'ere work, twopence a day more. But if I don't come out breaking stones, I don't get that twopence, see, and I amn't worked this past seven days. My lodgings alone is sixpence a week.'

Edward's mind reeled at the significance of such small sums. How was it possible to live on so little? 'You'd surely be better in the Workhouse than this poor living; its walls would at least give 'ee some warmth.'

'No; 'tis kind of you to think of me, Mr Capern, Sir, but I'd not go in that old place if its walls were made of gold. All my life I've earned my support with my own two hands, see, and I like to have the fields around me and the sky above, and 'tis like a gaol in there, see. And besides, I can't be parted from my Susannah. But thank 'ee, Sir.'

How could he be treated so cruelly? Edward's rage rose.

'These men on the Board of Guardians, you worked for them all your life, you say? Bringing in their harvest and filling their granaries and making them rich? And this is how they serve you now that you're helpless!' It was barely believable. Did these men see their former worker by the side of the road and pass him by? 'Give me your hammer now. I'll do the work for 'ee.'

He vented his anger on the pile of stones, aiming blow after blow at the society that abandons the very people it should revere, and at the men who scorn the needs of the poor although their storehouses and granaries are full. The hammer fell again and again with deadly precision, splintering the large rough stones and he wished that the members of the Board of Guardians would at this moment pass along the road.

When the pile of stones was finished, he climbed into the adjacent copse to find some sticks of firewood, then he helped the bent old man back to his dwelling, a small cottage above Edge Mill where his sick wife lay on a low bed beside a small, smouldering fire. A brightly-coloured rug was on the floor and some blue-and-white china arranged on a shelf, relics of past years when strength and health could earn a few extra shillings at harvest time. He spoke kindly to the man's wife and made up the fire for them. 'Let's pray that spring soon drives away this frost.' He took Mr Copp's hand. 'You take care, my dear, you and your wife.'

'Thank you, Sir, you'm a good man, Mr Capern.' He began to cry again. 'I'll lie on the bed now and us'll try to keep warm, the two of us together.'

Edward went on his way. He was late, but he could blame the weather for that. Breaking the stones had warmed him and his anger still burned inside. What could he do to change this heartless society? He was helpless; he was not even allowed to vote, so could not show support for those who might be more compassionate.

But he could write. If his poems were to be published, he could open the eyes and the hearts of those in power. He walked as if in a dream, barely hearing his bell echoing along frozen farm tracks because the lines of his next poem were ringing in his head.

Up in the village the icy wind pierced his layers of clothing and made his eyes run, and he remembered the local story that even the devil caught a cold when he came to Buckland Brewer. The only exception was the forge; he could see the red glow of the furnace through the half-open door and the heat melted the ice right out into the village street. Joshua Page, a huge heavily-muscled man whose sleeves were rolled up above the elbow despite the exterior temperatures, was shoeing a pony and roared out his usual greeting, and they exchanged stories of the weather.

Edward delivered the village post quickly and felt the welcome rush of warm air as he opened the door to Grace Ley's cottage. All three women jumped up to take his coat and plump the cushions on the chair by the fire. Grace continued to fuss over him even when he was settled with his dinner and Polly and Ann had returned to their sewing.

'Your boots, Mr Capern, take them off to dry now, your stockings too.'

He put his almost frozen bread and cheese aside and did as he was told. 'Mr Ley isn't out thatching, surely?'

She arranged his stockings on the fender. 'He's over the shed, preparing the straw. 'Tis too icy for ladders.'

Polly looked up from her sewing, her eyes bright with excitement. 'Be the river frozen still? And folks skating?'

'Yes, up towards Landcross they'm skating, but I didn't see Jesse Gay!'

Polly blushed. Jesse Gay often called at the cottage on some pretext, hoping to see her, and Edward liked to tease her about him. She looked particularly pretty when a flush came to her cheeks. 'I've told you, I don't care about him. I only wondered about the skaters.'

'Well, they'm the only ones I saw enjoying themselves. The only benefit of this frost is 'twill kill off the cholera if there's any still about, otherwise 'tis all bad. Many people are having a hard time of it.'

He told them about the old stone-breaker and the suffering of the day labourers, and Mrs Ley told him about old Moses Cole who had lost his stored potatoes to the frost and had no money for bread.

'What little they have, they'm using for coal. Moses is too crippled up to go looking for wood, and besides, the sticks has all been cleared from the woods nearest the village. Us is trying to help out when us can, but soon there'll be no more flour to be had and the road's too slippy to bring more up.'

Ann joined in. 'Mr Fulford came by – he said there's little enough hay left for the cattle.'

Edward warmed his hands on the mug of tea Mrs Ley had brought him. ''Tis a disgrace that such as old Mr Copp should suffer so; those with money should look after the poor at such times. Listen, I'm writing a poem about him. It can be printed in my book and I'll *make* the world sit up and take notice!'

He took out his notebook and read the lines he had written so far. Polly always took a particular interest in his writing and he had rather taken her under his wing, sometimes lending her one of his precious books to read. She seemed to have a natural talent and sometimes, when he could not find the right word for one of his poems, she would make a suggestion which was just what he wanted.

He finished his reading then looked up. All three had stopped their work and were watching him intently.

'Oh,' said Mrs Ley, 'I can just picture him, the poor old man.'

Polly had a faraway look in her eye.

'What be 'ee thinking of, maid?'

'You could make it like he's talking, telling you the story, just like you told us.'

'In his own words, you mean?' He thought about it; Coleridge had done something similar in *The Ancient Mariner*. 'Yes, that might do. That's another good idea of yours, Polly! Listen, I already have the last verse.'

He stood up and read it with all the fire and bitterness he felt towards the men of the Board. 'That will make them reconsider their cruelty!'

After another cup of tea, he prepared to go. He had only had a short break owing to his late arrival but he was keen to set off in good time, the steep lanes through Littleham being much more treacherous than the turnpike roads. He stood in the cottage doorway as he blew the first blast on his horn, then turned to say goodbye to the Ley family. Polly had put her sewing in her lap and was watching him. She blushed when he met her eyes.

Chapter Fifteen

Jane sat in her chair by the fire darning Charlie's socks while she listened to Edward and Mr Rock talking. The thaw which came yesterday had enabled the trains to run again, and Mr Rock had sent word that he would travel on to Bideford by carriage.

He was really very nice. He had shown interest in Charles's little collection of birds' eggs, had played with Milly and made her giggle, and both the children had sung beautifully for him. She had imagined Edward would take him to the top room so was rather alarmed to hear they would be in the kitchen all evening. Mr Rock used so many long words that she was afraid she might say something foolish in reply; but now that they were looking at Edward's poems together she could get on with her work and listen for the shop bell.

She was glad the visit wasn't as disruptive as the drawing class that now took place one evening a week in the top room. It had come as a surprise when Edward came home from the first meeting of his new Mechanics' Institute and announced that the Reverend Charles Kingsley was to teach a weekly drawing class, right here in their house! At such an inconvenient time, too. The first week it happened, she was just putting the children to bed when she heard loud voices and tramping on the stairs; she had to open the bedroom door to show Milly that they were just men and not monsters. So many men! Nine, plus Edward and Mr Kingsley, all carrying chairs up the staircase so they could sit down to draw. She could hear the chair legs knocking against the walls and knew they would be leaving marks. Then they all came tramping down again two hours later, waking the children with their noise.

Now, Mr Kingsley made sure they came down very quietly. Jane liked Mr Kingsley. He always stopped and said some kind words despite his dreadful stammer. The sixpence a week that was paid to hire the room helped to pay for Charlie's school fees, so it was worth the extra work of sweeping the room and the stairs.

Mr Rock was sitting at the head of the table with papers arranged in front of him. Edward was alongside, rocking on the edge of his chair in the way she was always reprimanding Charlie for, and trying to tell Mr Rock about his most recent poems.

Mr Rock held up his hand. 'Before we start; I have consulted with some literary friends and they agree that your poems have sufficient merit for publication. They also concur that neither I nor anyone else should have the power to alter the poems but that I should, with occasional advice from others, have absolute right of rejection. It is not always easy for the author to be the best judge of his work, so to give the best chance of commercial success, I will make the final selection.'

Jane thought it was so good of Mr Rock to help Edward that it seemed only right that he should make whatever decisions he wanted. He started showing Edward the poems he had chosen so far, and she allowed her mind to wander a little. Mrs Maxwell wanted a new hat for a wedding so she had promised to think up some designs.

'Mama! Mama!' It was Milly calling from upstairs. The children had both been so excited by the presence of a visitor that she wasn't at all surprised they had not gone to sleep yet.

Mr Rock stopped reading and looked up.

'I'm sorry, Sir, I'll go and settle the children again.'

'No need to apologise! It is I who should apologise for disturbing the routine of your household!'

Jane went upstairs to find Milly kneeling up in bed and bouncing up and down with excitement.

'Mr Wock, Mr Wock, stopped the clock, tick-tock!' She collapsed on to the bed giggling helplessly while Charlie, snuggled under the blanket, lost his battle to seem disapproving and joined in.

Jane quickly closed the door. 'Sshh! Be quiet both of you, he'll hear you!' It was hard to be really cross because they looked so adorable in their nightgowns with their faces rosy with laughter.

Charlie tried to look grown-up again. 'I told her she must go to sleep! Her wouldn't listen!' But then his sister caught his eye and her infectious laugh reduced him to giggles again.

'Charlie! I know quite well she wouldn't think up those silly rhymes herself! Now settle down to sleep. Daddy and Mr Rock can't do their work with all this noise from upstairs.'

'Mr Wock. He making book for Daddy!' Milly lay down, putting her thumb in her mouth, and her dark-fringed eyelids quickly started to droop. Jane tucked the blanket around her, smoothing the long curls back from her face. 'Yes, a book with Daddy's name on the front. Time for sleep now. Settle down, Charlie.'

He cuddled up to his sister then looked up at Jane. 'And everyone will know Daddy's name, won't they, and he'll be very important because only important people have their names on books, don't they?'

'Yes, he will be quite important.'

She sang quietly to them until Milly fell into a deep sleep and Charlie was drowsy, then she tiptoed out and down the stairs. It was correct, she supposed, that Edward would be famous. She felt both immensely proud and full of trepidation. The truth was that the idea of the book had rather gone to his head so that he seemed to think all their troubles were over. Being naturally more cautious, she wondered whether the book would make any money at all; but he had already bought himself several books to read, as he felt befitting to a published author, as well as a flute which he was learning to play. Their finances really would not stretch to such luxuries, but he just brushed away her concerns.

As Jane came into the kitchen, Mr Rock was leaning back in his chair, looking intently at Edward.

'Mr Capern, you have something here. You really have something here. Tell me how you came to write it.'

She glanced over his shoulder and saw that he was holding *The Lion Flag of England*, the poem about the war taking place in a foreign country. It was not one of her favourites but naturally Edward looked delighted at Mr Rock's reaction.

'Well, Sir, sometimes as I walk along I read a little of the newspaper when I have one to deliver – just a few paragraphs that I can see, you understand, without unfolding it – and I read of the battle of Balaclava and the terrible losses amongst the brave soldiers of the Light Brigade. I saw visions of the battlefield as I walked along the banks of the Torridge – I felt so strongly for the soldiers and I was sure that England could still vanquish the enemy if they did not lose heart. I wanted to tell them so, and the words just came to me, Sir, in a rush. Do you think it's good?'

Mr Rock was reading the poem again and did not answer at first.

'I do, I think this one will meet with much favour. Every verse rings like steel; there's a stimulant in it like the sharpening of swords, or the rush of armed men to the charge. I can think of many men who will be interested in reading this poem and it may be that showing this example will help to raise subscribers. But I stand by my decision to leave out *Apostrophe to the Sun*.'

Edward was shuffling through more poems to show Mr Rock.

'Here's a very new one, Sir, and one of which I'm proud! 'Tis the story of the old stone-breaker I see on my round.'

She glanced up, seeing Edward's impatience as Mr Rock read it through once, then a second time. Jane liked the poem; she had felt so sorry for the poor old man that she had knitted some warm socks for Edward to give him.

Mr Rock looked up. 'It is a fine poem in many ways but I fear it is too forthright for public taste. Some of our subscribers might be offended by the implication that they are uncaring of the poor.'

Edward's face fell. 'But they *are* uncaring! It's precisely because such people are only concerned for their own wealth that there are poor unfortunates like the old stone-breaker amongst us! My purpose is to raise awareness of their plight – you have already omitted *The Blind Coal-Carrier*!'

Jane put her work down and stared at Edward, hoping to meet his eye so she could frown at him. He must not talk to Mr Rock like that!

'Now, Mr Capern, you know we agreed that I should have the final say on selection. If you were to omit the last two verses I might reconsider, but I think it would be best to leave the poem out altogether. Please understand that I share your sympathies but there are plenty who do not.'

'Exactly, and they are the very ones I wish to influence! I *must* have this poem in my book! I want my work to soften hard hearts and alter ways of thinking, to bring about a fairer society!'

'I know, but you could damage your prospects in the process. If no one buys your book, you will have achieved nothing. Now, let us move on. There are more poems in your notebook, I see.'

He picked up the book but Edward stared unseeingly across the kitchen. Jane could see he was really cast down, and angry too. She willed him to look at her, anxious that there should not be another outburst. She could understand how disappointed he was about the poem, which he considered one of his finest, but surely Mr Rock knew best. Both men sat in silence, then she realised that Mr Rock was reading slowly to give Edward time to calm down. Finally he spoke.

'Now, this very recent one, *Winter 1855,* is an interesting poem. How well you conjure the biting cold and the silence of the frozen landscape! And in that last verse you make us aware of the suffering of the poor in a subtle way that will make rich men want to help. This one can certainly be included! I think we have almost enough now to make a book.'

Edward's mood had gradually softened. She put her sewing down.

'Mr Rock, Sir, would you like another cup of tea?' He seemed to be very fond of tea.

'Thank you, Mrs Capern, I would like another one. Now, Mr Capern, it will soon be the tenth anniversary of the Institution. Would you be willing to come to the celebration in Barnstaple and read one of your poems? It will be a large and appreciative audience!'

Edward was happy again; the evening had, on the whole, been very successful. Jane carefully measured out the tea leaves and lifted the kettle from the fire.

A few days later she sat at her table in the shop opposite a young girl whose staring eyes reminded her of a frightened rabbit.

'So Harriet, can 'ee tell me what you'd do first when you clean the drawing-room?'

Edward had again paid for a small advert for 'Mrs Capern's Registry Office' in the *North Devon Journal;* one of the three responses was from a lady in Weare Giffard wanting a housemaid. Jane always had a list of girls and women seeking work, but most of them were unsuitable: married women who were only used to rough work, or young girls with no experience. In truth, Jane had only a hazy idea of what was expected in a large household, but she had read a magazine article which described the duties of the various servants and considered herself a good judge of character. She would send the best candidate to meet the employer, but it would not be this girl; she could not even understand the questions.

'I've nothing suitable for 'ee now, Harriet, but I'll write your name in my book in case I'm asked for a general servant.'

Harriet thanked her several times, almost tripping up as she left the shop. Mary Blight came in for two pennyworth of treacle and a pound of rice, then Jane continued trimming a bonnet with mourning ribbon, while Milly played and chattered at her feet. As her needle flashed up through the black ribbon and down through the plaited straw, she glanced frequently at the window. Each time she saw a gentleman on foot she flinched and once she had to rethread her needle. She was, reluctantly, expecting a visitor.

Last night, she had not heard Reverend Kingsley coming down the stairs after the drawing class. When he looked through the kitchen door to thank her, she was leaning on the kitchen table and he must have seen from her face that she was in pain.

'Mrs Capern! Here, l-l-l-let me help you.' He took her arm and led her to a chair.

'Thank you, but I'm all right, a bit tired, that's all.'

He sat down next to her then questioned her gently. Had she seen a doctor? She had had a difficult day and his kindness made her tearful, otherwise she would have managed to brush away his concern. He insisted on asking his friend Dr Ackland to call; it would be no trouble, he said, as he lived just along the road. She tried to explain that doctor's fees were too expensive but he insisted that he would pay the doctor himself.

When Edward came downstairs, she told him what had happened. 'I really don't want the doctor to come! Would you call round to his house and tell him there's no need?'

'Well, 'tis very thoughtful of Mr Kingsley. He *is* kind; he's promised to ask a friend to talk to the Mechanics' Institute about the Court, Nobles and People of Russia.'

She pulled a face. 'Will that be interesting? Anyway, there's no need for the doctor to come. Please go and see him!'

Edward was sitting by the fire, looking at a book Mr Kingsley had lent him. 'I don't know; I don't want to upset him. Now, I want to read a few of these poems before bed.'

Jane had not mentioned it again. He was too involved with his own affairs to listen to her.

She knew Dr Ackland by sight because he lived with his parents on the corner of Chingswell Street, just opposite the water pump. It was said that he was walking out with the Rector's governess. She would be happy for him to see the children if the remedies she learned from her grandmother did not work; but she could not possibly talk to him about the cause of her own pain.

Being immersed in these thoughts, she was unprepared when the shop door suddenly opened. She jumped up, knocking her pincushion to the floor.

'Here, allow me.' She stepped back in alarm as Dr Ackland crouched down at her feet.

'There. You are expecting me, I think?' He smiled pleasantly; his eyes were gentle and kind. 'Is there another room we can retire to, away from the public view? And this pretty little lady can accompany us.'

He was on the floor again, squatting down beside Milly. 'And what is your name, little one?'

Milly put one finger in her mouth and stared at him, then losing her shyness she gave a little flounce and said, 'Amelia Eliza Cook Capern'.

'That is quite a collection of names!' He stood up and smiled at Jane.

'My husband chose it,' Jane blurted out. She had not even greeted him; how rude he must think her. 'It's not... I'm not ill, just that Mr Kingsley... I didn't mean him to call you.'

'No matter. Is this the kitchen? Can we go through?'

She followed him, feeling too miserable to refuse.

He sat down at the table; reluctantly she sat on the opposite side. He had fashionably trimmed whiskers, and she saw when she glanced up that his overcoat was of very good quality wool, and he wore a fine silk scarf.

'Mr Kingsley tells me that you are in pain. When did this start?'

His kind voice invited confidences, but what could she say? She could not speak of such things to a man.

''Tisn't bad, not really.' She hesitated. 'I've become accustomed to it, you see.'

'And when did it start?'

She looked down. Her hands were tightly clasped in her lap.

'Was it when this little lady came along?'

'Before that.' He waited. 'I have a son as well.'

'So, when your son was born, was that when it started?'

'Yes, Sir.' She almost hoped he would not hear her whisper.

'And where exactly is the pain, Mrs Capern?'

She glanced up, and his dark eyes, gentle as they were, seemed to see right inside her as if he knew exactly what was wrong.

'It is very fatiguing to be frequently in pain, is it not, Mrs Capern? The simplest chore can seem daunting, naturally one feels irritable, and of course it will affect a woman's ability to be a good wife. I imagine that you would prefer to be as you were in the early months of your marriage.'

His gaze was sympathetic. She remembered how it had been to feel attractive, to feel energy and laughter bubbling forth. What she would give to feel like that again!

'Mrs Capern, I may be able to help you but I need to know exactly what the problem is. I'm sure you understand the necessity of an examination.'

She looked away. It was unthinkable.

'We would need to go upstairs so that you may lie down. If you wish, a woman friend can be present, or your husband.'

Jane was appalled. The thought of anyone else being there almost made it worse. Her stomach was a tight knot and she could barely breathe.

'No; no, I said... I don't need... the pain's not that bad. Thank you, Sir, but I can't. I can't.'

There was a long silence.

'It is your choice, of course. Would you like to discuss it with your husband tonight?'

She shook her head.

'Well, you know where I live. If you change your mind, call in and let me know. There would be no further fee.'

She could not meet his eyes as she showed him out. When he had gone she returned to the kitchen; she sat there for a long time with her face buried in her arms.

A week later, Edward closed the Post Office door behind him and looked up at the sky. Throughout the day thundery clouds had been threatening to soak him, but the showers had come when he could shelter in a cottage kitchen or mill doorway. Now that it was twilight, the wind was rising while large drops of rain beginning to fall were clearly the forerunners of a prolonged downpour. A man hurried up the High Street holding a sack over his head. Edward turned into Mill Street and walked quickly in the direction of home.

He had only gone a short distance when he heard someone running up behind him.

'Edward! Edward, wait!'

He turned and was immediately enveloped in an affectionate greeting; he had to extricate himself to see who was so happy at their encounter.

'John! What are you doing here? My old friend, 'tis good to see you!'

John Gregory, the young shoemaker of whom Mr Lock had so disapproved! Edward held his friend at arms' length and stared at him in delight. Then he realised he was looking rather gaunt, and his clothes were threadbare. When John finished his apprenticeship, he moved to Bristol in search of better prospects than Bideford could offer, but it appeared he had not been entirely successful.

'Come back to my house and meet my children! Come now before we are both soaked!'

They walked quickly along the street where shutters were hurriedly being closed to keep out the storm. Jane was behind the counter in the shop, talking quietly with Mrs Prust.

'Jane, you remember John Gregory? Here he is, back in town and come to meet Milly and Charlie!'

He took John through to the kitchen. Charlie looked up from his slate while Milly leapt from her playthings on the floor and skipped towards him,

'Daddy, Daddy, Daddy!'

He lifted her up. She wrapped her arms and legs around him and buried her face in his neck, a bundle of warm body, petticoats and soft hair.

'This pretty creature, John, is my own Milly, my little cherub! And here's Charlie hard at work on his sums; there never was a cleverer boy at just six years old! Charlie, come and shake Mr Gregory's hand. Now, if I can untangle myself from this little fairy, us'll go upstairs and you can tell me where you've been all these years.'

They sat in the top room, wrapped in their coats as the fire was not lit. John told how he had only found casual shoemaking in Bristol so was constantly seeking more work. He had returned to Bideford to visit his sick father and planned to look for work in South Wales.

Edward was sorry to hear his friend had not met with more success, but was bursting to tell him the news. He had recovered from his disappointment and had barely been able to sleep, so excited was he about the book.

'John, I'm to be published! A book of my poems!'

John knew of Mr Rock's reputation as a benefactor. Edward described the latest developments.

'He has done a great deal of good, helped many people on the road to self-improvement and plans one day to provide a recreation ground for Barnstaple – perhaps for Bideford too. He knows many wealthy people – Earls and Dukes and Members of Parliament. He'll ask them to commit to buy my book so that sufficient money is raised for the printing of it. And I shall ask the people I know here in Bideford, those that can afford it. He's confident that we shall meet with success. Imagine, John – me, a published author!'

John jumped up to embrace Edward. 'Will 'ee still be my friend, even though I am poverty-stricken? You will, I know, because you have always championed the cause of the poor working man, and I guess that to be the subject of some of these poems!'

Doubt washed over Edward again. He explained the situation to John.

'But 'tis not up to him to choose your poems! You can't let him dictate to you – what are you, his lap-dog, doing his bidding, sitting up to beg? If *I* ever publish poems, I'll be the one to do the choosing!' John strode up and down the room, his eyes flashing angrily. Edward felt weary. All the excitement of his news was gone.

'But, John, a book of my own! And they *are* my own poems, without alteration or addition, only that a few are left out. Mr Rock is a good man, I would never be where I am today without his help, and he knows what to do to make the book a success. I can't turn him down!'

Eventually John grudgingly accepted that Edward had little choice if he wanted to make some money for his family, but continued to insist that he would never capitulate over *his* beliefs.

When he had gone, Edward felt very downcast. He gave Charlie his lessons and taught Milly a new little song while she sat on his knee, but his mind was elsewhere. He resolved to talk to Reverend Kingsley; he was himself a successful author and he understood working men.

His opportunity came after the next drawing class. It was difficult to concentrate on sketching the flowers from the conservatory at Northdown Hall, even though Mr Kingsley kept up an amusing and instructive dialogue which entertained the other men. When the class finished, Edward asked about the progress of the new novel, *Westward Ho!*; after all the young men had left he was able to bring the conversation around to his desired subject.

'I've told you, Sir, that Mr Rock is arranging a book of poems for me. He's told me he won't allow my more forthright poems to be included, and I don't know what to do! You have read them, Sir, so you know how much passion I have poured into them! Should I tell him I won't go ahead with the plan? It means so much to me to have my poems in print – I can't tell you how much!'

Mr Kingsley sat down. He usually seemed possessed of tremendous energy and Edward had noticed that he calmed himself by smoking. He took his long clay pipe out of his pocket, lit it, then stared at the floor. With his beak-like nose and fierce look, he reminded Edward of a hawk. Eventually he looked up and his expression softened.

'Mr Capern, you l-l-love Nature; you write of f-f-flowers, and birds, and these poems give you a g-great deal of pleasure, do they not?'

'Yes Sir, they do, but –'

'Your p-p-poems will give pleasure to others, and that is a great thing. Treasure that! Mr Rock is correct that r-r-revolutionary poems will not meet with favour. It is a subject I have studied in some depth. My novel, *Alton Locke,* is about a working-class writer who follows the r-r-radical path. I will give you a copy if you think it would interest you.'

'Thank you, Sir, it would. But, I see things that those in power don't see, and I want to make them realise how unfair it is, the way men struggle all their lives on low wages, then are thrown aside when they're too old and feeble to work!' He paced up and down the room. 'If I can put those poems in a book I can get my message across! Bring about change!'

He had hoped for support, an ally against Mr Rock's decision; but Reverend Kingsley merely sighed and smoked his pipe, sending clouds of smoke out into the room. It was some time before he spoke again.

'When a working man becomes conscious of l-literary ability, the effect of it is usually to throw him into fierce h-hostility with the social system which restrains him, and he boils with f-f-fierce but impotent fury. It is not for working men to confront those that rule them, to do so will lead to failure and d-despair; it is sad, but it is true. Even I have fallen foul of those in power through activities they consider unbefitting to my class and, believe me, I would not wish the experience on a-a-anyone. At best, the poems would be ignored and you would not achieve the desired sales. You must think of your wife and your dear children, Mr Capern.'

His gaze was deeply sympathetic, and Edward warmed to him. 'Then you really think I should accept Mr Rock's terms?'

Mr Kingsley puffed slowly at his pipe. 'When you share your gentle poems and songs with the cottagers you meet, the r-rhymes will ring in their ears and cling to their imagination; they will give relief to sadness and receptiveness to pleasure. That is the best way for you to help them. Let others take the r-r-revolutionary path.'

He puffed at his pipe again. 'To be able to publish poems you have written from the heart, that is a great opportunity.' He looked up, then fixed Edward with an intense stare. 'Take it, Mr Capern.'

Chapter Sixteen

Edward stood in the entrance hall of the Barnstaple Literary and Scientific Institution in a pool of light cast by an ornate cut-glass gasolier. Through the open door came businessmen and gentlemen in tail coats and top hats, smiling and laughing together in anticipation of an enjoyable evening celebrating the tenth anniversary of the Institution. He hoped to see someone with whom he could converse instead of again wandering alone through the crowded exhibition rooms. He stepped forward when he saw Mr Galliford and Mr Bale, but they did not appear to recognise him. It was, of course, eight years since he lived in the town and they would barely have noticed him, even then.

The new arrivals sauntered under an arch of laurel and holly to long tables presided over by ladies handing out tea, coffee and cake. Edward had tried coffee for the first time but found it bitter. The cake made up for it and he would have had another slice if his stomach did not ache so, whether from hunger or nerves, he hardly knew.

He had been one of the first to arrive and Mr Rock had quickly explained the programme for the evening.

'At seven o'clock the guests will assemble in the lecture room after perusing the exhibition. The Mayor will open the meeting; the Secretary, Mr Chanter, will read the report of the last ten years, and there will be addresses by Lord Ebrington and myself. Then a break of three-quarters of an hour during which refreshments will be served and Miss Gould will play piano accompaniments for flute and violin.

Then we will return for the votes of thanks and your reading. You are going to say a few words before the poem, are you not? It will be quite a crush for three hundred people but I think we will manage.'

Edward thought he had misheard. 'How many people?'

'Three hundred.' Mr Rock noticed his expression and clapped him on the shoulder with a laugh. 'Look not so palely, my friend! If you read your poem with all the dramatic fire that you mustered for me last time, you will have nothing to worry about. They will love it!'

Edward's throat constricted. 'But, I thought there would be a small group, thirty perhaps. I've been anxious about reading in front of thirty! But three hundred – I can't do it, Sir, not for so many, and some of them gentlemen of taste and discernment! They'll find me laughable!'

He had paid someone to carry out his postal round; he had hurriedly written his column for the newspaper and travelled by carrier's cart to Barnstaple eager for the evening's events, but he had not expected such a grand occasion, nor such a huge crowd of people. All those eyes and ears focused on him! 'I can't do it, Mr Rock!'

'Come with me; we'll look at the lecture room and you'll see it is not such a daunting prospect.'

Mr Rock stood with him on the platform and made him read the poem to the empty room.

'Now, please do not let the side down. You are the best example of the Institution's achievements and the Committee are looking forward to your contribution!'

He could not disappoint Mr Rock but standing there in the entrance hall, he felt almost frozen with nerves. Still more people were coming through the door. Edward walked quickly back into the room which now bore a sign over the door declaring 'Photographs and Nature Prints'. The whole building had been given over to an exhibition of paintings, engravings, scientific apparatus and specimens of local manufacture which surely rivalled the Great Exhibition in London for variety, if not scale. He had moved restlessly from room to room but could not concentrate on the exhibits.

The wall at which he stared bore a display of daguerreotypes depicting views of Athens and the architectural wonders of Venice, which had been loaned by

Dr Budd. Next to him, two gentlemen were looking at an adjacent picture.

'You would think it was a painting, would you not, but I am told it is a chromo-lithograph.'

Edward turned and looked at the picture. Under a bright blue sky, a man was leading a donkey on which his beautiful dark-haired wife and child sat side-saddle alongside panniers overflowing with luscious fruit. The woman reminded him a little of Jane. How he wished he could be the man in the picture, walking through sunlit countryside with his family instead of here, where he would be an object of ridicule.

He turned and walked quickly up the elegant staircase, past the Library where microscopes were displayed and stopped in the doorway to the lecture room. Small groups of people were already beginning to gather in the large room, the walls of which were completely covered in large gilt-framed paintings depicting distinguished men who seemed to look sternly down at Edward. What was he doing here? He would never have his portrait painted. He belonged in the company of cottagers and other unassuming folk out in the Devon lanes.

He leaned against the door frame, out of the way of the gentlemen coming into the room. Could he tell Mr Rock that he was going to leave and return to Bideford now instead of waiting for his lift? But what would he tell Jane, and his sisters? They were so looking forward to hearing about the evening.

He had not wanted to go to his very first interview with Mr Rock, all those years ago. He had not believed he could be a member of the Institution, but his mother insisted that he attend. He remembered what she had said to him:

'They'll soon see that you are cleverer than any of them. They'll be honoured to have you.' He seemed to hear her words again, and her voice was just as sweet and low.

And was she not right? Here he was, a guest of the Committee – he had not even had to pay for a ticket as others had – and he had been asked to read a poem, a poem which would soon appear in a book with his name on the cover! How proud his mother would have been. He had to do it, for her sake.

By seven o'clock the room was packed full of men standing shoulder to shoulder; Edward was sure he would never have managed to push his way through if he had not been following in Mr Rock's wake. He found himself sitting on the platform with three hundred upturned faces gazing at him, and quickly looked down at his shaking hands until the Mayor started his address. He had expected the declamatory tones which were familiar to him from Methodist ministers and speakers on temperance, but the Mayor stumbled over his words and did not give them the emphasis they deserved. Edward's spirits began to rise a little; he could do better than that, surely.

He found it difficult to attend to the other speeches until Mr Rock spoke, and he saw how he worked the audience, encouraging them to respond to his words with cheers and applause. He then told them that there was to be a contribution from a poet who was said to be comparable to Burns, Clare or Bloomfield. Edward looked around in surprise. Who was this? Mr Rock was smiling at *him* and the audience was cheering! Fortunately, before he had time to decide whether he should respond, the musical interlude commenced.

He stepped down from the platform and several men approached him to congratulate him and ask him how he came to write poetry. He enjoyed joking with them about the difficulties of combining the literary life with his postman's duties; by the time he had to return to the platform, he felt heady with excitement. He had not had time to seek refreshments and was feeling very hot from the crush of the crowd; he longed to loosen his cravat and remove his jacket, but the gaze of the expectant crowd was on him again.

Lord Ebrington proposed a vote of thanks to the Mayor and then Mr Rock stood up. Edward felt himself trembling. Mr Rock read the letter in which Eliza Cook described

Edward's war poems as amongst the best ever written, and then it was time for him to stand.

He held up his shaking sheet of paper. 'I appear before you with mingled feelings of pleasure and regret; pleasure at the scene I see before me, and regret that I am called upon to read my own poetry.'

His voice sounded croaky and unsure, but the crowd cheered. He took a deep breath and his voice strengthened. 'My friend, Mr Rock, might have trod the beautiful paths of poetry, but he chose that of commerce, and succeeded.' There were further cheers; as Edward looked up to meet the gaze of the audience for the first time, he saw that they were with him; they liked him. 'I write poetry because it pleases me, and I believe it pleases some others, and especially it pleases my wife.'

The laughter gave him courage. He reached the end of his address and the cheers drowned him out. He took the sheet containing the poem from his pocket and announced the title. He paused, then he took a deep breath. When rehearsing the poem, he had decided to start reading quietly and build up to a crescendo.

> 'The Lion Flag of England;
> Say, Britons, shall it wave...'

The audience was listening carefully now; when he stopped to take a breath, he could have heard a pin drop. He was tingling all over with excitement and nerves.

By the start of the third stanza, he let his voice rise.

> 'Have faith in dear Old England!'

He threw his arm out in emphasis as the crowd murmured its appreciation. He reached the fifth stanza, when he demanded:

> 'Who staunched the patriot's blood?
> Who? England, at the battle-cry
> Of "Liberty and God!"'

They were cheering loudly; he had to wait until he could make himself heard again. He was quivering with exhilaration by now, and so hot he could feel the perspiration running down the back of his neck. On he went, louder and faster as the drama of the poem increased; when the paper flew out of his hand as he flung his arms out effusively, he carried on from memory until he reached the final stanza and he thundered out:

'Fight on, keep heart, look up, be firm!'

The crowd roared its appreciation. Edward inhaled deeply, threw his arms skyward and declaimed the final line, but then he heard shouts of disquiet and everything went black.

The next thing he was aware of was a forest of legs around him, and Mr Rock looking anxiously into his face. His head ached terribly.

Mr Rock took his hand. 'You passed out, my friend. I'm afraid the excitement was too much for you. But what a triumph!'

It was late by the time he descended the steps from the carriage in Bideford. The horses tossed their heads impatiently and the driver wished him a 'good night' as they set off at a fast trot. He stood for a few moments to enjoy the stillness, such a contrast to the noisy conversation and suffocating atmosphere of the overcrowded carriage. The inns along the Quay were in darkness; the only sound was the distant barking of a dog. From the broad stretch of blackness beyond the gas lamps he could hear an occasional ripple and splash from the fast-flowing river, then the high, bubbling call of a curlew, and he felt the anxieties of the evening dissipating. He turned and walked slowly up Cooper Street towards his home.

Jane gasped as he walked in. 'Your face! Edward, what have you done?'

He felt exhausted, lowering himself carefully on to his chair. 'I'm all right, had a fall, that's all. I fainted and fell right off the platform!'

She jumped up and examined his face. 'Fainted! Why? What happened? You're going to have a bad bruise here – I'll make a poultice with cabbage leaves like I do for the children. Why did you faint?'

He took her hand and pulled her on to his lap. 'Janie, I read my poem to three hundred people! They liked it!' He could still picture their faces focussed just on him, and feel the heady excitement of bringing his poem to life for them; but beneath it all, he felt a deep sense of satisfaction. He put his arms around her and held her close.

'Mr Rock told everyone about my book. Do you know, I feel now I really am a poet.'

Chapter Seventeen

'Milly, put your boots on again! What are you thinking on, chiel, 'tis time to go!'

Jane threw some ash on the fire to damp it down and hurried to the mirror to put on her bonnet. She had re-trimmed it in autumnal colours. It suited her dark hair, and her eyes were shining with excitement at the prospect of an event that the whole family could attend together. She had sewn horsehair braid around the inside hem of her best dress to stiffen it and give a fashionable silhouette, and the children were ready, until Milly decided to remove her boots.

Charlie was tying his sister's laces for her.

'Good boy, now let's go and see if Daddy has finished work. 'Tis a pity he hasn't got time to change out of his working clothes.'

They stepped out into the street and she locked the shop door. All the shops were closing for the afternoon. Everyone wanted to see the first train arrive in Bideford.

'Show me the leaves! Show me the leaves!' Milly was jumping up and down with excitement so Jane picked her up to show her, yet again, the evergreen garland that Edward and Mr Purchase from Potter's Lane had strung up between their two dwellings. The children had helped to attach the branches of scented pine and ivy to a long rope and Edward had been out until nearly ten o'clock the previous night hanging it.

There was a stream of people making their way to the event; Jane guessed many of them to be from Northam and Appledore. Eliza was standing at the bottom of Hart Street, watching.

'Aren't you coming, Eliza?' she called, although she could see that poor Eliza looked too weary for the walk across the bridge.

'I'm not fussed about seeing a train.'

Many of the houses in Mill Street bore streamers and flags, or banners declaring 'Steam: The Wonder of the Age.' The family were admiring the decorations outside the Post Office when Edward came out smiling and swung Milly up into his arms. 'Quickly now, we mustn't miss the arrival!'

They turned on to the Quay where they met a crush of people, horses, carts and carriages. Jane stopped and held tight to Charlie's hand. 'We'll have to watch from here! We'll never get across.'

Edward looked up and down the Quay. Suddenly he gave a shout, and waved at a man in a farm cart. 'Hello there! Mr Hockridge! Can us have a ride?' He turned to her. 'Do 'ee remember Mr Hockridge? – where Thomazine and Lewis used to lodge!'

Jane clung to Edward as he pushed through the crowd to reach the cart. He leapt up with Milly before turning to help her and Charlie, then she found herself crouching on a bed of straw alongside a young couple who were Mr Hockridge's neighbours. She smoothed down her best dress and tried to make herself presentable; fortunately the straw appeared to be clean.

The crush was so great that Mr Hockridge had to lead the horse through while Edward took the reins, but even so the cart started to rock dangerously half-way across the bridge, and he had to shout at people to stand back. They managed to find a position in Barnstaple Street, which gave them a good view of the track coming from Instow and of the station, which was decorated with flags and banners.

Jane had never seen so many people. It seemed every inch of ground was taken up; she could even see people leaning from first-floor windows on the far side of the river, and on the water a fleet of small fishing boats sailed up and down, vying for a good position. Nearby there was a whirligig which attracted the children's attention, and stalls selling sweets, gingerbread and coffee, all of which added to the holiday atmosphere.

She pointed out the railway track to the children. Edward had told her that there were plans for a new road to Instow; the embankment, built to ensure that the track did not flood at high tide, would also provide protection for a road. Jane explained to Charlie that it would bring further improvements in transport: 'All the letters that Daddy delivers will come by train now, instead of the Royal Mail coaches!'

Edward was calling out excitedly to people he recognised in the crowd. Jane was glad to see him so animated. He had been most aggrieved that he had not been given a free ticket to ride on the train, despite being the Bideford correspondent, and had even spoken of resigning from the newspaper. When he eventually got over his disappointment he admitted that the occasion was sufficiently important to be covered by the Barnstaple reporters, but he still felt that he had been snubbed.

They had drawn up alongside another two-wheeled farm cart with five children in the back. Jane soon fell into conversation with the farmer's wife, whom she knew from the pannier market, while Milly clambered over to play with the children. Charlie, intent on the track which ran off into the distance below them, was determined to get the first glimpse of the train.

Suddenly a shout went up and everyone stood for a better look. At first Jane could only see a gathering cloud of steam; but suddenly there was the engine speeding along the tracks by the river, with all the carriages behind as if drawn by half a dozen galloping horses. The engine gave a sudden prolonged shriek which made everyone cheer. She and Edward held the children up to watch and she laughed to see Charlie; he was motionless in Edward's arms, his eyes and mouth wide open with astonishment and pleasure. The cheering and clapping reached a crescendo as the engine blew its whistle again and clanked slowly beneath the evergreen arch on the approach to the new station. It came to a gradual standstill, panting under a cloud of steam, while the church bells across the water started to ring and cannon-fire was heard from the hill behind them. The cheers were deafening, and Jane joined in until the noise became overwhelming and, like Milly, she laughingly covered her ears.

The train was much bigger than Jane had expected; the paintwork gleamed like the glossy coat of a horse and it puffed gently as if breathing. She had read an article in a magazine explaining how a steam engine worked, but she had not expected it to seem so *alive.* When the doors of the carriages started to open, their windows flashing in the afternoon sunshine, it seemed magical that people should emerge from such an extraordinary beast.

They had hoped to go into the station at Cross Park for a closer look; but as the passengers joined the crowd and started to move towards the bridge, it became clear that it would be impossible to push their way through. Edward was sanguine about it. 'Never mind, us'll come tomorrow and stand right on the platform to watch it come in. And one day us'll have a ride on it!'

'Tomorrow, Daddy, can us ride on it tomorrow?' Charlie and Milly were jumping up and down with excitement, and Jane had to restrain them as the cart was beginning to rock.

'No, not tomorrow, my chicks, we must wait until Daddy has some more money. That won't be long!'

Jane gave him a warning look. He frequently spoke of all the money he would have when his book of poems was published, and this worried her. The list of subscribers was growing but the book would only be published if enough money was raised, and it seemed to be taking a very long time. She preferred to wait until the money was in their hands.

Edward took the opportunity to give Charlie a lesson in geography. 'Now that the railway has reached Bideford, it runs the length and breadth of the land, from the German Ocean to the Atlantic Ocean. Do you remember I showed you on the map?'

Charlie nodded obediently, but his gaze kept drifting away.

'So Bideford is now properly connected and folk can cross the country in only fourteen hours. Many people will come to visit because they will read about the town in Mr Kingsley's book, *Westward Ho!* The railway can now go further west to Holsworthy and Launceston and Plymouth and 'tis to be hoped that landowners will give the land – they *should* because it benefits them as much as anyone.'

'Daddy, can us ride on the whirligig now?' Charlie was standing on tiptoe to see the small fairground.

'Come on then, let's have a closer look.'

'Edward, don't you think it'll be too expensive!'

Jane had to buy in more stock for the shop and there was barely enough money to do so; but Edward was already lifting the children out of the cart and thanking Mr Hockridge.

When they reached the foot of the hill, Edward suddenly grasped her arm. 'Look! There's Mr Bragington, Chairman of the Bideford Extension Company. I hear he is a subscriber to my book! And Mr Avery too!'

There was quite a crowd of gentlemen in top hats coming out of the station, smiling and laughing as they turned to look back at the train waiting for its return journey.

'There's a dinner at the Guildhall this evening for mayors and councillors from all over North Devon. I'm going to speak with them! I may be able to persuade them to find more subscribers!'

'But Edward, will they know you? It'll be humiliating if they don't.'

But he was gone, striding towards the group. She knew from her efforts to develop the millinery business that being too assertive was not effective; wealthy people liked to be in control. She took the children's hands as the crowd pushed past her, watching apprehensively as Edward approached the gentlemen. Mr Bragington, a stout man with fleshy features, regarded Edward quizzically as he gesticulated eagerly, while the other gentleman looked away as if bored. Finally they shook their heads and walked on; but Edward approached another group, and she saw that he was producing some subscription sheets. He always kept some in his pocket.

For the last few months he had thought of nothing but poems and the progress of his book, sometimes becoming very downcast when he feared that the list of subscribers would not be sufficiently long, and at other times wildly excited. It *was* exciting when letters arrived from Mr Rock telling them of the progress he had made; The Earl of Portsmouth had ordered four copies, Lord Clinton four copies and even Viscount Palmerston, the Prime Minister, wanted a copy! And the day that Edward heard that Charles Dickens had ordered his book, he was so thrilled, he claimed he ran all the way to Buckland Brewer.

There were times when he felt so positive about his prospects, he believed he would soon be able to give up his postal round, and he spent every spare moment writing poems and songs to put in a second book. At other times he was almost consumed with anxiety at the thought that, once published, the book might be greeted with scorn, or that an insufficient number of orders would be received, and all the eminent gentlemen disappointed.

She saw that two of the gentlemen were reluctantly taking the proffered papers, and she wondered whether they would discard them when Edward was gone.

Charlie was pulling away from her hand. 'Mama, I want to go on the whirligig *now*!'

He freed himself then pushed through the crowd to reach the contraption, so she had to follow him. It was a circular device the size of a small cottage, with a central pole holding up a red-painted roof from which roughly-made wooden horses were suspended on chains. A barefooted boy ran round and round, pulling on one of the chains so that the whole thing spun on its central axis, giving the children who sat on the horses a giddy ride. The faster the boy ran, the more the horses flew out sideways, threatening to unseat their riders.

She explained to Charlie how unsafe it was, but he stamped his foot angrily. 'But I *want* to go on it! I won't fall off!'

'Charlie, 'tis expensive and dangerous! Come this way, look, this stall's got jam tarts and biscuits and currant buns. If you're a good boy you can choose one.'

But Charlie ran off and tried to climb on one of the horses as it came to a stop, then Edward suddenly appeared to help him. As he sat clutching the chain and waiting for the ride to begin, he grinned at her and shouted rudely, 'There, I knew Daddy would let me!'

She kept a firm hold of Milly's hand and turned away to stare into the crowd. She didn't want the afternoon to be spoilt. She started to move towards Mrs Prust, but then glimpsed Dr Ackland with his wife-to-be, the Rector's governess. They made a very attractive couple as they strolled arm-in-arm down the hill, and she saw how he surreptitiously caressed her hand. As they approached she turned away, not wishing to be noticed, but Edward strode forward. He shook Dr Ackland's hand and thanked him for subscribing to the book. Dr Ackland looked somewhat taken aback when Edward pushed some leaflets into his hand, asking him to pass them on to his friends. He cast his eyes over the crowd and, seeing Jane, bowed his head politely to her before she had time to look away. She felt herself flush with embarrassment.

When Charlie was lifted, dizzy but content from his ride, she asked Edward to please stay with the family and not to talk to anyone else about subscriptions. He agreed, and the remainder of the afternoon was passed pleasantly enough, but she continued to feel an undercurrent of anxiety for Edward. If his book did not meet with favour, she wondered how he would live with the disappointment.

1856-1863

Success

Then will I sing mine own true note,
And wait the inspiration
Which gives out to the listening world
The echo of creation.

Chapter Eighteen

Edward turned down the track to Watertown, whistling as he walked. It was a fine June morning and the sky was of the deepest blue when observed through the bright green foliage of the oaks.

He had to shield his eyes from the sun, which was just beginning to lift the dew from the grass and to draw flashes of light from the River Yeo rippling over its stony bed.

He paused to run his hand slowly across the soft heads of buttercups, white stitchwort and red campions. The lush vegetation through which they thrust their stems was made up of astonishing variations in green, and was tallest at the base of the hedge where the ground was always a little damp, perhaps from an underground spring. He could hear the rustlings and squeakings of a mouse or vole tunnelling its way between the long stalks. This small area of hedge alone contained sufficient jewels to hold him spellbound all day and provide the subjects for half a dozen poems, but there was work to do, so he marched on.

The black-and-white sheepdog at Watertown heard his footsteps and trotted out, giving a series of short sharp barks, while wagging its tail to reassure him that it meant no harm.

'Hello, Shep, what's all that noise about, then?'

The dog turned to walk back with him, pressing close against his legs while he caressed its head. The geese sidled and cackled when they saw him but they knew him now, and he reached the farmhouse door without being threatened.

''Tis just bills today, I'm sorry to say, Mrs Partridge.' He rested his bag on the long deal table and took out two letters. 'This one looks like Mr Tardrew's writing and this one's from Mr Parsons, the veterinary in Buttgarden Street, it's got his name on the back, see?'

She wiped her hands on her apron and peered at the letter, 'Oh dear, yes, that'll be for the calving that was such a trouble. Never mind. Now will 'ee sit down for a minute and have a cup of tea? I've some cut-rounds fresh from the oven.'

The smell of baking was tempting and there was a chair with cushions by the fire; but Edward had already lost time talking to the bargemen down by the river, so he declined the offer.

'Well then, would 'ee mind just singing me a verse of our song before 'ee go? I have the words written down here but the tune has gone out of my head again. My other niece is coming to visit and I want to be able to sing it for her.'

He had written *The Lass of Watertown* for a niece who was now married and living in London. She was a very pretty girl who had rather taken his fancy. Mrs Partridge, with clasped hands and rapt expression, mouthed the words along with him as his voice resounded around the low-ceilinged kitchen.

He hummed the tune to himself as he followed the track down to Landcross Mill. He had composed half a dozen ballads in the last few months. The truth was, it was not always enough to be writing words alone. He had so much joy in his heart that he needed music as well as poetry.

What a time it had been! It was such a relief to hear that five hundred people had promised to buy his book, including his Graces the Dukes of This and the Right Honourable Earls of That, all his well-wishers in North Devon and eminent authors too; and finally the extraordinary pleasure of holding the book in his hands! Jane had been rather affronted when he said so, but the thrill really was as great as holding his children for the first time. He caressed the green embossed cover and ran his finger over the spine which announced *Capern's Poems* in gold lettering. It scarcely seemed possible that those words meant him, but on the frontispiece was the declaration, *POEMS of Edward Capern. Rural Postman of Bideford, Devon.* So it must be true.

As he descended the steep path in the sunshine, grasshoppers leapt from under his feet and landed amongst the poppies that grew on the rocky edges. Deep purple columbines, scarce elsewhere, grew in the high hedges and elderflowers scented the air. Three or four swallows wheeled low over the river and a pair twittered sweetly from the top of the waterwheel, a favourite place when it was motionless.

'Mr Guard!'

The miller appeared with a spanner in his hand and Edward took two letters from his postbag. 'It's a fine morning! Good day to you!'

He crossed the bridge, pausing to watch the dark-red cows drinking from the river shallows, and the sunlight that flashed on the drips of water when the cattle lifted their heads to stare at him.

At first, the delight he took in his new book had been mingled with fear that reviewers would find the poems ridiculous. They would ask why a mere postman imagined he could write poetry; they would declare that flowers and birds were not worthy subjects; they would scorn the choice of words and the simple rhymes. But then, the first reviews were printed in the newspapers:

'*Mr Capern is a real poet.*' '*A man of genius of a very high order.*' '*His verse is as delicious in sentiment as it is melodious in utterance.*'

He had almost fainted with astonishment. The reviews came from every county in England as well as from the national press, and after the reviews came the orders. After only a few weeks, Mr Rock told him that the one thousand books were almost sold out and there was to be a reprint. It was beyond his wildest dreams.

And then there was the letter that meant so much to him. The great poet, Walter Savage Landor, having subscribed to the book, wrote to him praising it in the highest degree and enclosing a treasured volume of his own poems and a present of five pounds. Five pounds! He could not earn so much in eight weeks. And even better, Mr Landor's latest book, *Antony and Octavius*, carried a printed dedication: '*To Edward Capern, Poet and Day-Labourer of Bideford, Devon,*' for the whole world to see; as well as a promise that any profits from the book would be given for the support and education of Mr Capern's children. Almost every day brought something new and, after opening a letter in the sorting office, he had several times run back down Mill Street in excitement to tell Jane the good news. Their little house was filled with joy again.

As he marched steadily alongside a meadow where glossy-coated cows with heavy udders grazed knee-deep in a golden blaze of buttercups, he heard the triumphant, ringing calls of buzzards overhead, and paused to watch a pair of the broad-winged birds circling together against the bright blue sky. What a privilege it was to be out, to be here, on such a perfect day!

Perhaps the greatest relief for him and for Jane was hearing that the first edition would bring a profit of £150, which Mr Rock strongly recommended should be used to purchase an annuity on their joint lives. As they realised the significance of the news, they held each other and cried with relief. Never again need they worry about going hungry in old age; never again would they fear dying in the workhouse.

It was no wonder that he sang as he went about his work.

He strode along the turnpike road until he reached South Heale Cottage and climbed the steps to the front door. He knocked, then turned to look out over the river, keeping his hand and the letter hidden in his bag. This was one of the sadder aspects of his job.

'Morning, Mrs Beer.'

The elderly woman who opened the door did not reply, but stared at him anxiously.

'I'm sorry, but 'tisn't good news.'

When he took the black-edged envelope from his bag, she covered her mouth and looked at him fearfully, and he spoke gently to her. 'Would 'ee like me to read it to you, Mrs Beer?'

He followed her into the cottage where he sat at the scrubbed deal table while she searched for a knife to open the envelope. Tears filled her eyes when he read the announcement. The woman was her cousin; they had been brought up together.

'If 'ee like, I'll come again tomorrow and write a letter for you, maid. Send your condolences.'

She thanked him, then stood at the door as he went on his way.

He continued in a more sombre mood. He was given frequent reminders on his round that many were less fortunate than he. Deaths were inevitable but poverty and hunger were not. Should he be content to bring a little pleasure into people's lives through his joyful poems, or did he have a responsibility to raise awareness of suffering?

At Edge Mill Mr Davey appeared, looking dusty and hot. He took off his hat and fanned himself with it. ''Tis dry old work, this. Any news of our soldiers?'

Edward took Captain Archdale's newspaper from his bag. 'Us can read most of this column here without unfolding the paper. It says they'm on their way home, but whether they'll have leave, I don't know.'

The miller studied the paper and handed it back. 'It's been a bad old business. What them men have been through! And all to defend their country – and us, every one of us!'

Edward carefully put the paper away. 'And they'm the ones coming back. There's plenty isn't.' Was he doing enough by writing about the soldiers' bravery? Perhaps he should have enlisted, despite feeling it must be the hardest trial to be so far away from home.

He walked on until he came to the corner where the old stone-breaker worked. The old man was in rather better health now that the weather was warmer, but the work still taxed his strength. As Edward approached, he saw how the stones flew out from under the hammer as often as not, and how the old man shifted uncomfortably on his unforgiving seat.

'Here, Mr Copp, let me do a few for you.'

It felt good to use his strength, which was not much needed in carrying letters. Swiftly, he broke a small pile of

stones with sharp, rapid blows, and swept them aside to leave
a clear surface for the old man.

'And how's Mrs Copp, my dear?'

'Oh, her's a little stronger. This weather does a soul good,
and us have some vegetables from tilling now. Us is still
alive, so us just has to carry on.'

Edward wished him farewell. He too had often felt life to
be almost unbearably hard, but look at him now! As a
successful author it would not be necessary to find subscribers
before publication of the next volume, and this time Mr Rock
would not make the final decisions on selection. If he was
careful, he could include a little of his more radical work
among the happy poems and songs.

A pair of trotting horses came into view, the sound of their
hoofs echoing along the valley. As they passed him with
tossing heads, the coachman raised his hat to Edward and a
voice called from the open window of the carriage. 'Good
morning, Mr Capern!'

It was Mr Kirkwood from Yeo Vale Mansion. Edward
turned round and waved as the coach turned the corner. 'Good
morning, Sir!'

Yeo Vale was not part of his postal round, yet Mr
Kirkwood knew him! And why not? Throughout the country
people had read the poems and knew the name of Edward
Capern.

He finished delivering to the valley dwellers and started the
long climb to Buckland Brewer, ringing his bell to warn the
farm households of his approach and whistling as he walked.
The tune was one he had been working out on his new flute
and he had some words to go with it, but was not yet happy
with the marriage between the two. He knew that when the
true subject came to him, both lyrics and melody would fall
into place.

It was a glorious day. When he paused to regain his breath,
the view back over the valley to the hills beyond brought

pleasure to his eye and warmth to his heart. Sunlight flashed from the blades of scythes in a distant field where labourers had commenced the hay harvest; skylarks sang high above him. He would never tire of it! He tipped his head back, drinking in the sun's warmth and the caress of the breeze on his cheek, and knew that this, *joy*, was the subject of his song.

His deliveries in the village quickly completed, he looked into the forge to see Joshua Page. He had let his fire burn down for the midday break, and was leaning on his anvil to talk to the gamekeeper from Putford, Ezekiel Leach.

''Tis too fine a day to sit indoors for dinner – I'm off down to the dell!' Edward told them. 'Do 'ee want to come? I've my flute in my pocket and a new song on the way – bring your fiddle, Joshua!'

The two men agreed readily, picked up their dinners and joined him.

Edward put his head round Mrs Ley's door. ''Tis such a beautiful day, I'll have my dinner out today. I'll look in for a cup of tea later!'

The two girls were, as usual, working at their glove-making but Polly's face lit up when she saw him and she jumped up. 'Can me and Ann come? Will us sing songs like last time?'

He regarded her affectionately. 'Of course! Be quick then!'

When walking the lanes, he had discovered the little dell a short distance from the village. It was surrounded by a tangle of shrubs and trees and seemed possessed of an eternal stillness. A bright brook murmured as it found its way between twisted roots and innumerable tall ferns, while sunlight flashed through the interlaced branches forming the roof, giving the place a cool, green and mysterious light. He thought of it as a sylvan palace, and when there alone would not have been surprised to see fairies dancing by the brook or pausing to gaze at themselves in its green-framed mirrors.

The three men strode down the lane together with the two girls following shyly behind. Joshua's loud laugh echoed over the high hedgerows; he found fun in everything and had become one of Edward's closest friends in the village. While he could not be described as bookish, he had a fine ear for music; they enjoyed playing fiddle and flute together while he taught Edward local songs. Ezekiel was less well known to him but his gaze was confident and frank, as befitted one who had enjoyed the freedom of daily contact with nature, and Edward liked him already.

They followed the narrow path to the dell. Edward brushed twigs and dead leaves from a mossy log and indicated to the girls that they should sit down. 'Here's a throne for two princesses!'

The men sat on an adjacent log to eat their dinner and exchange news. Whenever Edward looked up, he caught Polly watching him, but she quickly turned away and pretended to be interested in the fern fronds that Ann was plaiting. Amongst much laughter, he told Joshua and Ezekiel the story of the man who had wanted to walk the round with him but was exhausted before they even reached Hooper's Water.

'He was a strabbly fellow with legs no stronger than a spider's, and when he saw the size of the hill up to Buckland, "Oh," he said, "That looks a dull walk," and later I heard he'd begged a ride home. Next day he limped around the town claiming he'd walked all of twenty miles!'

Ezekiel joined in with a story of a young gentleman who had been knocked right down by the kick of a gun. ''Tis being indoors three parts of the day, you see, that and too much drink and vittles. They've no strength, these gentlefolk!'

Edward chuckled. 'Joshua makes up for ten of them in strength!'

He turned to Polly to share the joke but stopped, arrested by the sight before him. Ann had untied Polly's fair hair so that it lay in waves over her shoulders and breast, and was placing on her head a crown made from the starry white flowers and curling tendrils of bryony. Framed by the sun-dappled bower, Polly looked as beautiful as Titania.

The girls did not at first notice how he stared because they were laughing together, and the laughter made Polly's eyes shine and dimples appear at each side of her full mouth. When finally her eyes met Edward's, she fell silent, holding his gaze for a moment before blushing and looking away.

'Well, no longer the two princesses; 'tis now the Queen of Ferny Dell that I can see!' He kept his voice light and they all laughed; but he felt quite unsettled by her beauty. It was the first time he had realised that she was no longer a young girl, but a twenty-year-old woman.

Joshua asked to hear his new song. Edward sang the lines he had thought of so far, expressing the joy he found in nature. 'But I haven't got all of the chorus yet. *Goodbye to care, for here I feel* – what? *The joy the sun can bring,* perhaps?'

'As happy as a king.'

He looked up in surprise. She was every inch a natural queen, and wasn't he the king? 'Polly, you're right! That's just the line I want!'

He sang the verse again to try it out. When they all joined in, their voices and instruments must surely have been heard up in the village.

After a few more songs, Edward knew he must return if there was to be time for a cup of tea before his long walk home. As Polly started to take the bryony from her hair, he remembered something Jane had told him.

'Be careful now; don't put your hands to your mouth. I've heard the juice from that plant is poisonous. Here, let me help you.'

Joshua stood up. 'I must be off. There's a donkey coming in for shoeing.'

The rest of the party started to walk back along the path, while Edward moved close to Polly and carefully untangled the tendrils of bryony from her hair. She sat very still and he could feel her breath on his wrist. The little white flowers gleamed. It seemed strange that something so beautiful could do harm.

Chapter Nineteen

The next day was overcast. As he walked up the hill to the village, a heavy drizzle arrived with the south-westerly breeze. He barely paused on the two-mile climb and kept his head down, but it was not long before he could feel water running down the back of his neck. Although he regretted the drenching, the rain brought a sense of freshness and growth which was very different from the dismal winter rains, while the swallows skimming above the surface of the road in front of him and diving over the hedgebanks provided further confirmation of summer.

He called out to a labourer hoeing mangolds in an adjoining field, ''Tis good refreshing rain this, amn't it! A blessing to the earth, you can see the new growth emerging, almost!'

The man straightened up, scratching his head through his frayed and misshapen hat. 'More work's all I see.'

Edward wished him a good morning and continued on his way. A poetic temperament was a rare thing in the Devon labourer but nevertheless he felt a close affinity with the men who worked the land.

He tried to concentrate on the lines he was composing. Try as he might, he kept picturing Polly with the flowers in her hair and the way she looked shyly up at him. The memory would not leave him. He had passed a restless night, hating himself for allowing seductive dreams of Polly to disturb his rest while Janie lay innocently beside him. Sitting in the cottage to eat his dinner today would seem banal when compared to the events in the dell yesterday; but it would be best, he felt, to put them out of his mind. He should just be grateful that the occasion had produced a good poem. He was blessed to have as a friend a young woman who possessed both beauty and fine sentiments, but he must try to put all other thoughts of her aside.

In the village, the sun breaking through the diminishing drizzle sent a rainbow arching over the vivid green fields to the south while the call of a cuckoo echoed through the landscape – a rare and special concurrence of events that thrilled him. There were too many subjects for poems! Perhaps, he thought, he would leave that one for someone else's pen.

He left the letters for the outlying hamlets with Martha Withecombe, then started his village deliveries. There was a letter from Canada that would be passed to all members of the Wesleyan chapel, but it must go first to Mr Bartholomew Fulford.

His wife opened the door of the small farmhouse. 'Ah, another letter.' She did not sound very pleased and he looked at her enquiringly.

'Each one that comes makes him more determined that more members of the family must go. I'll just have to get accustomed to it, but it's a wrench. What's a letter compared to having a body around all the day?'

Edward frequently heard similar stories. There were good livings to be had in Canada but it was hard for a family to be divided by an ocean.

Now that the rain had passed, the village women were carrying out their washing again, spreading it on hedges and garden walls to dry. He greeted them all by name and handed out two or three letters. He pushed open the heavy oak door of the Coach and Horses. When his eyes had adjusted to the dim interior, he hailed the two men who were sitting at the bar with their half-pint tankards. 'Where be Mr Lake then? Two letters for him today.'

The two men stared at him gloomily and one of them shook his head. ''Tis a bad old business, Mr Capern. Little Annie's not too viddy, Mrs Lake was up all night with her and they'm fearing for her life.'

Edward was saddened by the news. Annie was a delightful child of nearly a year old who often sat on her sister's lap on the low wall outside the inn. Just two days ago he had coaxed a smile from her. She had been well then. As he stood at the bar, Mr Lake came down the narrow staircase, looking drawn and anxious.

'How's the little chiel, Mr Lake?'

He shook his head and could not reply. They walked out together and stood outside the door until he could find his voice. 'Her's struggling for breath, poor little maid. It cuts me in two to see her suffer so. Look at that!' He gestured at the thatched roof where a robin perched on the apex. 'Hear that? "Weeep, weeep," all the time; 'e's been doing that since yesterday. '*E* knows what's gwain to happen and cries for it! Us don't hold out much hope.'

Edward felt a chill run through him. The robin was quite motionless, uttering a plaintive little whistle which it repeated three or four times a minute. He knew of the local superstition that a robin weeping on the roof or wall of a cottage was a sure sign that a young child in the dwelling would die.

He put his hand on the innkeeper's shoulder. 'You mustn't believe that old story. How could the bird know of it? She'll rally, you'll see. When they'm little, they come up as fast as they went down.'

Mr Lake's voice shook a little. ''Tis against sense, but I've known any number of cases when it's been proven. The birds just seem to know somehow. The dog too; 'e was howling in the night.' He sighed. 'I must go back inside, though there's little enough I can do.'

'I'll ask my wife tonight if her can send something; her's very knowledgeable with children's ailments.'

Mr Lake closed the inn door behind him. Edward stood in the road, looking up at the robin on the roof. From the small open window under the thatch, he could hear the baby crying and her mother's soothing tones. The robin held its head on one side and uttered its sad cry again. Edward walked slowly to Mrs Ley's cottage for his dinner.

He glanced at Polly as he went in. She was wearing her usual grey dress but had a bright blue ribbon at her neck which emphasised the colour of her eyes. He noticed that she concentrated hard on her sewing while Ann chattered about the fine time they had in the dell yesterday.

He started to tell them about little Annie Lake, but they had already heard the news.

'I've often known it to be true that the robin knows what's coming,' said Grace. 'It was so when Clara Squire died, and little John Harris.'

Polly looked up from the silk glove she was sewing. ''Tis just an old story, Mother, surely. I don't believe in it and I'm sure educated folks don't.' She met Edward's eyes. 'There's always robins about and folks shouldn't read meaning into it when there's none there.'

'Well, us'll hope you'm right, Polly,' said Grace. 'I s'll pray for the poor little chiel.' She turned to Edward. 'Is it tonight you'm going out to dinner with the gentlemen, Mr Capern?'

He had been invited to dine with Dr Pridham and there was to be another doctor present who took an interest in head size and brain development. Edward had explained the theory to the Leys.

Ann looked up, bright-eyed. 'Will he measure your head tonight? 'Tis large as heads go, so maybe that's why you'm so clever!'

He laughed. 'I don't know that he will, but I shan't mind as long as he *does* think me clever!'

He finished his dinner then worked on the poem he had started on his way home yesterday, although it might have been wiser to set it aside. He did not, on this occasion, share his work with Polly. If she knew of the feelings that had been aroused in him as a result of the episode in the dell, he suspected he would be tempted into deeper waters.

He was careful not to meet her eyes when he left.

As he walked out on to the village street to blow his horn, he noticed a small group of people standing outside the Coach and Horses. With a sense of dread in the pit of his stomach, he went along to speak to the women staring up at the window.

Mrs Parkhouse turned to him as he approached. 'Look – 'tis over, poor little maid.'

A white sheet had been hung at the window, a sure sign that a death had occurred. 'But you hear the robin singing? 'Tis singing for joy because her's with the angels now.'

He stared in wonder at the robin, which was indeed singing its quietly joyful little song on the inn roof, an entirely different sound from the sad notes it had been uttering since the child had fallen ill.

That evening, he changed into his Sunday suit, and as Jane brushed him down and straightened his cravat, he kissed the top of her head.

'I wish you could put on your best dress and come along with me; I could walk in with 'ee on my arm, the most handsome couple there!' Wasn't that what wealthy people did? He would have felt so proud to have his Janie walk in with him.

She studied him doubtfully. 'I don't know that I'd want to go even if I'd been invited. Will other wives be there?'

'No, probably not. Maybe Mrs Pridham. Dr Pridham wants to introduce me to his friends, especially the phrenology doctor I told you about. Because he found so many subscribers for my book, he feels rather proud of its success, I think. I hope the food won't be too fancy.'

'Will there be cakes, Daddy? Will you bring us some?'

Milly heard her brother and jumped up and down with excitement. 'Cakes! Bring us cakes, Daddy!'

He picked up both children, whirled them around and kissed their soft faces. They laughed at his ticklish whiskers so he kissed them again, then Milly a third time because she looked so like her mother. 'If there are cakes, I promise I'll bring you some!'

Dr Pridham's house was hidden amongst trees at the end of Potter's Lane. He had been there once before when the doctor was seeking subscribers for the poems. He had been very helpful in that regard, although rather distant in his manner. He rarely looked at Edward as he talked, or asked his opinion, but perhaps tonight would be different. As he walked up the long drive, he wondered at his good fortune at being invited to meet gentlemen on equal terms. They would all be educated men so he hoped to be able to converse about the books he had been reading and perhaps be given recommendations. His friends at the Mechanics' Institute had even less access to books than he did himself; few were interested in poetry, so opportunities for discussion were limited.

A maidservant opened the door and showed him into the drawing room. He held his head high as he walked in. There were four gentlemen in the room; Dr Pridham immediately stepped forward and put his hand on Edward's arm.

'Now, this is the man I have been telling you about, gentlemen, and a most interesting case for you, Mr Rumball. He has met with remarkable success for someone of his background, largely due to my efforts. He was brought up in Tiverton where his father was a poor baker and was sent to work in a factory there at a very young age.'

'No, Sir, that's...'

Dr Pridham carried on regardless. The three men standing with wine glasses in their hands stared at him curiously.

'However, he had been taught to read and write by some old woman and he pursued his studies despite many privations. After trying a number of low occupations, he eventually became a humble letter carrier, an occupation he pursues to this day, which he claims gives him the time and inspiration for writing poetry. The remarkable thing is, gentlemen, there really is some merit to be found in the poems and that is not merely my opinion; reviewers up and down the land have agreed that the achievement is noteworthy for a working man.'

All three murmured their approval while Edward tried to look intelligent and composed. He did not know whether he should speak; Dr Pridham did not seem to expect him to do so. Was he to be a mere exhibit?

'Now gentlemen, I believe dinner is served, so if you would come this way?'

When Edward stepped back to let them go first, there was a crash behind him then he found to his dismay that he had knocked over a small table, a tall, spindly object that seemed to serve no useful purpose. He apologised and picked the thing up, relieved that there had not been an ornament on it, as there was on every other available surface in the room. One of the men raised his eyebrows in a sardonic manner as he passed. Edward followed, feeling hot and uncomfortable. He wished he could remove his jacket.

The silverware and cut-glass on the long table glittered in the light of the candelabras. Edward accepted a small glass of wine, watching surreptitiously to see which of the spoons arranged next to his plate he should use first. Soup was not the easiest thing to eat quietly but he knew what Jane would have said to him and he did his best. The talk was mostly of medical matters that would have been difficult to follow even if Latin had not been so frequently used. The little he did understand made him feel queasy; Dr Pridham was the coroner for Bideford and the details of his work did not seem a suitable subject for the dinner table, even if there were no ladies present. The situation was not improved by the pea soup being a most bilious colour.

During a lull in the conversation, he gathered his courage and spoke to the man opposite. 'Have 'ee had the opportunity to read any of my poems? I know Dr Pridham has a copy.'

The man looked rather surprised and looked over his glasses at Edward as if he had only just noticed him. 'Poems? No – no I can't say I have.'

'But you like poetry, no doubt? Have you read much Milton?'

'Good God, Milton? Not since my schooldays.' And he turned to his neighbour. 'I was most interested, Mr Rumball, in your claim that phrenology can prove moral insanity in murderers. Do you really believe that pardons should be given on such grounds? Should not our prisons then fall empty and our madhouses be full?'

Mr Rumball was the only guest whose name Edward knew. He wished he had been introduced to the other two, but it was clear that they were also medical men. It seemed he was not expected to take part in the conversation, so he tried to enjoy the food. The third course was roast ducks but he felt he would sooner have had Jane's potato and bacon stew. Ducks were fiddling things to eat. Dessert was announced next, which proved to be gooseberry pudding and was very nice indeed. It was served with some small biscuits which he managed to slip into his pocket to take home for Charlie and Milly, confident that he would not be observed. No one was showing the slightest interest in him.

After this the gentlemen pushed their chairs back and relaxed. Edward declined the offer of port, the earlier glass of wine having already made him somewhat light-headed, but had to suffer the smoke from others' cigars. Dr Pridham proposed a toast to the railway which had enabled his friends to pay him a visit; no one noticed that Edward had not even a glass of water to allow him to join in. He wished the evening was over. The speed of the witty responses and the loud laughter were making him dizzy, and the smile he maintained in order to look interested made his jaw ache.

He realised Dr Pridham was looking at him.

'Now then, Mr Rumball, are you ready to examine our subject's head? Do you not think there is a resemblance to Oliver Goldsmith? We'll be most interested to hear whether there is such a thing in nature as a poet's skull!'

Without so much as a 'by your leave', Mr Rumball came to stand behind Edward and started to feel his head. The sensation of the hands running over him was disconcerting, while being stared at by the other men did not make the situation easier. He felt compelled to say something. 'I hope you won't tell me I'm insane!'

'I think that's not likely,' Mr Rumball replied seriously. 'Well, gentlemen, this is a most interesting case. The areas of veneration and consciousness that you see here,' he prodded the top of Edward's head, 'are unusually well-developed, and benevolence and ideality – here, you see – are also strong. There are distinct bulges in those areas. Cautiousness is weak which suggests that impulsivity may be a problem, but that can give rise to self-determination which may be useful in a man born with few material advantages. It is a most interesting head. Mr Pridham, see whether you identify the areas I have indicated.'

One by one the men came and prodded his head while Edward sat in silent discomfort. Not one addressed a remark to him. Finally he could take no more. 'Perhaps I might take my turn now and examine your heads! I'm sure mine must be black and blue from being poked and prodded.'

'I think not,' replied Mr Rumball, 'the skull is most resilient. It would have been interesting, gentlemen, if you had told me nothing of this person. I think you can see now that I would have identified him correctly without prior knowledge.'

They went on to talk on other subjects. After a few minutes, Edward had had enough and stood up.

'I have to make an early start in the morning in order to earn a living. I wish you goodnight.'

Dr Pridham rang for the maid to show him out.

Once out on the driveway, his anger rose. They had made a fool of him! As for imagining that he was being invited as an equal – nothing could be further from the truth. He had been an entertainment for them, no better than a freak at a fair. He picked up a stone from the verge then stared at the house with its large lit windows. How satisfying it would be to break the glass that sheltered those four doctors and shock them out of their complacency! As he stood on the drive battling with his resentment, an owl called from amongst the trees, a soft wavering plea that intensified the deep silence when it ceased, then came again, thrilling him with its otherworldliness. The owl knew more about poetry than all those doctors put together. What use was violence? It would not change them. He lobbed the stone harmlessly into the bushes and turned for home.

Jane opened the door of the top-floor room and sighed. As usual the table was covered with drifts of paper, books were left open on the chair and piled up on the floor. The bed in the corner where Edward's now frequent visitors slept was rumpled and untidy. He would have a meeting in here tonight; she ought to get the room ready now while he was minding the shop before going to work; there would not be another chance.

She put down the broom and stacked the books on the shelf in the corner. It was becoming a proper library and she felt quite proud of it, although she wished Edward would keep it tidy. More books arrived every week; some were volumes sent by friends with whom he corresponded, others were bought from Mr Honey in Grenville Street. Edward was not slow to spend their increased income so she had recently persuaded him to keep to a weekly limit. He had even talked of giving up the postal round to become a full-time author, until she sat down and showed him the sums.

He had returned from Dr Pridham's in a bad mood last night and came up here to read his reviews again. Instead of cheering him, they had depressed him further.

'I'd only taken in the good parts when I read them first!' he had declared, brandishing a paper in her direction. 'Listen to this! "*He is but a humble postman of Devon.*" "*Here is an untutored rustic.*" "*Mr Capern has a heart, though he is only a postman.*" They're making fun of me, that's all!'

Jane had done her best to reassure him and had read the good parts of the reviews to him. 'Edward, no; listen. "*Here is an untutored rustic, with ear so ex-, exquisitely attuned to*

melody, that he produces rhymes equal in harmony to" –
what's that word?'

'Metastasio. He was an Italian poet, I think.'

'Well, there you are then! You have to read all of it! They
are good and I'm very proud of you.'

He had cheered up eventually, but had left the papers
scattered all around the room. She sorted the newspapers into
a pile and picked up his notebook which was open on the page
he was working on. She glanced down before closing it.

'Sweeter, richer is the bliss
Awakened by her kiss.
If I am her slave to be,
Welcome, sweet captivity.'

She felt a coldness in the pit of her stomach. She sat down and
read some more.

'Can the eddy in the stream
Brighter than thy dimples gleam?'

The poem wasn't about her. She didn't have dimples. But, *a
kiss*? He had always admired pretty girls, but she had never
imagined he would be disloyal to her. She read the poem
again.

She could guess for whom it was written and her anger
deepened. He often talked about the hours that he spent in
Buckland Brewer in the middle of the day and the warm,
maternal welcome he received from Grace Ley, of whom Jane
had become quite fond although they had never met. And he
talked about Grace's family. And Polly.

Jane had started to feel that she heard Polly's name too
often. Polly liked his new poem. Polly had made wonderful
progress with her handwriting. Polly thought of the perfect
word to complete the verse. But s*he* could not think of words
to help him. She had to clean his house and scrub his clothes
and cook his dinner; she had to run the shop, look after the
children, mend the clothes, trim bonnets and interview
servants. *She* hadn't got time to sit around smiling at his
poems and, even if she had, she didn't have dimples.

She had never seen Polly, but now images came to her of Edward smiling down at a pretty, blue-eyed girl, his gaze warmed by the knowledge that her youthful body was undamaged by childbirth.

She slammed the notebook shut and hid it under a pile of books, knowing he would want to take it to work with him. Suddenly everything was changed. She stared angrily around the room. Quickly she ran a damp cloth over all the surfaces, polished the windows and swept the floor, banging the broom against the walls.

Edward was serving a customer. She stood just inside the kitchen where he would not notice her. Milly was standing on a chair next to him so that she could scoop tea on to the scales, and her tongue poked out between her lips as she concentrated. That morning, Jane had tied red ribbons in Milly's dark hair to match the red braid on her grey dress; her innocent beauty and Edward's tender concern for her made Jane want to cry. They had been so happy since the success of his book, but all that was spoiled. Now that he was so well-known, would lots of girls admire him and let him kiss them? What importance did *she* have, now?

Edward found the coins for Milly to give to the customer in change. 'And now what must 'ee say to Mrs Waldron, Milly?'

Milly turned her face coyly towards her father rather than address the woman directly. 'Good morning Mrs Waldron and thank 'oo for your custom.'

The shop door closed. Jane had to face him. She could not carry this knowledge all day. He smiled indulgently as she came in. 'Did 'ee hear how clever Milly was? Weren't you, maid?' He picked her up. 'You'll serve customers all on your own before long. But her'll have to start school soon, Janie.'

'Edward, I've read your poem.'

She hated her voice sounding cold and hard, quite unlike his, which was warm and loving.

'Which poem, my flower?' He brushed the spilt leaves from the counter and replaced the box of tea on the shelf.

Liz Shakespeare

'Your latest. It's about Polly, isn't it.' It wasn't a question.

Milly started to dance across the floor, singing 'Polly, dolly, dolly, Polly.'

Jane couldn't bear for her to hear them argue. 'Milly, fetch Mama's cloth from upstairs. Quickly!'

Edward had turned away, carefully straightening the boxes of sugar and rice on the shelf, as if they needed to be at precise right angles. He usually replaced them haphazardly.

'Edward, tell me!' Her hands were shaking.

He fussed with the coins in the drawer. He couldn't meet her eyes. 'It's only a trivial little thing. I may not finish it.'

She struggled to speak. She did not want to cry. 'You kissed her!'

'Janie.' He came to her and put his arms around her so that he looked over her shoulder rather than into her eyes, and she felt herself to be rigid with anger. 'It was nothing. Just a moment's affection. She's a girl! She means nothing to me.'

She pushed him away. 'Well, that's not the way it sounds in the poem!'

Milly came carefully down the stairs with the cloth in her hand.

'Janie, I have to go to work. Come now, give me a kiss.'

She hardly knew whether she wanted to cling to him or push him away. 'And is that what you'm going to say to her too?'

'No.' He held her face in his hands and looked into her eyes. 'Of course not. I'll be having my dinner in the cottage and her mother and sister will be there.'

Was that the only thing stopping him? She did not know how to reply.

After Edward had left without finding his notebook, she fetched it from upstairs and put it in the cash drawer so that she could look at it between serving customers, when she should have been sewing. She searched for hidden references to Polly. There were poems to Ruth and Kate and Patty Rowe but he had shared their stories with her, tales of love between young people he met in the countryside. Although she knew he enjoyed talking to the girls, she had rarely felt threatened by his admiration for them.

Polly was different. Polly was clever. She was in his company every day. Although she had an admirer, Jesse Gay, Jane knew she showed no interest in him – and why should she? She preferred Edward.

Jane could hardly bear to look at him at suppertime. She snapped at him when he asked a question and busied herself with talking to the children, being extra attentive to the details of Charlie's day at school. Later in the evening, when she heard him coming downstairs from his meeting, she kept her head down as if she was concentrating on her sewing. She couldn't exchange pleasantries as if nothing had happened; but he acted as if there was nothing untoward, telling her about the amusing intrigues at the meeting and humming to himself as he glanced through the newspaper. She felt a tight knot of anger inside, hating herself for it. Polly wouldn't be like this. Polly would join in with his laughter and be affectionate and amusing. When he started to sing under his breath, she could hold back no longer.

'Did 'ee speak to her today?'

'Who?' He looked at her innocently, as if he didn't know what she was talking about. She could not look at him, or say Polly's name.

'Oh, Janie. Of course I spoke to her, how could I not? I was in the cottage for at least two hours.'

He came and knelt beside her. She reluctantly let him take her sewing away and hold both her hands in his.

'Janie, you'm my wife! No one's as important to me – you'm the whole world to me!' He pulled her closer and his familiar warmth and proximity released her tears at last.

'Promise me you'll never cheat on me, promise! Please, Edward!'

He drew her on to his lap and she realised that he was tearful too as he swore that he would never be disloyal.

'I couldn't live without you, Janie; please, don't be cold to me anymore. I want us to be loving and happy again, like us used to be with one another.'

Slowly her anger fell away and she relaxed into the warmth of his embrace. His anxious brown eyes shifted their attention from her mouth, to her eyes, and back again. Then she leaned forward and kissed him, rubbing her chin back and forth on his soft beard. He stroked her hair and his warm, melodious voice soothed her. 'I'll never stop loving you, Janie.'

Eventually they spoke of other things: Milly's schooling, Charlie's behaviour, the need to order more stock for the shop, until they were relaxed in each other's company again. When she grew tired and went up to bed, Edward promised to follow soon after.

The next morning after he had left for work, Jane found a paper on the kitchen table. It was a poem. Puzzled, she sat down to read. The title was *Why So Very Jealous Grown?*

So, that was it. *She* was a daisy, but you are a rose. She was a little star, but you are the sun.

> She was water, thou art wine,
> She was human, thou divine.

She sat back in the chair and felt anguish constrict her throat once more. She didn't know whether to laugh or cry.

Chapter Twenty

Walking up the hill to the village, Edward caught up with a heavy, lumbering cart piled with wooden poles, rolled sheets of canvas and wicker baskets. It was driven by a man in rough clothing with a large pheasant feather in his hat, while next to him sat his female companion in a mob cap and a thick yellow shawl to protect her from the chill November air. It was a struggle for the unkempt bay horse to pull the cart up the steep hill, so Edward was soon able to walk alongside and then overtake it.

He removed his hat with a flourish. 'Good morning! Come far?'

'Barnstaple,' came the laconic reply.

'Most will be set up already, I'd not be surprised.'

'Ah, I know it. Mebbe they habn't such a master long way to come.'

It was the day of the fair and great market in Buckland Brewer. Preparations had been well underway when Edward left the village the previous day; livestock pens had been erected in the fair field, and the pedlars and itinerant traders who had already arrived would have spent the night in their carts, or in village barns for the fee of a penny or two. This morning he had already been overtaken by a farmer's boy driving half a dozen sheep, another with a couple of heifers, a pedlar leading a packhorse laden with jars of miraculous cures and potions, and groups of high-spirited young men and women who had been granted a holiday to attend the fair. He knew that the roads from Torrington and Stibb Cross would be equally busy.

'Good luck with your trading!' He overtook the cart and strode on up the hill, humming in time to the rhythm of his footsteps. Although he had to work, the day felt as much a holiday to him as it did to everyone else, because the village was transformed by the twice-yearly fairs.

He swung his bag to the other side to ease his aching shoulder and his humming changed to whistling. He had cause enough to be happy. The Prime Minister had praised his poem *The Lion Flag of England* and sent copies printed on broadsheets to soldiers serving overseas. The Postmaster General, impressed by the success of one of his most humble employees, had promised Edward relief from Sunday working and an increase in pay from ten shillings and sixpence a week to thirteen shillings! Both he and Jane had been overwhelmed by the news. At last they would be able to go to chapel as a family, to eat Sunday dinner together, to walk out into the country, he and Jane and the children together, at last. And he was to be paid more for the privilege! He could barely believe his good fortune.

Today, Polly's cousin was to take the return mail to Bideford so that Edward could stay on in the village with Joshua Page and others who played musical instruments. They were to set up a tent on the green, and play while members of the Temperance Society served tea and cordials to tempt people away from the stalls selling ale and cider. The fairs always led to events that some people, led on by the availability of strong drink and the presence of unprincipled strangers, had cause to regret.

Arriving in the village, he found the roadside lined with horses and carts, pedlars' goods laid out on cloths, and village women who hoped to make a few shillings from their home-baked pies and pasties. Martha Withecombe was waiting for him outside the postal office, impatient to start the deliveries to the outlying hamlets. She had grown into a rather plump girl with an open, trusting face; he liked to tease her so he could hear her deep, infectious laugh.

'What, Martha, not at the fair yet?'

She looked indignant. 'How can I afore you give me the letters – I have to do my work first! Quick now, hand them over! I'm already in my best clothes to save time later.'

'Mind you don't get pushed in a ditch then, maid; the roads is packed with folk!'

''Twon't be me as gets pushed in a ditch!'

He watched her fondly as she hurried off. He had a handful of letters for the village; and he chuckled at the first, which was addressed to 'My dear aunt Mary what lives tother side of the road to the Coach and Horses.'

His deliveries finished, he went to the fair field where the serious business of the day was almost finished; only three or four inferior horses and a few scrawny sheep were yet to be sold, watched over by huddles of farmers who liked nothing better than criticising their neighbours' stock.

Most people had moved from the livestock area to the stalls and tents set up alongside. Edward exchanged cheerful greetings with people every few yards as he strolled through the crowd to find something to take home for the children. He passed by a tent selling crudely made wooden toys, and stopped at another to buy gingerbread and two lollipops. Women flocked around a stall selling printed cottons, so he pushed through to investigate. He would have liked to buy something for Jane but she would have a better choice in Bideford, and he did not know whether the prices were competitive, despite the persuasive tones of the pedlar.

'Come on ladies, you wouldn't see better if you went to London town!'

The village woman murmured appreciatively to each other; they rarely, if ever, went to Bideford or Torrington and knew no one who had been to London.

He felt a soft hand on his arm and turned to see Polly, her eyes bright with excitement. 'I didn't know you were here so soon! Have 'ee seen them pretty prints? I be going to ask Mother if I can buy a length.'

He looked at the display, then back at Polly. 'See that blue there? That would suit you.'

She held his gaze, and he could not look away. 'If 'ee think so, then that's the one I want. I'll be back soon.'

She disappeared into the crowd.

He walked on. Since June, he had been careful not to spend time alone with her, much as he would have liked to. He did not want to do anything to upset Jane, and tried to ignore the little voice telling him that she need not know. In the cottage, however, he and Polly had fallen back into their easy companionship as he read his poems to her and taught her his songs. It was a particular pleasure to sing together. He guessed that her feelings for him were the reason for her lack of interest in village boys and although the knowledge flattered him, it also made him rather uneasy. As he wandered through the crowd, he could not prevent his gaze from seeking her out.

There was a greater range of goods than in previous years; knives and other sharp-edged tools from Sheffield, glassware from Nottingham, cheese, claimed to be 'the best in England', from Cheddar in Somerset. It was the arrival of the railway in Bideford that had made such trade possible.

He was attracted by an infectious tune ringing out from a barrel organ. The uniformed man turning the handle was accompanied by a monkey with a little, pinched, human face. Edward stood amongst the village children staring in awe at the animal which, in turn, scrutinised them nervously and uttered a little chittering noise from time to time.

'What do 'ee think of that, then, William?' he asked the small boy next to him.

The child was silent for a moment or two, before asking fearfully, ''Zit a man?'

Edward laughed and pointed out the long tail, but in truth he was himself rather unsettled by the creature.

Suddenly, Polly was at his side. 'Look. I bought the blue, like you said.' She opened the paper bag to show him. Someone in the crowd pushed him up against her, and when he inadvertently put his hand on her waist to regain his balance, he felt her move closer to him. He detected a warm smell of cloves and soap. Reluctantly, he stepped back.

'Have 'ee seen the hoop-la?' She looked up at him as she spoke. They had not stood so close since the time in the dell. 'There's wonderful prizes you can win. Will 'ee help me?'

Imaginings flashed before him: he and Polly strolling arm in arm across the field, her hip brushing up against him and her soft voice in his ear; his expertise in winning her a prize and her grateful, loving glance; a walk in the woods together, away from prying eyes; Polly, pliant and willing, in his arms.

At that moment a familiar voice called to him from across the field. 'Edward! There you be!'

Joshua strode towards him, grinning. Being broad-shouldered and a head higher than those around him, the crowd parted readily to allow the blacksmith through. He clapped Edward on the shoulder.

'All right, boy? I be going to try the target shooting; come on with me and us'll see what us can win!'

Edward had no interest in shooting, but he agreed readily. As they headed for the booth, he turned to see Polly trailing after them.

Amongst the group of men alternately cheering and jeering at the efforts of the participants, Edward recognised the fashionably-dressed young man as Thomas Tedrake, a photographic artist who had recently arrived in Bideford. As the first photographer in the town, he was creating quite a stir. He had attended the Mechanics' Institute to offer his services as a speaker, and seemed to have opinions on many subjects despite coming from a poor background.

'Edward! Might have known I'd see you here!' He shook hands.

'Be 'ee here to pursue your trade?' Edward asked. 'Mind, not many in this village could afford to have their likeness taken.'

Thomas had a charming smile. 'No, 'tisn't a working day for me today, but I like to get to know the locality, especially when there's fun to be had!' As he spoke, he seemed to be constantly looking out for people he knew, or would like to know.

Edward took his turn at shooting but found it an awkward and dissatisfying experience and missed the targets altogether. Joshua had more luck, winning an orange after hitting the target three times.

'That be a present for my Ann,' he said, putting it in his pocket. 'Now, must be time for us to set up with our instruments – there's John come to join us.'

As they set off for the village green, Edward turned to see Thomas Tedrake talking to Polly.

The musicians were a mixed bunch. Joshua was the most accomplished fiddle player. William and John had been church musicians until the installation of an organ made them redundant, but both were now rather deaf and didn't always notice when their fiddles were out of tune. Frederick played his grandfather's bass viol which he had found in the attic and Edward found it easier to play the flute on his own than keep up with the group. Despite their shortcomings, an audience soon appeared because it was not often that the villagers had the opportunity to listen to music.

After the slower tunes, as Edward sang his song, 'The Old Grey Thrush', he noticed feet tapping and people clapping in time. Outsiders were strolling over from the fair field and several people pointed him out to their friends.

'That's Mr Capern.' 'There's the postman poet!'

He began to relax and enjoy himself.

After a break for tea, which was much appreciated by those who had been drinking ale all afternoon, they played reels and hornpipes. Men unbuttoned their waistcoats and women removed their bonnets as the dancing commenced, and when the sun disappeared behind the hill, someone lit a lantern to illuminate the musicians.

Edward tried to keep up with the tempo, as he peered out at the couples galloping hand-in-hand along the row of stamping, grinning dancers. It occurred to him that the intention of luring people away from the ale stalls, while successful, had been achieved too late; many people had already had too much to drink before joining in and the dancing was becoming even more frenetic than was usual at village teas and weddings. Two cheerful-looking women in brightly-coloured dresses, strangers to the village who had run a stall selling cheap trinkets, were much in demand as dancing partners. Their return journey would not be possible until the carrier's cart came the next day; Edward imagined he was not the only one who wondered where they would be spending the night. Several other strangers were dancing with village girls, including the owner of the shooting range who was whirling around with a laughing Martha Withecombe, his hand closer to her breast than her waist. Then Edward saw Thomas Tedrake dancing with Polly. She was allowing herself to be spun around but looked uncomfortable, and kept glancing over at Edward.

He tried to concentrate on his playing, but after a few more tunes he leaned over to Joshua. 'Think us should call it a day, boy.'

'Yes, they'm enjoying theirselves a mite too much now. 'Tis us as will get the blame!'

By the time they had put away their instruments and helped take down the tent, there was a steady procession of carts passing down the road as traders and folk from outlying areas made their way home, some facing a long journey by lantern light. Small groups remained on the darkened green laughing and talking loudly, while two lovers embraced against the churchyard wall. One of the strangers was staggering and flinging his arms about as he told an amusing story, and Edward saw he still held a tankard of ale in his hand. Neither Polly nor Thomas was anywhere to be seen. He knew he should start the long walk home but decided he would first call in at Mrs Ley's cottage.

Ann was sitting in the candle-lit kitchen with her parents, but Polly had not yet returned.

'Oh, her'll be out gossiping with her friends!' said Mrs Ley confidently. Ann's expression told him that she had an inkling of her sister's whereabouts, but she remained silent. After a brief discussion of the day's successes, Edward made his farewells as if to return home, but instead he turned the other way and walked along the village street. Murmurings and dark laughter emanated from the drangways between cottages where silence usually reigned. Where was Polly? He could discern singing and laughter from within the thick cob walls of the Coach and Horses, where many of the drinkers from the fair would have gravitated. He listened for a moment or two before retracing his steps and turning down towards Gorwood.

The darkness in the deep lane was intense; he had to follow the line of silhouetted hedgerow trees to avoid stepping into a ditch. After passing a couple of labourers' cottages, he heard low voices then a girl's laugh from the other side of the hedge. A dry, dark night was an advantage for lovers, and although it was November the air was not cold. Edward had fond memories of walks with Jane after darkness but on this occasion he felt uneasy. The presence of strangers in the village created risks for the local girls, and he hardly knew for whom he should feel sympathy. He paused, listening carefully. That was not Polly's laugh.

He had only walked a little further when he heard footsteps coming in his direction, the quick, short steps of a woman in a hurry, then the slight figure was almost upon him, walking fast with the swish of a skirt and the shadow of a bonnet.

'Polly!'

She let out a little scream and jumped back. 'Don't touch me!'

'Polly! 'Tis me, Edward! Be 'ee all right?'

'Oh!' He could not see her face but she was breathing heavily. Something was wrong. She started walking away and he followed her. 'Let me take your arm. 'Tis very dark.'

'No! I'm all right.'

He caught up with her and they walked silently side by side until they reached the main street.

'Were you on your own?' he asked quietly.

She stopped and stared at him. The sky shed a little more light here, and he saw that she was pale and her eyes wide and frightened.

''Tis nothing to do with you.' She turned and walked quickly towards her home.

It was a long walk back to Bideford. He was tired, too tired to think of phrases to describe the things he saw and heard; the immense night sky, the low swoop and call of an owl, the scream of a rabbit. He tried to relive the pleasure of singing while people pointed him out and said his name, but the thrill had gone.

When he crossed the River Yeo, the murmur of the water told him that he should be glad if Polly had found a lover, but he was not glad. As he climbed the hill out of the valley he asked himself what sort of lover Thomas Tedrake was to frighten such a delightful girl; and as he walked through the silent hamlet of Littleham he indulged in a wild imagining in which he arrived on a white horse, like the knight in the old story, to rescue Polly and take her safely home. But he knew that he had not helped. He had not helped her at all.

Chapter Twenty-One

Jane grated some more flakes of soap into the bowl of grey water, grasped the laundry stick in both hands and stirred the heavy fabric around. It was a mystery to her how Edward's clothes got quite so dirty; he must surely sit in the mud to write his poems.

Ever since she got out of bed at five o'clock, she had been fetching and heating water, lifting, stirring and wringing and now rain was starting to fall. Yet another wet washday!

'Charlie, put your boots on *now*, please, and fetch me some more water like I told 'ee.'

'Can't. I'll be late for school.'

Her irritation grew. He was becoming more difficult and rude by the day. 'Charlie, go *now*. Your father will be back in a moment – what do 'ee think he'd say if he heard you talking to me like that?'

Edward came in at that moment. 'Do as Mother says, there's a good boy.'

Charlie walked to the door but made a rude face behind his father's back. Jane gritted her teeth as she wrung the soapy water from the clothes and dunked them in the rinsing water.

'Five today!' Edward was as excited as a child by the letters that arrived for him each day. He fetched them from the post office early so that he could open them before returning to sort the mail for his round, claiming that he could not wait until he had finished work.

'Who are they from, Daddy?'

Jane's mood lightened a little as she watched Milly climb on to her father's knee.

'Can I open one?'

'The knife's too sharp, chiel, but you can pass them to me one by one.'

Jane lifted the washing to let the clear water stream through while she watched Milly proudly holding out the letters. It was a relief to see her looking alert and interested again; the 'flu had laid her and Edward low for nearly two weeks. He had returned to work a few days ago despite having little strength, knowing that they could not sustain the loss of earnings any longer.

She twisted a shirt until the water ceased to run from it, shook it out and draped it over the back of a chair. She had not told Edward that she had been unable to pay for the last delivery of dry goods.

She carried the heavy bowl of rinsing water through the shop, tipped it into the outside drain and straightened up to ease her back. Charlie dawdled into view, kicking a stone along the street and slopping water from the bucket on to his unlaced boots at every step. She resisted the impulse to shout at him.

Edward had already opened two of his letters. 'There's one from my friend Mr Mortimer in Braunton and one from a lady in Sussex who thinks my poems "touching." Next one, Milly!'

Jane leaned on the table to watch.

'This one is from –' he turned the envelope sideways to read the return address, 'Miss Burdett-Coutts, London.'

'And who's she, when her's at home?' He had rather too many letters from unmarried ladies for Jane's taste.

'I don't know, maid. Let's see.'

He opened the letter and two pound notes fell out.

'What's that!' Jane exclaimed. 'Does her want you to send some books?' She waited impatiently while he read the letter.

'She says she's sorry to hear that I've been unwell and she hopes the enclosed will go some way towards making up the lost earnings…'

'It'll do more than that!'

'…and she says Mr Charles Dickens has assured her that I'm worthy of support – Mr Dickens!'

'What, Mr Dickens the author?' Edward had read each instalment of *Oliver Twist* to her.

'Yes! This might be something to do with Mr Rock – he knew I was ill. And, she says she may be able to be of help to me and wants to know whether I plan to write more poems.'

'Well, you've nearly finished your next book! But who is she?'

Edward promised to ask any gentlemen he met on his round whether they had heard of Miss Burdett-Coutts. He handed the notes to Jane. They would pay for the previous shop order, and the next one.

It was still raining when Edward left Buckland Brewer. His coat and trousers were almost dry after two hours next to the fire. Mrs Ley had been most concerned that he should not fall ill again so had given him a pair of her husband's trousers to wear while his own pair dried.

He nodded to Martha Withecombe who was standing on the village street deep in conversation with Delicia Veal. He would like to have talked to Martha but it did not seem fitting. Both young women were heavily pregnant. A few months after last November's fair, three unmarried girls admitted that they were expecting; the perpetrators of their condition could not be found. The occasional village girl giving birth out of wedlock was not unusual but three at the same time was extraordinary. It would not be Catherine Cole's first child, but the other two girls were young, and had been innocent. Edward rarely heard Martha's infectious laugh now. Her mother would help to bring up the child, but it was less likely now that Martha would ever marry.

Polly had remained stony-faced when the news broke. Edward could not help wondering how close she had come to being the fourth victim. He knew Thomas Tedrake had called to see her from time to time but, as far as he could tell, she took no pleasure in his visits.

The rain became heavier before he was halfway down the hill and the road seemed to stretch endlessly in front of him. Since he had been ill, every step was an effort so that he feared his health might break down completely. He had seen it happen so often: a serious illness, and within weeks the entire family could be in the workhouse. At least he and Jane had their annuity to fall back on, but if they drew on it now, there would not be enough left for old age. Might the day come when he could turn his back on this work and earn his living as a full-time author? He was still receiving a small income from sales of his first book and had almost enough poems for the second volume; but it was impossible to know whether it would be successful and, in any case, it would not provide a steady income.

He paused in a gateway to look out across the newly-planted field. She was still there. This morning he had noticed a small girl wandering barefoot over the dark-red soil, singing a little song to herself which she alternated with a loud clatter from the bird-scarer she held in her hand.

He called out to her. 'What, still here then, chiel?'

She looked up in surprise, her reverie disturbed, and picked her way over the muddy ground towards him. He saw that her hair, which seemed from a distance to curl prettily around her face, was matted and her dress torn and dirty. Rain dripped from the battered brim of her hat on to the sack which was tied across her shoulders. She squinted up at him curiously.

''Tis a long day for you, chiel. How old are you?'

She had lost her front teeth, causing her to lisp.

'I be six.' She pushed her bare toes into the mud below the gatepost, still humming her little tune. She seemed unfazed by her long hours of solitude, although just a year older than Milly.

'And what time do you go home, my flower?'

She looked at him curiously. 'When 'tis dark, 'course. Else the rooks will come. Will it be dark soon?'

Poor little mite. 'Not just yet, chiel. Will 'ee sing your song for me?'

She sang a couple of rounds in a sweet, high voice:
'Here, clapping every day,
I scare the robber-rook away.'
And she finished with a little skip and a shake of the bird-scarer to provide the loud rattling chorus. When he gave her an apple that he had in his pocket, she snatched it before he could change his mind. He walked off down the hill and, looking back, saw that she was standing behind the barred gate, staring after him.

She would probably never go to school or learn to read. She was destined for a life of rough work because she would lack even the skills needed by poorly paid glove-makers. His Milly, although only five, could already read well, sew nicely and had fine manners. She could pass for a lady one day; she might even marry a wealthy man. Most importantly, she had enough to eat and a happy home. Perhaps a poem about the little scarecrow girl would help to make those in power aware of the evils of child labour. He was determined to include some more radical poems in his next collection but he had to be very careful not to offend his readers. He intended to write a careful Preface to make his intentions clear.

He had been planning a very long poem about Hubba the Dane, a ghostly story that had come to him after reading Coleridge's *The Ancient Mariner*, but friends with whom he was corresponding thought he should produce another book of the short poems and songs that people loved. He had already amassed a collection of the lyrics that tripped so easily from his tongue, and it was difficult to find the time or concentration for a longer, more complex work. There was his newspaper column to write each week as well as numerous letters.

He paused to listen to an old grey thrush singing loudly and joyfully from the top of the mountain ash alongside the drive to Orleigh Court. Truly, the thrush was the king of the wood. When he first became a postman, he had been struck by how frequently the labourers and young women he met on his rounds launched into song when resting from arduous tasks. He was amazed, however, that his own songs should prove so popular. Recently he had sung a new lyric to two or three people in Bideford; within a week, while passing along a lane near Buckland, he was startled to hear a voice on the far side of the high hedge singing his song! He stopped to listen to the words interspersed with the chop, chop of a shovel being used to clear a ditch, and when the verse came to an end he called out. 'Hallo there! What's that you'm singing, boy?'

The disembodied voice replied, 'I dunno the name of it, Sir, but William over at Bearah teached it me.'

His spirit soared to know that his melody was being passed so quickly around the countryside. He was known as a song-man now; he had recently been asked to sing at a wedding and also at a sheep-shearing party. The artist Mr William Widgery had asked him to pose for a portrait, his post-bag on his shoulder and his pencil in his hand. The handsome painting that resulted was hung in the window of Bideford Post Office for all the world to see. He had never dreamed that he would be important enough to have his portrait painted, but now was able to admire himself every morning when he arrived for work. How he loved his life!

As he climbed the old cart track towards Littleham in the steady drizzle, he had to pause to regain his breath, something he rarely did before he was ill. From the gate where he rested he could see on the far horizon the towers of four village churches, reminding him that he must ask the rector of Littleham if he knew the name of Miss Burdett-Coutts. None of the gentlemen in Landcross or Buckland had been at home to ask. Whoever she was, she seemed a very kind lady.

There was a letter addressed to 'my dear Father in Littleham, at the white cottage with a green gate,' which he delivered successfully. Two letters were brought out when he blew his horn, and there was a bundle of post as usual for the Rectory.

He was now far too wet from the incessant rain to be invited into the Rector's study, but when the housemaid opened the front door, the Reverend Harding was passing across the hallway.

'You wish to ask me something? Here, come in and stand on the mat.'

The rector was a rather forbidding man with a distant manner. Edward cleared his throat. 'Sorry to trouble you, Sir, but I've received a letter from a Miss Burdett-Coutts in London. She says she may be of help to me. Do 'ee know who she is?'

The Reverend Harding looked over his glasses at Edward. 'Miss Burdett-Coutts? I don't know her personally of course, but everyone knows her name!'

'Well, I didn't, Sir! Is she important then?'

'Important? She's the richest woman in England! Did you say *you* have received a letter from her?' He spoke as if Edward had been most impertinent by daring to claim such a thing.

'Yes, Sir. And she sent me two pounds because I've been ill! And she says she can help me some more. Why would she do such a thing?'

The Rector looked impressed. 'How extraordinary! But I have heard that she is most generous with her money. She inherited a half-share in Coutts' Bank but is apparently more interested in supporting worthy causes than indulging in a lavish lifestyle. She opened a home for fallen women with Charles Dickens, and follows his advice on matters of charity. She also supports the Temperance Society and provides decent housing for poor people who are prepared to work hard – indeed I have heard her called "The Queen of the Poor." But how did she come to hear of *you*?'

'I don't know, Sir. Perhaps Mr Rock may have spoken to Mr Dickens, or the Prime Minister may have told her about me. Did you know that he has read my poems, Sir?'

'Well, Mr Capern, you are a very fortunate man!'

Edward completed the two mile walk home along Littleham's muddy byways in record time. He could hardly wait to tell Jane. The richest woman in England!

As summer passed into autumn, several more letters were exchanged. Edward told Miss Coutts of his plans for the new book and, in response to her encouraging remarks and enquiries, described his humble home, Milly's pretty singing voice and Charlie's good progress at school. Whenever one of the gentlemen on his round passed on an old copy of *The Times*, he searched for references to Miss Coutts and was rarely disappointed; she had provided a lifeboat for Margate; she was visiting a new library for which she was a benefactor: she allowed a young suicidal girl with a criminal record into her reformatory in London. Each time a letter arrived with her address on the back, he was filled with anticipation – but quite what it was he hoped for, he could not say.

Jane ran her finger down the columns of her account book. She knew exactly how much money Mrs Prust owed, but she always wrote the figures down anyway so there could be no argument.

'Mrs Prust, it's up to four shillings and threepence already. You did tell me you would be able to pay off a shilling this week.'

Mrs Prust looked like a little mouse seeking a means of escape. She could not meet Jane's eyes. 'I know; I know I did. I'm sorry, I really am, but he went to the Ring of Bells again last night and took the money I'd minded to give you. And as I said, I thought if I could just have a twist of tea for the children...' She shifted her grizzling baby on to her other shoulder. He was her seventh and a sickly-looking child.

Jane sighed. She felt so sorry for Mrs Prust. Her husband occasionally did some farm work but they lived mostly on the rent from some land he owned at Hartland. His income would have been adequate if he did not drink, but he did and it did not agree with him; Edward had intervened on more than one occasion when he heard screams coming from the house, and once Mrs Prust banged on the shop door in the middle of the night, in fear of her life. Edward said that they were not even married in the eyes of the law, as the first Mrs Prust had run off to America where she had supposedly died, but then she reappeared in Bideford after his second marriage.

Jane looked down at the figures again. 'I'm sorry, but I really can't let you have any more. But I'll *give* you a little tea of my own. I can't say fairer than that. And next time, bring the money straight in to me before your husband takes it.'

Mrs Prust thanked her over and over before scuttling away. Jane had pleaded with Edward to try to do something for the poor woman. He had spoken to Mr Prust on a number of occasions about coming along to the meetings of the Temperance Society or the Mechanics' Institute, but to no avail.

She went over to her work table where she was working on a wedding bonnet for a young woman in Landcross. She had used a new design, with a high front brim decorated on the inside with white lace flowers. Her gaze drifted again to Edward's letters lying next to her box of pins on the table. He had left early this morning, so his personal letters had been delivered here in the normal way. He would be pleased to see the one from his brother Thomas in America, but more important was the one on top of the pile. It was from Miss Burdett-Coutts.

This was the fourth letter they had received. She was still amazed and thrilled that someone so important should ask after the health of Jane Capern and seem genuinely interested in the children. Miss Coutts had even said that she was sure that Jane was a very talented milliner. What would she have to say in this latest letter?

Just as she completed the last lace flower, Charlie and Milly burst into the shop and she jumped up to greet them.

School was still new for Milly, and Jane spent much of the day wondering how she was managing.

When Edward came in he opened the letter straightaway, standing there in the shop with his coat and hat still on, while Jane waited eagerly to hear what Miss Coutts had written. She watched as he carefully slit the envelope open and started to read. His smile faded, and he frowned.

'Edward, what's the matter?'

'I can't...' He looked up at her in amazement, then down at the letter again. 'Have I got it wrong?'

'Edward! Read it to me!'

He read slowly, trying to make sense of the words. '*It has become my pleasant duty to forward you the enclosed letter. Lord Palmerston, having heard me express the pleasure I had derived from reading your poems and the interest I felt in your history, has most kindly given me the privilege of transmitting to you and your family His Lordship's intention to transfer an annuity of £40 for you from the Civil List.*'

They stared at each other, stunned. Jane could not take it in. 'Forty pounds?'

Edward had gone quite pale. 'The Civil List. Can it mean... You remember I told you about the pensions some authors are given? Can it be that? Look, there's more, there's a letter from the Prime Minister.'

He read it out. Surely there was a mistake? 'You must have got it wrong, Edward! The Prime Minister's not going to give us forty pounds! Why would he do that?'

Edward had tears in his eyes. 'Yes, forty pounds, but not just that, chiel, a Civil List Pension, forty pounds a year, every year! That's what it says here! And, listen, Miss Burdett-Coutts says, "*It will gratify you to learn that the favour is wholly unsolicited and springs from Lord Palmerston's own thoughts*". And I'm to write to him, she gives me his address. It must be because of *The Lion Flag of England* – we know he liked that! Janie! Janie!'

He was crying openly now, and she started to weep too as they held each other tightly, there in the shop. But she still couldn't believe it. 'Forty pounds *every* year? For ever?' That was more than Edward earned as a postman!

'Janie, it's such an honour! Mr Wordsworth had a Civil List Pension! And Lord Byron! And Mr Tennyson has one, and now me!'

'Edward, sit down! Come on.' She was afraid he might faint; indeed, she felt very shaky herself. They need never worry about money again! They already had the annuity for old age, but this was to start now.

She took Edward's hands in hers as the tears ran down his dear face. She had always been proud that he was so different from other men, so clever with words, so kind and loving, but she had never dreamt when they married that he would meet with this level of success. How could she? She had never known that a poor working man could be so fortunate.

'Edward, we must tell Charlie and Milly!'

They called upstairs to the children who came running down, but stopped in confusion when they saw their parents crying. Edward held out his hands to them. 'Come here, my little chickens, Daddy's not sad, these are tears of joy! That kind lady, Miss Coutts, has sent Daddy such good news!'

It was a day Jane would remember all her life.

Chapter Twenty-Two

Edward saw the train waiting on the platform as he turned to hurry his family along. If his calculations were correct, they had ten minutes to spare, but he had waited so long for this day, he would happily have boarded the train several hours earlier.

'Quickly, come on! See the engine there, Charlie?' It was a pleasure to see the smile on his son's face.

'Can us look at the engine first, Father? Before us gets on?'

He glanced at Jane because he knew she was anxious to get settled into a compartment, but she nodded to him, 'Just a quick look then.'

As the children stared wide-eyed at the handsome black engine, it hissed gently as if to demonstrate its tremendous, yet entirely benevolent, reined-in power. Edward had confidence that it would carry them safely. 'See the piston there? Do 'ee mind what I told you of its workings? And there's the whistle; here Milly, I'll lift you so you can see.'

They found an empty compartment and the children rushed in to sit next to the window. After much deliberation, he and Jane had decided to buy second-class tickets, because they were concerned that the children might develop chills if they made such a long journey in a third-class compartment with no glass at the windows.

Jane sat nervously on the edge of her seat and he leaned forward to take her hand. 'Don't 'ee worry, my flower, you'll like it when us starts.'

She met his eyes affectionately, giving his hand a little squeeze in reply.

He had travelled by train as far as Barnstaple on two previous occasions, but this was the first trip for the rest of the

family and a huge adventure. London! He had thought he
would never be able to go to London.

The idea had taken root when the Prime Minister informed
him of the Civil List Pension. He wrote to him, of course, and
to Miss Burdett-Coutts, thanking them in the warmest terms,
but he also expressed his desire to visit and show his gratitude
in person. When his publisher suggested he might visit Fleet
Street to discuss the final selection and layout of his new
poems, he determined that the whole family should go to the
capital.

Milly was bouncing up and down on the hard wooden
bench, the ringlets that Jane had so carefully fashioned each
side of her centre parting in danger of springing out of shape.
'When is us *going*?'

'Soon, chiel; hush now and sit still. Show dolly the view
from the window.'

Milly obeyed solemnly and proceeded to engage the doll
in conversation, while Jane enumerated the contents of the
newly-made canvas bag in case Edward could think of
anything they might have forgotten. They were already
wearing their new clothes so there was not too much to carry.

The guard suddenly blew his whistle, and the children let
out cries of astonishment and pleasure as they felt the train
begin to move and the rhythmic puffing of the engine
gathered pace. Edward leaned back to observe the reactions of
his family; it was pure pleasure for him to see Jane's face
light up as it used to when she was a young woman, and to
watch the children's excitement, knowing that it was his
achievements that had made it all possible.

Although he had been on a train before, the sensation of
such rapid movement was still extraordinary and the children
looked astonished, holding tight to the seat as the carriage
jolted. Eventually Milly started to giggle as she bounced and
swayed in an exaggerated fashion, her laughter so infectious
that they all had to join in.

''Tis as well us has the compartment to ourselves because
there'd be no peace for other folks!'

He pointed out Cleave on the far side of the river, where he used to deliver letters on his first postal round. There had been no trains, then. 'Don't forget, my beauties, you mustn't fix your gaze on things as us is speeding along; you don't want to injure your eyes.'

'Can't us look out the window then?' asked Charlie.

'Yes you can, my lover, but you must let your gaze travel with the speed of the train so that your eyes aren't strained.'

Jane had heard that the speed might affect their digestion, but Edward had enquired and was told that this should not be a problem providing they avoided rich food.

Appledore came into view with its merchants' houses along the waterfront and rows of white cottages gleaming in the May sunshine. He pointed out the ships moored alongside the Quay and the fishing boats heading out over the Bar. 'Don't it look pretty and tranquil with the tide high and the sky so blue?'

He should perhaps be writing a poem about the journey, or about the River Torridge in all its moods. Its banks were now strewn with daisies as if it wore 'a frock of Whitsun-white.' Before he had time to think of any further lines the engine shrieked, making them all jump and laugh, before it puffed to a standstill alongside the Instow platform.

The journey took on a new and exciting aspect once they passed Barnstaple and he could look out at a wholly unfamiliar landscape. The Taw valley was truly beautiful, but as he gazed out at the river winding through water meadows bright with yellow iris, he could not help feeling that its serenity had been destroyed by the heavy throb of the engine, its fierce scream, the dust and the smoke. The railway was a great invention which had revolutionised the nation, but he preferred corners of the countryside that were beyond the sound of the engine's whistle, and soft green hills that had not been violated by tunnel-builders.

When the ticket collector came into the compartment, Edward told him their news. 'Us is going to meet the Prime Minister and have tea with the richest woman in England!'

The man looked at him dubiously. 'Are you now!'

'Yes, 'tis true! Seems unlikely, I know, for a working man like me but 'tis all because of the poems I write, see.'

Once the initial excitement of the journey had died down, he was able to enjoy the company of Jane and the children without thoughts of work. Although they now spent Sundays together, Jane always had the dinner to cook and mending to be done, so it was delightful to have her sitting opposite him, looking so pretty in her new clothes and bonnet and so willing to talk and laugh with him.

In the months since they received the news of his Civil List Pension, Edward had been much occupied with writing letters, attending meetings and giving lectures, including two talks on working-class poets, a subject close to his heart. Now that he was, in effect, paid to be a literary figure, he felt he should prove that he was earning his money; but he and Jane had snatched a few moments now and then to talk about their future. At first he had imagined he might give up his postal round, but Jane had pointed out that they would not then feel the benefit of the extra money. He would in any case miss many aspects of the work although he was beginning to find the long walk rather irksome, especially since he had put on some weight. He hoped that in time the Post Office might grant him an allowance for a horse and cart, as was sometimes the case for longer rounds.

'I would like a bigger house with a garden for growing flowers and vegetables,' Jane had said. They agreed they would both be happy to give up the shop in order to have more free time in the early mornings and evenings, and the loss of income would not be great. Jane would carry on with her millinery in a reduced way but did not need to be in the town centre now that she was well-known, so the new house could be on the outskirts of the town.

It was exhilarating to talk through these plans again, with the countryside flashing past the window of the cosy compartment, as if they were speeding towards a better, happier future.

'I think us should wait until the right house comes up,' Jane said, 'there's no rush. But perhaps us'll run down the shop stock anyway.'

Charlie was listening keenly. 'Can I have a room to myself in the new house?'

Milly sprung up and climbed on to his lap. 'Daddy, can I have a kitten? Please, Daddy!'

She snuggled up to Edward as he smoothed her hair and kissed her soft cheek.

'The answer's "yes" to you both! A room for you, Charlie, so you can do your work in peace without this little minx chattering to you, and a kitten for Milly! What shall it be, a little grey kitten with blue eyes? A pretty tabby?'

There was always something of interest to see from the window of the train; red-and-white cows quite unlike those in Devon, an open plain without hedges or fences, a cluster of children waving from a bridge or the excitement of drawing into a station. They ate the dinner Jane had packed and drank a bottle of cold tea between them. Edward checked his timetable and the platform clock at every station. 'Only three-quarters of an hour to go now!'

Jane laughed at him. 'You'm more excited than the children!'

He would not have known how they should get about in London or where they should sleep, but Mr Rock had, as usual, been most helpful. He had explained that the Prime Minister and Miss Coutts lived within a short distance of each other on Piccadilly, so recommended a hotel in the same street which would be suitable for families. They were to travel from Waterloo Station by hackney carriage which, he said, would be preferable to the cheaper, overcrowded omnibuses.

Edward smiled at Jane. 'Did 'ee ever think us'd stay in a hotel?' And then, as a sudden thought came to him, 'Have 'ee got the money safe?'

When she nodded and patted her lap, he remembered that she had made a special purse which she wore under her new hooped skirt. He gave her an arch look but she frowned and told him to behave himself.

Eventually the railway tracks converged with others and the train passed the backs of grimy terraced houses, row after row of them, and grey-faced railway workers who stood back to let the train pass. The sun had disappeared behind thick cloud. Could this be London? It was not as grand as he expected, and he began to feel a sense of foreboding.

When the train drew in to Waterloo Station and he opened the door of the carriage, the noise was tremendous: the slamming of doors, trundling of trolleys, panting of engines and shouting of porters combined to form a cacophony that almost deafened him. He helped Jane and the children down from the train and they huddled together as people pushed purposefully past. The air was thick with steam and dust but when he looked up, hoping for a view of the sky, he could only make out a high roof.

He held Milly in his arms; Charlie and Jane stood very close to him and he knew they were feeling as anxious as he was himself. 'Now, my chickens, this way.'

He had no idea which way to go, so followed the crowd along the platform. When they reached a large hallway, the crush was even worse. People pushed past from left and right, porters made their way with trunks held high on their shoulders and new arrivals were greeted by waiting groups; ladies, gentlemen and poor working people were mixed together without discrimination. Milly clung to him tightly and Jane took his arm. 'Edward! Whatever shall us do now!'

He did not know what to reply. He had never in his life seen so many people and had no idea how to find a cab – what madness it was to come to London!

'Daddy, where's the horsie that'll take us to the hotel?' Milly whispered in his ear.

''Tis here somewhere, chiel. Us'll find it soon.'

He tried to address passing strangers but was ignored, until eventually a porter paused. 'Cab? Out there, mate!' He gestured vaguely and was gone.

Edward summoned his courage and they set off, keeping as close to each other as they could while they were jostled this way and that. After a short distance he could see through the crowd to a high archway, and passing underneath they found themselves on the street. He stopped in astonishment. The chaos here was just as great! Hansom cabs, curricles, carriages and handcarts wove in and out to the accompaniment of shouting and cracking of whips, while people on foot took their lives in their hands as they ran between the carriages to reach the far side of the road. People clambered up ladders to reach the top of dangerously overloaded omnibuses, and a woman screamed when a spirited horse drawing an open landau shied and was only controlled with difficulty. It was a few minutes before he realised that there was a line of carriages drawn up alongside the pavement a short distance away.

'Look, Janie, they must be the cabs!'

The first few were hansom cabs drawn by a single horse and suitable for only two people, but a little further along was a larger two-horse carriage. This must be one of the Clarences to which Mr Rock had referred.

The first driver he approached waved his hand vaguely, looking away when Edward asked for Hatchett's Hotel, but the second climbed down and opened the carriage door. 'One and sixpence, Sir. Up from the country, are yer? Do yer want me to point out the sights?' The accent was unfamiliar so Edward had to ask him twice to repeat what he said.

His relief was intense as they settled into the cab. They were safe. They would soon be in their hotel. Charlie, who had been unusually quiet, let out a big sigh. 'No wonder the French were defeated at Waterloo, I thought us would *never* get out!'

Soon they were trotting along a main thoroughfare and the driver leaned towards their open window. 'Westminster Bridge now, Sir!'

'Oh my!' Edward remembered Wordsworth's poem and looked out. The river, although remarkable for being at least twice as wide as the Torridge, had dubious-looking rubbish floating in its dirty grey water, and the stench from it soon drifted up to their open window. It was very disappointing. 'Mr Wordsworth said "Earth has not anything to show more fair." Whatever was he thinking!'

But the driver called out again. ''Ouses of Parliament and Big Ben ahead, Sir.'

Now, this was more like it! The building was bigger than a dozen churches put together and Edward was very impressed by the intricacy of the stonework towers and pinnacles and the thousands of small windows. And Big Ben! A grander clock there surely never was. They all took turns to lean out to admire the prospect, and he looked back at it until the cab turned a corner and the sight was lost to him.

''Oss Guards on yer left, was the 'ome of the Duke of Wellington.' Edward was beginning to comprehend the accent now and translated for the others. Trafalgar Square was quite as grand as he wished, then they passed along Pall Mall which caused Milly, who already found 'Piccadilly' amusing, to wonder why streets in London had such silly names.

''Ere y' are, 'atchett's 'otel.'

Edward climbed out and helped his family down on to the pavement.

'That'll be two shillings.'

'But you said one shilling and sixpence!' He had the money ready in his hand.

'I've showed you the sights along the way, Sir. Two shillings. Can't say fairer than that.'

Edward was shocked; he knew from Mr Rock's instructions that they had travelled by the most direct route, and he had thought the driver had named the buildings from the goodness of his heart. He reluctantly handed the money over. 'Well, 'tis not the way us treats folk in Devon, that's all I can say.'

He felt better when a kind man welcomed them into the hotel, made a fuss of the children and showed them to a comfortable room. Jane examined the beds for bugs before she would let them anywhere near, but when they were pronounced clean, he sat down with relief. The hotel was exactly the right place for him, because it used to be the starting-point for all the mail coaches heading for the south-west. They were to eat downstairs in the dining-room, so there was no need to go out again until their important engagements the next day. What a day it would be! He doubted whether he would sleep.

Jane woke just before dawn. A little pale light was finding its way through the dark-red curtains, and she could hear a low rumble. She propped herself on one elbow to look over at the children's bed; Charlie had his arm around Milly and they were fast asleep. She eased herself out of bed and tiptoed over to the window. The noise from passing traffic had kept her awake for an hour or more last night but the street had gradually fallen silent apart from the occasional shouted altercation and, once, the sound of galloping horses as a carriage was driven past at a high speed. She pulled the curtain aside. The room was on the third floor and she was again taken aback to see how far it was to the ground, and how far to the grandiose buildings across the wide street.

Now she could see the source of the rumbling sound. A large market cart piled high with cabbages and potatoes toiled slowly along with creaking axles. Both the horse pulling the cart and the man who walked alongside looked as if they were half asleep; it could not be after four o'clock. As soon as the cart passed, another came into view, this one carrying cabbages and carrots; and then a third, until they formed a steady procession. The men accompanying them had a rustic look, at odds with the appearance of most London people, and Jane guessed that they must be bringing their wares in from the country to one of the big markets.

She went back to bed but slept fitfully, being filled with anticipation of the day to come. It was fully light when Edward and the children started to stir, and she drew the curtain aside again. There were now many people on foot hurrying along the pavements, mostly young women in neat black dresses, shop-girls perhaps, and carriages and omnibuses bringing people into the city centre. She heard a clock strike seven. It was time they made themselves ready.

When they had breakfasted, it was still too early for Edward's appointment. He was to meet the Prime Minister at eleven while she walked in the park with the children, then they were all to take tea with Miss Burdett-Coutts at three. Jane was glad she did not have to meet the Prime Minister, but it did not seem to worry Edward at all.

News of his Civil List Pension had appeared in every newspaper in England plus one or two in America, and had resulted in a stream of visitors. People now realised that they could reach Bideford by train to visit the scenes described in Mr Kingsley's book and could meet the famous Postman Poet at the same time.

At first she worried about the visitors. Edward didn't have the manners of gentlefolk. *They* spoke in quiet, measured tones, rarely displaying their emotions; but Edward beamed at everyone, clapped the gentlemen on the shoulder, held the ladies' hands, spoke volubly and laughed loudly. However, she soon realised that they were charmed by him, especially when he recited his poems and sang his songs for them. Visitors sometimes accompanied him on his postal round, although most turned back after a few miles, while some became friends and exchanged many letters with him. Others wrote articles in newspapers praising his 'frank, open countenance', his 'broad, manly bearing', and remarking that he was admired by rich and poor alike. This resulted in yet more visitors. She would be glad when they had a new house with a parlour so that she wasn't constantly interrupted in the kitchen.

It was fortunate, in any case, that Edward had become so used to meeting people.

'Tell me again what you're going to say to Lord Palmerston.'

They were sitting in the hotel foyer. Charlie and Milly were trying to do as they had been told and not bounce on the deep leather sofas, while Edward, very smart in the new suit she had made for him, was looking out of the window and springing up every time he saw something of interest.

'Edward, sit down, do. You will mind you'm going to tell him what a difference the pension has made to us, won't 'ee?' She brushed some dust from his trouser leg.

'Of course, my bird.' He took her hand. 'I'll tell him that he has given an already happy family a secure future and I'll promise that to earn my pension, I'll never stop writing poems.'

Jane felt so proud of him. She wished she could be there, not to meet Lord Palmerston but to watch from a distance.

'Now, look at the time!' Edward jumped up. 'Us must go!

They held tight to the children's hands as they walked along Piccadilly's crowded pavements to Green Park. The shop fronts seemed to be made entirely of glass, and some were lit by dazzling gas-jets. By contrast, the pavements were very dirty though Jane was more shocked by the state of the road, which was a couple of inches deep in mud and horse-dung mixed with every sort of imaginable filth, so that pedestrians had to walk close to the buildings to avoid the muck thrown up by horses' hoofs and carriage wheels.

Edward would have to cross the road. 'Edward, you can't walk through that! You'll tread mud into the Prime Minister's carpets!'

Edward peered up and down the street. 'Look, people are crossing over there!'

They walked a little further and saw that a dirty, barefoot boy was sweeping the mud away to create a clear passage across the road. He paid no attention at all to the horses and carriages; some stopped for him and others almost ran him down. Jane noticed that people using the crossing handed him a coin for his labours

'Here, you must go. Good luck!' She gave Edward a farthing for the boy and he set off across the road, turning to wave when he safely reached the other side. The Prime Minister's home, Cambridge House, was a very grand building set back from the street; Jane saw a man in uniform speak to Edward before letting him through the gate into the forecourt. She looked down at the children. They were watching wide-eyed as their father disappeared into the imposing edifice.

She took a deep breath. 'Come on, us'll go in the park and Daddy'll come and find us when he's finished.'

Green Park had lawns stretching almost as far as she could see, interspersed with avenues of tall trees. Ladies and gentlemen strolled along the paths. She hurried after Charlie and Milly who were racing towards the first tree.

A man carrying a tin can came along the path towards her, shouting something at the top of his voice. She could not make out the words at first, but as he passed she was able to see into the can and then his words made sense.

'Pies all 'ot! Eel, beef or mutton pies! Penny pies, all 'ot!'

Charlie was calling Milly away from a muddy area so she would not dirty her clothes. He had been such a good boy since they had been away.

A group of men in fashionable clothes stood talking and laughing loudly in a haze of blue cigar smoke. One of them, who had one foot on a bench, wore trousers so tight it was a wonder he could get them on. As she wandered along the avenue, two young ladies simpered towards them and appeared to strike up a conversation; one pointed her toe delicately as she talked, revealing an ankle. When the other one moved very close to one of the men, he laughed and put his arm around her waist. They all seem to know each other very well. As she got closer, Jane saw that their dresses were very low-cut and their faces were painted. Suddenly realising what they were, she turned and walked quickly away and called to the children to come with her, but when at a safe distance she continued to watch them.

It was quite a relief to see Edward striding through the park gates; the children ran to him and she wasn't far behind.

'Daddy, Daddy!' Milly flung herself into his arms and he whirled her around with her petticoats flying.

'Edward! Did 'ee see him? Did it go well?'

Edward was beaming. 'It was wonderful, Janie, he is such a nice man! I thanked him the way I'd planned but he said no, he must thank *me* for giving him heart and hope during one of England's greatest trials, and for raising the spirits of the soldiers. He liked all my poems, he said! He had wanted to give me a bigger pension but £40 was all he had left at his disposal, but he said I was to remind him to increase it at a later date. I recited *The Lass of Watertown* for him and described the Devon lanes with their flowers and birds and he said he'd like to visit one day. So then I sang *The Old-Fashioned Plough* to remind him of the hard-working men of Devon. At the end he joined in the chorus – that made all the servants smile!'

'*All* the servants? Were there many in the room with you? Was it very grand?'

'Oh, any number of them, footmen and I don't know what else. And grand! I never thought to see such a place Janie, a veritable palace, chandeliers the size of a house and the floors so shiny, you'd think they was glass.

'We talked seriously as well. I told him I supported him one hundred per cent in his fight for the abolition of slavery and we agreed it to be a very great evil. I told him I have written a poem about it. And in the end he told me he thought I must be a very good postman and he would like his letters to arrive with a song such as mine!'

There was more excitement to come in the afternoon. Jane felt very apprehensive as they walked along Piccadilly again and turned into Stratton Street. It was a narrower street and the buildings were so high, there was little sky to see.

'Here we are, number one,' said Edward. He hesitated at the bottom of the steps. Jane guessed he was feeling that it was presumptuous to ring the bell of such a very grand house.

She took the children's hands. 'Now, don't forget, you must sit very still and good and only speak if you'm asked a question. And don't touch *anything*. Promise?' She straightened Milly's bonnet.

Charlie was craning his neck to see to the roof. 'Seven floors! Can us go to the top, do 'ee think?'

'No, that'll be bedrooms and suchlike up there,' Edward replied, 'though why she needs so many, I don't know. Right, us is going in!' He marched up the steps and pulled the bell.

A maid in a smart uniform showed them through a very large entrance hall and into a light, airy drawing-room. 'Mr and Mrs Edward Capern, Ma'am.'

There she was! Jane curtseyed and from the corner of her eye saw Milly give a sweet curtsey of her own, while Edward and Charles bowed. So, that had gone as planned.

'Come now, no need for that! We meet as friends. Come and sit down with me, and Lucy will bring the tea. Now, tell me, how was your journey?'

Jane found herself sitting with the children on a chesterfield upholstered in gold. So this was Miss Coutts, the lady who had transformed their lives! As Edward described their journey, Jane took the opportunity to study her. She sat very upright in her chair and was very thin, too thin – surely she had enough to eat! And her complexion was not good. But her manner was direct and unassuming and there was kindness in her eyes.

'And how do you like London? It is exciting for Charles and Amelia, no doubt!'

She had remembered their names! Jane found she was not too nervous to speak. 'Yes Ma'am, thank you, it is very busy but us – we – had a walk in the park this morning.'

'I would like to have asked you to my estate in Highgate. It is just outside London but I thought the travelling might be difficult for you. It has a very lovely garden in which the children could have played. I prefer it there because London is so very dirty and the smog in winter is atrocious.'

She had a clear silvery voice and was rather younger than Jane had expected, perhaps in her forties, so only a few years older than Edward and herself. She was wearing a dress which was simply styled but of the highest quality embroidered silk, with some fine old lace at the neck. *She* did not go in for very wide crinolines. The room, however, was much fancier; everything was decorated in gold and white and the curtains were silk brocade. A huge vase of exotic-looking flowers stood in the middle of a polished table.

Edward was starting his carefully prepared speech. 'Ma'am, we have come across the country but we would willingly have come across the whole world for the opportunity to thank you for your kindness.'

Miss Coutts raised her hand to stop him.

'No, Ma'am, excuse me, but I must have my say. You have increased the happiness of our little home and I promise that you shall never regret the kindness that you have shown to me and my family. It is because of you that the anxieties that often kept Jane and I awake are gone, and because of you that our children need never go hungry. I thank you, Ma'am, from the bottom of my heart.'

He was close to tears, while Miss Coutts looked quite uncomfortable, so it was a relief when two maids arrived with the tea.

'Now then!' Miss Coutts clapped her hands. 'We have a special little table at which the children may sit to eat their tea because I thought it might be difficult for them to balance plates on their laps.'

Charlie let out a whispered 'Jove!' when he saw the stand of iced cakes but Miss Coutts just smiled kindly.

The time passed very quickly. When Jane joined in with the conversation about the Poor Law and Miss Coutts' plans to build decent houses for poor working people, she found it almost as easy as talking with an old friend. There was much laughter between them and Miss Coutts included Charlie and Milly in the conversation when she could. After the tea-things were cleared away, Milly stood up and sang *Come List*

My Love while Edward accompanied her on his flute, and then, after Miss Coutts requested another, he sang *The Old Gray Thrush*. Jane noticed that when she was not speaking she looked quite dejected, especially when she was looking at the children. It was sad that she had never married. Edward had heard that she had any number of suitors but she believed them to be interested only in her money.

'There is one more favour I would like to ask you,' Edward said when he had finished his song. 'I know you'm not enamoured of being in the public eye but I would like very much to dedicate my new book to you. It's a book of simple ballads such as I have sung to you today and it'd do me the greatest honour if you would allow me to do so.'

She was almost pretty when she smiled. 'Of course you may! But only if you promise to write to me if you ever find yourself in any kind of trouble. I'm sure you know I would be pleased to help if it is within my capabilities.'

The next day Edward set off to meet his publisher. He was walking with Jane and the children as far as Piccadilly Circus, but there was somewhere he wanted to visit on the way.

'Here it is!'

Hatchards was said to be the best bookshop in the country. He could feel his heart thumping as he pushed open the door, and once inside he held up his hand to his family. 'Wait, now. Just look!'

The atmosphere was hushed. It would not have felt right to stride in thoughtlessly, just as one would not rush up to the altar in a church. He stood and breathed in the delicious scent of leather and paper while his gaze drifted over the oak shelves that stretched from the floor right up to the ceiling. On every inch of every shelf were books. There were ladders to reach the highest books and a staircase leading to an upper floor where, no doubt, there were yet more books. There must be tens of thousands. And in every book were words; words of love, words of great wisdom, lyricism and intellect. He could happily have spent a week in here.

'May I help you, Sir?' An assistant in a dark suit had approached. Edward intended to buy Mr Longfellow's new book, but there was something he wanted to do first.

'Would you show me the poetry books?'

Holding Milly and Charlie by the hand, he followed the assistant to the back of the shop, then he ran his finger along the shelf until he reached the letter C; Campbell, Campion – and there it was! *Poems* by Edward Capern. It was a proud moment.

He left Jane and the children in Piccadilly Circus, where they were to visit Swan and Edgar's emporium, and he took an omnibus. The experience of riding on the top deck was exhilarating, but he thought twenty-five passengers far too many for two horses. He alighted in Fleet Street – the source of the printed word! He stood at the door of number 86 to relish the moment. Inside this building were the hills and woodlands of North Devon, the beauty of the Yeo valley, the song of the thrush and the cottages of Landcross, and all described in his words.

Mr Kent was warm in his welcome but keen to settle down to business. The shelves in his office were piled high with manuscripts which drew Edward's eye; he would like very much to have looked through them.

'There are just two poems I would advise you to omit,' Mr Kent was saying, 'here, you see, and here. I feel they are not up to standard. Rather than have you work on them further, I would advise instead including the six poems we added to the second edition of *Poems* which can then revert to its original size for its third edition.'

'Third edition? You'm going to reprint *Poems* a third time?'

'Indeed; they are still selling well and I envisage a resurgence of interest after this new book.'

Edward stood up and shook Mr Kent's hand. 'Thank 'ee Sir, thank 'ee for having such confidence in my work. I shall endeavour to do you proud.'

Mr Kent smiled. 'You do realise, do you not, Mr Capern, how fortunate you are? You have talent but you also have some very good friends, and the success of your first book was due in no small part to the extraordinary list of subscribers Mr Rock and others managed to acquire for you. These manuscripts you see around me have been written by men who desire the sort of success you enjoy, but the vast majority of them will never be printed. Of those that are printed, most – especially those by self-educated men such as yourself – will sink without trace, leaving their authors embittered and despondent. Many, having glimpsed the possibility of a more fulfilling life, turn to drink when they fail. I see it every day and it is a hard business.'

It was chastening to hear such stories. How would he feel if this next book was not a success? 'Do 'ee think, Mr Kent, that the public'll accept such poems as *The Old Stone-Breaker*? Mr Rock advised me to leave it out of the first book.'

'I think there is no harm in it. Reports of your warm personality and the perceived romance of your occupation have captured the public imagination. I think your readers will excuse you being a little outspoken in one or two poems.'

'I don't want them to excuse it, I want them to listen!'

Mr Kent sat back in his chair and stroked his beard. 'Mr Rock's advice was good. Be careful. You have written a Preface for this new book, I think, which makes reference to this subject. Let me see that now.'

Edward took the paper from his pocket. 'This is what I've written.

"I have sought that no word of mine should tend to provoke class jealousies; and, whilst singing of the sorrows and the trials of the poor, I have never forgotten how many there are who, prosperous themselves, sympathise with such sorrows as much as I."

'I've also written that I know readers will judge the poet this time, not the postman, and that they must understand that these are simple rhymes that country folk like to sing. Will they be expecting work of greater seriousness, do 'ee think, Mr Kent?' The sight of so many unpublished manuscripts was making him feel apprehensive.

Mr Kent took the paper and quickly read through the Preface. 'No, that will suffice. Have confidence, Mr Capern! Now, as to the title, I would suggest *Ballads and Songs*. It is simple and descriptive.'

When the business was complete, Edward shook Mr Kent's hand warmly. 'Please, let me sing to you before I go!'

He smiled. 'Thank you, but I have another visitor now; perhaps another time.'

The next day, Edward sang three songs for Mr Rock. The family travelled by train to take tea with him in Greenwich, where he lived with his sister, and they had a convivial meeting around a well-laden table. Edward watched Charles proudly. He looked charming as he sat very upright with his new bow-tie and his carefully brushed hair.

'No, when I grow up I want to be a man who invents things, like Mr Stephenson did. He made the first steam train.'

Mr Rock smiled. 'Indeed he did, Charles. And what will you invent?'

Charles's eyes shone with pleasure. 'Well, I don't know yet, but I do know I'll live in London. I shall live in a big house with Milly, like you do with your sister, Mr Rock, 'cos I wouldn't go away without her.'

Jane laughed. 'What, both my children in London!'

Edward was moved to hear him speak so self-assuredly. 'When I was your age, Charlie, I had to work all day and half the night in the lace factory and if it hadn't been for Mr Rock's kindness, I would never be where I am now and you would not be able to go to school.' He turned to Mr Rock.

'Without education, I might have ended my days working in the tanner's yard. What I want to see is free education for every child, at least for a year or two to set 'em on the right road. Will that day ever come, do 'ee think?'

Mr Rock assured him that he believed that it would come about, perhaps not too many years in the future.

It was with a deep sense of satisfaction that Edward travelled back to Bideford on the train. He had thanked the people who had transformed his life, and London was all very fine, but he was glad to be back in Devon.

Chapter Twenty-Three

As Jane walked along Mill Street with Edward, she slipped her hand into her pocket to clasp the key and ran her thumb over the brass indentations. Its weight was reassuring; perhaps this time they would find a house that met their expectations. It was more than a year since Edward had received the news of his pension but the few houses that had become vacant were too small, too expensive or too distant from the town.

The children had run ahead and reached the junction with High Street as a large brewer's wagon drawn by two heavy horses was passing.

Charlie grabbed Milly's hand. 'You must look where you'm going, maid! Those great hoofs would flatten you!'

Milly was now six and would never run out on to the road but Charlie's concern was touching nevertheless and Jane exchanged an amused glance with Edward.

He took her arm. 'I won't be able to stay long; I have to write my newspaper column tonight.'

'Well, you must stay long enough for us to decide. Us don't want to miss this one.'

They walked along the path that led past the church and into Lower Meddon Street. There it was. The first house in a terrace of three, it was much bigger than their present home and had only been built a few years ago. As they looked up at it, Jane hardly dared to voice her thoughts lest doing so should lead to disappointment. They walked through the little front garden on a path lined with columbines. Lily of the valley grew near the wall and their scent drifted up as she took the key from her pocket and unlocked the door. The children looked in, wide-eyed.

'No running about, mind. Stay with me and Daddy and us'll look at the rooms one at a time.'

Together they tiptoed into the hallway. It was very quiet, as if the house was waiting for them.

'Look, a tiled floor! That'd be easy to clean.' The spacious front room had a tiled fireplace and a bay window. 'Edward, this'd make a lovely parlour. Somewhere to bring your visitors!'

A passage led to a large kitchen. She stopped in the doorway and gasped. A black cast-iron stove stood in a large chimney breast. 'Edward, there's a Bodley! 'Twould be wonderful to have a stove!' She opened the oven door. 'Just imagine having an oven! And the hotplates here, look.' She stood and stared at the stove. She almost forgot the rest of the house, so absorbed was she by the possibilities it conjured.

'Mother, there's another kitchen!'

She hurried after Charlie. Sure enough there was a good-sized scullery which had a large sink with a drain running from it, but Charlie was calling to her again; beyond the scullery was a wash-house with a copper for heating water and a water pump. She could hardly believe it – just imagine never needing to fetch water again, and having a special room for washing without filling the kitchen with steam! By now, Edward had unlocked the back-door and was out in the yard.

'Janie, look! A water closet! No more digging out of the privy!' He strode across to another door. 'Oh, my goodness.' He sounded very serious and Jane hurried to join him. It was a stable, and next to it was a large, well-built carriage house with an entrance from the street.

'Janie, I could keep a pony!'

After several letters to the Post Office asking for an allowance for a pony and trap, his request had finally been granted, but he had been unable to find a stable to rent. Here, the pony could be kept in their very own yard. Edward was finding walking increasingly tiring and Jane worried about his health.

Milly pulled at Edward's hand. 'Daddy, *please* can us have a pony? I'd feed it oats and brush it and give it water. And a kitten? A little grey kitten!'

'Mother, look up here!' Charlie's voice came from above, so they hurried up a staircase which was twice as wide as their steep narrow stairs at home. At the front of the house was a sitting-room with views of the river, and there were three good-sized bedrooms.

Charlie's voice echoed down from another, narrower, staircase. 'Two more bedrooms up here!'

These were cosy rooms with sloping ceilings.

'Can me and Milly sleep up here? 'Twould be like a little house of our own and I'd take care of her!'

Edward ruffled his son's hair. 'So you've decided us is having the house, have 'ee?'

Jane started down the stairs. She wanted to look at the other bedrooms again, and the stove and the water pump, but first she admired the view from the sitting-room window and imagined how the room would look furnished. They would need a lot of new furniture, but she had been careful with money during the previous year and hadn't spent much of Edward's pension, despite giving up the grocery business. She looked around at the walls and the ceiling; the house was in very good order – she wouldn't have to do any whitewashing. This room would be their very own, and the parlour downstairs kept for Edward's visitors. One bedroom could be for his guests and another could be his library.

She turned to Edward, who was galloping down the stairs with Milly shrieking excitedly on his shoulders. 'Edward, let's go this moment to say us'll take it. Us can't do better than this.'

It was a house where they could all be happy. The years of heartache and anxiety were behind them. They had arrived.

They had only been living in the house for a month when he saw the advertisement in the paper. '*A very handsome black pony, gig and harness. Pony 13 hands, 6 years, safe and quiet, and harness in good condition.*' He showed it to Jane. 'I'll go to see it tomorrow. Don't tell Milly!'

Two days later, he waited outside in the road, leaning against the wall of the carriage house. It was a fine July evening and the street was quiet but for the cheerful voices of children playing further up the hill. The melodic notes of a thrush in the churchyard must have drifted up through the open window to the room where Milly sat playing with her doll, because he heard her high, childish voice:

'O give me the thrush with the speckled throat,
The king of the ringing wood.'

He hummed quietly along with her. Charles had finished his studies for the evening and had been allowed to visit a friend. Edward wanted the pony to be a surprise for both of them.

This part of the town was peaceful compared to Mill Street. He could almost believe he was in the country, yet within two minutes he could be at the Post Office in the High Street, and a few steps, which he took now, gave him a view of the Torridge. As the sun dipped behind Bideford's western hill, the golden cornfields beyond the broad tranquil river drew in the last warm rays, and the only sound was the plashing of oars as the last barge of the evening returned to its mooring. He murmured a few words and scribbled them in his notebook in an attempt to match the perfection of the moment. He felt a deep contentment. Jane was delighted with the house and it thrilled him to see her happy and singing as she went about her work.

Ballads and Songs had created less of a stir than his first book but had met with considerable success nevertheless, enabling Mr Kent to arrange a second printing. Although it had received fewer reviews than *Poems,* he had been especially pleased with a favourable one from The *Examiner*, a paper that was known for publishing scathing criticisms. A philanthropist was so taken with *The Old Stone-Breaker* that he made financial arrangements for the old man, ensuring that he never had to work at the harsh, back-breaking task again. An admirer had invited Edward to give a lecture at the Working Men's Institute in Newport, Wales, and he had spoken on two consecutive nights on 'The Poets of the

People.' He was told that it was a most entertaining talk, and certainly he had managed to make the audience laugh. His fee did little more than cover his railway fare and the pay for his Post Office replacement, but he felt he was justifying his pension by disseminating the knowledge of poetry.

At last he heard trotting hoofs turning in from the Quay. As Mr Dennis climbed down from the cart, Edward held the reins and patted the pony's neck.

'Hello there, Billy boy! Here you be, then, here's your new home!'

The pony snuffled at his hand, then tried to put its nose in his pocket.

'No apples in there, boy! Us'll have to find 'ee one dreckly.'

'You'll have to watch him,' said Mr Dennis, 'he'll eat for a pastime, that one, and it don't do to let him get too fat.'

They led him into the carriage house where Mr Dennis demonstrated how to remove the harness, then they made him comfortable in the stable with the straw and hay that had been delivered earlier.

'Behave yourself now, Billy.' Mr Dennis turned to Edward. 'He's a good beast and will serve you well as long as he knows you'm master.'

When he'd gone, Edward leaned on the stable door and watched as the pony tore hay from the rope net and chewed contentedly. The advertisement had not lied, he was indeed a handsome pony, pure black with a long mane and tail, and a stocky build that suggested he would manage the Devon hills with ease. No one in Edward's family had ever owned a horse. What an adventure!

He winked at Jane as he came into the kitchen. Charles had just arrived home and was searching the pantry for something to eat.

'Charles, Milly, would 'ee come outside for a moment? I want your opinion on something.'

They went outside and he stood with his back to the stable. 'I've been thinking that if us was to pull down this stable and carriage house, there'd be more space for a garden. There's little enough at the front.'

He observed his family's reactions. Jane was trying not to smile. Charles frowned, and Milly's face fell. 'But Daddy, you said you'd get a pony!'

'Well, I don't mind to, now. 'Twould be too much trouble, I think.'

'But Daddy… I wanted a pony…' Milly's voice trailed away. She looked distraught.

'Well, 'twould be costly. Us'd be better with more garden.'

At the sight of her eyes filling with tears, he began to waver, but at that moment came the sound of a stamped hoof and a low whinny. Milly's expression changed to doubt and then astonishment. When the whinny came again, he reached back and pulled the stable door open.

She was in there as quick as lightning and before he had time to warn her to take things gently, had her arms around the pony's neck while it blew gently into her hair.

'Billy, meet Milly! And here's Charles.'

She turned on him and slapped him playfully until, laughing, he had to hold her hands to save himself.

'Daddy, you'm very naughty to trick me like that!' And then she was back, stroking Billy's neck and talking to him and tidying his mane.

Charles wanted to know when they could go out in the cart together. Edward leaned against the stable door and put his arm around Janie. 'Us can go out on a Sunday, see the countryside together just like I've always wanted!'

Life had never been so good.

The next morning he harnessed Billy with Milly's help. When they had him ready, she raced upstairs to wave as she did every morning, and he blew a kiss to the little face at the window before climbing with some trepidation into the cart. The pony seemed unperturbed by the change of location and driver and set off willingly when Edward shook the reins. What an unfamiliar and thrilling sensation it was to be driving his own pony and cart! He stopped outside the Post Office and tied the reins to a lamppost for safety, although Billy did not appear interested in wandering away. When he came out after sorting his letters, there was quite a crowd of shopkeepers and friends waiting to see him off.

''Tis the Royal Mail coach!' shouted Mr Squire.

'The Flying Post!' cheered another.

He would show them what the pony could do! Laughing, he jumped aboard and cracked the whip. Billy shot off at a gallop, almost unseating him and causing the onlookers to leap out of the way. Before he knew what had happened, the pony was galloping on to the bridge and he had to use all his strength to pull him up and turn back on to the correct road.

'Whoa there, Billy boy, us isn't in that much of a hurry!' They settled down to a steady trot and he began to regain his equilibrium. He would have to drive more carefully. 'You got to take care of me, Billy, just as I'll take care of you. I'm new to this business, see.'

The pony's ears flicked, and with a jangle of harness he tossed his head.

It was a fine morning with the promise of warmth in the air. From the increased height of the cart, Edward could see over all but the highest hedges. Swallows dashed and swerved above the river, almost skimming the glassy surface before wheeling high above his head again. As he gazed up into the sky to follow their path, a line came into his head and he leaned back on his seat to rearrange and perfect the words in his head.

> 'I would sound a note of joy,
> Through the vales of Devon...'

After a minute or two it seemed to him that a stillness had fallen. He sat up. Billy was standing with his head in the hedge, tearing away mouthfuls of lush grass and chewing noisily.

'Hey there, Billy, come on sir!' He flicked the whip gently and they set off at a steady trot again.

As usual he had a book in his pocket – the poems of Shelley, it was today – and it occurred to him that he could read a little as they travelled along. By the time he reached the foot of the first page, he realised that the pony, sensing that his master was distracted, had again wandered off to the side of the road, but they made good enough progress despite these setbacks.

This new means of transport would renew his enjoyment in his work. He had calculated that he had walked more than thirty-two thousand miles since he became a postman, so it was not surprising that he had begun to tire of the long daily walk. The Post Office had brought in new and irksome regulations requiring him to record the exact times of his departure and arrival; he was to supply detailed records of dog bites – attempted dog bites even! Should he also record the sting of a wasp and the song of the thrush? Absurd. Perhaps he should send the records in the form of poems; that would show them.

Though he had to admit he had been treated fairly. When he complained that he was developing varicose veins from the long hours of walking, in recognition of his fame as the Postman Poet he was offered employment in an office in London; but of course he would hate such a position. He preferred the open air of his native hills – he was not to be caged! Jane had persuaded him to apply to be the new postmaster in Bideford following Mr Lee's death but he had not been successful, Mr Lee's son obtaining the post instead. He did not mind; he would have missed the journey along the deep lanes and the friends he met on the way and now, with this pony, the arduousness of the job had been taken away.

In Landcross he met the milkman, William, whistling as he passed from house to house with the milk cans swaying from his yoke. William stopped dead when he saw the pony and cart and pushed back his weather-worn hat to stare. 'What's this? You'm gone up in the world! Is this how you mean to go on now?'

'I've had my fill of walking! Put your foot up here on the running board and I'll give you a ride up to the Rectory.'

Billy put his ears back at the rattling of the cans then tossed his head and trotted on.

As they continued on the road to Buckland Brewer, labourers, cottage girls, gentlemen on horseback and playing children all stopped to exclaim when they recognised him in the cart and Edward was very pleased with his new status by the time he led Billy into Mr Ley's stable.

It was a Sunday morning in August, and the second day out for Jane in the pony and cart. The determined little pony drew them onwards alongside hedgerows bright with honeysuckle and meadowsweet, past hamlets of thatched cottages and up hills which gave her a thrilling view across fields to the immense blue ocean and distant sailing ships. A fortnight ago they had visited the great pebble ridge and for the first time in her life she had walked beside the sea; and now they were heading for the fishing village of Clovelly.

'I hope it don't rain,' Jane said. 'There's some dark clouds up there.' She was wearing her best bonnet.

Edward was in a jubilant mood. 'Rain? On our day out? Of course it won't rain, I said a special prayer this morning.'

She looked at him amusedly. 'I don't know why the Lord should look kindly on us as far as rain is concerned, when us is out enjoying ourselves instead of sitting in chapel. But soon you won't care if it rains because I'm looking to get you one of those new waterproof coats. Folks say they'm marvellous.'

Charles was sitting on the narrow bench behind Edward. 'I'll have a carriage when I'm grown. Then it won't matter if it's wet or cold.'

Edward flicked the whip as the pony snatched a mouthful of grass from the hedge. 'You'll have to work a lot harder to afford that, boy. You'm no more suited to working with your hands than I was. To break through to join the middling sort who work with their heads, you've got to study morning, noon and night. 'Tis time you saw the seriousness of it, Charles.'

Jane glanced back at Charles. He was glaring angrily at the back of his father's head. His teachers were pleased with him, but he was almost eleven and Edward felt he still had a long way to go before he was ready to be launched into the world of work, and frequently told him so. The pressure on Charles and the resulting distress was the only blot on her happiness.

She woke every morning feeling their new house must be just a dream, and got up to walk from room to room in renewed wonder. Each day brought something different; a chair bought at an auction, the discovery of a new flower in the garden, the delivery of a mangle. The burden of anxiety that she and Edward had carried all their married life had been replaced by joyousness that spread throughout the house.

After two hours of steady trotting, they came to a rustic gate next to a lodge house, where Edward slowed Billy to a walk. 'This must be the Hobby Drive, I reckon.'

They turned off the main road to take the rocky, sun-dappled track through the trees. Jane had heard about the enchantment of the carriage drive that led to Clovelly, and certainly the deep wooded ravines and bright sea glimpses were exceptionally lovely. When she turned back after calling to Milly and Charles, who had chosen to walk for a while, she saw that Edward was scribbling in his notebook and the pony heading for a grassy bank.

''Edward, you must look where us is going! Here, let me take the reins!'

She hadn't driven before but it surely couldn't be hard. Billy responded to a shake of the reins and resumed a straight course. After a moment or two, she saw the white of his eye as he turned his head a little to see who was in charge.

Edward stood up suddenly. 'Look at that view out over the bay! Can 'ee see the sea birds wheeling round the cliff?'

'Edward, sit down! You'll topple us both out!' She pulled at his arm and he started to write again.

'I must get down as many impressions as I can: the boom of the surf on the rocky shore below; the shady pathways between the trees and the little streams running down the narrow valleys!'

She smiled to see him so animated. He had often told her of the sights he saw but she had rarely been with him to see the excitement which inspired his writing.

'Mama, look at all the flowers I've picked!' Milly was trotting alongside the cart, holding up a posy. Her face was framed with dark curls as glossy as the pony, and was a picture of happiness. 'I want to climb up again!'

Jane pulled gently on the reins as she had seen Edward do and the pony stopped obediently. She let him eat from the verge while Milly hitched up her dress to clamber up and cuddle in between them.

'Daddy, why are you always *writing*? You should be having fun today!'

'I *am* having fun, my flower! This is what Daddy likes doing best, save for spending time with you.' He put his arm around her. 'Now tell me what you can see that I should put in my poem. Shall I put in all these flowers you've picked?'

'No, 'cos you always write about flowers. When I'm grown I shall write about all kinds of things, not just flowers, and I'll put them in a magazine like Miss Cook does.'

Eliza Cook had been spoken of very frequently since Edward's recent meeting with her. He winked at Jane over Milly's head. 'Of course you shall, chiel, because you'm the cleverest little maid that ever lived and why would I have named you after her, else?'

Jane glanced around to look for their son, and saw him trailing along behind, slashing at some nettles with a stick.

'But Miss Cook has no husband,' Edward went on, 'and that's maybe how she finds time for writing such wonderful poems. You need a husband so's I can have some grandchildren!'

278

'No, me and Charlie's going to live together. I don't want a husband.'

The village came into view below them, a line of white cottages tumbling down the steep hillside towards the protective arm of the harbour, and beyond, little red-sailed boats gliding on the placid sea. Jane stopped the pony again and called to Charles so that he might see it also.

The winding track led them eventually to the topmost houses, where they were offered a stable for Billy. The long village street leading down to the harbour was cobbled and too steep for even the most surefooted pony; but donkeys managed it despite the heavy loads of lime they carried up from the shore. Jane had to watch her footing, and almost tripped on a couple of occasions while she was admiring the flowering creepers that climbed up the cottage walls. Edward stopped to exchange pleasantries with the inhabitants, especially those that were young and pretty. She stood back, pretending to watch as Charles and Milly explored a side alley. She could not quite catch his words as he laughed with an attractive dark-haired girl; but he kept his hand on her arm a little too long and she felt a knot of jealousy tighten inside. She always listened carefully to his tales in case any particular name was frequently mentioned. She rarely heard Polly's name now and understood that the photographer, Mr Tedrake, was visiting Buckland Brewer more frequently.

She was not going to wait any longer and marched over to where he stood. 'Edward, would 'ee carry this basket for me? 'Tis getting rather heavy.' She smiled at the young woman who was, after all, quite blameless. As they continued down the street, Edward took her arm and she knew she could not be cross with him for long. Despite his dalliances, she never for a moment doubted his love for her.

When they reached the harbour he struck up a conversation with an elderly fisherman mending nets by the broad harbour wall, so she followed the children down on to the stony beach where Charles was helping Milly build a tower of pebbles. She leaned against a small boat that had been drawn up on to the shore and pulled her bonnet forward to shade her face from the warm sun. She half-closed her eyes to enjoy the comforting sounds of the tide lapping on the shore and the calls of the seabirds. How rare it was to be able to do nothing.

When Edward came to join her, he was in a more sombre mood. 'Come, us'll all sit down together and I'll tell 'ee the tale that's been related to me.

'Here, in this very house behind us, lived a woman named Kitty Lile. Every day she watched her husband go out to fish for herring in the bay and every day, when he returned, she took him in her arms and together they walked along this beach and withdrew to their house on the edge of the shore. During one fearsomely stormy night, she waited and watched for his return. The hours passed; other fishers returned bruised and battered by the storm and when they'd made their boats safe they walked up the cobbles to join their families who waited anxiously. But Kitty Lile remained at her window, and over the roar of the waves the villagers heard her shrieking her lover's name.'

The children gazed open-mouthed at Edward. Jane turned to look at the house, imagining the wind and the rain and the crashing of the waves on that dark night. Edward was silent for a few moments and when he spoke again, his voice was low.

'He never returned, and from that day until the day that Kitty died, she could be seen standing at her window or wandering the length of this harbour wall and always she waved a scarlet cloth which, it was said, was the flag from her husband's boat given to her as a token of his love.

'They call the house "Mazed Kate's Cottage."'

The waves washed gently on to the pebble beach in a repetitive sad refrain, and Edward began to hum quietly along with their rhythm. Jane rose and gestured to the children to follow her; she knew he would want to be alone to write his sad song.

When he joined them he was cheerful again. They clambered over the pebbles to reach a waterfall that tumbled from the wooded cliff and sat nearby to eat their dinner. When the meal was over, Edward and Charles stripped down to their undergarments and dared each other to dash through the sparkling water. Jane watched them fondly as they ran yelling and laughing through the icy water, pleased to see them enjoying each other's company.

They spent the afternoon wandering along the shore to find unusual small pebbles to take home, watching the red-sailed fishing boats winging their way across the bay, and staring up at the sheer cliff wall that stretched as far as the eye could see.

'I've a mind to visit Cornwall one day,' said Edward. 'It lies just beyond that furthest promontory. A man who trades along the coast has offered me a passage.' He gazed at the hazy coastline. 'I might undertake a lecture tour too, I've plenty of offers and 'twould show that I deserve my pension. But a week away from you, Janie, and from Devon, would be enough for me.'

At last they collected their belongings and started the climb up the steep cobbled hill. The children went on ahead to explore the drangways leading off the main street, but Jane and Edward paused frequently to turn and gaze out over the sea and regain their breath.

After one such rest, something caught her eye and she put her hand on Edward's arm as he started to resume his climb. 'Edward; wait.'

Out from a side alley came a small procession; six men in dark Sunday suits carrying on their shoulders a coffin that was not adult-size. Following on behind, the parents supported each other, then sombre-faced villagers came walking in pairs. She and Edward stood back by a little gate that led to a perfect cottage garden, and bowed their heads as the sad procession passed by. She stared down at the cobbles, listening as the measured footsteps and the muffled sobs replaced the previous happy sounds of lapping waves and birdsong. The sudden reminder of human tragedy was shocking, and Edward held her hand as they continued up the hill in silence. An otherwise perfect day had ended in sadness.

1863-1866

Sorrow

My heart is sad, I cannot sing
Those merry strains I sang of yore;
I hear the thrush salute the spring,
But music charms my soul no more.

Chapter Twenty-Four

Edward got up from his desk and strode over to the window. Neither the early morning sun catching the ripples on the fast-flowing river, nor the rhythmic clatter of a trotting horse which drifted up to him along with the scent of budding flowers from his garden below, were the focus of his attention on this fine May morning.

The question was, what should be the subject of his next lecture tour? He had completed several tours in the last four years, and now his friend Elihu Burritt was keen for him to visit Birmingham and Leeds again, but needed to know the topic before approaching the local societies. Last time he had spoken on 'Cornwall; its Coasts and Cairns', a talk he had prepared after his journey by boat from Appledore to Penzance. He had included several as yet unpublished poems and had been well-received apart from a few complainants who claimed they could not understand his accent.

'You should hear the way folks speak in Birmingham, Milly,' he said, attempting the local pronunciation.

Milly was curled up in his upholstered chair with her grey-and-white cat in her lap. She smiled up at him. 'Do the Cornish way of talking again, Daddy.' He tried it and succeeded in making her laugh. She had woken with a tummy ache and Jane had decided she should not go to school.

Perhaps they would not object to his diction if he were to sing. A description of the Devon countryside and a song for each month of the year, that's what he would give them! *Wayside Songs.* He must allude to the sources of his melodies. He picked up his pen again and jotted down the ideas as they came into his head; his tunes came from the rhythm of his footsteps, from the roundelays of birds, the laughter of happy children and the murmurings of brooks.

Giving lectures and writing new poems occupied so much of his time that he had decided, a while back, to give up his newspaper column. By a strange quirk of fate the post had been taken up by Thomas Tedrake. Thomas was now married to Polly and had opened portrait rooms in Meddon Street; they had a child, born somewhat precipitately after the wedding. He wished Polly a polite 'good day' when he saw her about the town, but now that she was a married woman, they could not indulge in the delightful conversations they once used to share. The gaiety had gone from her glance and he could not help wondering whether marriage to Thomas disappointed her.

Such matters did not cause him lasting disquiet. He was busy, and life was good! He had given talks in Barnstaple, Hatherleigh, Exeter and Dawlish; poems and songs continued to flow copiously from his pen so he intended to submit work for his third book before the end of the year. He had an ample number of the simple poems and songs that came so easily to his pen, but he had also written a handful of poems on the local folklore that was still widely believed and, following a challenge from his friend and fellow poet, William Bennett, he had attempted some sonnets. At first he had felt irritated by the constraints; why *should* he stick to fourteen lines – why not twelve or sixteen? And why should he follow such a complex rhyme scheme – birds rejoicing in the wood did not rehearse their songs! But he persevered nevertheless and was really rather pleased with the results.

'Edward, look at the time! You'll be late for work!' Jane's voice reached him from the foot of the stairs.

He put down his pen, pushed his notebook and a volume of Thomas Hood's poems into his pockets, and crouched down to Milly. 'Daddy must harness Billy on his own today, chiel! Will 'ee be able to wave from the window in a few minutes?'

She nodded and he kissed her goodbye. She was looking a little brighter. When the pony, who knew what was expected of him, paused in the road outside the house, Edward turned to look up at the window and there was the cheerful little face and a waving hand as usual. He blew her a kiss.

When he set off from the post office with his bag of letters, his thoughts returned to the trip to Birmingham. Of the many friends he had made since his success, Elihu Burritt was one of the closest. Born in America to working parents, he became apprenticed to a blacksmith when his father died and embarked on an intensive programme of self-education which made Edward ashamed of his own paltry attempts. Elihu learned different languages which enabled him to find work as a translator and to travel throughout the world, speaking on abolition and peace and writing many books. They had in common a passionate interest in poetry, natural beauty and social justice, and when Elihu had visited they had talked late into the night despite the early start they both had to make the next day.

He stopped the pony as he drew level with a strange, bowed figure. Blind John Westcott was walking back to Littleham, bent double under a large sack of coal. He made three trips a day to earn a few pence, using a long ash stick to feel his way along the turnpike road and up the steep, stony tracks leading to Littleham. He lifted his sightless eyes enquiringly towards the cart and Edward jumped down to shout in his ear, for he was hard of hearing as well as blind.

'I've a new song for you, John, listen! 'Tis about that field alongside the turnpike gate east of the water; you know they always say that when it's cut, a storm is sure to follow.'

And he sang '*Jemmo's Curse*' while the old man listened intently, smiling beatifically and waving his hand as if conducting an orchestra. Edward knew he would only need to hear it one more time before he was able to sing it for the family in Littleham who looked after him.

He hummed the tune while he retrieved Billy from the grass verge alongside the river. His songs were sung by ploughmen and dairymaids, farmers and blacksmiths. They were taught to children in Devon schools and shared at harvest teas. Since the publication of *The Devonshire*

Melodist two years ago, they were sung around pianos in drawing rooms throughout the land.

The preparation of the book of sheet music had not been easy. Mr Murby was to transcribe the melodies but rejected most of the best songs on the grounds that they were untutored, rustic and too coarse for middle-class taste. The ones he chose, Edward considered rather bland, and he then changed many of the melodies and added fancy accompaniments. Never mind, that was what the people that had pianos wanted, it seemed. At least they could enjoy his own unaltered words. He had felt vindicated when a review in the *Illustrated London News* praised his verses but criticised Mr Murby's melodies as being artificial and laboured.

He heard voices and stood up in the cart to see over the hedge, bracing his legs to balance as Billy trotted on. 'Good day to you! And what a beauty it is!' He took off his hat with a flourish.

The two labourers straightened up from weeding turnips and, stretching their aching backs, called out, 'And to you, Mr Capern!'

He approached Nethercleave and rang his bell in case there were letters to collect. When he reached Buckland he would continue his letter to Elihu. His friend had offered to find employment for Charles in Birmingham because suitable positions in North Devon were very hard to find. He would soon be fifteen and needed to make a start, but Jane was reluctant to let him go. Never mind; all would be well. The valley was alive with birdsong and the hawthorn buds were opening on the wayside trees. He started to sing to himself:

It was the golden harvest time,
And life went merry in the fields…

Two days later Milly still did not feel well enough to help Edward with the pony. Jane insisted she stay in bed and gave her peppermint tea to drink. It was just a childhood upset, Jane said. But when he arrived home the next day and walked into the kitchen, Jane was not there. He called up the stairs. The tone of her reply told him something was wrong and he took the stairs two at a time.

Milly was curled tightly on her side and looked pale and tense.

'Chiel, what's the matter?' He sat on the edge of the bed and took her hand in both of his. 'What is it, my flower?'

Her normally bright and mischievous eyes were dull and filled with tears when she spoke. 'It hurts, Daddy.'

He knew from the exaggerated calmness of Jane's voice that this was serious.

'The pain got worse about an hour ago, Edward. I was thinking maybe us should ask the doctor to come? Just to make sure.'

He felt himself go cold. 'Yes. Yes; I'll go now, shall I?'

He met Jane's gaze and for a second the extent of their fear was acknowledged. As he reached the door, he heard Milly cry out in pain and he turned in horror. Jane looked up. 'Go! This is how she is.'

He tried to resist the urge to run as he dodged between a donkey cart and a brewer's wagon on High Street and he barely heard the greetings of friends as he hurried along Mill Street. He strode up Dr Pridham's drive for the first time since the night he had met the phrenologist, and he hammered at the door.

The maid would give him the message, she said.

'Is he at home? I've got to see him, now!'

'Who *is* that?' Dr Pridham appeared from his study. Edward told him about Milly as best he could but the words tumbled out and he knew he was barely coherent.

'She is conscious? No convulsions?'

'No. No, but...'

'And she is what age?'

'Ten. She is ten years and six months.'

'Then I will be there in about an hour.'

'No, Doctor, please, you must come back with me now...'

Dr Pridham lifted his chin and stared at Edward, his spectacles glittering coldly. 'I am busy at present. I will be there in about an hour.'

If it were only sixty minutes, they were the longest minutes Edward had known. He paced from Milly's bedroom to the front door and back, giving terse answers to Charles's anxious questions until finally he saw Dr Pridham crossing Lower Meddon Street and coming up the garden path with his leather holdall in his hand.

He was kind and gentle with Milly but Edward hated to see a man touching his daughter. When he pressed on her abdomen and she cried out in pain, he took a step forward to intervene, but Jane grasped his arm and held him back.

Finally Dr Pridham straightened up. 'She is certainly in considerable pain but a draught of opium will bring her relief; she is of sufficient age to benefit.' While searching in his bag, he issued further instructions and stated that he would return in the morning.

While Jane busied herself around the room, straightening the bed covers and making everything neat, Edward sat with Milly and stroked her hair from her forehead. As the opium took effect he saw her face relax, and she smiled at him.

'Is that feeling better now, chiel?'

She nodded drowsily and curled her hand around his finger, as she used to as a tiny child listening to his bedtime stories.

He met Jane's gaze and knew that the relief in her expression matched his own. What a blessing it was to be able to call the doctor without even having to consider what the fees might be! How magical was this medicine that it could so easily and swiftly take away her pain and make her well! They left her to sleep and went downstairs to reassure Charles and talk over the details of her illness and the fear they had felt. Every time he or Jane checked on her as instructed to make sure that she was not developing a fever, she was sleeping soundly.

He woke early but Jane was already up. Milly was awake and did not seem to be in pain, but was still too drowsy to speak.

'Her hands are cold, and her feet.' Jane seemed puzzled.

'Here, Daddy'll warm them for you.' He rubbed her hands gently in his and thought he saw a little smile. It was natural that she should still be drowsy from the opium.

He was reluctant to go to work before the doctor came, but Jane insisted that he should.

'Her'll be fine when you get home, you'll see!' He knew she was being brave, but Milly really did seem to be recovering.

The pony stopped in the road below the window as usual and he could not prevent himself from looking up, although he knew that she would not be there to wave to him. Something else caught his eye. A small bird was perched on the garden wall and he caught its subdued, fleeting call, 'Weeep.' He stared in disbelief. The strength seemed to go from him and he almost stumbled as he got down from the cart and walked towards the wall, thinking, '*it cannot be; she is getting better.*' But he was not mistaken.

'Get out! Go away!' He ran towards the robin with his arms flailing wildly and it flew on to a higher sill and uttered its sad little cry again. He picked up a stone and threw it, not aiming at the bird, which he had no desire to injure, but hoping to frighten it away to another wall, another house. It cocked its head on one side to regard him curiously, and cried again.

'Get out!' He could hear the desperation in his voice. 'Us don't want you here!'

He was bending to find another stone when the door opened and Jane appeared. 'Edward? Whatever be 'ee doing?'

What could he say? He could not frighten her by telling her what he feared and he felt foolish standing there with the stone in his hand.

'There was a stray dog. 'Tis gone now.'

290

He climbed back into the cart as she returned inside. When he glanced up at the house, he saw that the bird was still there, and it uttered its sad little cry again.

All the way to Buckland he berated himself for his foolishness. Probably the robin was there most days and he only noticed it today because Milly had been ill. Once in the cottage, he quietly told Grace Ley of the new developments in Milly's illness and of the incident with the robin. She was reassuring, telling him that his daughter had undoubtedly turned the corner and that the stories about robins were no more than ignorant superstitions. They even managed to laugh together at his foolishness and he promised her he would tell Jane the story once everything was back to normal.

Arriving home, he felt almost cheerful as he stabled Billy and paused to watch the swifts screaming over the rooftops before he went into the house. Probably Milly would be sitting up in bed; they might even be able to sing together.

The house was silent. The sun shone in through the stained glass panel above the door, catching dancing motes of dust in its beams and casting intricate patterns of colour on to the tiled floor. Perhaps Milly was sleeping again. He called quietly up the stairs but then the parlour door opened and Jane appeared.

'Edward…'

She looked different. Something was wrong. They stared at each other and he felt as if the floor beneath his feet was slowly falling away, and Jane's face crumpled as she ran to him.

'Edward, her's gone, our Milly's gone!'

Gone? From habit he took her in his arms, and from habit he held her, and when Dr Pridham came from the parlour and put his hand on Edward's shoulder and said that there had been nothing he could do, that peritonitis was invariably lethal, he thanked him and closed the front door after him. He stared at the door until Jane led him into the parlour. Charles was sitting silent and rigid on the sofa and Mrs Bate from next door and Eliza Elliott were weeping. He could not fathom why they were here, but sat down with them. Jane started to talk to him and he took her hands in his, distressed to see her so upset. She told him that Milly had developed a fever soon after he left for work, that the pain had come on again just before the doctor arrived.

'He told me 'twas serious, Edward. He said he would do his best.'

She told him that the doctor had bled Milly in an effort to remove the poison from her body. She broke down and could not, for a minute or more, continue. He stared at her.

'The pain was so bad, Edward....'

She had wanted to send for him, but could not leave Milly's side. Eventually the doctor told her there was no hope, and he gave opium to ease her passing.

Mrs Bate stood up. 'Come now, come and see her.' She held out her hand to him and he looked at it, unable to comprehend her meaning. 'Come, her's beautiful now. Peaceful.'

'Yes,' he said automatically, 'Yes.'

He followed the women up the stairs to Milly's bedroom. They obscured his view of the bed at first, then Jane stepped aside. He looked down. His eyes were swimming and at first he could see nothing, but then his vision cleared. He stepped back in shock, and felt someone's hand steadying him. This was not his Milly. His Milly was vital and smiling and mischievous. Her eyes were full of laughter and she reached out her hands to him. This body on the bed, this shrunken doll, this was not his Milly. He turned on his heel. He found himself in his study and gripped the back of his chair in an attempt to still his shaking hands.

The days passed in a blur. The house seemed always to be full of people; neighbours, his sisters, well-wishers from Buckland and Littleham. Once, when he went to his study to escape them, he found Charles lurking there. They looked at each other for several long moments, then Charles left and he heard the front door close.

The visitors spoke of Milly having passed to a better place, of being held in Jesus's arms, but he heard her happy laugh at night when the house was quiet; he saw the flounce of her dress and caught the scent of her long hair as she ran past; he felt the light touch of her arm around his neck.

The funeral took place in the Dissenters' cemetery in Old Town. The grave seemed very deep for such a small coffin and he found himself wondering at the difficulties the gravediggers must have experienced. He expected to find Milly at home to greet them when they returned.

That night, he held Jane in his arms for many hours as she talked of Milly's loving ways, of the things she said and of what she would have become. When eventually she slept, he turned on his back and gazed at the moonlight filtering through the curtains and playing on the ceiling. Perhaps he had just woken from a dream. If he went upstairs, he would see his daughter sleeping in the moonlight, her hair curling on her cheek, her hand clasping a corner of the blanket the way she had done since she was a baby. He thought he heard a rustle, a creak from the room above, and he got out of bed and climbed softly up the stairs.

First, he saw her doll sitting on the chest of drawers and the outline of her books lined up on the shelf, then he discerned a rustle from the bed and a long shape in the shadows where she should have lain; Charles, face down with his arms hugging her pillow. As Edward watched, his son drew a long shuddering breath and deep, wracking sobs rose up from the very depths of his being.

For a few moments he stood and watched Charles. So, this was still a dream. He had not woken. He turned and went back to bed.

Jane paused with the heel of her hands pressing on the bread dough. Milly used to help by greasing the bread tins before she went to school. When she'd finished, she'd tear around the kitchen, picking up her books and saying goodbye to her cat.

Will 'ee buy some more fish for me to cook for her, Mama? You like fish, don't you, Tibby?

Then she would come for her kiss – her pure, clear skin, her eyes full of laughter - and disappear through the doorway with her hair flying. Jane stared into the hallway. She could almost hear the front door close before the empty silence settled in the kitchen once more.

She continued kneading. There was the bread to finish, the ironing to do, the stairs to sweep, the kitchen floor to scrub. She had let things go.

For a week after the funeral she was so tired she could hardly lift a finger. How would they have managed if Thomazine had not stayed on? Edward could not have any more time away from work. All she could do was sit in the chair while those dreadful hours of Milly's suffering played out again and again in her mind. If only she had given her peppermint tea when it first started. If only they had sent for the doctor earlier. Jane was the one who knew about childhood illnesses, she was the one that people turned to for advice. *Keep her warm, just some peppermint tea, no food, she'll soon be vitty again.* If she had got it right, Milly would have been sitting up in bed in the morning, stretching, smiling. *I feel better now, Mama.*

Stop; stop. It did no good to dwell on those thoughts again. Dr Pridham had explained that there was nothing anyone could have done to save her. *You must not blame yourself.*

She left the dough on the table and went out into the yard. The stable door stood open, as Edward had left it when he went to work an hour ago. When she stood here to shake a duster or beat a rug, she would hear Milly's high, musical voice talking to Billy in the stable, chiding him for stamping his hoof, laughing when he whinnied. She would come into the kitchen.

What be 'ee after?

Just a carrot for Billy.

Jane returned to the table, divided the dough, pressed it into the tins and put them next to the stove to rise. She swept the kitchen floor and emptied the sweepings into the dust-can in the yard. A thought came to her and she went out into the front garden to push aside the stems of the columbines, being careful not to disturb the bees that worked amongst the flowers. Yes. There were the lilies of the valley, their perfect bells just opening to release their heady scent amongst the glossy, dew-laden leaves. She picked some to take to Milly's grave; she would go when the ironing was done.

She went every day. Sometimes a friend went with her, and Charles came once. It upset him dreadfully; he allowed her to put her arms around him and they wept together, but since then he avoided opportunities to talk about Milly. Almost fifteen; almost a man. He had begun to find his way in life but now, without his sister, he was lost. He was out most evenings; she did not know where.

Edward had not visited the grave since the funeral three weeks ago. She had pleaded with him at first but he always said he had letters to write. When she looked in at his study door, he would be standing at the window or sitting in a reverie. He was taking no interest in his reading or writing and seemed to sleepwalk through the days; he ate very little and she was really afraid that he would make himself ill. The three of them sat around the table in silence at suppertime pretending not to notice the empty chair.

Mr Hearn had called in. He was worried about Edward, he said.

'I was working near Orleigh when something caught my eye in the lane a couple of fields distance, so I stood up on the hedgebank to have a see. The cart was veered right across the road, blocking it 'twas, and Mr Capern was sitting there like a mommet while the pony ate from the verge. I carried on working but after half an hour he was still there so I crossed the field to see what was up. Well, Mr Capern was that confuddled, he didn't seem to know what he should be doing or where he was gwain. I gave the pony a slap and on they went to Buckland.'

Another day Mr Lee came to apologise that Edward had received a written reprimand for unpunctuality.

'Naturally he's all of a mizmaze, I can see that, but you see he'd signed against his arrival times and didn't care for me to change it. If I could have stopped him getting that reprimand, I'd have done it. I just wanted to explain to you, see, but I'm afraid 'twill happen again, the way he is.'

So, Jane could not let her grief get the better of her. Edward and Charles needed her; they had to eat, they needed clean clothes and a welcoming house to come home to. They were still a family, the three of them. She had to hold them together.

She shook her ironing blanket out on to the table. Mrs Bate came in with her daughter yesterday and they did all the washing. People were so kind. Friends looked in to see her several times a day and often brought some little gift; a few flowers, some buns. She lifted the first iron from the stove then tested the heat with a wet finger. The iron hissed on the damp sheet as she swept it forwards and backwards across the table. The day was fine; she could hang the ironing out in the yard to air and by the time she came back from the cemetery it would be ready to put away.

She finished both sheets and she reached into the basket for the next item. She pulled out a chemise; the fine white cotton; the drawstring at the neck; the small darn on the sleeve where a moth had got at it. She stared at it for a moment, uncomprehending.

Mama, this chemise is too tight.

You're growing so fast! I must make you a new one. You'll be a woman before I know it.

It wasn't meant to be washed. Mary Bate must have picked it up by mistake. Jane sat down abruptly, clutching the chemise to her face. She had found that if she sat on Milly's bed and closed her eyes and held the chemise close to breathe in the delicious little-girl scent, she could believe for a few moments that the warm body of her daughter was lying next to her, wriggling a bit to get comfortable.

Move over, Mama, you'm squashing me.

Is that better, chiel? Go to sleep now. Sleep well, my lovely.

Now, the chemise smelt no different from the rest of the washing. Milly was gone. She rocked forward as the breath was forced out of her in long, shuddering sobs that would not stop. Milly was gone; she was never, ever coming back.

Edward wandered through the long grass to the hedgebank where campions, buttercups and stitchwort grew and he started to pick them automatically, taking no pleasure in their blooms. Here were wild columbines and scabious; he added them to the bouquet. The pony's harness jingled as he greedily cropped the lush grass; the nearby waterwheel clattered and a cuckoo's call drifted down the valley. Jane had asked him to pick flowers for her and he had felt a pang of conscience; never before had she needed to ask. Had he grown cold towards the one he had loved so deeply? If so, it was because something inside him had died; he felt his heart dwelt in perpetual darkness.

He let the hand holding the bouquet fall to his side while he stared at the green steep-sided valley that was alive with birdsong and the voice of the sparkling stream. He had thought it a Garden of Eden, once. He walked back to the cart and put the bouquet on the seat. He should go. He had to follow Moreton Drive, and then New Road into Bideford, and he was probably already late with the post. Instead, he wandered aimlessly along the stony track towards the old barn.

A sharp chis-*ick!* just above his head made him glance up. A swallow with a glossy dark-blue back and long tail streamers dived past him then shot away, uttering its alarm call again. On the lower half of the barn door four small birds, paler than their parents, sat huddled together. As he moved quietly aside to watch them, a memory returned to him. He had stood in this exact spot a year ago, watching entranced as the baby birds shuffled sideways along the old wooden door in the evening sunshine and cocked their heads to regard him quizzically with beady black eyes, vulnerable little bundles of promise with wide baby beaks, cream downy breasts and dusky blue wings. When the adult swallows swooped in to land abruptly next to their young, the babies set up an insistent cacophony of rasping calls until a fly was dropped into the nearest gaping beak.

He had hurried home and called out to his family; it was a beautiful evening, they *must* come and see the fledgling swallows at Upcott Mill. Jane had been too busy and Charles disinterested, but he and Milly had set off together with the pony and cart. When they were out on the Torrington Road, he had allowed her to take the reins and she sat upright and proud, shaking the reins as she had seen him do.

Walk on, Billy! Good boy!

He had shifted sideways on the bench so that he could admire the calm, confident way she drove the pony, her glossy dark hair pulled away from her face and falling down her back, the little smile that played around her lips.

When they were near the barn they had climbed down from the cart and walked quietly towards the door, where the young birds were beginning to flutter their wings and hop up and down in an experimental fashion.

Oh look, Daddy! Be 'em going to fly soon?

Soon, my flower, and when the summer's gone they'll fly all the way to Africa.

And us'll never see 'em again?

Oh, we will, chiel. They'll be back next year to nest in this exact same place. Shall us come and see 'em again?

Yes, and the year after and the year after that. Let's always come to see 'em, Daddy, even when I'm a grown woman and you'm an old man.

And she had slipped her hand into his.

And now she was dead. His Milly was dead. She lay deep in the cold, dark earth. He stood and watched as one of the young birds launched itself and followed its parent into the clear blue sky, first fluttering and then gaining strength and height until they soared together, while the tears ran down his cheeks. The tears that had been so long coming would not stop, not even when he rode into the town, not even as he settled Billy for the night, nor when he stumbled into the kitchen to find his Janie.

He fell into her embrace and for the first time they cried together, sobbing until he felt that both their hearts would break.

It was a long time before he could speak. 'What be us going to *do*, Janie? How can us live?'

And she put her hands on his shoulders, holding him at arm's length, so that he could just make out her face through his swimming eyes and hear her tearful words.

'Us just has to carry on, Edward, for each other, for Charles. And you know what you must do? You must write. Write about Milly, write about our loss. Please; do it for me, Edward.'

Chapter Twenty-Five

On the first anniversary of Milly's death, Edward led the way up Meddon Street to the cemetery. He clutched a fragrant posy of lilies of the valley, Jane and Charles carried handfuls of violets and white-faced daisies. As he walked slowly past the terraced houses with the scent of lilac drifting from gardens and swifts screaming low over the rooftops, he thought how cruel it was that his favourite month of May should now always be wedded to thoughts of loss, yet how fitting that a time of youth and gaiety should be devoted to Milly's memory.

Jane leaned in close. 'She's up there, watching us; I know it for sure. She feels our love and our thoughts.'

'Yes, my sweet. She does, of course.'

Jane's faith had strengthened since Milly's death and she was perfectly confident that she would one day be reunited with her daughter. Edward longed for that certainty. He too felt Milly's presence but feared that it was only their love that kept her memory alive, and on his darkest days when his prayers met with silence, he believed God to be cruel and heartless.

He glanced back at Charles. He dragged along behind carrying the flowers down by his side as if wanting to disown them.

Jane leaned in again, guessing his thoughts. 'Don't judge him too harshly. He visits the grave on his own, sometimes twice in a week, mind.'

'Visiting on his own is no good. How many times have I told him that he must be strong and help to hold the family together?'

As usual, Edward's sorrow welled up as they followed the path that ran between the lines of weathered grey stones, spilling over into tears by the time they reached the grassy mound. He put his arm around Jane and together they struggled to control their sobs until they could speak again.

'Do 'ee remember how she'd lie in her cradle and smile every time us looked in? She hardly ever cried.' Jane's voice shook a little.

He looked down at Milly's cruel resting place and tried to see the delightful child she had been. 'And her laugh. You remember, Janie, how she'd chuckle? No one could hear that laugh and stay serious.'

They stood for a while in contemplation until Jane asked, 'Will 'ee read that poem now, Edward? Then us'll scatter the flowers.'

He had chosen the poem that carried Milly's name, one of many he had written for her in recent months. He struggled to read with a steady voice from the crumpled paper, but his voice gained strength as he went on.

> We welcomed her to earth's green isle,
> And gave the little thing a name,
> We call'd her Milly, and we thought
> We never heard so fond a word.

When he had finished all the verses, Jane said a prayer and he placed the lilies of the valley in a jar at the foot of the stone. 'Now, strew the daisies and violets; let her lie beneath a blanket of flowers.'

Jane scattered the flowers lovingly but when she had finished, Charles, who had stared at his boots throughout the proceedings, thrust his flowers into her hand. 'You do it, Mother.' And he turned on his heel and walked quickly out of the graveyard.

Later that night, when Jane had gone to bed, Edward sat at his desk working on the poem entitled *The Anniversary* in which he was attempting to record the complex emotions of the day. All the poems he had written in the last year focussed on recollections of Milly and her death because he could think of nothing else, but the effort of writing brought him fulfilment and the poems brought comfort to Jane. He thought he might include some in a future volume in the hope that they might console others who had suffered a bereavement; but he had not yet responded to his publisher's frequent requests for a third book.

He heard the front door close and footsteps mount the stairs. He frowned. Charles had not returned for tea – on this, of all days, when the family needed to draw together and share their memories of Milly. He walked out on to the landing. Charles, looking dishevelled with his jacket undone and his cap askew, clomped up the stairs with his head down, and did not see Edward until he had reached the top. Their eyes met and as Edward saw his son's expression change to one of veiled embarrassment, he felt a pang of disappointment. Why could they not share the loving-kindness that had come so easily with his daughter?

'Where've 'ee been, Charles? Your mother's missed you. You upset her, walking off like that.' This was not strictly true; Jane was always ready to excuse Charles's behaviour.

'Oh, just out in the town. I met some friends.'

Charles tried to continue on to his room but Edward grabbed his son's arm. ''Tisn't good enough!' He had pulled Charles close and detected a familiar smell. The shock caused him to let go and he stared at his son's face in amazement.

'You've been drinking! You've been drinking alcohol!' He could scarcely believe it.

Charles tried to pass him. 'I haven't. I'm going to bed.'

'Charles, don't 'ee lie to me! What have things come to, that you'm out drinking? You'm neglecting your studies – how are you ever going to get on if you carry on like this! This is the last time, from now on you'll be here in this house each and every evening!' He was almost shaking with anger and disappointment. Charles shrugged and carried on upstairs to his bedroom.

Edward slept badly that night. The next day, he sat deep in thought as Billy pulled the cart along the lanes and steep valleys, while the rain dripping from his hat and running down his neck suited his sombre mood. Since Milly's death, the plan to send Charles to Birmingham to work had been dropped, because neither he nor Jane could bear to lose their only remaining child. Suitable employment was hard to find in Bideford. Charles was passed over for the few clerical positions that were available because he was only a postman's son, despite Edward's success. And now he was falling in with an unsuitable crowd. Was his son to waste his life?

After tea, during which he and Charles sat in stony silence despite Jane's attempts to lighten their mood, he sent his son upstairs to study. He had already told Jane what had happened the previous evening.

'Us can't go on like this, Jane. He's a clever lad and I can't bear to see him throw away all the opportunities us have given him. I've made up my mind; he must go away. Elihu Burritt can find him a good position where he can make something of himself. 'Twould be selfish of us not to let him go.'

Jane stared straight ahead, her mouth a grim line. He saw for the first time how she had aged over the past year.

'Janie, think of all the work I've done for the Temperance Society and now my own son is drinking! Us don't want him to go through all the hardships us had, but he'll have worse if he carries on like this.' He reached across the table to take her hand. 'Even when he gets back on the right track, there just aren't the jobs for him in this town.'

After a long pause, she looked at him. 'You'm right, Edward, but I can't bear to lose him, I just can't. What would he do – lodge with strangers? And suppose he was to fall in with a bad crowd in Birmingham – us wouldn't even know! No; if he's to go, us must go with him.'

He stared at her. 'Us? Go to Birmingham?'

'You'd have your pension; it might even be increased as Lord Palmerston said it might. You'll be due a pension from the Post Office if they'd let you go. You could write all day then.'

He could not take it in. ''Twasn't the money I was thinking of, not straight off. Us leave Devon? Janie, I don't know that I can. I've never had a mind to leave Devon.'

'Well, I will, if it means us can be with Charles. I can't countenance being without him. You've been to these places, you know what they'm like. They can't be that different. They have houses and people and food, don't they? Trees and fields too, I don't doubt.'

How could he explain to her? 'But they'm not home, Janie. They'm not where us belongs.'

She gave him a straight look. 'Us belongs where Charles is, that's all I know.'

Months passed. Edward planned a new programme of study for Charles with a strict timetable which kept him off the streets, but did not solve the problem of his future career. Arrangements had to be made for him but, for Edward, leaving Devon would be like a second bereavement and he could not bear to think about it.

But then Elihu Burritt came to stay, and he was very encouraging. There was no need to live in the city, Elihu told them; they could find a home near him in the village of Harborne and Charles could travel into the city where he could obtain a position as a banker's clerk. People were welcoming so Jane would easily make friends. He could introduce Edward to other writers who would not be prejudiced by his humble beginnings; there would be greater opportunities to give lectures; they could walk together in the countryside he had named The Black Country and Edward could write poems about the social conditions endured by the workers there.

Charles asked a lot of questions, pleading with his parents to allow him to go. Gradually Edward began to see that he had to choose between his love for his son and his love for Devon.

By the end of the year their minds were made up.

It was some time before the final preparations could be made and a house in Harborne sought, for there was much to do in the meantime.

Edward visited London to prepare his third book, *Wayside Warbles*, for publication. Twenty-three of the one hundred and six poems in the book were about the loss of Milly. As he worked on the joyful poems and songs written before her death, changing a word here and altering the rhythm there, he feared he would never be able to write such pieces again. His mood had changed and besides, it was the Devon countryside that had inspired him and made him what he was; now he was abandoning it. The only poems he had been able to write recently concerned his regret at leaving Bideford and the lanes and valleys he knew so well. But when the book was published, it received many favourable reviews from newspapers throughout England; on a sunny day in October as he wandered along deep lanes bright with hawthorn berries and golden autumn leaves, he thought he might perhaps, one day, be able to write such poems again.

Elihu Burritt, now United States consul in Birmingham, made enquiries for a position for Charles. Edward read the latest letter from him as they sat around the breakfast table. 'Elihu has spoken with the manager at Lloyd and Company, and he would like to meet you, Charles.'

He looked over his glasses at his son. Charles seemed to have turned a corner since the decision to move to Birmingham was made; he was more even-tempered, more helpful around the house. Edward was beginning to feel proud of him again. Look at him now, his face lit up with expectant pleasure! He had grown up so fast.

'Can I go, Father? Please say I can!'

'Of course you shall go, boy, and I'm going with 'ee. Us can look at houses while us is there. But mind you don't get arrogant with all this talk of city life; don't forget your old friends in Bideford.'

Even so, Edward was still beset with doubts. 'How can us go and leave Milly behind, leave all the places where the memory of her's so strong?'

He knew that Jane, too, found this very difficult. 'But us must, Edward, because Charles is our only family now. He's our future. And us'll visit every year, won't us, on the anniversary?'

'She was the best of daughters, wasn't she?' He felt his sorrow welling up again, and Jane leaned over and kissed him. She always knew how to comfort him.

'She was. Us was lucky to have her, even if 'twas for such a short while.'

At Jane's instigation, Edward wrote to the Post Office to enquire whether he could retire. He had received a hint that, due to his fame, a request might meet with a favourable response, but the reply stated that there would need to be medical reasons for retirement at the age of forty-five. He read the letter to Jane, who was trimming a bonnet at her work table in the sitting room.

'Well, you could tell them about the veins in your legs that have got so bad, that's due to all the walking you've done, for sure. Then there's your eyes, your sight has got worse, hasn't it?'

He was dubious. 'Yes, but I can see to read the addresses, it's the distance vision I have trouble with. And as far as my legs are concerned, I don't have to walk anymore.'

'There's all the climbing in and out of the cart.'

He sighed. 'I'll miss it, all of it. Except the rain. And the rules. When the new rules come in, I'd not even be allowed to hand a letter to someone if he's away from his house, and I mustn't push letters under doors. It don't say what to do about these new slits some folks have been cutting in their doors.'

She looked at him sympathetically. 'You'll miss all the friends you've made.'

'Yes. Yes, I will.'

There were forms to fill in and an examination to undergo, but eventually he received a letter telling him that if he retired as planned in January 1866, he would receive a pension of £8 9s 5d a year. It would help, but would mean a drop in income of £25 a year, and Elihu Burritt had told them that everything was more expensive in Birmingham.

Jane reminded him that the Prime Minister had promised to increase his Civil List Pension.

Edward had sent him a copy of *Wayside Warbles* and had received a very kind letter in return, but he did not feel he could write to him about the pension. On a visit to Barnstaple, he met the newly-elected Liberal M.P., Colonel Acland, and mentioned the matter to him. Colonel Acland very kindly drew up a petition which was signed by all the principal nobility and gentlemen of Devon, asking for an increase in the Civil List Pension to enable Edward to retire from letter-carrying. Within just a couple of weeks Edward received a letter from Lord Palmerston informing him that his pension would be augmented by £20, making £60 a year. It was said by all the national newspapers to be one of the last things that the Prime Minister did – within a week he had died, having driven out without a greatcoat in inclement weather.

The day after the news of his pension appeared in the papers, Edward was driving up Buckland Hill in the grey drizzle of a November morning, wondering how he would be spending the day a year from now, when he saw young Richard Ashton loitering on the corner. When he saw Edward, he took off at a fast sprint towards the village and, soon after, the church bells started to ring. That was strange; it was not Sunday, there were no weddings. As Billy trotted around the corner into the village, Edward saw a large group of people in the road cheering and waving, and it was not until he made out their words that he realised that the celebratory peals were being rung in his honour.

'Three cheers for the postman poet! Congratulations Mr Capern, another pension from the Prime Minister!'

He felt quite overwhelmed as he climbed down from the cart. The Reverend Colling stepped forward to shake his hand, shy Betsy Prance and rosy-cheeked Fredrick Smale clutched his arm while others clapped him on the shoulder.

'Well done, Mr Capern!'

'Us'll miss 'ee when 'ee go, us really will. Who'll sing our songs for us?'

'Thank 'ee, Mr Colling, thank 'ee all!' His voice wavered too much for him to be able to say more, but he shook hands with everyone, then ignored the new Post Office rules by handing out letters to those present before leading Billy to his stable.

In the afternoon, he was more prepared when the church bells began to ring as he drove into Littleham. How he would miss those happy chimes! They took him back to his early days as a postman when he worked a seven-day week, one village's music fading as the deep lanes drew him away, only to be greeted by further peals from the village that lay ahead. City bells would surely not give such warm welcomes.

Christmas Eve was his final day at work. The day passed in a haze of confused emotions; delight at his good fortune in having wonderful friends who came out from every cottage, farm and mansion to wish him well, grief at having to part from them and from the hills and valleys he loved so much. He shook every hand and patted every child's head and promised to visit each year. As he drove for the last time down the steep stony track that led to Upcott Mill and Bideford, with the calls of peewits echoing from the fields, his heart ached at all he had to leave behind.

That night he gave a supper for all his fellow postmen and they spent an amusing evening exchanging stories of their experiences delivering mail. He loved each and every one of them – Joseph Young with his rather pedantic manner and liking for the Rule Book, William Abbott with his infectious laugh and wealth of amusing stories. When, at the end of the evening, they grew serious and made a little speech thanking him for his friendship, then presented him with a handsome book of Devonshire views, he was overcome with emotion and could only express his thanks in a few broken sentences.

There followed three months of final preparations. A week before the move, he was invited by the Mayor to attend the Council Chamber for a farewell presentation. He dressed in his best black coat and stood in front of Jane for an inspection. She straightened his collar and brushed some dust from his shoulders. 'Before you go, come through to your study and us'll see how much more packing there is to do.'

Every room was cluttered with packing cases, the walls were bare of pictures and the rugs had been rolled up, making their footsteps loud on the bare floorboards.

'Edward, you've hardly started!'

He had tried to pack his books, but how could he know which ones he would want to look at again before they left? He had spent much of the afternoon picking them up one by one and running his hands over their covers. When they came to Bideford he had three books; he now owned nearly five hundred.

'Us've only got a few days and there's still a load of things to do! *Please* pack up your books in the morning!'

He promised her that he would.

He walked around the corner to the town hall, passing the churchyard where his old friend, the song thrush, piped a tuneful melody from the top of the yew tree while the evening sun dropped behind the hill. His senses were alert to every impression; everything he saw, everything he heard made him think, *this is the last time*. He could hardly bear it. He took a deep breath and walked into the grand surroundings of the Council Chamber.

He was shown to a seat of honour. As the proceedings got underway, he looked around at the assembly with some self-consciousness but also with great affection. There was

Frederick Lee whom he had known as a boy and who was now Mayor; there stood Reverend Kerr-Thompson, Dr Ackland, Mr Cadd the postmaster, Mr Rooker who had been secretary of the old Mutual Improvement Society that had set him on his way; there must have been upwards of forty men present and many of them stood in turn to praise him.

He was told he had done much good for Bideford, both as a newspaper correspondent and by making the scenery famous through his poetry, the effect in bringing the town to the attention of tourists being second only to Mr Kingsley. He had already made a name for himself and, through his move to Birmingham, his fame would spread still wider. One after another, the gentlemen stood up and he hardly knew where to look. References were made to his poetic genius, to his many illustrious friends, and Jane was alluded to as the best of wives and the best of mothers; Mr Cadd spoke of how many enquiries were made at the post office for 'the Rural Poet'; letters were read out from Mr Maxwell and others who lived too far away to be present.

Finally he was presented with a case and urged to open it immediately. His hands shook a little but he was overcome for a few moments when he found a gold watch and chain. How often had he longed for one when walking his postal round! His thanks were heartfelt.

When he stood to deliver the speech he had prepared, he was greeted with such applause that he momentarily forgot what he had planned to say.

'Those who know me best,' he looked out fondly at the sea of beaming faces, 'know that I am the last man to disguise my feelings, and I would lay myself open to a charge of folly were I not to say I am very proud of the honour my friends have done me.'

There was more applause, giving him time to recollect his planned words, and he managed to get through it tolerably well; the formality of the occasion did not lend itself to emotional scenes but his voice wavered as he recollected the beauty he had met on his rural walks and his fondness for his adopted town of Bideford, 'The river-parted town which smiling sits upon her pleasant hills.'

Finally, the last words were spoken and the last hands shaken and he strolled home in the cool evening air, caressing the watch which had been secured to his waistcoat.

Bideford would always have a special place in his heart, but it was time now to look to the future.

Epilogue

Braunton, Devon, 1884

The night after their long journey from Birmingham back to Devon, Jane woke in the early hours. There was no hint of light at the window and the unfamiliar shadows in the room confused her, until she remembered where she was. Devon. Back again after eighteen long years. She listened to Edward's deep, slightly laboured breathing and smoothed the quilt up over his shoulder. A tawny owl out in the lane made a sudden, sharp exclamation which was followed by a soft, tremulous reply; but that wasn't what had woken her.

'Where are you?' A tiny voice. Jane slipped quietly out of bed so as not to wake Edward and crept to the door. A child stood on the landing, the glow from the night-light on the chest of drawers gently illuminating her white nightgown and wistful little face, and for a moment Jane's heart seemed to stop.

'Milly?'

'Grandma?'

'Ilfra! Here I be, sweetheart.' Jane picked her up. 'Here I be; what are you doing out of bed, my pet?'

'I didn't know where you were.' She sounded so plaintive. Poor little mite; her life had changed so quickly. Jane gave her a hug and carried her back to bed, then fetched her a cup of milk and sat with her while she drank it, the childish gasps for breath between the loud swallows seeming almost loud enough to wake Archie, asleep in the adjoining bed.

'There, you sound like a little lamb drinking its milk!' Ilfra giggled and snuggled happily down to sleep, while Jane stroked the dark wavy hair away from her forehead and waited until her breathing slowed and deepened.

Jane was wide awake now. She picked up the candlestick and crept down to the sitting room. A half-moon shining through the window created just enough light to make out the shape of the furniture, and she eased her aching hips on to the sofa.

Had they done the right thing in bringing the children to live in Devon? Was there anything they could have done to prevent this tearing apart of the family? In the last few weeks she had been so busy caring for the children, packing up the house, and saying goodbye to all her friends that there hadn't been time to think. Should they have tried to stop Charles going to America?

She and Edward had gone to Birmingham because of Charles. How could they have stayed behind? He did well; in time he became the manager of the bank. They were so proud of him. And then he married Alice.

Jane went to the window and stared blankly out at the darkened landscape. Everyone said it was a good marriage. Alice was from one of those well-to-do families.

She put the candlestick on the mantelpiece and searched through the packing cases on the floor until she recognised the shape of the framed photograph. She unwrapped it from its protective piece of blanket and held it up to the candlelight. There were the four children, bless their hearts. Archie looked mischievous as usual, and Ilfra a little lost, as well she might. Dear Lilian, looking so grown-up at eight years old, and holding little Hilda's hand. Jane allowed her gaze to linger on the faces of the two girls; would she ever see them again? And there was Charles, tall and proud in his fashionably tight trousers and cutaway jacket, the fine man that he was. And Alice; her ornate hair arrangement and usual air of dissatisfaction.

A good wife makes a good marriage through love and hard work and support for her husband, that's what Jane believed. It doesn't happen by riding all around the town in a carriage wearing a wide hat and white gloves, nor by staying out until all hours without her husband while the children were put to bed by a nursemaid. But there were stories about Charles too. People stopped their whispering when she came along but she had guessed: when word got out of his move to America, the newspapers spoke of his 'roving nature.' Edward said it meant that Charles liked to travel.

As far as she could tell they had been happy when they were first married. The first baby had come along quickly and they had all loved little Milly. Edward chose the name, of course, as he did for all his grandchildren, and it was natural that he should want to call the new baby after their own precious daughter. When Milly died at eight months of age, old wounds were reopened; it was dreadful to see Charles and Alice suffer in a way that she and Edward understood only too well. Perhaps that was when the marriage went sour. Alice seemed afraid to love her children, but she did love dressing-up and being away from home.

It was partly due to money difficulties that Charles and Alice had to leave the country to avoid disgrace. When the severity of his son's problems became clear, Edward was so angry he made himself really ill. But he was firm in his resolve that two of the children should remain in England; it was unthinkable that they should lose all their grandchildren as well as their son. As Lilian was closer to her mother and doted on little Hilda, it was logical that those two should go with their parents and Archie and Ilfra remain in England. Charles had been reluctant but knew better than to argue with his father; he could not dispute that the children were more attached to their grandparents than to their mother.

And then it all happened so quickly. Edward suggested that they return to Devon immediately, and Jane agreed that it would be cheaper for them to bring up the children there, and better for everyone's health to be near the sea. Saying goodbye to Charles and the other two children was dreadful, and Edward took it so badly she was really afraid that he would fall ill again.

Poor, dear Charles. She didn't even know whether they had all arrived safely in America. Please God a letter would arrive in the post tomorrow to put her mind at rest.

Edward wandered out into the small front garden on the morning after their arrival. The air was fresh, with the sense of lightness that spring brings, but what struck him most was the silence, disturbed only by the mellow song of a blackbird. He closed his eyes and took a deep breath of Devon air. He was home, at last. Harborne was a village, but it was nothing like a North Devon village. The tumult and strife of Birmingham reached out to it, sending carts rattling along its streets day and night, drowning out the birdsong and making its inhabitants anxious. He used to stand in his garden staring at the blanket of smog hanging over the city in the distance, and thinking of the people feeling their way through the unnatural darkness, all of them intent on pursuing profit at the expense of their poverty-stricken neighbours. That was what was known as civilisation. He called it cold and unkind and he infinitely preferred Devon's simple, innocent ways. The city brought degradation and dishonour. It corrupted its people. It had corrupted his son.

He groaned inwardly. He must not think of Charles, or of his darling Lily and Hilda; that grief was still too raw, he could not face it yet. All their lives had been turned upside down. But Ilfra and Archie were here; keep them happy and innocent, nothing else mattered.

He sighed, and eased himself down to sit on the garden wall. Eighteen years. They had not all been bad. In the early years he had enjoyed walking expeditions through the meadows of Staffordshire and the industrialised landscapes of the Black Country with Elihu; he had thrived on stimulating conversations with new friends. There had been many successes; *Sungleams and Shadows* had received good reviews and a second edition had been printed after just a few months; he had been much in demand as a lecturer, and the name of the Postman Poet was now well-known throughout the Midlands and beyond. But as time went on, he began to feel that he was viewed as a loveable oddity, an eccentric old man with a strange accent who spoke of green lanes, wild flowers and other old-fashioned things. He did not belong there. As the effect of city ways on his family became clear, many of the poems he wrote were dark and sad, and an increasing number voiced his longing for Devon. He had feared he might die before returning.

No more lecture tours now. It was time to retire from all that. He would give local talks when asked and he would write poems and songs when the fancy took him, but no more books. Four was enough for any man.

He looked up as he heard the cry of a gull and murmured the familiar words as he watched the gleaming white bird float towards the estuary.

Bird of the Ocean,
Graceful in motion,
Swift in thy passage from inland to sea.

That was a sight he used to miss in Harborne. Years ago, he and Jane used to dream of a cottage alongside the River Torridge in Weare Giffard, but this house would suit them better now they were older; it was close to a proper Devon village with thatched, cob houses but the station and a few shops were at hand. There was a school for the children, the sea was nearby, and they were in the midst of the Devon countryside they both loved.

But Charles was gone; in disgrace. Could anything make up for his loss?

'Grandpa, Grandpa!'

'Ilfra! There you be!' He laughed as the small girl skipped down the steps and launched herself into his arms. 'Come on, chiel, up you come!'

She squirmed to make herself comfortable on his lap and he wrapped his arm around her solid little body, holding her buttoned boots still to protect his shins. Her hair carried a scent of almonds and the loving glance from her dark eyes was worth a hundred good reviews.

'There, my flower.' He kissed her hair. 'The first day in our new house, the four of us together. What shall us do today, then?'

She looked up into his face and frowned; a delightful picture of childish solemnity. 'You know Grandma says we have to make the house tidy and you, Grandpa, have to help!'

He teased her, 'What, me? No, I be going for a walk along the lanes! Will 'ee come with me?'

The door to the adjoining cottage opened and a woman with a baby in her arms came out, followed by several young children. 'Oh, Mr Capern, you'm here!' The news of his move to Braunton was in the papers, she said, but she knew already that he was a poet. 'Us used to sing your songs in school!'

When Jane came out to meet their new neighbour and converse on domestic matters, Edward stood back. Some of Jane's cares seemed to fall away as she talked and he was amused to hear her Devon accent strengthening. While living in the Birmingham area, they had both modified their pronunciation in order to be understood.

Archie came running out of the house to see what was going on, and Edward watched as he edged towards the children who gathered wide-eyed at the cottage door. Ilfra hung back and glanced up at her grandfather appealingly. He crouched down near the children and drew the smallest girl close.

'Now then, can 'ee tell me your first name? Charlotte, is it? How old do you think her is, Ilfra? Around five years old, same as you?' Ilfra pursed her lips and looked at him coquettishly, but wouldn't reply. 'Well, I think so. So, Charlotte, meet Ilfra.' He joined the girls' hands together. 'Now, skip together down the lane to that gate and back again.'

The two little girls reached the gate and skipped enthusiastically back, then started to plan their next game without his assistance. There, Ilfra had a friend and Archie, always the more confident, had already disappeared into the house with the other children.

Edward sat back down on the wall. He had much to be thankful for. He was home again. He must try to keep these oppressive thoughts at bay.

Two months later, Edward sat at his desk and signed the letter to his friend with a flourish. It was the latest in a correspondence expressing their mutual appreciation of William Barnes's poetry and gave him a great deal of satisfaction. As he replaced his friend's letter in the drawer, he paused to run his hand affectionately over its contents. His desk held thirty-five years of correspondence from dear friends and valued acquaintances, literary men and cottage wives. How many men could count themselves as lucky as he?

Charles's second letter lay on the desk. He would not answer it just yet. The first had spoken of the long and trying journey by ship, this one of settling in some distant city, and the prospect of employment. Lily and Hilda were well, but of Alice there was no mention. He had replied immediately to the first but this one could wait a little longer. Edward could not yet forgive his son but, in time, perhaps he would become accustomed to his changed circumstances.

He closed the drawer and allowed himself a moment to gaze at the view of which he never tired – mile upon mile of North Devon countryside laid out before him; here the soft pastures, on the horizon the green uplands, and between them the sea and that band of silver which he knew to be the Torridge estuary, reminding him of the tide that ran in to bathe the arches of the dear old Bideford Bridge.

He added a few more words to the poem he was writing and pushed himself up from his chair; he had spent the morning digging the vegetable garden and was paying for it now. The book-lined walls of his library caused him to pause again, because he could not pass them by without selecting a volume and reading a few lines. Today it was John Gregory's *Idylls of Labour*. His old friend had waited many years to be published but had produced poems of uncompromising quality. After perusing a few pages, Edward put it into his pocket for later.

Jane was resting in the sitting room.

'I've a letter to post, so will take a bit of a walk, my flower. Be the children playing outside? They can come with me if they've a mind to.' He rested his hand on her shoulder and caressed her cheek. With her glance, all the years seemed to fall away. They could be young again, as young as that day when they met by the stile. How strange that they should now be living such a short distance from that place.

She patted his hand. 'Which way will 'ee walk?'

'Oh, up Buttercombe Lane, I think. 'Tis one of my favourites.'

Archie bowls his hoop along the road ahead, tapping it with an ash stick and urging it on as if it were a horse. Ilfra takes Edward's hand and together they stroll along the sunlit lane until they reach the red postbox.

'Can I post it, Grandpa?'

'Yes, chiel, let me lift you up.' She is warm and heavy in his arms. 'Us didn't have these postboxes, years ago. I used to ring a bell to let folk know I was coming.' How long ago it seems. 'I had a long, easy stride in them days. Come, us'll go this way now. Archie!'

Archie picks up his hoop and sends it back in their direction. Edward ruffles the boy's hair as he passes by. What better place than Buttercombe Lane to spend an hour or two?

It is a fine afternoon in late June. In a meadow high on the hill, haymakers in white shirtsleeves are making the first cut, the sun flashing on their scythes, the dark horses standing patiently by the waiting wagon. The old man and the two children wander up the narrow lane between high hedgebanks of oak, ash and hawthorn, the boy hopping left and right over the grass that grows in the centre of the road where no cart-wheels pass. The small girl holds on to her grandfather's hand and it can be seen that the two are talking together as they point out orchids growing on the banks, and inhale the scent of the meadowsweet that grows like cream lace above the foliage. Their laughter drifts now and then across the field, hers high and childish, his a deep chuckle. He lifts her to see something concealed in the hedge, a bird's nest perhaps, and from time to time all three turn to look back at the patchwork of fields and the distant sea glimmering beyond the sand dunes. Once he crouches suddenly to point out a family of swallows flying high in the sky, the newly-fledged young fluttering bravely after the agile, glossy-backed adults. He and the children watch them until they are lost to sight in the distant sea haze.

As they stroll on along the steep lane, a cuckoo's call echoes down the hillside; a song thrush rejoices from the tallest tree. Not to be outdone, the old man begins to speak in rich, musical tones, his distinctive words ringing out over the North Devon hills.

Here is a man who is truly at home with his Muse.

Buttercombe Lane

O, the beautiful, beautiful Buttercombe Lane!
How it calls up the scene of my first meeting Jane,
With its ink-spottled orchises, hawthorn and fern,
And blush of red robins at every turn.
What a joy to be there, and saunter at noon,
When the meadowsweet perfumes the zephyrs of June,
And the bonny speedwell meets the wayfarer's eye
With its greeting o' blue newly sent from the sky!
While the lark in the welkin, the merle in the wood,
And the mavis, and cuckoo in rapturous mood,
Make the solitude vocal with songs of delight
And hill, plain, and sand dune, and sea charm the sight;
The wise will abandon the tumult and strife,
That make the soul sicken, and weary of life,
And if there is aught that can sweeten its sour,
'Tis Nature at peace in her Buttercombe bower.

by Edward Capern
Published in the *North Devon Journal*. June 18th 1885

Historical Note on Edward Capern.

Edward Capern died in Braunton on June 4th 1894 at the age of seventy-five, four months after his beloved Janie. In his final weeks he was nursed by his grandchildren, Archie and Ilfra, aged sixteen and fifteen. His son Charles returned from America for the first time to attend the funeral.

Edward and Jane are buried in Heanton Punchardon churchyard, a short walk up a steep hill from their home. Edward's postman's bell is incorporated in the headstone, which is inscribed with a verse especially written by Alfred Austin, the contemporary Poet Laureate. Baroness Burdett-Coutts asked to be allowed to pay the funeral expenses.

From the churchyard there are panoramic views over farmland and the Taw and Torridge estuary. Edward described the place he would like to be buried in *The Poet's Grave*, a poem published when he was only thirty-seven years old.

> Near a village church, and shady grove,
> Where I've listened to Janie's tale of love…
> On the lonely brow of yonder hill…
> Where the boatman, as he glides along,
> May look upward and chant his plaintive song,
> Singing my dirge; with the waving tree
> As Nature's sweet symphony –
> Just there!

THE POEMS OF
EDWARD CAPERN
Selected by Liz Shakespeare

In 1857, just a year after his first book of poems was published to national acclaim, Edward Capern was awarded a civil list pension for his services to literature. He went on to write three more volumes of poetry and a collection of songs which have long been out of print.

This new selection, published alongside *The Postman Poet,* gives the reader the opportunity to discover the passionate verses of this self-educated Devon man, poems that celebrate the lanes, resplendent with flowers and birdsong, through which he walked on his postman's round, and poems demanding a fairer society for the impoverished labourers he met.

In recognition of Edward Capern's commitment to social justice, £1 from each copy sold will be donated to the Northern Devon Food Bank.

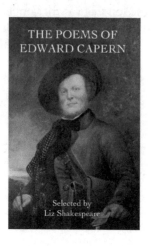

Available from www.lizshakespeare.co.uk

THE SONGS OF
EDWARD CAPERN
Performed by
Nick Wyke and Becki Driscoll

The Songs of Edward Capern. A selection of poetry from the 19th Century Rural Postman Poet set to music by North Devon musicians Nick Wyke and Becki Driscoll. Inspired by the local folk music of the time, Wyke and Driscoll have carefully crafted their melodies and arrangements to enhance the character of the poems, and have included two of Edward Capern's own tunes, originally published in "*The Devonshire Melodist*" in the early 1860s.

For more information please visit www.englishfiddle.com

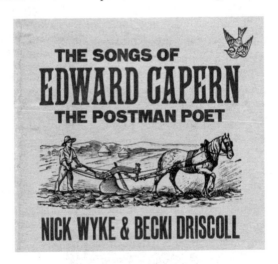

C.D. available from www.englishfiddle.com

ALL AROUND THE YEAR

Liz Shakespeare

These twelve poignant stories, deeply rooted in the Devon landscape, are each linked to a month of the year from January through to December. You will be transported from a sleepy village square to the wilds of Exmoor and from a summer beach to the narrow streets of a small Devon town, and introduced to a variety of memorable characters. In January, a young Croyde surfer tries to come to terms with her uncertain future. As signs of spring appear in the hedgerows, a farmer's wife starts a new venture. In August, a bereaved woman is deeply affected by an unexpected sight on Lynmouth beach. A Bideford man searches for a special Christmas present. All are at a moment of reckoning in their lives as they experience the subtle but significant events that make up everyday experience.

These stories of love and loss, of separation and reconciliation, will stay with you throughout the year.

"Sincere, emotional, touching; just three words that describe the stories in this book. Believable characters and the situations of everyday life which affect them are written in a moving and heart-warming way." *Devon Life*

"Liz Shakespeare's latest book is a collection of charming and compelling short stories rooted in the Devon landscape." *Exmoor Magazine*

"*All Around The Year* is a tribute to North Devon and to the people who live here." *Western Morning News.*

Available from www.lizshakespeare.co.uk

THE TURNING OF THE TIDE

Liz Shakespeare

Devon, 1871

Young and vulnerable Selina Burman from Clovelly and her two young children are confined in the harsh environment of Bideford Workhouse. She can only observe them from a distance and despairs of a better future. Her prospects improve when she meets Dr Ackland, a popular G.P. committed to social change. He employs her as a servant in his own household, despite the doubts of his wife and the Bideford community, for whom any connection with the Workhouse is a source of fear and shame. Selina's work gives satisfaction, but her search for love and security does not conform to the expectations of a middle class Victorian family and threatens to damage both her own future and Dr Ackland's career.

Set in Bideford and Clovelly, this novel draws on newspaper articles, letters and census returns, and powerfully brings to life the factual origins of the story.

'An immensely engaging story that captures the reader from the first page.' *Historical Novel Review*

'A clever combination of fact and fiction, this book both illuminates and entertains – an extremely gripping read.' *Family History Monthly*

'Liz Shakespeare understands the period perfectly well, describing the deprivation of the Union Workhouse as though she had suffered it herself.' *Devon Family Historian*

Available from www.lizshakespeare.co.uk

FEVER
A Story from a Devon Churchyard

Liz Shakespeare

How many of us have wandered through a country churchyard and been moved by the memorials to young children? In this book the author sets out to discover the truth behind a number of graves dating from just one year in a nineteenth century Devon village. Her compelling investigation reveals the harsh reality of life in a small village before the days of effective medical care. By skilfully weaving social history, research and imaginative reconstruction she builds a sympathetic portrait of a community in the midst of adversity.

We hear of strange remedies, the attempts of the clergy to help the stricken village, and the desperate poverty and over-crowding in farm labourers' cottages – the same cottages which are considered desirable today.

It is a story common to many rural communities; it is impossible to remain unmoved by the knowledge that this story is true.

'Fever is a good read, well-researched and dramatized with sensitivity.' *Western Morning News*
'A mixture of social history, research and imagination produces this sympathetic portrait of a community struggling to survive in harsh conditions… this book is a valuable reminder of how hard life used to be.' *Devon Life*
'This book gave me a great deal of pleasure to read. Liz Shakespeare has carried out her research very thoroughly.' *Devon Family Historian*

Available from www.lizshakespeare.co.uk

THE MEMORY BE GREEN
An Oral History of a Devon Village

Liz Shakespeare

When she first moved to Littleham near Bideford, Liz Shakespeare decided to capture a vanishing way of life by recording the memories of elderly men and women who were born early in the twentieth century. Farmers, housewives and labourers tell stories of oil lamps, outdoor privies, communal harvests, cattle drovers and the arrival of the first tractor. They describe in their own words the days when families kept a pig to supplement a simple diet and water had to be carried from the village pump.

In this remarkable book, the voices of a generation who are no longer with us reveal changes in village life which have been reflected throughout Devon and beyond.

'As generations die out and people's memories are lost to posterity, books like this with their invaluable eye-witness versions of village life in quieter times, form an important part of our literary heritage.' *North Devon Journal*

'People with modern 'romantic' views of pre-war rural life should read this book to obtain an insight into the reality of the experience.' *Western Morning News*

'It is a fine example of the value of oral testimony and how it can unlock memories stored away and ensure that the lives of ordinary people are not forgotten.' *Oral History*

Available from www.lizshakespeare.co.uk